BRIAN O'

A WICKLOW Girl

A Wicklow Girl

Wholesale discounts for book orders are available through Ingram Distributors.

Cover illustration by Peter Kim.
Shutterstock Stock photo

Tellwell Talent
www.tellwell.ca

ISBN
Paperback: 978-1-77370-092-2
Hardcover: 978-1-77370-093-9
Ebook: 978-1-77370-094-6

Dedication

For Paulie

PREFACE

The book is prefaced by an editorial review.

"Suffice to say I read it spellbound. The novel is perfect, A classic, satisfying love story. Being language driven, the love story itself is transformed into an epic. Regardless of any plot or theme, it's the voice, the acerbic, relentless observations, the exhilarating metre of sociological dissection, the skewed homecoming poetry of it, the anger and energy and bitterness. **It's superb, every word of it held me enthralled**. Making this the fuel of a love story is a supreme achievement. It's more than the great Irish novel; its very language is dependent on a narrator's voice corrupted by his wandering in both the physical and written world. You take a scene to its linguistic origins, refract its meanings and create myth, it goes beyond Modernism because the voice is contemporary and so compelling in its delivery. **It's everything a serious reader would want from a novel.**"

"Delighted in the puns, the literary and cultural references, the brilliance of the wit and one liners, the put downs to die for and the absurd and crazy, surprising twists of storyline, from the nun to the house visit, and all the wanderings between, uphill and tower, down town and up trees. You've serious and comic themes going off like fireworks in the box; the current state of Ireland, the risk of a wanderer returning to his stifled beginnings, the traumas of going back, the mid-life crisis of a wounded man surrounded by drink and Catholic redundancy. All written with Joycean sensibility but in the language of hand reared bitter. **Every sentence a beauty and a beast**; the tension tears itself apart amid lyrical totality."

"Yes, it's very Irish too, a pub crawl novel deluxe, and there's not much in the Irish tradition that isn't referenced. It's also a kind of rake's progress, for bb is not a particularly sympathetic man at all times, often just a woodworker with balls in his brain- a man of book and brothel, bothy and booze."

I love the fact that it defies definition, shifting between identities, always surprising, always astonishing. You've a word for everything, a phrase for everything. My only explanation to a third party of what the novel is would be to read the whole thing out to them, it's that big, major. But just as a blistering study of a society it must surely be recognized; the way you paint Ireland as county dick, the sink of porter, a land torn between lonely drunk farmers and city braggarts against a backdrop of superstition and boom and bust. It feels real to me, even though I haven't been it or seen it from the cobbles myself. So the Irish identity, while special, is saying much more about the state of the world, the male behaviour, its backwardness and lack of insight; the art of self-pity so mightily observed.

Reviewer from Writers workshop, England (abbreviated).

http://www.writersworkshop.co.uk/index.ht

ABOUT THE AUTHOR

Born in Dublin. Presently living in Toronto. Also enjoyed living and working in London, San Fernando, North Carolina and the Jersey shore. Cleaning bumper cars all summer long.

This book was written in one hour on a dark night. It took only 10 years to polish it.

Do not attempt to read without a glass of wine (or beer).

Do not drive or operate machinery while reading this book.

ACKNOWLEDGEMENTS

Thanks to the reviewers at Writers Work shop, U.K. In particular Dexter Petley. Dexter many thanks for the many encouraging words.

They kept me going!

A work of fiction. Characters, events and incidents are product of author's imagination. Any resemblance to persons, or events purely coincidental.

(Caution if you have an overactive imagination)
Gratuitous copious bawdy abound.

A WICKLOW *Girl*

CHAPTER 1

That warm afternoon I left the city of New Orleans and drove the coast roads and grand river trails of old Dixie wondering what God had for me. Down south Louisiana it's fishing towns with marinas, seafood places and gas stations. Far out on the horizon oil-rigs parked in the ocean sucking our planet dry. Drill baby drill, for I had a set of traveling to do. I stopped in Galliano for late lunch. The usual fare with gumbo, jambalaya and crab cake washed with amber draft. Never keen on lobster, seemed like too much work for so little, like dating catholic girls in the days of my youth. At the end of that road I was riding through Plaquemines parish, arrived in Grand Isle and pulled into the 'Shady Nook' motel parking lot. Not grand nor shady, just your clapboard tourist place, seedy joint with dodgy plumbing and frayed carpets. Art decrepido, tatter patched by handymen committees but balcony rooms faced the ocean, good enough for my likes. My bag and pipes had long seen their best of times.

'*Welcome to Grandy! Owned by Pickens family more than 30 year*', read from faded sign. Katrina and blowhard relatives had gotten in good licks over those years. In family owned places, always imagined shepherd's pie grub so good to lick your plate clean. It had a Shamrock bar next door and that's why I stopped. An Irish pub, for I needed my ration of grog. Beach outback reminded me of Courtown in county Wexford, sandy dunes and memories of better times. Behind the counter in the lobby was a bikini-top woman sucking diet Coke through a straw. Across the counter veneer saw sheen on athletic legs. She'd spent summer in the ocean. Had an appreciative gawk, well she knew. Some lucky lad landed that lottery and loved those golden tanned legs. I could hear light rain starting on a tin roof, noticed tiny beads of sweat on her upper lip. Nowt like having a woman in the tropics, perspiration drips down breasts as juice from ripe mangos, low hanging fruits sure you can't never be a day thirsty. Lot on my plate, I was thinking.

In that faraway place 'Bikini-top' was on the phone. I was fascinated to hear her accent from Ireland's east coast. As I read her nametag, wondering if those breasts were tanned like the rest, in Ireland they'd be turning pale given time of year. Surest sign of autumn in land of pale sun, golden delicious Dublin mott back from Majorca. Memories of tan lines fading on brown skinned Irish girl, by Christmas it was all white. Wonder of the world, never needed Copernicus to tell me something was going around. High cheek freckles, short hair and as I looked her eyes were laughing. *Golden rule, she who has the gold rules.*

"Mairead I'll go, sure I've a Canadian fella giving me the eye."

Air Canada tags were there on a suitcase, the maple leaf.

"Noreen," she said as we shook hands.

Krakatoa moment for me. Touching her.

"Howya sure we get loads from Toronto."

Noticed she was giving the eye, but maybe only my mind's eye.

"Yeah, and Baile ata Cliat?" I asked.

"You know I was thinking."

Thinking because my pale Irish mug, plain Irish mug truth be told.

"Sure I'm Wicklow."

"Climbed the Sugar loaf once."

Blurted out as a cat got my tongue, many thoughts seeking attention head to tail. From garden of Ireland no surprise I was smitten. As she handed the registration card I inhaled warmed coconut.

"For one?" she asked, oblivious to my beating heart being that short of air.

"Yeah, a night to fill. Out traveling down God's highways."

Some guests appeared and with she distracted I hefted my bag and on my way, till she changed my world forever.

"Brian will you be in the bar later, sure we could have the grand old chat?"

"Okay," all I could muster.

I'd sold my soul, knew a devil's deal done with hell's tariff to pay.

"Frozen beer for Canadians," she laughed.

"Hey, I'm Irish," I corrected.

I've that pot mess of confusion, Paddy's boy Irish stewed with Micks and Billys, green and gold. Sinn fein and our Union. Scattered together, afraid and separated on one wee isle, only home by end of days. We curse and swear but love our wretched island. At least on that we have our brawny hands. Lying on bed, contemplating with ocean waves through an open door. How did she escape the clutches of culchie showers back home? No ring, but beautiful birds are caught and caged, she was never alone.

"I never see anyone from home," she had said.

There'd be bubba boy lurking, she'd show up with surly fellow. Good old boy chewing 'baccy, dragged out to hear paddies blabbing about far away island. Anything else was too far fetched.

'Y'all ever see a leprechaun over there?' A sole contribution.

Downed mini-bar Baja wine encounters with gaels never prospered. Other than we fled our windswept misbegotten bog land, there was nothing. Through the years I formed no lasting relationships with paddy's abroad. Pipes banging and shaking I got the warm shower, brushed my teeth thinking you can never shove pyroclastic flow back down a volcano. A friendly mirror, but departed with low expectations, going with flow in land of the delta.

'Cold mugs of Beer' cajun's promise, she won't be there. I was anticipating cold beer for a mug, sit silent with a few Sam Adams and leave for the double bed. Past the end of season bar was quiet and dark, but on a bar stool was Noreen, lip sticked and fresh faced. Lit in neon from Hollers Moonshine sign, short red dress and painted toes in flip-flops. A sight for eyes of any man. Forgave her piedement faux pas, wanted to tell her I missed her as she grabbed my arm.

"It's great to see you," I told her.

No hubby, no main squeeze, no partner, no other body just her body. Gob smacked with she by her lonesome. Saints be praised and marching in.

"Nick, this man is a famous Irish writer," she told the stout bar man.

I gave the raised query eyebrow.

"Have to be careful in this motel business with dangerous fellas," she laughed. "I looked you up. You've more degrees than a thermometer."

"I wrote one book, me mother insisted on edgeimications."

Copying the Almighty as Christian Brothers fretted my limitations.

"We love Irish in Grandy," Nick says with a hippy handshake.

Saw through that bon homie and knew what he was about, messing like an extra mongoose at the party. Looked like he had a thing going for Noreen. Maybe some previous.

"Our Cher is always telling us about Ireland." Some mirage beyond the waves. "My friend, a toast to the island that gave us Noreen."

He lined up shot glasses.

"Slainte and Eireann go brea, mud in your eye."

Italian cock blocking action as ever. Fair play, and me messing on his turf with a girl from the old sod. I sank his cheap rye.

"Nick, go away and don't get Brian drunk. I need to talk."

We sat at a table, vamoose pal you heard the chick. She was drinking from the bottle of Dixie beer, I'd last of the summer ale.

Move along pops, I'm rapping with Wicklow babe with wicked thighs. Them are ties that bind.

"So Professor why are you here?"

Sick and tired of working, then times God gives me a kick in the arse.

"Roll by coast day to the sea side, carnival rides." Zipper and dipper.

Too long in New Orleans smokey clubs waiting for decree nisi and decree absolute. Now carnal rides on my mind, zipper and dipper.

"Ireland should keep girls like you, not away down these bayous."

"What was your book about?"

"What makes a woman change and hurt the man she loved. Romance as young fellow, it finished. Departed old Eireann with broken heart. Heard even men were reading."

I'd written about a young fellow leaving Ireland, as many before and after.

"So you still miss this girl?"

Typical broad question. Here I was carrying flames for young one from years past. She'd think I was daft in the head but romantic like a poet.

"Both from Dublin streets, knew lots about each other." I shrugged. "Sometimes."

Paused to let early loves gravitas fill the air, blend with country music. If man takes a ride he must learn how to fall.

"Falling in love with an Irish girl seems deeper." Having that old tumbling feeling, deja vous working again.

Back then I was just a kid with no place to hide. Who knew how to deal with that? Like snorkeling and skating in that transition from boy to man.

"Nobody explained those consequences," she nodded.

Like she understood the romance business, told me as a teenager in Avoca she had an affair with a married fellow, laughed and put her hand on my knee. That bird from Pelican state gave me goose bumps. Maybe there was a reason she was in deep Louisiana, Mick and Kate wrong side of the pond with the same motivations. She leaned close mad spirit in those eyes.

"It was hopeless. Still did think of him even when I was married. Mad with emotions terrible like that."

Ultra surly Nick gave us more beers. I could feel she wanted to reveal her secrets. Nancy whiskey had taken over and then I kissed her, one of those just because moments.

River warm duck know first, so quack, quack for 'two blushing pilgrims' Took a gamble knew not too soon.

Then we talked like we had always known each other, ties and thighs loosened. She left Ireland at nineteen and fell in love with Ferrice, son of the motel owner. Noreen swapped her mother's house to make a home in a trailer park on Gulf coast. Returned to Wicklow only to tell mammy she'd not do the Kevin street hotel course but was heading back. Her father had died and her mother could do nothing to stop this. Now divorced, her 'ex' was away with their son in Biloxi down the coast. She never finished her leaving cert.

"Ferrice had his customized knucklehead Harley, king and queen seat, and sidecar. We would be out over Florida panhandle. Past fields of Texas blue bonnets and bob wire fences, hit the black top on the archipelago to Key Largo and on to Key West. After I never worked on rooms. They hired Dora a black girl only spoke Gullah from Georgia sea islands. Loved Key West, Caribbean music and steel bands, a gas time. Jugs of real orange juice from the trees. That was for me, I wanted to stay."

Ferrice, her wheeler dealer fellow. She liked that ride.

"My God-mother left me a house in Howth, right on the head. Not sure what to do with it." My grubstake.

I lobbed that in the mix, life smelling of roses. Needed to bamboozle, flummox, boast and cheat as any decent man. Blow her summer dress with hot air, climb the bamboo, be Brian Boru. I won't whack a World series home run nor see my name scratched on Lord Stanley's cup. Frankly my achievements do not amount to a hill on the plain bogs of Allen.

"Oh my god you're lucky. Amazing a house on Howth head! Very impressive, rich man living in the high cotton."

"Remember as a kid in the tent, hearing fishermen below the cliffs, cursing about nets with rough seas beyond. There are caves underneath. When waves rush in you feel the earth shake."

'*Through caverns measureless to man.*'

"Will you rescue me? I can make beds!"

Laughed at her crazy notion, stared in the bar mirror, brushed the fringe from her eyes. No middling woman. A smasher, an eye catcher in my round specs.

"So will you go back?" she wondered.

Only searching for a road home, as always.

"I'm thinking."

Only a eunuch sees clear. Dangling sac, everyman's Achilles heal. I knew Ireland could be that lonely night or day.

"Don't you have to be a Professor?"

"I'll quit. Got cash from the book."

Money in banks, build potemkin village. Deluxe life, large chips and two rock salmon, fruit on the table with no soul poorly.

"Sometimes I think of Wicklow and home," she said.

Yeah? Real home, not this carpetbagger state. Crocked place full of alligators and reptiles, storms and slick oily fellas from barges and real dangerous fellas in motels. Scallywag life. Even the land was fickle, a will of the wisp place. Swamp and bayous and houses built on stilts over sandbars of the delta. Forever changing, shifting sands, slivers of land with only a bare width of road, here today and gone tomorrow. Gone with the wind in ablink of hurricane eye. Every year the storms come with no time to ever recover. Louisiana was nothing like the rock hard place from whence she came, that timeless land that made her. Wicklow was hard granite rock a thousand miles deep, anchored to the earth. There's no crack in that ground, in that tectonic plate. Even Dublin's river Liffey flowed down from those Wicklow mountains, we were crafted of the same stuff; Celt, Saxon, Norse and so much worse. Elemental my dear, Liffey's children we both were.

"But then I know it's too late and difficult. So many things. Maybe for you it's easier. I'm hanging on like hair on a biscuit."

Things complicated. Women were always with others to look after. She left for few minutes. I was feeling good in family style. When you don't have nothing to hold it's easy to travel. Took a swig from her bottle with the taste of lip gloss. She returned and sat closer, lost love song on the jukebox by her silver dime. Randy Travis to second my emotions.

"Oh it's good to talk about home. I still feel a stranger here, even though folks are friendly it can be lonely."

"Going into exile is traumatic we all suffer with that."

Querencia, I was with thinking. Those who journey overseas change sky and their souls.

"I think we want a lottery win and head home, be done with it," she offered.

She ran her fingers through my hair, breasts pressing on my arm. She'd have beads from Mardi Gras, impressed I was.

"I can layer it, two days I'll be back at my place in the quarter. Will you be around?"

"Sure, I can arrange things."

With me in white water above a fall and no escape, attracted like steel to a Swiss hadron magnet. It was that rapid. I'd be that happy croppy boy.

"Brian, let's go down to the ocean. This time of the year is best. Ca-va." she waved Nick goodbye. "Allons."

Avoiding eye contact with the man, I gave him a tip but he already knew all about me. Outside on the wooden path she took my hand, by shoreline and beneath light of a harvest moon she pulled me close.

"I'm glad you came by this way," she told me. "For the sea-side rides."

We kissed by that Gulf of Mexico and again on a wooden bench nearby. She took a small bottle of rum from her purse, took a sip and handed it to me.

"Wicklow girls taste nice," I whispered.

What life is about, my brain tuned to turmoil, warm and dark as I stripped and went for a bathe in the salty ocean. She laughed and warned me to watch for sharks.

"Weather breezin up," she said and ran for towel.

Swam that sea, my dip in the nip with a rudder for her in the sand dunes. We went to my 'Villa room' and spent that night together. Windy season was ending but Grand isle was a wild place. I wasn't crowing but we made the earth shake, made easier on shifty soil. We lit the lamp bright on that night. It was hard, to tell.

Could hear waves but crows woke me morning after. An angel lying on pillow, hair tousled from the night. Wondering if I'd crashed on the road, maybe on morphine drip, then felt curve of her bum.

"Told the devil for one night he'd have my soul."

"Because of me?"

"A good deal."

"How did Satan know I'd be so crazy!?"

"He knows about you." She had sinner ways.

"That divil made me do it." She jumped from the bed. "I've to run, a woman's work never done with fellows around. Oh laissez les bon temps rouler."

Her son James was back. Early morning, her mother-in-law had brought the lad from Biloxi. At the door she waved her finger.

"Better not be a one night-stand buster, I'm a convent girl from Wicklow, don't have me a sinner. Y'all come eat when you hear breakfast bell. Sorry no white pudding, just biscuit flapjacks and buttered grits today."

She tucked in the bed cover and kissed me again.

"I could get to like you. I've black satin sheets in my chamber a coucher on Decatur. You better come visit, good Lord willin' and creek don't rise." Heard her humming as she ran away. It was not the blues.

I lay back with my brain in topsy-turvy land. Only evidence remaining was an empty rum bottle and mosquito bite, *September mozzies have iron mouth.* In life I only ever needed half a bed with a woman to call my own. An hour later in the kitchen she introduced me to her son, James. Sitting together around the kitchen table.

"Brian, my friend from Dublin," and that no lie.

Young fellow told me firmly his name was Jimmy. Bright kid of twelve years, he had Noreen's unguarded eyes but not her bones. I shook his hand. He looked so much like his mother but smaller than a normal kid, had some undiagnosed wasting disorder and was in wheel chair, caught me looking. Feel infinite sorrow when young ones are in trouble, too hard to contemplate for us all, he don't got all what belongs to him. He replied with his eyes.

'I know I'm in a tough spot but I'm brave, I'm doing my best. So no pity okay? I have my mom and she will always be with me.'

Jimmy told me he had been to Wicklow with his Dad.

"Best looking girls are from Wicklow but they've too many freckles." Could hear his mother's Wicklow accent in Jimmy.

"James!"

Kid had an opinion. I gave thumbs up.

"Wicklow girls are the best!" On that I'd testify.

"Not just you Mom, I saw them on the beach in Bray."

"I'm jealous. my boy checking out girls." She hugged and kissed him.

"On the beach here they tan more even, Celtic Irish people are most white, Mom I read that."

I drank my coffee, ate the dreaded grits and laughed.

"I swim okay in the sea but better in the pool."

"James got his first kiss from his girl friend at the pool in Arklow." Noreen was so proud. He waved away his mother's remark. No time for that trivial talk.

"He writes poetry to her!"

"Don't go an dog me Mama. Mom I write poems but not all to Jenny, also write to Stephen Hawking. Jenny writes a lot, she might visit next year. My Dad says I could maybe swim for Ireland in para-Olympics, obviously my first choice would be Louisiana. Need to train really hard."

Noreen looked at him humming like she was bursting with pride.

"I liked the Sugarloaf took a lot of pictures. If I get my leg muscles stronger I could maybe climb it. It's only 1644 feet high."

Later that morning I sat with Jimmy on the end of rickety pier out over the mighty Mississippi. Fishing for catfish with a long fishing pole furiously waving at the captain on the bridge of passing oil barge. Noreen had asked me to video her son. We watched waves break around oil freighters led by pilots.

"That's Eldoridge from Texas goin up river to Kansas. Reckon they're two days late Seymour?" Jimmy said.

Elderly fisherman Seymour Stanley had on a Yankees baseball cap, stood alongside Jimmy. A black face lined like a wicker basket, chewing a wad of tobacco. Seymour, I guessed, was Jimmy's best friend.

"Looks like they got cleaned up somewhat. Must have gotten held over dry dock in Pensacola, I sure heard she needed repairin."

"And she's ridin low," said Jimmy. Now he was all deep Louisiana and happy when captain responded with the foghorn.

"Sure enough. Gotta make sure those folks in Kansas got their heaten for them cold winters," Seymour replied. "We ain't all fortunate."

"Someday! Someday I'm gonna ride those barges movin that crude. Eh Seymour! Ain't I? Ain't I Seymour?"

"Sure Jimmy, you'll ride on the barges. You'll move the crude from Pecan island to the end way up north. If you sets your strong mind to it, I figure you can do anything you wants. Mark the twain for safe waters, sand gravels always changing. Like the time Jimmy."

Slowly the Eldoridge barge moved past, up and around bend in majestic river.

"Okay Jimmy we gotta be movin. Your Dadda's boat comin anytime soon."

Seymour walked slowly with the aid of a cane as he pushed Jimmy.

"You can bet on it, Seymour you can bet on it!" said Jimmy.

"Yeah you can bet on Gamblin Star sure enough. You ought to be on stage just you and your Dadda."

"Catch you fellas on flip side." Last thing I said.

Ferrice was coming back so later that morning I left. At the side of the motel Noreen discreetly hugged me. Driving back to the city of Nawleen I was in a trance and could not wait to see this unguarded colleen again. God's plan always involves a fork to change direction, that's how our universe works. Sometimes God will pass a bouncing ball. On that road trip I had my epiphany after my precious years of debauchery, spending time with honky tonk angels. Those priests of school days were correct. You need emotional bonds with the woman and not babes looking for a wad of cash in your wallet. In our brief encounter she put me in a mental place I'd rarely been, like batter man with two sugars in his tea, three balls and no strikes.

CHAPTER 2

An Irish lad in Toronto, advised by a perceptive prescient fellow, had warned me about going home.

"It's your optic delusions. Silly fellow, you can't just drop back in on a Dublin social scene. Not malarkey of having a pint, cead mile failte my arse. You'll always be a 'come from away' geezer. Never works a whit. You've never done the time; blow in misfits like you always a weird kettle of fish, a pacific mussel in Great lakes. They won't take to you."

Transplanted emigrant Mick laughed at me.

"Didn't climb on their social ladder, what Dublin's all about. They'll learn you, they've a lot invested in status their whole life. You think you can be their equal? Returning is like an oil painting, ugly closer you get." All craquelle and no craic.

My Toronto sneer went on.

"You'll be out of time as paddy boys in fifties orange Toronto, jobbers out. Indian men with haberdashery suit cases roaming Dublin streets. As out of time as a pinsetter boy, gandy dancer checking on rail roads, pedestrian potboys. Elevator operator, bobbin boys, Esperanto, tallymen with spiel tanglers, okay?"

It was crystal balls the seer man had. He'd find dark lead in certified silver.

"Guaranteed you'll sit on your butt end alone or with another returned Mick. Like dustballs losers find each other, accretion gang of geezers. New York cop or worse a liquor store git bursting with lifetime stories from liquor warehouse world, retired early. Apart from a sister in Mayo knows nowt. In a heart beat you'll be off to Switzerland to drink the juice to end the misery of it all."

"What should I do? Perceptive fellow?"

"Sell that place you have in Howth, go to Vancouver, get yourself a Chinese chick, walks in the rain in Stanley park, love her on the beach in Maui. Irish women are too choosy and trouble. The place is a royal pain in the arse, you know all that."

In that spare Toronto coffee shop, the man paused to wet his whistle on Timmy Horton double-double. He spared me no hopes, crossed the man's palm with crunchy bear claw.

"As for women in Dublin there's not one available. You'll be on shank's mare. In Oz they've the great white shark, Dublin has the women. Them with sensors for the job and full pension, like silky night owls tracking the mouse for dinner. Middle class Dublin broads detect the poor. They want a healthy bollix and periscope for making the childers and that fat wallet. For their endless days of easy leisure. For god's sake man, they've little trophy photos at the lawn bowling club in their best mohair and you're not in any."

My persistent fellow had issues with Irish women, got discouraged and scarpered with scars. In Toronto he married above his station and wasn't moving anywheres now.

I'd endured a long unhappy marriage to my Canadian wife, told her I wanted back to Ireland after twenty years of Toronto. The siren songs heard over ambulance wails in those caverns, the fabled pipes calling me home.

Pray to St. Paddy never be concrete
where condo canyons block light of the day
create winds of hurricane in Toronto.
Tight fisted Bürgermeisters
offered not a downtown fig leaf
no blades of God's greenery.

With full agreement, she chose the frozen land over further occupation of our marriage bed. Decided not to wait till 'death do us part' that had been taken care by barren Dominion coast to coast to coast. We reached that turn along our ragged road and both took the opportunity of making new life. Separate futures and commonwealth settled in a Toronto divorce court, madam judge from Africa with jagged knife gave missus a healthy chunk. Gavel slammed down and doings of legal beagles restored freedoms, put a fork in that relationship done door to door. But entitled she was.

"Uhuru," I'd hollered fist in air, a word for freedom in Swahili. Madam gave the blank stare, likely a Zulu lady. Easy peasy mistake on my part. Doors of the marriage penitentiary slammed open and I felt breezes of change on that Toronto day, likely mixed with the bitter north wind. Demobbed, I landed back down on civvie street. Bachelor ways beckoned again, back where I started but robbed of years as a happy citizen. Headed my unshackled corpus for an exit and nearest jet plane. Mustered out, streaked east across Newfoundland munching a ham sandwich, felt as Mandela leaving Robben island. Perhaps wiser in the ways of women but one size never fit them creatures, mystery bunch of all sorts.

Whatever, our planet meanders unperturbed
teeming with bunchberry dogwoods, rhododendron
chokecherry and wild cherry and all of us in cottonwood.
Summer wind will blow across Indo-Ganga Plain
sirocco sweeps an acqua tide in Venetian Lagoon

but that year I'd nowt more be stuck in a Dominion.

A feeble University of Ontario career tanked in blink of an eye. In physiology class, for pure devilment, I shook on my long bamboo pointer and posed a question.

"What organ in man's body grows largest when attracted to his lady? Over 10 times bigger! Make no bones about it."

In front, a young blondy got upset with my bare facts of life. Iris McCoy was her title.

"You should not ask those questions and like that," she says.

Quite the looker she was, gave her a nod and a wink and outrageous shake of the stick.

"You see, pupil of the eye," I says, without leering.

A laughing class, the young one flushed. Oops so stupid me for I'd not let her be.

"Aye aye, you'll be mighty disappointed on your wedding night." Declared with my wonky grin.

Rightly distraught she hotfooted, mates tagged along, my pupils shrinking. Wasp lawyer was blondie's Dad, old orange stock had his pile of fieldstone bricks in Rosedale, no time for inappropriate green taig likes of me.

'Humiliated and traumatized', the faculty bald heads announced. Shown the door, escorted off campus by security, no longer saw eye to eye. A month later I got a Bulova watch in the mail 'for university service rendered.' Threw it to a fresh faced bum on Yonge street, he'd more time than me.

Even an Ontario summer is a cold wasteland and I despaired for having squandered those years. So I moved to the house on the rock of Howth where I became accustomed to lonely evening cocktails of wine and valium, sitting in the wind garden making fresh daisy chains on Howth head. Left with only beans on toast and transient euphorias, I knew what was missing in life of a spaded dog. Divorced fellows are Moonies with brains rewired, accustomed to life with a broad. Us old lags desperate to be back in that jail, hobbled and hitched with the woman. Forever done sowing wild oats, farmer days were over. Several pathetic attempts were made to contact fellows I'd known all of twenty years previously. Scanned the phone book till I found a few familiars. Call a fellow, have a few pints, catch up with things.

'Hey cara amigo what's happening? The man's back in town.'

What was wrong with that? Fit right in with a gang, on the pig's back. I had this image of card games, toking cigarellas of a rainy Friday evening. Doing stuff with sophisticated Dublin folk, drinking bottles of Babycham, Madeira brandy and coke. Getting langered having a laugh. Even dusted off my old handy black book for Dublin birds raring to go. Catch them on the second go round.

Mott at 4 Provinces dance, pitch and putt Step-a-side
carousing Feis ceols, boxing at National stadium.
Grey hounds at Harold's cross, coffees in Bewleys with tipsy cake,
Portobello sing along shindigs, bouncy train rides to Newry,
horse racing at Leopardstown. Boozing all the way.

My sister tells me high faluttin Mister Michael Ghosh was living on the rock, heard he was now top prof at Trinity-Kildare Institute, Philosophy was what she said. We were at secondary school together although never amigos. Now homies we were. He was the popular kid, played scrum half, always had the old college try stashed in his locker. His last gasp try won schools cup in Lansdowne. If Ireland had jocks he'd be living ivy league large. I still hear cheer leaders chants in those old stadium stands.

'Go Ghosh. We love you Michael.'

'Gosh Ghosh, thrilling win!' Evening Press lame headline on the day.

Grew thick beard at sixteen and became a legend on peckin order with the ladies. Found himself high on their totem pole. Uncanny then to have observed those surging female instincts, whatever he had what they wanted. '*Something whereof they knew and I unaware.*' Mighty dangling pairs on all involved, I'd observed.

His old lad hailed from Calcutta, mother from Paisley, always with bluenose airs and graces about no easy fit for Dublin streets. Strained tea leaves, sugar cubes and butter curls, toasted on both sides, wax fruits in a bowl, grand holidays away in Rimini. They had friends in Foxrock, those mean old biddies with Buckingham palace white pillar disorder, suede and fur coat swells in Abbey private boxes. Ghosh hallway distinguished by plaster paris reclining lion, more class than porcelain wall ducks. Of course, his old lad drove the Audi, boasted of weekends with stately 'fine dining' hoteliers in Kennymara, held the ritual family toast for Queen Victoria's birthday. I could agree Michael cut a striking figure. Even rivaled Sharif in his prime. Black hair and brown skin, scattered red hairs in the moustache to betray his roots. Irish women took to drooling, I'd witnessed them all. He liked to play bagatelle and badminton, master with shuttle cock, cocksman on dodder rowing team. The man never a moment regarded a gurrier friend, nor threw young pecker discarded bones. Fair enough. Them days of failure mise fishing with wrong hook and pole.

"Call him, often see him around town. MG knows lots of people out there. He's interesting, knows how to cook fish." Claims of my sister.

From that opening 'Ahouy' of my call I knew my quest to be a train wreck. Still, never pickle dropped from emperor's table for wretched pints of plain. Now in these years he was still hog high, he'd no truck with me. His old lad had done well for him, he now occupied a palace top of the hill.

"Sure I'm Napoleon in St Helena out here on this causeway." I laughed. "You'd go nuts talking with rabbits and seagulls. Out here."

Our twenty year separation not long enough, he claimed he barely remembered my ugly pus. I could hear Maggie Thatcher's accent, Dublin's version where beat up, down trodden Walkinstown was crammed into priestly over educated uppities in Ballsbridge, like Brits imperial empire butting into old India. More off-set than an Ingo bike, no 'where have you beens?' from him. Immediately felt the need to abort a futile effort, but struggled on despite indifference to his old school mucker.

"Dia dhuit a cara, maybe we could meet for a village pint? Catch up."

One pint of plain, one black and tan.

'Filled with mingled cream and amber
I will drain that glass again
such hilarious visions clamber
through the chambers of my brain
quaintest thoughts, queerest fancies
come to life and fade away.'

"And then do what? Morosely stare at the pints? I've a busy academic life."

Well you teach philosophies, mostly a load of old chutney. It's Howth not Acropolis, no Plato in the Parthenon. Spiraling down, I persisted being reasonable, accustomed in ways of docile Dominions.

"Okay, you take life very serious, just a pint."

Me with no gift of gabbers, another spudnick sausage and potato fellow. To our shame, given a chance, we do parrot absurd English upper class like toadies.

Once had a froggy named polly, he was awfully awfully jolly.

"Like I say I have other things to do. Meeting you would serve no purpose."

The man gave me heeby cheeby chills, brawl by the cut of his tongue. No qualms with notions too familiar with Kant, no simulacra in our philosophies.

"We could watch porpoise Marvin cavorting chasing minnows and laugh and laugh." My last gasp. *'Up jumps a dolphin with his chuckle-head.'*

I put the phone down to dial tone, mortified. Rejected by that clown, I needed desperate silence.

"Alleluia my brother," I hollered to gulls and daisies. "I'll keep notes in case I ever write a book on pillocks."

Posh git, preposterous pretentious parvenetti displaying undesirable social manners, characteristics inherited from erstwhile conqueror's abroad on their mainland. Had the Indian sign on me, accessing him was Himalaya too high for Howth, descendants from toady Johnny Bull maharajahs in jewel of their empire. Lad so high up bamboo I could see his rude red arse. Talking with me was Mozart playing piano for a cow. I was a git useless as yokes on a nun. I'd planned to say, 'well you're a prof and I'm a prof', let's do dialogues. But there were to be no ivory tower anecdotes. Bores don't change what he was thinking. No tales of misdeeds, treasured encounters with a pretty post-doc or two. Alls I knew I didn't ever want to meet this dreaded fellow, his rudeness my very salvation. Shocked I slid under the couch blanket replaying the nightmare, mad doggin my sister for weeks after. If I could sue for lazy shoddy advice I'd be hiring bewigged barristers to impoverish a wayward sibling. The experience resurrected harrowing insecurities of dire high-school, propelled everyday into a morass.

School friends, never were friends
uniformed uninformed hard labour
me dullard mates of every class,
distress mitching, itching to be free
trapped waiting for Leaving cert
long days serving time marking time
wasted my time with them,
till finally when I was still me.

Ju know warra I mean?

And free on that last day.

Later, I saw him abroad on the hill dog walking. Each with radars whirring we managed to avoid intersecting. No tip of hat nor ditchside chats, he resembled his long haired mutt. On village streets he drove a speedy MG sportster, still handsome son of a bitch.

Another call proved equally upsetting.

"I'm looking for Charlie?" Fellow from same dire school.

"Yes, well Charles is my husband."

Harvested from the disco, lassoed as biggest buck in the litter. Remember a night at the club, he dragged his sorry ass there after some other mini skirt had dumped him. A shy lad, said he'd not do the dance. I showed him my moves and he scored while I sat on the bench riding pines. Life is that ticky tacky.

"Barbara?"

But Barbara could not recall and Charley boy was not home. Inconceivable she'd not remember, even bores we dredge up just to avoid them.

"If it was only a pub acquaintance afraid I'd not recall." Barb let fly, burst my homey bubble.

She'd calculated futility of renewal, still waiting for her Charles to call. Hey, her very kids were on the planet because of me. Toronto's Nostradamus on the money was not a fellow to wager against.

"You'll be back in Hogtown. General whiff of an Irish man but all Paddy whackery with yankee doodle dandy paraphernalia. They'll not be having ye one iota. You know that."

Them's my shibboleths. Official Oirish man with green blazer, roaming me homeland like a chupacabra.

"St. Paddy wallowing those misty pasts and oike hokey ballads. Right friggin mess, chalk scrapped on blackboard for them. Rent the house here, don't sell. Don't talk to them about Ontario. Remember we were raised on the film bored of Canada. Jeanette McDonald and Nelson Eddy musicals on RTE, and don't never mention those failing cedars."

But 'away' was no home for me. Heel of Dominion could reign o'er me no more. Before returning to Ireland I'd tried that Florida trip a few months. Ended up ocean side patio bar in Cape Canaveral drinking dollar beers from styrofoam cups. Me and bar 'buddies' gazing over at NASA rocket's red glares, listening to country music and wanting every day to leave. Bar maid Mandy, killer body and sun-beaten face, liked the way she called me 'boss'. Midday, after six styros on empty stomach, I was thinking about asking her out. Motivated by a belly full of blue balls blazing, sometimes better to be neutered. Then I'd got the call from a solicitor in Fitzwilliam square waiting for me to pick up keys of 268 Hedge road in Howth. My aunt Tassy, dear old lady, had handed her pile to me. She knew I'd return to our beloved Erin.

"Quite the valuable property," he told me, "best spot in the county. Lucky man, count those blessings."

"Sure, that's grand but you never know."

Connemara lonesome, I'd not survive long on me tod. Head over them cliffs of Moher. I left Mandy, it gets hot by that cape try a hat.

Pitiful man neglected recluse chancy looking roaming the hill
pig on his own as ever, picayune monkey peeling his banana
with me hobo bindle and cup unkempt hedge lonely wild grass
garbage piles disturbing villagers, they'd peg rocks at me,
procrastination curse of my life, lazier than Angwantibos slow Loris,
stress and strain come what may. No body ever to come down my lane.

Trips in my youth to stoney Howth loaded with Rathgar family gossip paid off. The best teenage times were spent there. I knew trail-ways and byways of the county from walks with my aunt. Blessington Poulaphuca waters to Pine Forest and sands of Malahide tram up

Howth head, Shankhill strand and Bray to Eagle's nest. Aunt Tassy was a philanthropist, supplying fivers and tenners to develop my philandering ways. Slow learner, but I stuck to the trade, could feel the rewards. She'd welcome my latest fling, if no approval welcome mat would read bye-bye. Satisfactory middle class tonal sounds and wine would flow, mott entertaining grand style. When a bird she liked did not re-appear I'd shrug under her glare. I'm the bait, let's face it, a wriggle worm but they ain't always biting.

"Aunty it ain't easy. Slings and arrows Dublin men bear cloth like Matt Talbot."

Our parish priest assumed church was getting the pad for silent retreats. At least there was occasional banging when I was there. Summer tent by cliff face when even calm nights ground was rocking.

Back then, a Dublin quare one dumped me for holes in me favourite purple jumper, not best bib and tucker. Said she was 'so embarrassed', I took off looking for New Jersey. I was propelled to drunken nights in Camden town, then nights listening to snow ploughs on streets of the new world, raising children in a northern American town with no shared culture. When torn from roots you lose more than you gain.

CHAPTER 3

I spent those months alone in Howth, women-wine-weather my only concerns. For those days I was a desperate sailor on the Bounty observing bare breasted Hawaiians, Romans bidding for Nordic blonds, the cleared felon studying a pole dancer. Late November, looking out on a grey turbulent Irish sea, gloomy feelings crept heavy those evenings. Those long days.

Hard moments alone in Howth village church. It was quiet there except for aches and creaks among olden rafters, ancient woods forever drying in sea air. Wooden pew benches fierce on the bum, hundred year oak hardens with age. An insistent sea breeze on my back, expecting smell of rains, dose of drizzles on the air. An aroma of incense permeated from past thurible benedictions, stations of the cross and lighted candles. Palm Sunday sermons with hours standing before Easter, not for the faint hearted with starving pains. Medley stained windows provide a glimpse of spirit for my soul. I was not an aficionado of the church organ. A lot of promise with pipes blowing, huffing and puffing noises like Bordello Ranch whores intent on giving weak bums the rush. On a week day flat capped citizens were off in factories making stuff, knackered for few punts. Lads smithing and forging, melting charring welding bricking fishing tarring ironing, black boot polishing, wall paper hangers and bag men patrolling. Reddlemen in fields, if lame horse needing shoeing I'd have cobblers. I'd toiled another land so now sat my arse down to benefit from their labours. I was feeling for ploughman's lunch.

'Wringing bread from sweat of other men's faces.'

All the while I'm eyeing red velvet cushions in confession box awaiting a padre. What a dawdle. They know who done who, easy life with soft hands. Box ticking soldiers, creativity not encouraged, they'd boil heretics in oil. I'd not apply no John Servitius, seeing as I've fear of wraths of God. Often churches are leaden spaces despite the pageantry within, but it's grand they leave them open for sinners, an oasis of solace for solitary men. Most countries they'd loot the space, brass plates from pews, lead from drainage and divils take the souls. Fear of those wraths mostly keeps Dublin gurriers at bay, only I hoped they'd kept golden chalice under lock and key. Once I did a dinky toy from Woolworths in Grafton street. Still owed a decent Meath fellow a fiver in old money for a pocket watch. Never clumped no one. Never a gambler for me. No good with the numbers.

I made a dash across to the confession box, closed the door in case peeping shawlies came to light candles with shuffling and muttering. In the box I was twisting my arse wishing for Marilyn on an old Pirelli calendar. Just a zucchetto hanging on nail. Put on my head it seemed fitting. My legs were dog tired from walking, living on hill. I took the weight off, heavy curtain, pitch dark, dozed in my wadi hole dreaming.

"Are you in there father?"

Disturbed awake, awkward, plain confused and dozy.

"Aye indeed I am."

Frosted slider pulled back, had a gander. Crucifix on rosary, anxious, collar deferential. Thirty, those wide eyes could not see me, thinking I'd see through her.

'Yes my child?"

Best Galway like my old fella, I'd sweaty palms. Give it a shot for the craic, a snake behind glass.

"I'm from nunnery in Bruges, I knocked rectory door. Would you have room for one night? I'm on my way to Knock in Mayo for special intentions. I'm Sister Aniky."

Lucia Santos at Fatima, Bernadette at Lourdes, children at Medugorje and old folks in the rain at Knock. I was not comfortable mocking the bird.

"Arra now, my house keeper Mrs Murphy would have a rare old fit. A wandering young one in the house! There's grand b and b above on the hill with Spanish arches, run by nice fellow divorced many the year. Rascal does the head tour, back home from Americas. Tell him I sent you and demand stiff tariff deductions for clergy. Take scenic paths by the cliff."

"Can you hear my confession?"

Ex nihilo, out of nothing, the sins of a nun - expecting none.

"Once of a morning rose for vespers at 4.30 instead of 4.00, skipped angelus what with orphans in snow storm.'

"Go ahead now."

"I'd feelings for Father Victor Salvaldor from Malta. They sent him off to Brazil. I'll leave nunnery behind and travel on to Rio."

Her lover high-tailed, now she in hot posse pursuit. Well this revelation set me off bang nutty lunatic with mouth open spouting full of nonsense.

"Leave that poor fella alone now. Don't be going tempting a good man from the celibate oath. He fled to keep his vocation to get away, so get your mitts away from him. Women and their wiles, terrible temptations depriving men of eternal life and salvations. Took his celibates with his own vocabularies. Fierce powers youse have to tempt fellas, it's under burkas youse should be and no mistake now. Only ways to stop. I'm not having a bit of it."

Shipped off Salvaldor nunnery malarkey
shenanigans, she's set adrift in doldrums.
Host the wet sail she's coming,
sailing down on the windrush
defrocked on Ipanema in her bikini.
All arise. To attentions. Straighten up!

Saints above, impersonating a priest, serious mortalers and with coveting a nun. She'd a cool hat, I'd tell her keep it on. Rightly should boil galoot like me in fish and chip oil or have me jig on Tyburn gallows. What devil gets into you, all upside-down? Maybe lead in old water pipes. She thinks her soul cleansed white, what if flattened by a truck? No wonders I live out days lonesome on hill tops.

"Away on the head now, don't neglect your rosaries."

"Sorry father. Thank you, father."

I watched her in daylight through a chink of curtain. A woman that would kneel nails for indulgences. Healthy young one, tantalized eyes, nice appendages. No nail polish or rings, double dutch, celestial icy star dust debris aggregated nicely with good form in firmament. Her rapid footsteps in tubular socks left the church.

I was through side door like a bullet, up fields, leaped over the slurry ditch. The gravel cliff road would take her past my hacienda. Still time for a quick comb of hair, brush teeth and gargle, change of shirt then sit in the garden chewing peanuts and polishing me spurs. In minutes I was the brylcream boy with a gleaming harp lager, following her progress with binoculars. Life's as hodge-podge as a dingo going walkabout. Even an old man Orangutan in a Borneo forest goes to search a mate. Blind squirrels will find few nuts. I remembered a school trip as a twelve year old to curraigh of Kildare.

"Can we see the stallion and mare fucking?" I asked the stud master. Brother Edward treated me to a whack on the ear hole.

"Watch that fucking language." So he was entitled. Our parents paid for a full term of wallops.

Suddenly out back by the cliff face, down she went on steps to the rocks below. I watched from the cliff top. Shoes and back pack in vivo she marched into a cruel trashing troubling sea. In moments fierce undertow, sharp stones battering waves would dispatch her. I'd sent her over the edge. Only priests can perform that confession job. Lunkhead me had short circuited the business like a shark biting Marconi's transatlantic cable and leaving only doggerel distorted static buzzing above in the ethers.

"Ahouy young one. Get back, it's dangerous! You'll catch your death with cold."

She paid no heed up to unwise molars in rough waves. Narra attempts to float, only barely doggy paddle. I bounded down the steps. Aunt's tarred curraigh was moored upturned on a shard of rough sand. Crafted of wicker, cowhide and tar, Aran technology from darker distant ages where they never heard of robust fiberglass, hardy plastics and Loctite glues. I launched out the quarrelsome tub in currents, after damsel in wet dress. Bleeding craft was a nautical nightmare. Her head still bobbin in forty foot.

"Think of your children not yet born among us," I hollers.

Finally her reaction. Women with gra for young ones, works every time. Up came a shaking hand, grasped the wicked craft and tips kit and me in the oceans. It was iceberg cold that gray day, me knoby dick shrinking as cracked ice on skillet, Aniky grabbing tight me trousers, leather belt jammed together. Stuck to my ass like Y fronts. 'Twas a time of bobbins, no selkie woman on my hands.

'But he that is born to be hanged need fear no drowning.'

"Lets head to shore. We'll have tea with hot buttered scones and jam, with boiled eggs."

Egg crack inside bring life, otherwise omelette.

Crawled for shore arm over arm, waves the height of houses. Needed the strength of ten men, only blessed by an incoming tide we washed up on shore. Her nibs on dry dock weighed a ton. She was gaspin with swallowing, trying to catch her breath. Pants around my knees, round bare arse pointed towards cloudy skies.

"Not best for swimming. There's grand beaches across Rush and Donabate." Brain frozen I says, only jit-jit-jit jittering.

Frostbites on extremities, needed warm up squeeze,

no balls of brass monkey, no whale oil protections.

Blue Irish veins suitable for drizzles, not frozen calamities,

peeing ice cubes, under those circumstances.

Knelt on the sand, head bowed she made a sign of the cross.

"Sorry, I could have drowned us. Fit of sudden fuming madness, then got dragged out. You lost the boat?"

"Tide coming in, 'twill wash up. No loss anyways, task was over."

"Are you b and b man?"

"Aye, I'm Brian. Up the steps. Get hot whiskies flowing before we catch our sodden death. Logs aburning in the house."

At the bottom of the steps she hugged me strong, passed ancient aunt's sign to deal with metal scavengers.

'There is not 3 pounds and 8 ounces of gold buried here abouts, pass on by nothing to see.'

"You were so brave."

She tells me again she's Sister Aniky from Bruges.

"Some scarce monies got washed away. If I don't have breakfast do you charge less?" She says at the gate.

"Don't worry. Say us a few prayers."

Any charge would be on my soul for telling porkers.

"Your first born will see you right." Laughed hew-haw, moron's word to santificated nun, then led her up the garden path.

"Get wet stuff off and be wrapped up warm."

The favourite couch blanket I gave up. Upstairs palaver in my skivvies running her bath, hot dressing gown from the press. I'd throw in the towel. Kitted out in departed aunt's gear, she was smelling of youth and moth balls. She sat on the couch, further wrapped by aunts full length mink coat. We'd cloves hot toddie with lemon for thermal internals.

"Good for what ails you."

"Tomorrow I'll be off. I wants to be no burden."

Ears out, large teeth of butter faced chattering woman. With such a mug I had an inkling why she went the cloistered route. Giggle mug enough to make a stuffed bird laugh. Not lacking charms, beguiling a man with drink taken and mott balls, soft furs and uncovered thighs.

"Priest in church was unkind and angry," she sobbed. "Terrible things said in confession. Where else can I find comforts? I wanted a bed for the night to lay my head."

"That man would not know his very arse from elbows. Has that bad a reputation. Galway man busy distressing women folk. Not to worry, I've feathered pillows and eiderdowns."

Aniky constantly crunched kettle crisps. I'd lots more. Two fingers of *Scotch* disappeared, thereafter helped herself fistfulls. Irritated, I was, by her description of dreadful priest behaviours.

"Are you by yourself?"

"Single man, I'd a son Jimmy pass away in Louisiana."

Muddy waters easier catch fish. During house fire easy steal diamonds.

"I'm sorry, Vicar said you were best b and b."

"He'd tell no lie." In or out the box.

"For one night. I'm to Knock in the morning. I still feel cold," she says.

Hand draped on her shoulder she held me for warmth, embraced for defrosting. Could feel her jitter shiver, enjoyed manly attentions after all she'd fled the single bed.

"Saved with your swimming."

"Sure that's strength from these hills," I says.

In the blurry passage of times we konked out on the couch. Later untangled, buried her with blankets, I snuck up stairs. That midnight she came to my bed both still plenty jarred and each desperate as hump backs tackling fishing trawlers.

"Do you want I have favourire feeling?" she whispered. "Do what you want, wonderful to experience man desires. I had love before the convent."

All she said, no better words spoken on earth all that day, by a naked lady. Saints could not blame that one on me. Enough said, nothing dimmed my ardor. Lifers getting conjugals, better bite one fresh mango than basket of rotten ones.

Things moved slow, Aniky had previous with the willy but one swallow never made a summer. She lay like a log and toiling was involved, occupied tougher than lads cutting their winter wood. I took her there and then, shooting from the hip.

Busted my ass
licking my chops
humping a log.
'Choppers and sawyers
lay timber low,
skidders and swampers
holler to and fro.
Come sassy loaders
before break of day
come load my bully boy
get my wood away.'

Still that lass paid many a tariff, worked for her keep, long or short they all fit as a catholic school blazer. She was a grand kisser, considerate and finished in missionary. Days went by, Aniky developed a taste for the double bed. Attentions appreciated, one tree never enough for Canadian lumberjack. She cooked Netherland sausage, could have been worst.

"After Sunday mass I'll go to the rectory, deal with this Père. Saying the rosary is no penance. That's my life, I'll box his ears." Aniky tells me on the second day.

Finally for her own good I called the prioress of the cloister in Clontarf. I knew the place, over looking the bridge to Dollymount. Never could have left her to perish in the seas and spare parish headaches, but what choice did a guilty man now have?

"One of yours at b and b needs comforting prayers, she's never got tariffs. Find her most intoxicating to sooth my lonely spirit. My only guest presently. I'd not want her to be led into temptations with a sincere single man. Once married with kin across in Canada. 'Twould be best come and get her, save both our souls before any adulteries. She has tastes for Johnny Barleycorn, beggars belief we'd be on best behaviour. Can youse pay kitty for her nights?"

Of early morning, a gaggle of nuns appeared, Ballyfermot bruisers emptying from a black Range Rover. Reminiscent of Khrushchev shot putters, dispatched when a rogue savannah elephant needs relocating. They sequestered their wild rover, threw she and back pack in the jeep. Her jig was up. All in all, shame about her boat race and my momentary lapse of judgment.

CHAPTER 4

Always with empathies for early rising milkman, scared that morning until I recalled I'd had beetroot for dinner. Through early morning mists I watched a tall figure swift style by the cliff path. Ominous spectacle, seeing such rushed strident gait of grim faced church padre. Trembling visit coming for some unfortunate feudals who'd missed their tithe, or a knuckle rap for delinquent post honeymooners baking no oven buns, or attentions for creaky trawler widows to remember the Holy See. So sail on by, man of the cloth. I'm needing no salvations now. Come ye back when I'm old and greyer.

It was an unpleasant surprise when he altered his stride and headed in my abode. I was in me Y's and not attired for formal Vatican visitations. It was a warning to never scrimp on a hefty drawbridge, deep moat with sharp pikes and fortified barbican. Always have ample hired help armed with cross bows and heavy duty trebuchet flinging rocks. I'd hide in me oubliette below stairs if I'd a mind, with decent portcullis as ever. Naturally.

"Tis yourself," he says, me in a dressing gown on front steps.

Thin skinned, shaved countenance, like he'd descended from Mount Rushmore. Grey haired like every priest in the country.

"Come in Father McCracken," I says with my customary b and

b welcoming grimace, as Brezhnev messing Dubchek's spring. I recognized him from the local rag having Beetle whist drive to collect a few bob. Something leaking, plumbing, needing repairing, same church fixens since time of Nod in this land of rain.

Eskimo's fabled hundred words for snow, Hawaiians ridiculous 139 for rain, 'kilikili' for heaven's sake! Irish with just 'rain' or 'fecking rain'. It's always wet.

He sits in the kitchen, waves off any approach for refreshments or cup of Gold Lyons tea. Only fierce business was the order of his day, a personality harder to crack than the shell of a chinese walnut.

"I'm afraid it's not the social visit now, you are not a member of my congregation."

Northern man, Donegal I'm guessing. Such fierce men forever searching for troubles, serious by nature with dour Scottish inclinations, been all around the world and never left home. Belt and braces approach, different beast than sloths found down south.

"Not presently."

Give it time. Meantime a staunch buffet catholic. It'd been a while since I wore forehead ashes. Nowadays, stations of the cross were rush hour on DART railway. Charismatics drove me from the fold, congregating was never my thing. I gave up on Romans, formed no other allegiances, my hope for life immortal gamble that Cardinals were wrong with contraceptives. A leap of faith needed for any atheist leanings. *'Ain't no atheist in fox holes'.*

"We'd a bit of thieving with St Vincent De Paul's poor box last year. Stealing coins for crack, I'd mince meat those bowsies if I get hands on them. Useless rascals."

Padre had a powerful pair of fists, scar tear and wear visible.

"I had the recorder installed. Garda Walsh donated time and talent. This morning our curate gave me the recordings from the machine."

Bruce Walsh from the village bar, slicker than snot on a door knob.

A lad that strips big in budgie smugglers, a real honey badger. Now I was confronted by this collar's old machine on my kitchen table. Made in Albania, crafted from cast off any old irons, sounded like running on steam pipes and whistles.

"Wait now I'll push the lever for pictures."

Whirring and clacking silent black and white film with visions of mise inside the church, seated in pews, shuffling my arse. No concealing that cyrano nose and ugly pus. Then up I gets and sits on hard man's cushion in confession. McCracken had me nailed with Tirana technologies.

"Hope you were grand comfortable now." Hard man says.

"Having wee rest and prayer father, heavy day climbing. Bunions. Cushion nice on the arse for contemplations."

Visions of Aniky wandering aisles, lost waif darts for confession box where she entrusted her pious securities. Quiet time passed in empty pews, then Aniky comes out runs thru' front door. Sight of lummox me flying out back door, galumphing lunkhead.

"Enlighten me now, mister. What game are you busy playing? Hide and seek? What confusion you meddling at all? Two of youse scattered like dandelion seeds up the same hill. What did you do to yer one, stirring up her sacred troubles?"

The man's accent had me scared with flashes of O'Neil, Faulkner and Chichester-Clark politicians, Ulster TV nightmares from black and white static days of yore. *Stop children larking near bombs or vehicles parking.*

"She needed a place to stay the night with salty breezes, off to Knock. No sins committed. Pillow and pie, long and short. Sorry for despoiling the box, I'd no business with that." Gaspin I was with the seething fellow. "Lit a few votive candles and prayers for special intentions."

"That's not the end of it, not by a long shot now. I should be giving you knocks with my leather belt."

Was he watching activities with satellites and drones? Not only witnessed by whitecaps and small yachts from harbour, whipped by miracles St. Anthony could find anything.

"Michael Ghosh saw youse above on the hill. 'Watching her like a hawk stalking a mouse', he says. Then her off down cliff steps out in the waves. 'Terrible distraught, heading for drowning'. You in your aunt's boat. Do you have explanations for these activities? After she stayed these four nights."

"She was off down to watch seals cavorting in waves, to swim with them. Flippers, loved walrus and tusks. Desperate keen on pinnipeds she was. In Howth we all enjoy our sea creatures."

Hog tied, a man of paws, her bum covered in finger prints, guilty as Oswald and Ruby, O.J. and Eichman, Chessman, Wuomos and Abel. Worse cheater than 1921 Black Sox, none worse than that.

"It's Shady Nook b and b I'm running. For tariffs only." Aunt's tariff was once 'seventeen shillings and six pence, half crown for the minister'.

Ten days absentia and shawlies looking good, keep teeth in old lady. Between you and I, needed bit of trim your honour. But collars don't relate to that malarkey, no man to man with men of iron, my ass kicked sooner than later.

"Mrs Connolly at the chemist told me you were getting supplies. 'Rubbers by the lorry load'. I think the child came to the church in distress, looking for ministry and instead encountered the likes of you. What willy nilly devilment did you start? You'd jiggery pokery debauchery ways. Do you think I'm a damn amadhan? I know your ways and type. Satan has control of you boyo."

He tapped his pineapple nut, slammed his fist on the three planked oak table, mad maybe with chemist shops profiting from my carnal sins. Hard man had cured many a borstal juvenile from deviant behaviours with them hams. I was not prepared for any fisticuffs, nor wanting my skull beauchained with welts. I'd fold quicker than a sushi chef.

"Loaded to the gills, if I'd me druthers with youse two debauchers. I don't appreciate a galoot stickin his nose in my church business. Yer an I'm all right jack fellow. What's your business?"

"Odd bit of the writing, father."

Veins popping on puce papa, he was no box ticking man of cloth. I feared he'd explode like Betelgeuse.

"Good minds to put a few welts in, see who's mightier. Forty year calling to priests by Churchbridge parish at 12 year old, dedication vocation as sure as God made this very earth."

Appreciated hefty oak between us, ready to tip it and break his toe.

"Picking yer women in my church?"

Put corn whereever hogs can get to it. If monkey eats nuts let monkey eat nuts.

"Smart aleck behaviours, I'm a hard man, 25 years in Kinsale industrial school with borstal lads. Begob delinquents. Aye, I'd a few knockouts at Staidiam Náisiúnta in Dolphins barn. If I catch you with shenanigans down that church again I'll beat the living bejasus out of ye."

Bent nail needs straightened by hammer.

Figured on four steps to the sink, grab upturned frying pan, skull blow to floor him, five mile to airport. Exit on the jumbo. Not times to forget.

"Right there father, I'll drive across to Rush for me daily meditations."

Maybe less demented, better than belts on my hide. No debate.

"An altar boy many the year no harms intended. Sure I'll put few bob in yer poor box for them altarations. I'm a bit shattered."

Maybe it's Garda Siochana station I should be dealing with. Alls I'm saying.

"That's my business with you taken care of now."

He sat back, silent in his comfort, satisfied with right old scary rigmarole. Only tick tock and sea birds moving, caught his drift. Watching departed aunt's painting of Galapagos blue footed booby on living room wall, bought for few punts at county fair. He lit up a fag. The man knew his mind. Our Pax Dòmini, for entitled he was. Savoured my cup of Bovril, let things marinate.

"I've chill from morning mists. Put two decent fingers napper tandy, get a body down the hill now. Your good Aunt ran an Irish house, ball o'malt, grand breakfast."

While he was swilling four fingers of Courvoisier from tantalus crystal decanter, I wrote a cheque to stop his leaks and buy me karmas. He checked for zeros and location of decimal point.

"Right enough appreciated, that Rush is not up to snuff, Donabate is Anglican territory nuff said. Eating the blackberries. Say the few prayers, a years probation. Good day now, behave yourself. We've not only cameras, tigum."

Man upstairs also checking. Sound man, calling for back up. Fairplay.

"Church can always rely on my donations."

Off he went, mindful of inclinations. I was left only with blue kitchen-smoky air.

CHAPTER 5

Machez a mio called from village on that early May, Noreen arrived from storms of Louisiana. I was still halfway finishing kippers poached egg with buttered hovis. She waited by harbor wall beside Martello tower watching strong fellows on trawlers seeking shoal of red herring of which there were plenty. Slick sea lions bobbing and weaving anticipating bouncy summer beachballs. Bundled with silk scarf and winter coat my pale Noreen, green eyes gleamed like she had laser done.

"So long waiting, missed you." From me that was no lie.

"Brian, you'll never know."

Cheeks cold, not dry eye between pair of us maybe unaware we were strangers those many ways.

"Oh bb, I came to see you and the rabbit." Wiped those teary cheeks, and took a flyer on me.

On drive back said she loved the village and on St Mary's road the ancient church.

"I'll pay a visit say a prayer for us," she says.

"Occasionally find some comfort there from strife."

"Never traveled first class before very generous, fell asleep and missed the wine. They woke me for dinner, foie gras entrée. Soon as we arrived I'd a lovely pint."

Living high life on my dime, Blackpool carousel happy.

"No better pint going or coming, if Taosaigh I'd award free pint for the passport."

My boggy philosophy put every arriving manjack in good state. Failte romath a cara do tell of wild times and far away malarkeys. Many Sam Adams in tall glasses in San Diego departures at 7 in the morning, get nerves ready for jumpy rides over Rockies. What's that Johnny foreigner up to? Worse we'd always be expecting.

"I've special places to show you, Wicklow people think they have it all, travel very little in Ireland." She claimed.

Of the rest of thirty two they'd not give a damn, blessed by their own wilderness.

"bb I left with one suitcase and return with two, world's most pathetic creature! Right off jump street, can you handle me at all?"

"We're on the pig's back, Howth head is pot of gold."

By the house she pranced and laughed like swirling banshee not a care in the world, loved garden's wildwood flowers, path with steps down cliff to sea. Waved and shouted big 'Hello' towards mountains of county Wicklow where she was born and raised. Horrified to see tacky TV perched up in living room surrounded by cardboard boxes.

"We can't be having balloons what with sea mammals near by. Ones you watched were Horace pod, there's others all about. You see them pinnipeds in wake of car ferries. I'll get a kayak for summer but currents are that fierce. Not like peddleboats in Bray."

"Brian you're well stuck in with doings out here!"

"You get close to hill folk, watching out for each other. Weekends on buses tough yokes from city rough trade, took off with aunt's wee currach." *Howth summer time only fish in the schools.*

Aunts doings lay mostly undisturbed, studied carded instructions on grand polished table.

'Never use dinner crystal, once had visitors used best glasses

oh horrors visitor broke one, their day spent running to replace,

punts from their poor pockets, they never returned once.'

On fridge note from those long before days: *'careful picking mushrooms uncle Ted got the runs, do try on Prizwickies poodle first.'*

"When can we go?"

Take me home boyo was her message, start with living once again. She'd not stay on Jackeen hill, Howth fly over rock heard only on shipping forecasts warning of rough waves. Fish out of water, Atlantic salmon returning to wrong stream.

"Brian I can't believe I'm here! Only working Shady Nook that few nights when you showed up."

In time to learn I'd taken this chick to foxes and girls from granite county have hearts of stone, rocks for brains.

"Irish men will be glad to see you, do Dublin city world of good."

In the kitchen emptied her suitcase laden with gifts from bar flies, alligator heads, Mardi Gras masks, 'happy' and 'unhappy' face-mask worn in parades. Bobbled head Jazz bo Jims, voodoo amulets for juju, Buddha statue purported to endure emotional relationships and Zulu coconuts.

"They knew I was broke customers generous, wanted to get my sinners bench shipped but it was worn out!"

Too heavy to ship with her goings on, flashed wad of cash maybe a few grand. *Earn money needle dig sand, spend money water move sand.*

"People at work would say I'm too friendly. How can I be too friendly?"

No qualifications, get blue job somewhere, bet her bottom dollar on me? Beautiful birds never dependent on any man always candidates lurking, fellows eager for beaver only fool would think to cage this bird.

You're the fool, you're the fool,
no going dutch with this broad
parrot in my head knew summat
best eat rice one spoon at a time.
Tiki tacky mistake for little men.

"I'd dinners in every restaurant in town everyone wanted to say farewell even Ferrice. So much craw fish."

Famine food, pinch tail, suck head.

"Walked from Satchmo statue to Savannah markets to Riverwalk a hundred times. Look what do you think?"

Displayed her flat tummy, well appreciated tease, gazelle knew what she was about. On the couch we drank down Niagara Gewürztraminer and dish of pyella fried rice.

"It's overwhelming do they want us coming back in their lives? We left many years ago, is it possible to catch up after so long away? Brian I'm that scared now."

Not a problem for somebodys, that navel floated my boat. Naturally.

"On my visits home old friends would get out best china and fruit cake, I'd only ever wanted the cracked cup." Said she.

Best China worked many a time, but that day Noreen pulled me away from silk roads, back to rutted boreens where dark mountains sweep to the sea. Pointed my compass to green land time, journeyed back from Khyber's pass to Dublin's scalp hazard where rocks do fall on numbskulls. Enough wok bamboo and brown nipple babes, can't beat pot of mashed spuds.

Late afternoon wrapped around each other we fell asleep, when I woke whispered she was tired.

"Will you be long," asked as she climbed stairs.

Yeah sure. Well she knew cut of my jig with her.

"There's lots of bedrooms, bags of room altogether." Giving space, not pressures.

Aunt's bed room pilled high with dogeared Mills and Boon. I preferred rough and tumble under satin sheets, not imaginary.

"Are you mad daft? Are you an Irishman at all? I'm living a nun these many months, bb. I've traveled many miles not to sleep alone. Get up here and give a proper cead mile failte. I'm wanting my big time howdy!" She laughed.

Run off her feet, then rolled up my sleaves, although well she knew I had short comings. That night touching her felt like Franklin with lightning bolts, shaking bones and boner.

"Have happy time," she whispered in my shell like, fingers dancing on that belly.

Better than nun, experienced habits under covers, wive's tail all it was cracked up to be. Met again sugar more and sugar beig 'suck 'em like grapes' not grab like Japanese soldier with Shōchūt Shanghai lady once learned me. We'd fair rocking ruckus up and down like Wicklow county. Not a broad to lie down easy only try to hang on, finished hands grasped on her bum, sugaring off.

Dangerous gamble this woman game like climbing Matterhorn, sitting on Alabama public transit or having children. Everyday desired her that mattered most, life might never be this good again, I'd drink to very last drop. Our journies in Ireland started and entered an emotional place, hoped never to leave.

CHAPTER 6

It seems now that Waterford nuns in boarding school had them practiced in arts of deception. Cloistered ladies with no gra for man, their primary life decision a vow to avoid the likes. Men ugly design of human race, those one prick ponies. Not having sex a calling in our fertile land while down the farm, horses, chickens and bulls make pigs of themselves. Through nun's eyes their madrasah pupils developed misshapen ideas. Disaster of Noreen's father early passing increased perverse notions, clues were there dalliance with a priest at her sexual awakening, her 'married man', and heading down Big Easy for all seasons of bacchanalia.

Daft directions for Wicklow girl to locate in that wanton city, none was not for likes of her. My mother liked Noreen happy I found a Wicklow girl, old dear stressed relating to other cultures, I'd inflicted potpourri's of women from foreign parts. Japan, babes from China and Korea, mostly how I was oriented (crazed as Genghis Khan) away from celtic girls. Preferred chopsticks for my mother was gathering kindling beyond in pine forest. Noreen planted flowers, fixed middle of lawn fountain, polished black range in the kitchen, potted leafy plants with oiled leaves appeared in each room moved to ensure they receive rays of sun, 'pink lady's-slippers' what she said. Many days we walked stony Howth Head pathways on down to Baily Head lighthouse picking berries from briars, *'where seldom is heard a discouraging word and the skies are not cloudy all day'.*

McArthur the tower keeper took a shine to my dame, flashed her beaming smile his way, blackberries coloured her lips. Dim your wick laddie only for mise. Every day I told her how much I loved her, 'cause Mama didn't raise no fool. Maybe too much 'I love you', 'I love you.' Like dollar store shopping come with no value.

Out in Bray we rented a paddleboat, won and lost on slots in Arcades. On Bray Head a gurrier yelled her nipples stood 'up like lamp-posts' as I took snaps in cold wind. Spent weekend in a caravan at Brittas Bay, swam in cool sea then wandered through Dublin zoo, Japanese gardens and Victoria's way. Swam Forty Foot in Sandycove and rode waves from Liverpool fast ferry entering Dun Laoghaire harbour, there she laughed in shock as an elderly priest dropped his togs and presented a white hairy arse. We walked Vico road to climb the Folly, Killiney's Obelisk. She loved grand houses on those hills, escounced for life in those gilded lillied pads, those loaded folks must have oodles of side door money. On that sunny day told her view was better than Sorrento bay even though I'd never been there. Afternoon tea and strawberry cake in a restaurant in Powerscourt.

In Delgany spent the night in Vaughan's classy hotel. Next morning she had a massage in the spa with handsome muscled fellow, naturally I'd few pints at the bar.

"She's off having a rub from Rory. Am I safe enough do you think?" Says I to smirking pubman.

My pathetic laugh trying to communicate, never comfortable conversing publicans in any land. Country lad would not spare steam off his piss, 'Put a lid on it Jackeen,' said with haughty silence. Not a thing surly replied, left me sweating in me hush puppies. Dublin pubs inflict dour pin wearing teetotalers, down from bogs pouring pints of solace for solitary men, with no social groveling required for any gratuity pittance. Drive decent men to drink these silent bar men would, grim species unique to Ireland. Takes lifetime rejection of booze, spends that lifetime to dispense the stuff. Staunch canny business fellow, member of steamed Vintner and publican licensing trade. Measures words like quids worth, angry red face stock in trade. Disapproved of drinkers as hooker hates johns, but dollar is a dollar with their canny business mind. Barely control his contempt's as long as heavy brass fill the till, these being my poor contemplations as she appeared.

"Alan give us a big glass of white," says bold Noreen after mauled by Rory.

Surly Alan related in some county way, gave my woman a big smile.

"Worst friggin massage, I needed ten minutes with you this morning. At least a happy ending." She whispered.

Ten minutes would be mighty grand, I'd early departed our bed, famished for buffet at seven afraid fry ups would finish. Tend to panic, folly to my ways them days.

"Honestly we're staying in this gorgeous place and all you want is crack of dawn sausage."

Apparently what we had both desired.

"I heard you spent an hour reading newspapers, drinking coffee. I was swanning about like a widdy woman, flapping like fresh fish."

Feasting on buffet and toasted brown bread with fine honey from Offaly.

"All hotel luxury and you with rashers and pudding. Such a senior citizen."

Getting roasting over fry ups, needed to nip this babe in the bud.

"Alright Noreen, last night I over did it in the bar and wine in the room. You on the phone to your mother for the ages, so I conked out."

She too had been hitting the sauce with the yaking, two of us fair blotto.

"Brian you're stupidest man, I should charge."

Always her small fry. Her surly tapster refilled, keep her going on that awful tack.

"Like that Asia place in the French quarter and your brown skinned Belize Indian, that might get you interested."

Finished the pint with improved contemplations. Only dreaming of double headers, with full speed per head. *Happy as a gannet in a kettle of fish.*

In hotel shop bought a gold claddagh ring to be best friends, try to convince her I'd put my fork in old time activities.

Never be too happy, even sunny day bring umbrella.

One fateful Wednesday afternoon me and the mott were out getting airs in Dublin city. Grand day reclined on park bench in Stephen's green, our central oasis. Threatening rain but hung on feeding waddling ducks with stale croutons. Forever the twitcher bird watching gathering of students on the bridge over the pond. Dark, reds and blond, perched and preening like painted penguins by water's edge, Irish with palet of colours like no others. Posh Trinity voices, probably one time Sion hill convent graduates.

"Dog haired brigade bunch of mongrels we are in truth." I says to my foxy head.

Life perfect on daddy's easy coin, except for harsh exams. There in gathering a short-haired blue-eyed blond, gorgeous creature blessed by her creator. 'Kimi' I heard, got on the bike, slung backpack in slim body way. Looked Nordic but a Dun Laorite, on this island she could have a brother with jet-black hair. Why her to swot? Head to Monaco speak frankly, Rivera topless use beauty and brain. Find yacht fellow marry a frog, disappear from humble places let scion have what he needs, raise shortie blonds belted in the Merc on streets of St. Tropez. Meantime a bird toxic to hapless secondary school lad never to replace her, like losing Stradivarius in Gioachino Rossini's overture. None of the girls wanted Kimi swishing around wishing she'd skedaddle, except to be forever nagging in their minds eye. With side eyed glances girl friends stared fascinated for their reasons. Embarked on their journey with fewer tools, like journeymen watching young Dylan in Greenwich village, agreed with her boy's haircut to tame that beauty. My only chance to take a ride on those hips if she was to fall on low times and be high priced call girl. Worth each cent of hefty booty loot demanded. No doubt.

Jewish fellas watch basketball.
Young felon's arses with old lags,
Vermeer with his light of day.
Men get a lot watching the likes
tall legs clad in white stockings.
As Yahweh watches us all.

Kimi glanced about her technicolour world flashed victory sign and departed, never notice grizzled dogs like me. But poor form and me stuck like flame to a mott, seeing I was attached.

Best not covet young ones
when sitting with your mott,
eat beef still want dragon meat.
Them Brothers knew I'd slow side,
Brothers with talents to spot dossers.
Bonehead will yeas never learn?
(gurrier doing Kimigazi)

On the grass some auld ones circled two buskers, handsome lads singing with their antics. One moving guitar as jungle dweller waving his codpiece, disturbing for fat pond fowl, his mate rifting on penny tin whistle. Boyos had talents and varsity girls chiming the chorus, threw a few coins in the guitar case. Bridge birds flapping every move.

"Big opera on." Says I.

"Can any of you sing solo?" Busker asks his choir.

Aussie I'm thinking hybrid vigour of down under fellas. Admiring pied piper and how he'd roped one in, same move as rodeo cowboy in Fargo, regaled by the chaps. Bits of Samoa, not all black lot of what I would wallabie. Up jumps Noreen wanders off to 'down under', music men her aphrodisiac.

"Can you sing at all?" he says.

She takes hold of the lads long necked instrument.

"Can I have a go?"

Then belting out old time ditties, more moxie gusto than Maureen Potter in pantos. Never expected such likes from shy and a sober Noreen, with your man standing right behind for duets, bodacious carry ons from jazzed up Aussies. Crowing under my gaze, too close bumping up his codpiece too touchy feelie for them tunes. Waltzing matilders, Danny's boy, she hushed entire green park with Mountains of Mourne, lots of tight daft Dubliners throwing paper notes. Full pint Noreen raised on farmer's fields and music talents, I was half pint hodge podge tapped from Toronto slops.

"You've great voice, great craic. Rare old variations." Busker Ozzy tells her. "Give a big hand for Noreen from New Orleans."

She looked right pleased, Penny whistle handed over some paper lucre shared for her notes. Right then I'm thinking better get off my arse and straighten things, shrewd 'down under' digging on my chick. We both understood attractions, clear as bank holiday Blackpool winning extra time on bumpers. Every manjack sees me weak, figure Noreen's never serious with such likes. Up I gets to assert me prima nocta rights, get sheep shearers back off, tame them shrews boys.

"Hey wild life, enjoying big time busking."

Casual what I started, waded into their fray, picking on lads entertaining citizens upsetting pastoral ambiance.

"Koala keep mits off, she's not one of your shelias." I challenged him.

Telling myself I was over the top, 'only coddin' shouda told him with a wink.

"Take it easy matey," he says.

Noticing my prowess as roughian, shirt fronted him as shiochana Lugs Branigan.

"Hands off and we don't have significant problems."

Compared to this git I was skinny bastard on thin gruel, by normal rights should have been afraid, and stayed in deep bunker but scared of no woman's land, I streamed over the top. Who'd have thunk it?

'muscles of his brawny arms
are strong as iron bands,
his hair is crisp,
and black and long
his face is like the tan'

Only eyeing stout branch to give solid whack, couple of early hits needed avoid being pummeled, my battle plan rarely survives contact with enemy. Noreen all startled with my behaviours, sees raging disparity and jumps between us. She very cause of creating tough predicaments, now innocent as Mrs. O'Leary's cow in Chicago's fire.

"Brian just the singing," so now she claimed, "no jazz hands fiasco, wind your neck in, pipe down don't be acting all jangly batty."

So who threw her a peanut?

"I'm ju jitsu, purple belt taekwondo."

Stakes on that claim, leaping and jumping like wack job, wee fists dancing knuckle ball bringing knife to gun fight. I'd stepped on a mine field, tempered like dry wood explode with sparks. *'I'm a terrible creature sober or soused, unaccustomed to fear.'*

"Anytime Paddy ready for you." Koala warns.

"Stop it," shouting at me like she's U Thant, that she ain't. "Go home."

Yer man mits up, prancing like an alien.

"Boxing kangaroo, I'm a citizen your butt will be riding Quantas."

Disturbing peace would get him dispatched on the jet plane.

"Roughians dispatched to Van Diemens land is what we do." I warned gnashing on my choppers.

"I'm from Cape town," Ozzy claimed, doing his springbok bobbing and hopping.

"All youse shackle draggers look the same, I'm down from Dundrum looney bin a mad cuckoo fella. Climbed sycamore tree to get over those booby hatch walls this very morning." I laughed playing to the peanut gallery.

"For the love of God," she says. Hoping to diffuse dire straits.

Watching tweedle dum and tweedle dee bump vacant heads, shadow pummel each other then sort it later. Tin whistle comes at me, acting daft to deflect attentions.

"You'll be lying in a box in repose over on White friar street with Carmelites within the hour. You'll not be first I've dispatched." I warned busker. "I've warrants out for sicko behaviours. Circle the Goombahs, I'm a peddler skinning cats."

Right then fat ould geyser shouts over, he with thermos flask for tea. Wore Fidel hat, had old Raleigh with dynamo and pump with bursting saddle bags. Painting floating lilly pod ducks with pallet and brush.

"Youse disturbing peace, I'll be calling peelers patrolling on these very parts."

"Go ahead citizen call Joe Friday and Mc Alpines fusiliers, bone head here is cavorting with me mott." I calmly explained only festering. That's the facts.

"Yer one's doing cavortin from what I'm looking. You're a right four eye'd streak of bacon you've no control over your bit of stuff. Looks like she's taken her fancies to him." Heard his toothless weezle cackle.

"Thermos you'd not know yer arse from an easel, keep your snout in Sporting Life old lad. Mind your business or you'll be smoking those woodbines from your butt." *Kill chicken, control monkey.*

"I'll smoke that puke face of yours. Would youse disperse now I'm here's for me solitudes." Old geyser panting like a Ronnie Delaney long mile.

"On your bike go put guineas on Arkle's mother in BallyJames-Duff. A tanner on Freddy Gilroy and fiver on Stirling in the TT." I was pumped, as George with his dragon.

"That afrikaner fellow will smoke ya, watch now that fella is worse than balubas and mamluks combined." More ugly cackles from Thermos Joe.

Bridge motts on sidelines enjoying my ignominious spectacle, vultures had circled for the kill. Me mortifications coming home to roost. Monkey meets gorilla.

"Brian leave here, leave them alone. Leave immediately, you're as a mad as a waxy hatter." My mott says, sharing her own mortified fears of morticians.

"Noreen we're off to Poolbeg for a gig, they're paying come for the craic. Ditch old big bird." Afrikaner persistent as bowler hat Orange man with Iron bru coursing blue blood.

"I'll take him down would ya hold me specs, " I says to Noreen. "I've seen enough Bruce Lee movies, I'll belt him one shot. KO." Okay.

Manys an oriental bird I've pinned to the mat, must count for someth.

"Ditch grinch." Chimed those birds.

"Alright that's enough. Sorry Graham, I'll get him out of here." Noreen says.

Focused on south paw African, left and right with no place to turn. To my detriments I'd not kept keen eye on Tin Whistle did not have me full wits, only circling and crouching he was.

"Listen matey I'll give you five count to scarper .... five, four, three." So goes Africa.

On that fecking three count in blink of an eye Capetown Graham gives a shove, I tips over genuflecting Tin Whistle. Down under backwards, should have seen it counting, no whistle blower on my side. Flipped on me backside turtled arse over bollix, buskers had me grabbed quick as you like. Tin whistle got me in a head lock and frog marched to waters edge. Foot shove in arse from Africa I was floundering blind in pond foul ooze. Thankful Dublin had no hungry park hippos. Bridge girls laughing bear witness my humiliations, to a woman found the business great gas. All delighted seeing my butt ended in the pond holding struggling frog legs in my fist. Dublin women with quick eye, dowsers divining, girls solid admirations for Africa macho. Finally Noreen comes to water's bank, helps me from weed entanglements most foul and ducks disturbed. Walked drenched, sat outside park railings, things had not gone well. Stumped down on me hunkers.

"Lass run across to Dunnes by the green. Get the lad a T shirt, socks and trousers and a wee towel. Before he'll catch his death." Decent auld one tells Noreen. "His knickers must be that soaking."

Noreen ran off haberdashery shopping, those brief moments chill of clothes I'd a breakdown. Brain swinging in me vacant cranium as pendulum on stormy sea. Pond sick there on cements and grabbed iron bars, I'd to get a grip of traumas. Young Capetown and his mate pushed me over rubicon, mined unearthed bizarre behaviors. But faith hollering abuse at fit muscular African in public space was reckless. Full well knew I was nut job with previous form, neither did I feel emboldened getting away bones intact. Boyos back singing John Brown's body with me bedraggled. Emptying wet shoes, squeezing socks. Me gabardine coat supporting lest I collapse, bare bone skeleton in rags ready for bin men with dustbin vans. Then running back she was with dollar store garments and wee towel.

"Honestly can take you to no wheres."

Felt like wailing as a baby.

"Don't mix easy, Brothers told me mother. Long agos." Yapping like amadhan.

"Look at very states of you." She says.

Shuffled off behind the jacks, toweled off, changed kit. Recovering, two of us sat on street seat left for hackney carriage travelers.

"Can't take you out for walk in park, thought you were man of the world used to all sorts."

"Sorry it all happened so quick. He with paws all over you, don't seem right."

She hugged me in tight embrace, what good women do, a woman with four hearts as if incubating triplets. Committed Kimigazi but she was kind hearted. Then a sod of wet turf was hurdled, hit side of my crown splattered me visage with mud. Missed the missus by hare's breath, got befuddled bit muddled from desperate wack on me noodle.

"What the fuck are youse up to? You could have killed him, I've a good mind to be calling fecking guards." Mad Noreen turned on mucksters.

Standing tall she was, let buskers feel her wrath she with the right hump.

"Go feck yourselves, stupid hare brains."

Through mud in my eye sees Thermos flying off on his bike, she brushed dirt from my hair.

"You've a bad streak, where did you learn to talk like that? He was twice you, honestly, shitzu barking at mastiff." She lobbed and smirked.

Woman tired of her man forever going off half cocked, size of my bone haunts me.

"Skilled with Asian martial arts." I defends to that hilt. "Not happy and you cavorting with them candidates."

"First I saw you google eyed with that bridge lot, you were leering," again she counters. "Why were you even ogling that one on the bridge? It's ridiculous."

There was hurt in the eyes of your one.

"I was only thinking how monkey eat apples. Honest."

"Did any blood return to your brain after all gaga eye with that blond?"

She understood how sausages were made, ain't never pretty.

"Why should I put up with your rascals behaviours?"

Don't mess with heart of a woman, crass fool I was with ox brain. Not need for mystic meg to know there'd be reprisals.

"I'm a friggin nut job."

"You're a horse's ass." Not happiest girl. "How did ye get out of the bughouse?"

Then the phone dinged, Joe Lange on the blower.

"Brian, it's done," he says.

Saved by his jingle jangle, from that triangle.

"We're to go by Joe's on Camden street, pick up a wee parcel."

"Brian don't make me more disappointed."

Moody and tense Noreen dragged over those hard yards, given rope and hung myself, nowt more to say. Stopped outside Lange's jewelry shop, my father had been in business with Joe's father. Me best school time mucker, two lads running wild on those old streets. They'd come by parents house in Rathgar, matzo bread and creamy cakes for holidays, suspenders for Joe's waisted pants not the vision

I'd for myself. A few wisps of hair all that remained, introduced sullen Noreen. Gave Joe the nod, understood I was doghoused. Underpants still wringing with pond waters, in my drawers of water minnows tickling my arse. Me previous attire dripping in a plastic dime store bag. Joe had comfortable salesman presence, with suede sofas and deep carpet, office smelt of seedy opulence and cigar smoke, Sinatra on low.

"I'd mishap in the park, unbalanced with the divots." Explain me dollar store get up. "Got fronted by down under, tripped in the muck. Van Dieman maggots coming back to haunt us. Are we ready?"

"All kinds of strange yokes down the town these days." He says. "Noreen I've been busy, Brian had me working hard, told me all about you."

Treated to glass of fine cognac. Leery Noreen swirled liquor in crystal, but intrigued by jeweler.

"Brian is my old friend, I took special care. You will be the envy of every woman in this city."

Noreen's problem was figuring out who I was in her life. Switcheroo Joe, pawning off cheap napper tandy, crystal from Watford. Joe and I as teenagers worked removing fire-damaged goods from buildings, our fathers negotiated salvage deals with insurance companies, or Garda auctions of drug dealer houses. Joe opened the wall safe and handed me a velvet box, admired his style, schooled watching Hollywood flicks from up in the Gods.

"Voila, here," Joe says with a nod. "I pulled rank, favours owed for many year."

Wee blue box presented flipped open, inside scarlet diamond earrings.

"Noreen I picked these in Amsterdam. I'd have flown to Africa, this was a job I had to get right, I carried your photo around De Beers. Fire diamonds match redness in your hair."

So Joe claimed, took me for mashugana putz, I'd not blow that whistle. Joe hands her the loupe, described blood diamond stones, made stunning with ginger. Smelt the diamond, Joe once told me you could smell sock of African stone smuggler. Knocked zero off the cheque, phony as myself. She reached to hold my hand, our armistice, conflicted truce declared. Stones not from Amsterdam, maybe transported on skiffs by Somali pirates. More likely gems reset from estate of old biddy on South Circular, trousered on some side deal with wayward sibling. Dublin's large families had lots of them devil. Or property seized from molls of drug baron's armory, escounced on Costa Del Sol. Noreen well knew I was plying rough trade, no polish on my old facet. Cracked from sleaze days, as a gurrier.

"Boers you trust." More like Mogadishu swindler. "With your hair short my dear they were made for you, always be part of your beauty." Joe told her. "Noreen for these times you are why I'm in this business."

Joe laying it thick as cream on his tribes delicious cakes.

"I've never had anything like this," she cried.

Only glass beads from Mardi Gras awarded for displaying ample knockers. Entitled. Listening to 'My way", signed his bonus k'sierra, put zero back on the cheque, for sheer guf of that gab.

"Wonderful with my pearl necklace." she said, streaming with tears.

"Nice," I agreed why not? Sure, I'd a load riding on her.

Outside walked streets in peaceful state of mind, on train ride studying her face in the mirror.

"Brian should I dye my hair blond?"

Oh fuck, deep in that muck and me out of her league. Her insecurity my only security. Maybe being blond would even odds, take mentals down notches.

"You look nineteen. Noreen my behaviour is weird, I need to stay out on the rock."

Surrounded by shawlies no gorgeous Sion Hills, away from brawny troubadours loitering public spaces.

"Louisiana sun damage, ocean burns, fourteen years by Gulf of Mexico. My baby was right, Wicklow girls beetroot skin have many freckles."

With that memory of James I started to laugh and she laughed. Sure Jimmy I hardly knew ye.

"I'll have skin peel with the laser." She said when we were home.

"Noreen why are you doing this?"

"For me."

Marched to beat of her drum, tote her own load. Few days later she went off early and in the evening called to pick her up from a cosmetician. Face wrapped in gauze.

"I need to stay in the dark and take these." She shook a bottle of pain killers.

That weekend she unveiled, delighted with her glow and younger years, no Karloff vision from Frankenstein films. Went off and returned with shopping bags of new clothes, hair with blond streaks. In those weeks diet changed lost few pounds, dressing as University student, looks without books, stress or degrees. This would not end good. I'd not papered over my cracks.

"I like curvy." I told her. "Don't be zany crazier."

Did not need to advertise shop window wares. Already had sold out demand. Had her on the never never.

She paid no heed to my ways, Stephen Hawking warned SETI don't beam out bright lights attracting aliens of all sorts.

"Tips at work are improving, Brian you also pay much more attention." She laughed. "I've been counting." On manicured fingers. Did like blond streaks, more fun in the sack. Mastiff with her, pleasured to pay her piper.

There'd be no safety box for us

not only solid Wicklow land,
do you understand volcano?
Then talk to Japan people,
world with burning vents
Tsuami, better keep moving.
Like Celts.

CHAPTER 7

With most those days I'd clear view in white house on top of Howth Head, 'Mine field' named by my aunt to scare away neighbours. Across the bay from Kish lighthouse, Bray Head and white Sugar Loaf peak from among those Wicklow hills. Promised Noreen we'd climb all 1644 feet and leave Jimmy's photo on the summit, my brave lad might I take courage from you. But despite these sights preferred to see Noreen dressing in the morning, that brazen kind-hearted Wicklow lass liked to admire herself in her pelt, full of natures bounty. In our yellow-walled bedroom with orange window frames combed brown hair tinged with celtic red, with sunlight streaming.

Waking up together,
our raw I want you
so many decisions,
whose turn to go on top?
The cover, the cover!
Keep blanket in place
and she on her back
in that cold place.
Mostly she goes top,
harder dealing with.

A Wicklow Girl

You can still see it, house with three Spanish-style arches, wooden deck out back, hedge at the side. Love your neighbour but maintain dense high foliage. *No junk males*, Aunt's no nonsense red sign on front garden gate. Roscommon visitor once overstayed his welcome, 'Monster from the Dail', she said. Details not related but after sturdy locks applied to each bedroom door.

Noreen was thirty two, I was taller but once flattered when creole woman in a fish restaurant north of Grand Isle said I looked like John Lennon. In truth I'd already passed more sand through hour glass than found on Courtown beach, all my genes faded ripped patched pounded chiseled and dented. Maybe aged slower in Canadian winters where there is no life. Truth be told.

When that final day of my prime,
morning woke commence decline?
Little to realize, eyebrows grow again,
inch by angle libido in reverse.
Girls looked my way, glance no more.
After, every day I value less,
as brand new car off the lot.
No collectors item, days end.

Noreen took a gamble after fourteen years living over in 'land of levees' she lost on many bets. I her hero in escape from Louisiana. 'Forever feudin over money' her frequent Ferrice complaint. That lad her two cent loser, broken shoe one bowl rice money fellow lost all their marbles. Older sister Beth would visit, she and Noreen never close divorced her husband after few years. Face puckered liked sucked lemons, if a car she'd be an Edsel, as they say. Always considered Beth heartless different from her sister but monkey see monkey do, sticky viscous family blood can be vicious.

That summer Noreen had part-time job in Howth Arms below in village, relief from gruff creatures charged with dispensing pints.

Thereafter I'd see crowd lingering, bar fly malingerers staring and she as copper penny rubbed with sand, shinny object distracting attention of magpies. Bar banter as best friends not pub acquaintances.

'What was she doing with likes of him?' Pack of wolves wondered. *Oh they'd seen many likes of me, blind cat catch mouse, suckers.*

Noreen aroused passions in bowsies bunch of cute gaelic hoors. Hips swinging master of her universe she was in green blazer. Owner Harry adored her style for business, eyeing his barmaid like his old lad eyed prized heifers in Mullingar's livestock market. Takings good with her hands pulling pints and her ways with badinage.

"She's best," says Harry. "Now Brian don't take this wrong way ye need to keep the eye out. They're mad for her never witnessed the likes, I won't want to see you get hurt, you're a good lad."

Stating bleeding obvious Connemara man, Harry Einstein detected she was altogether too grand for plain likes of me, thinks I hail from Ballinasloe.

"Those bar fellows don't know our relationship, we've history in times before here." I told Galway man." *Together grow as rain with mushroom.*

People opened up, men figured they'd chances. Emotional balloon inflated needed pricks, always on hand in Ireland. Dog's bollocks Garda Bruce Walsh leader of that band of buggers. This ape, this gorilla, guerilla armed with sleazy charms. Pirated highwayman, vile raparee, his recorder queered my patch with staunch padre. Always called her Mac figured she'd be easy pickens to pluck from weirdo on the hill. Stand deliver your woman, I'm male man armed with what she wants.

Howth hill no tiger only have monkeys,
Hill with no tiger monkey is king.
Monkey always have king.

Contemptible fellow put his hands around her waist. So what can I do, how can fleas avoid wild honey? Put her in burka, shut in the house? She'd call garda, landing back on peelers bailiwick end in hoosegow, fitting zebra stripes in the jail house.

Woke late that morning feeling guilty with Noreen departed for work, when she left our warm bed I'd roll and bury my head in her eiderdown pillow. Doing nothing preferred occupation, I drank coffee slow. Women expect men be grafting, bone idle never fit well. Struggled to be ambitious while she wanted me improving nest in salaryman's hurly burly. Baile ata Cliat work force not on my dance card, do not wish struggles back in harness working for gombeen pimpled Irish creature, only making wages. Over hauling those days, determined to have productive day.

'So my man where do you see yourself in 5 years?'

'Maybe work at ape house, in the park. Then wind up in pine box ups on old coote hill.'

'... tired of planning and toiling
in the crowded hives of men.
Heart-weary of building and spoiling,
and spoiling and building again,
and I long for the dear old river
where I dreamed my youth away.
For a dreamer lives forever
and a toiler dies in a day.'

'Sleepy head cut grass', note stuck on marmalade jar. She'd dispensed with gardener Ron, now paid good fella for not working, long or short he with team of kit and kin. On the back she penned *P.S. 'I wanted you'.* Drizzle descending best rake not progress that morning, headed to town bumpkin toured capital city bothering no one. Wander streets, earwigging over pint in Slattery's, Dublin city grants every citizen a Bloom's day. As copy writer jotted down notes, smoke stained walls heard from generations of gurriers.

'Metal fellow spit in me porter.

Do you do short hand? Do you have any yokes?

I've the bedsit in Belgrave square for Nescafe,

give us a feel, give us the hand job then. I hate Man city.

That Jesus movie was too antisymmetric.

Me uncle has De Lorean in Aran islands, Inisman.

Brand new. I'm gone for slash, don't ye split.'

After decent steak and kidney pie in Bleeding horse, sorting through books in a stall on Nassau Street. Misery literature by an acre, bios I don't jot a care about.

Me auld fella left me Ma with bag of porridge, there was 10 of us. On the gruel.

Took a pass from Decko, did zigzag rifled a shot in off the post. Fuckin genius.

(They say books will be written by robots, that happened long ago.)

Found marked up copy of 'JFK, An Unfinished Life' and Jack the PT-109 pilot. Saw she called.

"I'm home early where are you?" Sounding exasperated with me out toiling, wobbling delicate ankles on cobble streets.

"In town collecting background, starting to like kidney again. I've photo of Felix Walcott watching over Kennedy, Wexford in '63. Amazing stuff."

Didn't she care a wit.

"Hurry come home, I'm back early and you were gone. I miss you."

"Off to Henry Street to get pants."

"They've pants out here for heaven's sake, bb come home get on a train."

"My favourite place with half sizes."

"bb champagne is in the fridge, I'm starting and lonely!"

Sitting on H train rounding smooth curve of bay, this babe chomping at the bit. Knew in those winters of Canada there would be la eile go brea times, phaorach getting fizzy wine. When I got back she rushed to the door pushed me against the wall.

"I told Harry I was leaving early, thinking of you alone."

"Out about getting it done, I can make it in this old back water."

With those white thighs no bone of mine would remain idle.

"Drinking pints reading ancient books?"

Getting a dressing down, so far so good.

"In the hustle baby starving, make me a sandwich?"

"Typical Dublin man and me expecting to be ravished, I've naked body under this dressing gown you should well know."

Quick as duck on June bug felt her breasts, cracked beer slaked thirst with cold draft.

"Throw in few radishes."

"I needed to come home, Harry said you are the luckiest fellow."

"I know."

Next to reveal sky is blue and wind blows hard. Didn't need no publican pontificating my fortune. Stick to ripping off customers as victuallers throughout the land, like they're dispensing god's golden nectar. We'd cup of tea and sandwiches sitting in cosy kitchen.

"Grass will get cut tomorrow, promise."

Let it piss rain again, easy bet up on that wild hill.

"I'm in love with you," so she claimed that very day.

Popped champers, sometimes ball finds the glove. Assumed she knew my feelings but with women you have to relate fidelitas everyday. Never glib, need hand on bible 'I love you'. Relationship emergency light always blinking, hidden rocks hiding there be dragons. Phone rang her oldest friend Mairead as ever.

"Having romantic afternoon strawberries with whipped cream, evening of wine and passions!"

Busy with babycham she'd rapted my attentions, as they musth.

"Mairead says it's only Wednesday."

Don't spare rod seven day adventist with Noreen, that young one not like dovetail furniture, screws required. Not wanting her with wandering 'aye'. That gleam about her always had that whip hand over me. Fair dues. In her round robin life.

"Mairead remember the tower our Cill Mhantáin wish? Maybe some will come true, I ran home he was out buying trousers."

Lots of laughter done with the phone.

"What's with the tower?"

"Arra as young ones, sixteen. They took us virgins up Glen da Lough's round tower. Very scary, a county thing so don't you go off telling. We left our wishes on walls for Malachy, they say he lives in the walls. I wanted so much to replace my Dad, I wished for a lad in love. I'd teach him."

Lords of a manor county to play with, I was never what she wished when sweet sixteen.

"bb I need to know you're not prowling streets, your head gets turned. I get lonely feelings when you're not here."

"Noreen you lived alone on decadent Decatur street?"

"If I walked it's length I'd meet a dozen folks or down Jackson square. Noise and life, here is solitude and you quiet more like St Kevin."

"There's a place on Clontarf road I'll take you. Family style, meat potatoes and veg. Full man chew. The Abbey I'll get tickets, we can stand on the terrace watch rugby in Donnybrook. Chick flicks at Ambassador, anything you want. Take off for la Fiesta de los Rondeles in Casarabonela, disco dancing." *Want every day be colourful, in that peacock time.*

"bb heaven's sake I don't need that, what ails you?"

After we'd dispatched rations of grape, we went under bed covers, she moved close on my pillow. Belting rain lashing panes, long grass in clover. Tickled that fancy

"I've to be at Mam's 'till Sunday."

Together time prairie puddle, mile wide centimeter deep. Left only without my slim pickens.

"What about missing me?"

"Doctor appointment in Bray for her pains, Mom wants a carvery roast beef lunch on Bray road. It's not easy I want to be with you, I'll buy pants in Tommy Keegan's emporium. Next week I'll tell Mam I've to stay here."

That morning as she was leaving, I confronted her.

"Noreen do you have somebody down there ways?"

Mott to old flames, I wondered?

"Of course not, not off with any gallivanting."

Down Avoca those O'Boyle women would sit in the mother's kitchen happy yapping. Gathering of those shrews. Pervasive lonesome hush of Howth head no substitute, knew better than restrict or be clingy. She needed nights out with her gang, fair enough. *I don't need no crowd, not going to kill tiger.*

'How can the bird that is born for joy, sit in a cage and sing?'

"I did a piece of cod for dinner." Appropriate choice.

Off she went high tailing on the train to go clattering about in Avoca, I was left with nervous sheep in fields. Later that night she called.

"We're doing karaoke, lonely without you," she shouted.

"Singing a storm with your lot?"

"Oh sure old blarney a gas old time."

I could hear heavy background noise of the pub and lots of carry on.

"Wish you were here," she said.

Tried to talk but she could hear nothing. Should have followed her down and been there with the craic. Previous sessions I could muddle through old 'Danny boy', after that many pints. Neither wanted to get hammered talking crap with O'Boyle men. Those boys formed the

LAMP club, topics were literature, art, state of matrimony and poetry and who was getting the next round.

'We are all met together here to sit and to crack, with our glasses in our hands and our work upon our backs.'

I had sat trying to fit in but constant complaints filtered back.

'Doesn't play well with others', Muckcross nuns had once explained to my poor suffering mother. *I'd irritate even black legged kittiwakes sequestered on Rockall.*

Wished for cider nights, discussions of Bathsheba and Tess and tales of old Wessex. One of those lads Derek had married her cousin. Red hair shaped by toilet plunger, mad gra for hard stuff two pot screamer and drunk to the rule, '*no mute inglorious Milton, just a rude forefather of the hamlet.'*

"I'm like Noreen's older brother," he told me. "My wife left me two years ago now it's back and forth with two kids. But I like the relationship, I surely need that."

Had a life not much blemished by success, many's the time talking through his arse. Struggle to read an Oxo cube, argue crows were white, insist cock make eggs. Wicklow fellow believed Noah busy saving wooly mammoths, giraffes, dodo and giant moa, aardvark and armadillo. Like he'd hammered planks on the ark.

"Are ye away in the head? You know feck all about Thomas Hardy."

Common was that refrain from drunken lad, repeat like panto matinee. My time to signal Noreen for rescue. No wonder I preferred wild winds on the head then listen to gargoyle opinioned ramblings from those gas bags, 'home schooled' without brain of Ramanujan. Let's farm and eat corn fellow.

On one of our car trips back from Wicklow Noreen had a right old rattle back at me, getting schooled on behaviours. Toe the line paddy, gurrier. *'Every mile of road have two mile of ditch.'*

"You're home let boys to themselves. You're an odd creature they're not accustomed parle with likes of you."

Noreen taken easier to green shirt on her back, I'd still an away strip. Each mountain have a song, don't sing song on wrong mountain.

"You see why I've no friends."

"Are you picking up what I am putting down?" Asked, but was telling. "You can be a know it all, don't so bubble yourself. Let them have an opinion, even agree sometime. We know you're Briany big banana. Herr Professor behind the podium."

If subject be 'eat banana', then monkey is expert not Plato.

Dose of right verbals, alien from Ontario lurking in their midst. Koala basking in Iceland's hot springs.

"I've personality like water fit anywhere."

"You've high faluten far away ideas they think you've lost run of yourself. Full of boom boom pralapaw as my Ferrice would say. Blowing off steams."

Don't put on airs seigniorial or climb high on bamboo so they see red arse. Remember dog mouth never have ivory. *Be like turtle, keep meat inside.*

"Okay so I'm just a phony."

Top table people preach boring and long, need check their selves. Under stage people open small meeting do their own yapping.

"You went on and on about abortion that's not wise, too many Canadian ideas."

Journey man returned, jarring as USA soccer commentators full of yankee doodle dandy, rubbing wrong way as left handed hand jobs, from Oz.

"Don't have Canadian ideas. No literature, no culture unless counting bios of hockey players which I don't. Or Victoria and Albert touring Labrador, pages used to start barbecues. It's cold in that place." Extreme on extremities.

Shelves of milktoast, Jasus Murphy make 'em aerodynamical fly in air on way to trash barrel. Don't care about any of youse or who your mother was.

"LAMP fellows read nothing all uisce baite learning."

"You told Gerry Mc Nally Irish were mongrels world never heard about and Irish clergy messed up Africa. Upsets people, priests were brave got malaria. Remember Biafra? You know better you've a quirky mind for here abouts. Why pontificate how condoms solve traffic problems, it's not Mexico city?"

Masses fomenting agin me, Noreen heard every crumb. Dicky dazzler fly boy don't wag tall tail in company of tossers. Men jealous my stripping her green kit, feeling Noreen's native born arse.

"It's debate, dumb opinions. In future under your thumb, silk purse or sow's ear you're the decider." I decided.

"You can be too much of a smarty pants. You know?"

Since I could fog a mirror. Irish with their gab then set up 'Committee on Evil Literature', writ by morons or monkey stenographers, censoring books, films and magazines. Teach paddy's line or get out, rid one oppressor, embraced worse sinn fein.

Such small island nonsense
tedious Japan tea ceremony
day's end, only cup of tea.
China no time to pour,
drink from spout.
Chop, chop. True.

'Sure I was born on Herbert street by banks of the canal', explained to Customs creature as he stamped passport with foreign crown. Visitor my arse, in my land with my hills and valleys, I was no having the likes, from six counties only stranger himself.

Get them off ye mise eire
show us yer arse,

with plastic eye look like normal
nothing to see.

Following karaoke's phone call I was away with nerves, fickle daughters of Eria find endless ways for divilment. Was she calling to make sure I was far enough away? Getting nailed by local handymen while I got hammered as cobbler's thumb in Howth. Hour later middle of the night with clean white shirt on my back headed along dark roads, that air stinking of burning turf, only beaten by skunk road kill in Ontario. Reached her mother's house tiptoed on creaky stairs, Noreen fast asleep in feather bed. Expecting some sturdy farmer snoring flagrante delicto with corpus delicti sowing oats on neighbour's soil. Nor wished to tackle combine-harvester's ménage-a-trois.

"Glad you're alone." I whispered.

A woman beneath sheets ready for right old knees up. Anticipations like Christmas eve as a kid, open every gift.

'En mi pecho florido.'

"What did you sing?"

"Miss you nights, When will I see you again."

Divil she did.

"A real come all ye, a hog boucheries, a bit of diddly eye musics."

That morning could hear the mother, all busy slicing brown bread, cracking eggs, crackling bacon on black pan. Being partial wandered down, slippers and dressing gown.

"Arra Brian how are you? Where did you appear from?"

"She left me again for yellow ferns of home."

Tumble weed like me, busy seeking road trip action.

"Out on the town with Craicioke won't see her 'till lunchtime. That's O'Boyle's, her father's daughter no less."

"She has the voice for that craic."

In a jiffy her mother dished up grand rasher omelette and strong tea, brown bread, salty county butter with fried spuds pepper and parsley, having Patricia Lynch life in spades.

"Great to have a man about the house. I see so much of Frank in her, Garda more than twenty year, Dublin man as yourself. She knows every mountain path in the county, off with sardine sandwiches and a flask of tea, of course Frank with the naggin. Seventeen and her heart broken, fine healthy man in one minute he was gone."

She made sign of the cross.

"Easy ways, a few pints he'd talk hind legs off a donkey. Big man with a pound for every pocket, generous with friend or foe. Manys the garsun he'd kept on straight and narrows, buy ticket for the Dublin bus."

"I'm too quiet, it's St. Kevin all she calls me."

An uneasy character truth be told, for this manor I was small fry.

"Listen now Brian it's not good she going off by herself, there'll be fellas have wrong ideas, right tossers. Keep an eye on her now, sure she can be a divil and no less. I was born a young one meself, once upon that lovely time."

To that manner born, fellas with wrong ideas bane for this world.

"Give her this when Princess appears, 'twill be dried out but she won't be caring one whit."

She left breakfast plate covered with tea cloth in the oven.

"I'm away off down to Arklow with Patty for shopping."

Mid-day noggin hung over Noreen appeared, dressing gown buttoned to the neck. Found her grub with foraging instinct, I made a strong pot of tea. Like many a breakfast she'd show up silent functioning just not up yet.

"So Nawleen heard old craic mighty good in Cricklewood?"

"bb you snuck in my bed like a wild animal if I was not dreaming, worse for the wear and jaded. What on earth? Men are mad daft fellas."

Cock up at dawn, being farm country. Wasted and laid with tossing, finished what nature insisted.

"Next time I'll take Quebec nipple syrup, sweet for Air Canada boy. We should get fresh air but I'm banjaxed, sit out in the sitting room and I'll bring coffee. I'll show you my little girl photos, if you laugh I'll hate you forever."

Table covered with photo albums.

"Nobody never sees these."

Another inner sanctum breached ahead of tossers, wandered through her halcyon times. That Wicklow place permeates the soul, you don't get off unscathed she'd ran amuck in those fields. Fein spear.

"I'd have carried your school books with you on the cross bar, shared chewing gum and gob stoppers."

"When I was 15 you were a 100 years old, angry Dad would have locked you up and threw away the key!"

"What would he say now?"

"He'd see I'm happy."

"You went to Louisiana, did you not fancy Wicklow garsuns?"

"If you'd seen me a shy thing, pale as a sheet and insecure. Fellas get off easy with your thingymajig doohickey bean sprouts, stand on two feet mumble and bumble. Girls are tadpoles takes a lot to make a woman."

Ran my hand high on her thigh and kissed her.

"Only that first summer away I'd interest from boys. Every lunchtime sunbathe on Gulfview beach, a gorgeous tan. On my own I'd go down the boardwalk of an evening."

She with tomboy ways, with that longing look, an eye for big boys.

"Sea taffy, frosted donuts, pretzels with mustard. Submarines, hoagies, cheese steaks and banana splits, Big boy hamburgers with pickles, roasted peanuts and fried chicken!"

"Sure you could wear anything, a bikini, cut off jeans and lip stick. Everyday pushing a trolley with sheets and water shimmering, so tempting, longing to swim in waves. Carnival music on the piers, fun of the fair tall boy beers and fellas! I wanted fun in that noise."

"Amazing you went by yourself."

"Away living in East Jesus so many a year!" She laughed.

The room fell quiet you'd hear a rabbit fart in the garden.

"Brian so what are you going to do? Will you marry me?" she asked. "One day."

Thunder so long, she didn't see rain.

As Luther nailed demands for church banns accept or reject, no negotiations.

One more ball of wool to finish that jumper else false idols await sorry ass.

She'd wanted quality relationship, last forever as Queen's hunting wellingtons.

Heaven help me never focused on weddings, both failed not flourished with those fiascoes. *There's no learnin with second kick of a mule.* Didn't want to repeat that palaver, smack that batchelor bean can down the road. Marry again? Sure early doors, there'll be time enough to seal them deals. Then ever after hated myself with stupidness.

Side step, schimmy dipsy doodle
too much pussy footing around.
She should have been strong and pushy,
Over ask.
Threatening fear of gods,
Over ask.
Should have signed on, indulge her.
'Yes,' a word never said.
'Nothing I should avoid so much as marriage,
I know nothing which brings manly mind down from heights
more than a woman's caresses and that joining of bodies
without which one cannot have a wife.'

Never considered her point of view, now know what I should

have said. After all also wanted a long term relationship not a temp thing. Serious motts repeat every transgression, dalliance, temper tantrum, foible, argument, error and memory lapse, every raised voice with nausea. After she'd never asked no more.

"Let's deal with that come September, need to finish things in Canada."

Trojan horse, blasé-blasé-blasé. Now is when she started tempting other candidates for that date with her. No doubt entitled she was.

"You told me it was all done."

"All unraveling not finalized, complicated issues with Will pension resolve and that, I've legal people working. Lots."

Calculus maths,
complicated like
the knights tour,
banking derivatives,
comb shifting in mane of Geldof,
fixing miserable folk in impossible six counties,
quantum photon entanglement, Hawking radiation.

Dodging negotiations more crooked conniving than carnies mangy dog, right old wheeler dealer. Didn't realize hurt she felt and underestimated my feelings, damn she'd never ask again. Stakes never even, when they fell pierced my heart. Some broads offer no second chance, no Hobson or Sophia, a Morton's Fork not even catch 22, only SNAFU. Such that was my dilemma.

She showed her special photo, Scottish terrier with two of them.

"High above Craig Leat near Lugnaquilla, Ramsey was his son."

"Why Ramsey?"

"Looked like a Sphinx watching for Dad to walk in the gate."

Peeling back onion layers, tears on freckled cheeks wanted each one of them for me.

"We wandered many trails, best childhood, sure when he was gone my troubles began. Lose someone you learn what love is."

"Noreen that's why you find comfort here."

My consolations only cold porridge. With feet bare on old shag carpet we dozed off into something wrong dream. Rastafarian eat fried chicken, where boffins wrongly pontificate bright light at life's end is imagination not our creator. When Mairead wandered in we were stuck together, she sat in the rocking chair examining pair of us.

"Brian don't you get weary of her?"

"Drove down middle of the night, lost without her."

Suddenly Mairead stood tall agitated, all argibated.

"Look, Noreen I'll not stand idly by with two of youse."

Irish girls most decent in all this world, God fearing honest woman. Good on collars and cornettes educating young ones, poorer land without devoted vocations. Thank them all, Vatican does craft fine souls.

"I don't want that Cathal Sweeney gobshite interfering."

Noreen flushed finger wagging at babbling buddy.

"Mairead! Stop this already, just mad fun the riot. My weekend vacation. Diddly squat."

"Brian don't even let her out of your very sight."

Woman's farsighted doubts with troubles now brewing, some barking dogs sense earth tremours ahead of the pack.

"Mairead I love my Brian, bb don't even mind her. Don't have him think I'm out flirting because I'm not. Don't be giving out for heaven's sake!"

Noreen kissed me softly on the cheek, maybe a Judas' sister. No tourist by this world, all onion layers are bitter.

"He's not cross, Murray's was packed, singing old county craic. I'll told him so already."

Packed with lads stalking and vacant double bed, watching mad one on the loose.

"Mairead you and Brian go for a tea, I need a nap from nights carry ons."

She stretched and yawned. Mairead and I wandered to café on Clarke Street, chilly rough tumble table and chair. Two grand hot cuppas with chocolate digestive.

"So what happened?"

"A tinkers yard over there a great let-out entirely." says Mairead. "That Cathal Sweeney, his wife passed away last year, Miss Nawleen sitting on his lap jarred to rafters and kissing. Can't keep his hands to his self for a sec. Way more than flirting whatever she bothers to say."

"Fancy that."

"Busy singing 'It's over' hit high notes easy. She'd borrowed Sweeneys shades, cheers like it was Roy Orbison hisself."

You'd not know friends until ice cracks, not tickled with the news.

"Better she watch out, I saw those sex activities on that Bourbon street where she lived. Behaviours what she has now in her own parlour."

Mairead disappointed, her friend adopting wayward goings on ways of foreigners.

"Dairy farmer, Cattle Sweeney they call him."

"At least didn't go off with him."

Get nipples milked.

"Brian so excuse me, you don't even realize half of it. Noreen Helen O'Boyle, you see I'm so mad, all hell broke loose, legless tooth and nail. From the pub dragged her down streets, she lost a leather shoe on Burnside street. Put her in bed, sat on guard outside the house for an hour. Can you believe the likes?"

Nothing good happens on dark streets, drinking women with

antics. Mount St Helene, tiger by the tail, scattered as chicken eats cracked corn walks only grand for blind fellas.

"I had to fight her, got this for my troubles."

Punching purple bruise marks on her arms, a war with tugs.

"What gets into her?"

"Polluted from rum, manky. That style she only learned away."

Sat in silence, not a time for long words.

"Mairead thanks."

Stout hearted in her moment dealing with friendly fire.

"Brian she is closer than my sister, I was not having her go on a Cattle drive. I dated him years ago above in Dublin 'till I found he was engaged.

"I was that glad to see your car outside only expecting his black Beamer."

Déanta in Éirinn shamrock tattoo on her rawhide, on heated seats.

"How old is Cattle?"

"Younger than you, more her age." Mairead laughed. "Sorry Brian."

Drank tea, Sweeney got a taste away then left on his tod. Use your loaf swallowed spotty dick bun, *still lucky bag with steelers.*

"He lifted up his hairy paw
with one tremendous clout.
He landed on the fellow's jaw,
and knocked the farmer out.
He set to work with nail and tooth,
and made the place a wreck."

"Should I confront her?"

My nighthawk on display hanging in bars, different page every day, Noreen and Book of Kells.

"No she'll very hate me, she was shouting 'he's all hat and no cattle' about you. It's not only Sweeney, broken marriages, lots of lonely boys in these hills attracts maggots and flirts with anything. She picked up a lot of nonsense being away, although never Saint Bridgid to begin neither. Brian you surely know that."

After Shady Nook harvest moon activities anything was possible. That's what got us to here.

"You're too casual, she said you dropped by the Arms. You ignored her? Not just a little hug?" Mairead shrugged.

Where copper boy had parked his Paddy wagon, should have told him to feck off. Instead only right feckless.

"Fellows ask, they don't see you with her."

"Mairead help me, what's the best way?"

Damn wide boy Sweeney with his acres. Feeling heat in hand-knitted gansey.

"Once me and her went to turn hay on her uncle's farm. Dead tired after an hour we dumped pitch forks and fled. Our worse day. Take her back to Howth don't have her come back alone, she's that scared of farming." Keep gardener Ron on hayroll.

Later that night headed over Dublin mountains, headlights showed the way. Through dark valleys past huddled peasants and pheasants fattened. This brazen Norleans frisky in the baro, but high spirits teeming with rummy spirits proves nowt else we'd all be arraigned before magistrates. She'd a storm raging longer than red spot on Jupiter, when that was done she'd be at peace.

Traversing females mind?
Like most men of limited expertise,
as ice cream seller a one trick pony.
Even winter, only make ice cream.

"What did you and Mairead talk about?"

None of your beeswax, curious baby.

"Easy talk knocked about, told me about growing up in Avoca nothing on darker side."

She'd divulged bar fella was feeling your thigh above black stocking south of Brazil, pale territory of Dublin jack not flinty cowboy. Had to rip you from arms of cow fella, expert at sucking tits. Booty on his lap, ready for fouling in rocky mountains. By midnight's chime.

"You always say how boring she is."

Don't worry farmer boyo, I'm hoeing and ploughing with gusto.

"I listen."

With Noreen checking out darkness.

"I sure miss this time of year china berry trees are turning, and watermelon wine. I would make gallons for holidays. Is a person who makes allegations an alligator?"

Brain twisting and turning light of day that dark night. Drunk people do stupid things, don't recall half. Pondered her travails, clearly my lady was the tramp. Imagine if she woke in farmer's bed and him down milking jerseys and frisons. Give aways on home turf the whole nine yards, family sleeping all about. Then off home deserted roads dressed to the nines. Mairead at sixes and sevens and me with no 40 winks driven to distractions on her single pillow. Sleep disturbed like fried dumpling on the pan, Mairead saved that fresco fiasco.

"Don't find Mairead interesting sexually, no distracting powers."

Not my bowl of rice.

"bb I'm a mystery to me and these silly carry ons. Are you obsessed with me?"

Ass chasing red carrot.

"Troubled and distracted."

Cattle boy must be mad having her snatched from his grasp. Many's a slip twein lip and cup, never count chicks before thatch be trimmed.

"You know Brian I feel sorry for you driven all your life by constant need to want us. Where does it get you?"

Mostly jack squat, jackeen forever chasing tail, pursuing thrill of that female species. Me and bonaboo. *Sure vive away whatever be that difference.*

"Noreen it's dark lonely world, with you days at peace. Be happy to live in Wicklow."

White flag aloft in battle, waving as Neville Chamberlin. Cowtowing.

'bound down by this disease of the flesh
its deadly pleasures were a chain
that I dragged along with me,
yet I was afraid to be freed from it.'

"Hay and barley, farm stuff hit and miss engines, tractors. Milking, full of hens. Just remember."

I could, grand father grew tomatoes, chickens, and blue tulip.

"Brian don't be silly, jeez what a nightmare. You with a farm? In a pig's eye. Milk pails, lifting bails. Meandering cows, wandering streets desperate to be milked. I'm well aware there's a part of you not screwed on." *Always needle in the cotton.*

"Moo, moo dear Mr. person need me a milking." She mocked. "Can't be exhausted with your demands and expected to farm, I'm okay in the pub mostly I enjoy it. I like tourists a nice class of folk, I don't want arm muscles and sun baked face."

Forgetting getting docked pay, when foreign fellow downed his pint, did a runner. Left ratty coat and hat on stool to fool her.

"Wicklow can be too crazy and wild to blow off steam, I like our walks a quiet life. Then Mam gets upset and Mairead telling you not true things. I like we go to bed early, need to take care of god's gifts. Even your sweaters needs darning."

Big shot in Cill Mhantáin whole place belongs to you. Over in Dublin you're outsider a stranger, a serf, pauper a spallpeen.

"If you like we can stay tonight in Bray."

Another night in beloved county as we were crossing the border line.

"Brian you're a strange person with a tin ear. You spent your time schlepping around wondering where floozies were kept. No surprise you ended with big arsed strippers on Bourbon street, shoving dollar bills in their knickers. Brian we live in Howth, why would I stay in a lino floor hotel smelling of stale food? You've chardonnay in the fridge, I want to sleep in our bed under covers with a man beside me. A woman needs to love and hold."

"And me to behold!" A treat for her.

"Move it buster we're burning daylight."

Then we laughed and laughed along the old Bray road. Maybe for her any man would do, but for now I was that lucky buck on cloud nine heading for ninety nine.

"There are hermit souls that live withdrawn
in the place of their self-content.
There are souls like stars, that dwell apart,
in a fellowless firmament.
There are pioneer souls that blaze the paths
where highways never ran.
But let me live by the side of the road
and be a friend to man."

CHAPTER 8

Barely recovered from Stephen Green ruckus, then one hallowed evening before Halloween Noreen came home with invitations to Fancy Dress at Hibernian Hotel out by Malahide. Cops and firemen from the bar organizing charity dance. She liked dress up scene, whereas mise a leaden footed eejit could jump and prance, not hot to trot.

"Sure okay sounds exciting, like that stuff." I managed.

Cringed at this nightmare in Malahide place crowded by all sorts, determined to feign sincerity, not grouch on her parade. In truth only women and gay fellows care about such affairs, still I knows what's good for me I'd wear the mask. She missed Mardi Gras parties on New Orleans streets with Ferrice parading down FQ to jazz and kaiso. Sparrow, Calypso Rose, Crazy and Penguin, all for fun on shores of Lake Pontchartrain.

"Jumping up with the band, get in a trance with hot men. I'd want to lick their sweaty bodies! Ferrice had to keep me under control, I was Cleopatra in Egypt!"

She turned and wiggled for bedroom mirror to West Indies beat spinning on a turn table, laughed like crazy woman off in her trance, fists flying and pumping away. Divil flowing in those blue veins beneath pale skin, Wicklow's girl learned to groove those hips to beats of African drums. Noreen singing with melody thumping. Go wine that body girl.

'Hop down front then doodle back,
mooch to your left then mooch to the right.
hands on your hips and do the mess around,
break a leg until you're near the ground
now that's the Old Black Bottom Dance.'

Cleo got the asp bite, this bird got her ass bit by Louisiana, she with beads enough to buy Manhattan. Flashed those breasts, bounce grandly they did humping to the din only on my mind.

"I'd see him drunk feeling up with those black women down in shebeens with their icy lime caipirinhas."

"You'd wild times."

"World's greatest show, the reason I'd go back on someday. I carried a leather rum pouch parading Esplanade and down Bourbon and Canal then party crazy for three days. Wild with music we'd be half naked," she laughed. "My kind of town."

Forever sailing fast currents of the gulf. La danse de Mardi Gras, flambeaux carriers providing light in dark ways.

"People moving bumping up all the touching a turn on, Jouvier morning, Ash Wednesday through Fat Tuesday pancakes sheer bacchanal."

Not Dublin's prim but proper St Patrick day parading cold March, old days pubs were dark, shut tight. Culchie barmen day off. There'd be no carousing with pints on Paddy's day declared our Free state, citizens parched as strayed pachyderms searching oasis. Only travelling man could get pints on the railways. Only time I'd get hankering to visit Ulster, day return. Condoms and pints, good on ye, Northern man. Good for sumeth worthwhile.

"With Ferrice we'd room at Sonesta."

Beggars to bandits she'd siesta at Sonesta, doing bomba jitterbug, hootchy-kootchy bellydance twisting and twirling with some lucky fellow. Can can, she could and do the dance if bit by Fer-de-Lance.

"Brian I've never heard half of what you were up to. I know you had a thing for that Indian from Belize, for a jackeen you got turned around with whores and strippers. You know those French Quarter alleyways betters than me."

New sheriff in town, ways of men she knew too much, need to avoid codswallop with this sharp tack. Figured lay of land without lugging a theodolite in hilly terrain, eye of the hawk, no tomfoolery she'd ferret nefarious doings. At least not promiscuous with my prostitutes, never wash rentals nor fall in love with ladies from Gentlemen's clubs. Carried on as debauchee blade held my edge as alley-gator. Woody serviced at Asia establishment, nowt more to relate.

"Where did you learn that behaviour?"

Never interested in Carnival, better off-season more bang for buckos like me.

"In Louisiana I'd find world's most beautiful babes." Not only alabasters.

That's how I put the spin on these activities. Workman's wage for all manner of ivory to ebony, as fast poured porter, separates cream from crop. By dark night all feel the same. Noreen out of breath all serious turned off the music, lay flat on the bed.

"Ferrice and me split for a while, forever losing money. What could I be doing?"

Jars of old smokey moonshine mucho nights feeling sorry staring thru' tears at moon beams rising over Pontchartrain.

"I lived with a mulatto fellow, his father owned a coffee plantation, only my fling. Eventually Ferrice came and took me home. Are you shocked with my nonsense?"

Sometimes broads get jumpy pants, figured Ferrice went through hell while she shacked with Creole gigolo.

"Phillippe would come back smelling of women and cachaça. On my birthday he sent his chauffer to have dinner, birthday cake with a driver! The very cheek of him."

From bedside cabinet she showed me a pearl necklace.

"His birthday gift, driver delivered with white gloves."

'Miss Pickens this here box is for you, Mr. Phillippe Chambron wishes you happy birthday celebrations.'

Hard balls on creole rejecting those pale cheeks. The way she handled the necklace still with dreams of guaguancó rumbas, flung by pearl tooth boy.

'To him that smiteth thee on one cheek offer also the other.' That she would.

"That night drunk on tequila I called, Ferrice took me back to Grand isle. He was crying the whole way, gambling days done for a while. Probably that night I got pregnant."

"I hit a jackpot when he lost with chips." My two cents.

Now winning punter wrapped around a slot machine.

"So what would we go as to the fancy dress?"

"Ravishing Bathsheba, low cut show off those boobs." I says.

Noreen engrossed with the mirror hardly heard my words.

'I wish I had feathers, a fine sweeping gown and a delicate face, and could strut about Town!'

"I'll be Victorian gentleman William Boldwood."

"Who are they?" Asked with her indifference, I let her know those folks from Hardy's 'Far from the Madding crowd'.

On Halloween we dolled up, costumes rented from place on Capel Street. Stunning charms on display, Victorian women that daring.

"bb let's have a great night, I'll not be thinking of any sad times."

However one disastrous evening horribilius started watching battered Merc arrive in the driveway. Beth and lard-ass boy friend from Derry an hour late, her fella Noel Mc Philips owned a nightclub, late-thirties long hair with the alice band. Beth with all class of lower leagues footballer's wife, no offence. Standing in hallway few things were obvious, he was drunk and no fancy dresses on these people, not a dickey bow.

"Beth a fancy dress! I fecking told you," Noreen explained.

"Noreen I'm trying my life is a mess, I'm stressed, driving dark and rain. He's drunk, that's all they're good at."

'Scuse me, I can pee and spell my name on brick wall, including an apostropee.

Beth with face of a fist and me imbibing wine for nerves, within brief moments hated them both. Maybe Beth dressed as 'ugly sister', jealousy fomenting many a year. In the kitchen an irritated yakdiddy yak banter between loving sisters, I was left to engage Ulster boy. Six county people have me sweating bullets fox smart and humourless, never pass velvet ropes at his club.

Sure well pardon us our partition Norlin Airlann from Eire,
whither gold or orange, glory twelfth or Easter march.
In tricks of island trading you say Nolan I say Gaybo,
whatever and wherever porter be porter and that George was all our best.

"How's old Belfast, all quiet by northern front?" I asked.

Once needed chemist shop on Malone road for johnnies, never could leave that creepy town fast enough.

"Wow," said Noel surveying the room, "One old shit hole, black and white forties and fifties. Betty Davis style dude, I heard this hill is a volcano." He said.

Stuck in art deco times, for some a dive, no glitzy plastic razzle dazzle, wrought iron and wood. With him eyeing stacks of unused china and mason jars filled with hen's coins halfpennies and salmon flóiríns all lined on shelves.

"They're still building furniture she's ordered. Cabinets, fancy armoire, futon for feet! Chaises longues from France. We'll be fully loaded all together. Grand style."

The man made no eye contact, bottle of Bushmills slammed on my shit acajou Queen Ann coffee table, delicate tiffany style candelabra took disturbed bounce. Needed Harland and Wolff come rivet his gob, ready to krakatoa this numb skull, wanted to kick his derry air way out.

"Nautical," I says, although surely knot.

Sprawled on couch took drag on his smoke, flicked ash on French polish. Maybe expected to buddy with Norn Iron, go marching on Garvaghy irritating one side of those maliferous showers shouting at squaddies. To man jack Ulster folk pernickety species, palookas could not stop fighting, regarding twenty sixers as Foxrockers perceive Ballyfermot. Churchill wily old soul kept us separated demonstrating in his way loving care for all Irish.

'we never laid a violent hand upon them, which at times would have been quite easy and quite natural,' regards from dear Winston. '*and take back our sentinel towers of the Western Approaches.*'

With blue hair Maggie only more of the shame.

"Noel my sister is pissed I'm not dressed as a slut and you're not got up as a scrawny fag."

To relax this stressed atmosphere Noreen explained costumes and god bless her peaceful heart.

"Bathsheba left old Boldwood for handsome Sergeant Troy."

What I told her. Of Hardy she hardly knew nowt.

"Yeah I remember from school." Beth said, feeling her sister handed juicy bone.

"Well Boldwood was only forty one." I'd swiftly countered.

"Oh, are you Boldwood's father?"

She and six counties laughed and laughed, squashed me like wobbly cockroach. So amused as if Groucho walked among us, guffawed like squady pack of bitches.

"So youse going as ball breaker and drunk fellow?"

Reckless zinger from the vine, Beth pondering to hammer me with half filled Bushmills only floundering I was.

"Noel we're leaving." Beth barked, gurning, face like smacked arse.

Well jeez mahogany, hard mouth woman. Whipped puppy dog McPhilips jumped, ran with bottle after the moll. In the hallway McPhilips banged the gong for guests, *bolan, bolan, bolan* echoed. Merc disappeared into that rainy night.

"You were rude, drive people away." Noreen says.

"I didn't."

In truth driven away more folk than would fill CIE double decker, abilities honed by Dublin's disco markets.

Telephone rang loud voice on speaker.

"Video is out on internets for everyone," hysterical Aniky from Bruges.

Only bad spells abroad that witches night, some broads you never shake loose. As the woman told her tale sounded madder than long-tail cat in room of rockin' chairs, madder than rosary rattler shawlees dispatched to hell fire, after lives of dutiful penance, and denials of life's wanton participations. Madder than T Rex with toothache impacted and no dental plan.

"You in the church caused everything, I can't believe and always thinking it was priest of the parish. Good innocent man never defile any woman. Nearly had me drowned then deceiving me, and me in your bed that very same night. Taking advantage and me a distressed way then you never took any safer precautions. I'm this seven months already with your baby, doctor with ultrasounds saying it's a boy and me not ready for this. All that whiskey and getting me drunk for your bed, Irish men and their drinking. So you could be having your ways.

Cold from the oceans, I'm a nun and now pregnant from you. The likes of you. You did all this to me."

Never want to grow more ear with that news. Neither me or poet Raftery could hear that coming.

Rightly good woman felt hornswoggled. That day late in October wanting mayday to abort that evening. Didn't move one inch in bed now hopping mad rightly exercised with hullabaloos grinding. *Radio off, I was facing the music.*

Whimsical philosophy
carry brolly no rain,
winter tire no snow,
pay insurance no crash,
wear johnnies now babies,
fool operating heavy tool
under foreign influences.

"I have to leave my dear Bruges and travel back to Ireland for birth. I've not told my poor mother with this affairs and my sisters. The prioress and all here are shocked with my behaviours. I've not any resources you'll be have to get the bed room in your house for the baby, I'll be sending lists. I know you can buy these things with all your hotel monies. I feel from our days that you've great passions for me, I think you wanted for this so I would came back to your bed. I did in my heart want your passions and responsibilities. I hope you will still want me and your son, and your son Jimmy pass away in Louisiana. Remember in games you said hands finds balls."

Stunned silence with bosom heaving's, only catching on. Disconnected candle stick phone above on the shelf had heard it all. But not that. Needed to toss tantalus canters in ocean and stay forever teetotaler, save trusting decent porter. Having to deal with Aniky's troubles was putting gas in car I'd wrecked already.

Always make things double hard, as blind man walking at night chop bamboo on the node, imbibing cialis-viagra cocktail

with Belize twins in the quarter, me holliers in Timbuktu.

Bad habits with frolicking, now visions of nappies and colic, that day wanted to chop my ears for working.

"You knocked up a nun?"

'Whosoever digs a pit will fall in.'

"Saying it that way sounds more bad."

'If you give me six lines written by the hand of the most honest of men, I will find something in them which will hang him.' – Cardinal Richelieu.

Felt me tremours coming, faced with right rhubarbs. Tell truth but keep one foot in styrup, first head show out hunter shoot.

"I left my home away, come all back here and you cheating with a nun that's having a baby. I gave that up for you and my dogs Odin and Thor. All for naught like this?"

Spewin she was, time's divil passage supplied shards of rope to hang meself. Kick away stool no leg to stand on, Noreen felt she had been bamboozled, worse than pearl tooth boy and me without grill or chauffer carrying precious gifts.

"If a dollar for every stray young one saying I put her in family way, surely I'd rattle only four quarters." Talking crazy.

Aniky need damn better show me Watson and Crick on the brat, remembered her telling I was never one to burst her cherry.

"You fool, you fool, damn you to a man fool."

Noreen would listen no more to old john like me.

"What did you tell about James?"

"Nothing that's definitely her misunderstandings. Befuddled she was and confused with translations. Waves addled her brain works, I'm not that fluent with phlemishes. Difficult language, better with Finnish. Hyvasti!"

Sheer frumpting, blowing more smoke than junky Moscovitch

cab in Havana. Chords stressed, straining to form words as they stuck in me craw.

"You've only taken that FQ behaviour of yours back here, now humiliating me."

To tell the truth I am a poor cheat, also not a good liar. A man in no where.

Saw her eyeing bayonet poker, have me head severed like strayed dogs in Bahrain, precious family pearls dangling precarious. As I reached out swung her arm to keep me away, her ring gouged me head as she pushed, accidental I'm sure. Ragged cladagh ring imprints on numbskull as I tripped over jagged acajou table, dizzy ditzy and dozzy. Saved more damage by door bell, Niall our one legged taxi driver for pick up.

"Are youse all right, I'm hearing a terrible ruckus?" One peg says.

"Nothing, having a clear out, getting rid of old garbage." She answers, and no lie.

Panting a distraught Bathsheba took off to the dance. Broad never finished her leaving, only learned to scarper.

Knock knock.
Who's there?
Knocked up nun
on road to Knock
got there but
never reached Mayo.

Took care of my cut with vaseline, the way Angelo plastered Cassius in the jungle. Lucky punched like a girl, although mad one with knuckle duster. God in his mercy created enough of them with beauty not brawn. Knew Father McCracken had no maliferous intentions with troublesome flick release, aware my constant ducats bought tarry gloop to plug church leaks. Some other divilment at work, that night of Howth's hollabulo. High-tech shenanigans had me trapped, Asimov seen them coming down the pike, hacked by beady eyed robots. Bruce stitched me up got me collared, twigged McCracken told him who Aniky was. There'd be no two finger tantalus salute for cassock hard man, although I'd wait till slates were slotted, obviously still needing me full karma blessings. Not wishing McCracken hotter under collar and be dispatched away to Rush Anglicans, with my hearts allegiance to Roma pontiff: *Roma locuta causa finita est.* Fair dues, more accustomed accepting their pontificating.

Taken over an edge with Aniky and Noreen, two broads with dangling sac to twist, well they knew where to find when required. Eventually I stirred, tail sequestered between my legs headed to night of fancy party frivolities. No more blubbering, not wishing to waste on the rental, departed dwelling, going dancing. In the taxi stubborn with hefty flask of whiskey to take further rough edges off.

Even smart folk can be stupid. Vicar paid a visit to Isaac Newton, brainiac's cat had kittens and he busy cutting a second hole in the door. One cat-hole smaller than the other to accommodate kittens. See that's what I am saying.

Old ballroom decked out witches and goblins that night, Showband lads playing Tennessee Waltz, costumers intent with circular culchie hustle laps.

'Spit on me dickie, go on ye ride.' God love'em.

With stove top hat hit drinking bar hard. Still tomcatting around, as God intended.

"Ye look like a wasted President Lincoln."

Says fat one at the bar giving the eye, dressed as Statue of Liberty.

'*Love width of your one,' hippy lament for heftys.*

"Saw ye in New York, you'd a torch for me. How ye holding up?" Says I figuring the fit of extra poundage.

Needed lady liberty sit her arse in Dublin bay for returns, maybe de Gauls could float us a spare. We'll forage the metals, empty beer cans to forge cobble and hammer.

"You've tomato sauce all over your face, flowing like Powerscourt's waterfall. Did you get done over in a meat wagon or rob a traveller's chipper?"

"Abe afters shot, in the hearse." I says, blood with gobs of vaseline streaking. "You should see state of me Áras. I'm only with swimming to Holyhead this very tonight."

"You're the gas man."

Right wound up wind bag.

"I'd skirmish over on the hill, damsel in some distress."

Gives her the wink with nothing to see, only me doing the hunting rounds. With she drinking the cider, I felt attraction or maybe it was only gravity.

"Ladies that know me do call me bold wood. Come guaranteed." With a flourish.

My thinking under many influences.

"Are ye boasting?" Fat Dubliner asks.

Fame in the saddle drifted far and wide.

"Me old lad was from Timfecktwo."

Muddled mess, whiskey was doing me blattering.

"Full of yerself are ye?"

"I'm only on me tod, chasing me mott she gone done a runner, disguised as Mrs. Booth."

"Well feck off then."

"I bid you fond farewell Miss Liberty, as I return to life's theatre."

Not feckless, I'd freed cotton slaves,
put my arse in barren hearse
wrapped in rough linens,
at fifty six years,
no three score and ten.
Me stone skull on Mount Rushmore.
For me troubles.

Cleaned up in the jacks wandered through the crowd, searching quarry with heart of stone. Short order sees garda billy bigboots Bruce and lackeys gathered around a table, there be his dragoons. Muscle head gym rats 'Can you spot me?', fawning toadies, lick spittle's, duck personality lads follow leader in Dodder at full flood. She with those dumbbells, himself dressed as 'mafia gangster', bogus costume black suit and hat, arm attached to Bethsheba, all adorned with pectorals. Bruce feeding rum she guzzled like baby from juicy teat. One of the mates decency to move his arse, I sat down. Noreen with elastoplasted knuckle, surprised I'd a neck to show a bruised face. True to form got Bruce stare, as duck talks to chicken, dual talents witty talk and cock of the walk. Well aware Bruce the lad with wheel barrow full of bullfrog. Plumb loco.

Felt like sixth fish finger on handy pack of five.

"Papiamento?" I asks.

Close to monkey, talk monkey language.

"I see you've come as an old fart," he says, tipped by perceptive Bathsheba herself.

For such offence Boldwood would throw gauntlet down challenge to duel. Pistols drawn at dawn, risk to lose leg from cads cannonball. Puffery fellow Mr. D.J. appeared on stage bellowing, Showbands given right heave ho their spotlight dimmed.

"Spain, Caribbean! Carnival time folks! Brazil, Trinidad, Aruba. Well hello New Orleans!"

Quisling song and dance man enlisted for machinations, eager to mess over a brother, big mouth well knew Louisiana fully represented. Caribbean rhythm's in Noreen's rum laced brain, Mafia man knew about this wild one.

"Nawleens, Nawleens," she was shouting two fist thrusting in air.

Off her damn rocker.

"Let's rock the joint," heard from Bruce.

Booming calypso steel pans thru' speakers, Noreen's gangsta parading his booty. Devil divil's all out about, expected on that night.

"Mardi Gras danse," Noreen shouting thrusting hips like daft one. "I want to go home to my Nawleens."

Them two alone on dance floor, never my private samba passistas dancer, beautiful attraction as he 'rolled his dame under and over'. Swirling, bedazzling, meshing colliding into something brighter. Soaring chemistry sucked oxygen like uisce buzzing sodium, hotter and hotter till it flamed. Gyrating side by side making love on bouncing dancing floor for Malahide pensioner parishoners.

She took a glance my way now only traveling her way, felt shivers from fear of cold sheets, flaying like Icarus. Trusting me that grand mistake, in life of errors.

Back on fat Tuesday trance of African beats,
bands on Bourbon Street, trim ass, hands of hot fellas.
Rummy mind full of creoles mulattos and blond skunks,
not boiled mashed praties like me.
Besotted like Bruce crapped Kohinoor diamonds,
maliferous tidings on my hide, calamity Malahide's night.

As calypso singing ended she fell into his arms, lick spittles bayed and crowed, warm pint of Tyneside porter tasted liquorish. Having whale of a time and me fish out of water, dealing with another alligator too close to the boat. In Canada hit a skunk on highway drown in tomato sauce to wash almighty pong, no solution unless I got him to Palermo and he gored by a bull.

Cast off me hearties down to Barbary coast,
live on galley ships, eat fishy gruel row all day
for I'll row no more with her.

Walsh had done me in, tracked my maid from Orleans, executed his move. Gangster now the maid's man, bold braggart gave thumbs up for Mr. D.J. mission accomplished. He and her cruising to tête-àtête alcove speak easy, rum bottle wedged in his pants. Both panting from jitterbugs, he ready to pop wadsworth as Moet after hard twist and no controlling on those knobs. Squeezed together in an arm chair, understood better Mairead's wrestle on Burnside that Avoca night. Maybe in his soul Ferrice relieved thorny Irish rose departed, I stood over pair of them.

"Hey buddy that's enough." I told him, he dispensing rum like from gutbucket in Bourbon street barrelhouse.

"I'm not even drunk," she protested, piece of work Missy O'Boyle.

"Go home to Ovaltine," your man says.

Mother Erin why you rear them eegits? Dropped the dime on me already, caught with three edged sword that never heals. Nescaf with dolup of Baileys favourite bed time tipple.

"Causing me troubles with McCracken's camera. Trying to help yer scared one and you with spying machines. In the fecking church doing me contemplations, is nothing so sacred no more?"

Freaking Bruges sees the flick creating conniptions, now out having babies.

"He was hanging round the church picking up nuns. Cameras caught him! Me and the ads boys put them in for yobs stealing candle stick monies, he got hauled in that net. Now the nun is up the pole. What you going to do Poindexter? Got the baby pram?" He queried but not sincerely. He wore an unpleasant sneer.

"Make your commitments?"

Right button pusher, sensed peril I tipped her glass, Boldwood style. Nobodies fool.

"Old man has a temper, getting to the boil. Careful don't have a heart attack old fart, high pressures rolling in."

I felt beetroot red, Noreen took swig from his rum glass.

"You've pissed on my parade. Go feck a duck," I says.

Bruce fingering her pearls, fighting bush war nothing fake except that love for me.

"Go home yourself, I don't care no more." Noreen interrupted. "You're the clown needing a circus."

Well trick or treat! Needling with the hump to breaking a camel's back. Head of steam. She with rights to get shirty, bold tits on display.

"I've another film with them boinking on the heather bare arsed." Enjoyed his crude revealations.

Fella was Cinerama Cecil B. De Mills, I tossed disposable Geordie ale caught him full on. Shirt drenched with brown brew, took a licking as trawler man in nor'easter and no sou'wester. Suffered loss of face, with psycho grin lunged whippet fast as JFK on Marilyn, as flea on varicose veins grabbed me rental. Ducked his sneaky Glasgow kiss butt, lost me stove hat, on his back like moss covered Mississippi tree stump, so entwined climaxed crashed to floor. Early head start grabbed his neck, arms pinned, enjoined in grotesque danse macabre embrace.

"Give's a fucking kiss," I says. "I'll make your guts garter for me stockings." Not required, as I had high top prim argyles.

Disturbed by his stubble, cologne sweat and beer, powerful chest, troubled by his heavy breathing. Never been close to a fella since a baby with me Dad, now capable fighting like a girl I pulled on his hair.

"Don't rip the thing, it's a rug." He croaked.

Fellow was a damn big wig.

"Well me fecking suit's only borrowed from Capel street."

Soiled rentals and rugs regretted punts to pay. Noreen screaming at lick spittle's to end brouhahas. Grabbed by door bouncers arms bent and stretched they jump-frog marched me from festivities, Walsh retarded by his posse.

"He's some class of a eejit." Drunk Lady Liberty explaining to our exit parade.

"Are ye up in arm agin me?" I says. "Gotta hail a crab."

"Needs a kick in his arse, fighting palooka." Her reply unhelpful with circumstances.

Pants half mast, okay with my shamrock knickers, shoved through lobby doors. No complaints, I'd started their kerfuckle.

Made right horlicks of it, by sandy Malahide my name forever mudd.

"Noreen better get this geyser away before we call the guards." Says bouncer boy with scary eyes, required tool of a thuggish trade. Likely part time job as get away driver.

"Youse will have to stop the bleeding," says taxi cab man. "I'm not havin it."

Claddaigh scar re-opened with blood pouring, she rams wad of tissues on my skull, stove pipe pushed back hard on my cranium. Me brain leaking, dripping pints could fill the hat. Feeling dumber.

"Niall don't bleeding try my patience," she yells to one peg.

Back seat of the cab miles apart, two of us cried all the way home.

"What in god's name possessed you?" She says.

Can't never teach monkey be human, easier human be monkey.

"I'm going back to clear up the mess, settle things with the guards. Don't want courts involved." No bewigged barristers, already occupied with Walsh toupe.

Got her back hand, then off to play new set of balls. Advantage copper, ready to serve her wishes. I went to bed solitare. Love zero. Rare old times when broad can be annoying, frankly I don't give a damn. Had my under duress nightmare, kissing arses in Pyongyang.

Late that morning, elastoplaster congealed me hairy skull, comb stuck in dread locks. Seagulls wailing jeering my woes.

'Away with yer skylarkin, don't youse have fish to dive for young ones?'

Mangaler O'Boyle drinking green tea, no offer of front page to fear an ti. I was her headline, already knew there'd been disasters.

'When the blast of war blows in our ears,
imitate the action of the tiger.
Stiffen the sinews, summon up the blood,
disguise fair nature with hard-favour'd rage,
set the teeth and stretch the nostril wide,
hold hard the breath and bend up every spirit.'

My Boyle was steamed by strange kettles of fish, once mad attraction now magnets poles flipped. Mise on trap door with knotted ropes waiting for the drop, eating cornflakes me hand shaking with pouring milk. Scardy cat rabbit hid white tailed arse, tension plants wilted. Wanted to say time of witches over, wondering where she hid her broomstick.

"You're too much to handle, with all them at the dance laughing at sheer carry ons. Every hound dog in this world knows your exploits. Now I'm Mrs Village idiot, should have known given your dreadful history of exploits in Orleans."

"Sorry for cursing". As if ever caused commotions in holy Ireland.

"Constantly fighting, no controlling temper or anything. We'll see what happens." Ominously was declared.

Sliced her brown toast buttered, with marmalade.

'You may not be interested in war, but war may be interested in you.'

"Better you chop off that flippin thing that causes shenanigans and now your pregnant women." Said with sheer wicked sneer.

As she got up I tried to touch her, faith 'tis aisier stop runaway train on top galloping horse.

"Leave me alone, I'm working."

Praying mantis stop chariot?
Centipede arm stop car?
No more change direction

than eye on stuffed bird.

That day hill of Howth no level playing field. Early morning spied from bedroom window denim shirt, fisherman sweater and jeans, back-pack like schoolgirl heading for bus. Blue collar girl finishing her leaving, never looked back, no crying over spilt milk, all *'Renee'* she went on that day, that was our farewell parted from my dear. She never wore jeans at work, bare legs fellas craved and tipped big. She'd slipped my bonds and left surly that morning.

Takes balls to bear pain of loss,
Napoleon on his arse in Helena
lonesome in Longwood.
Jackie watching Zapruder's film,
flightless dodo's wacked in Mauritius,
astronauts in their failed space craft,
Machu Picchu's see Iberians screw America,
Diana shocked by pearly gates
no deluxe Parisian five star.
Dakota Lennon cursing green cards,
Pius IX reading Darwin, with
Bestie home watching World cups.

Battered pillar to post, faith give me amnesty from chicanery or grant amnesia. I'd not be pulling her leg no more, that's the hitch in my giddyup.

CHAPTER 9

Next evening emerged for the walk feeling as worm after rains, dropped by the pub, slidering through that place full of couples nursing pints, '*many an eye that measures me*'. Once in bygone times King's press gang bopped lads heads with truncheons at those tables, taken to toil in antipodes and Indies and Dartford. She was nowhere to be seen, my black stocking beauty absent without leave. Instead nobbly blondy from out Bettystown way in industrial uniform, mighty busy on her shift. From Termonfeckin, a town twinned with Ecclefechan, only for a laugh. Eyes blazing voice loud on the job, share loathing fear of varmints, wild critters, attack minded centipedes and loud mouthed broads. Lathered with makeup, veneer over plywood, no friendly Mac. Life time member of ridden hard put away wet class, '*with eyes without light*'. No need for x-ray specs to imagine tattoos on that ass, I'd not be paying washers. Irritations but no pearls with such an oyster, I'd not take the bait. Telegraphed distain for customers, poured crap pint, beer so flat it could be served in envelopes as scousers complain. Saliva finger licking person as she counted me punts. Never fingered the change, let it sit evaporating.

"The head, sure didn't go order no black and tan." Muttered as mutated pint drip soaked the mat, charged for three only drank two.

Harry pulling fast ones, *vegetable in rice bowl not make rice.* I'd not look her in the eye nor be dragged into that bedraggled world, no truck with dent and scratch combustion Betty Attracta. Her old man bald and gray troll, failed rock musician out hustled by the world, music 'studio' in garden shed singing Bonzo Dog Doo Dahs. Scattered rusted Honda dirt bikes, busted Commer knocker car on cinder blocks. Claims he's a roadie drives a lorry to Belfast to deliver eggs for 'Breakfast all day' caf owned by the drummer. She and I repelled each other, don't pass on bad luck, receding could detect red shift. Spied erstwhile acquaintances, received 'no sit awhile and have good cheer' invite. Sans Noreen I was objectant with never a 'great to see you', tried to appear unconcerned to gloating prying eyes. Whatever a busy life, no time to chew the cud with buck eegits, maybe with luck that press gang would saunter by again, shift some unfortunates. Not that I was a loner people did not like my face, cap I was given to wear. Minefield that house where nobody came where I alone lived, in truth the quare yoke, but no desires to be Bhikku man. As somberly studied my pint suspected things were bad, maybe need to try harder.

Long fellow, leg in two boat, feeling woobly
dogs in street knew what ails me,
obvious as lice on head of bald man.
Two hooks dangle, single line
'chase two rabbits lose them both.'

So not a bother, folks could get enough of me even Noreen needed an escape, if for a while. Read in a magazine that women cannot love two men at once, they figured using prairie voles in West Virginia zoo. But that was West Virginia and voles, likely smooth moving Wicklow broads were more complicated with devil may care crazy emotions needing to take measure of a fellow. All such details not yet understood by the sciences, only yet reported by supermarket magazines. Dismayed over several more pints, felt patrons knew more from the way things telegraph along this blighted high land. Should have gone to gaunty Kelly's alehouse or stayed above in my lair judging lay of the land, didn't want them enjoying misfortunes for that's their Irish way. Gaelic word for 'bloody Shauden Froid' a worn down focal. To understand no need sixth sense, common fair enough. I read their miserable minds, faith one day I'll be reading Macnamara's 'Squinting windows' for the insight.

Big shot back from Canada with trophy bird. Not even married had her working round the clock and he on his arse. Never lifts a finger has a fella cut the grass. Living on her money, she off to the coalface everyday. What could she see in likes of him? That old goat.

Fair rubbernecking comment, I'm getting through life. A struggle.

Fine looking lass strong bones has lads interested, a young one would need to have ones of her own. Never a word out of him, he'll be alone now has a wife across in Canada. Writing dreadful things about the country, he knows where the midnight ferry is. Off back over there, doesn't have a friend only yer wan. Didn't take her long to scamper, lonely and quiet with likes of that fella, always walking himself. Ye'd think now he'd have a few bob away so long. A professor should be well set, not one for ponies or dogs. Every time with same wooly jersey, he's skint. The aunt gave him the place, lock, stock and barrel. He'll be worse for wear, never cope with loss that's men for ye. Weak as the day is long. Never miss water 'till well runs dry, a burden trying to coax her back. Musty not a penny spent since before the war. Gas masks stored in garage waiting Hitler's bombs! Bottled gas for the stove. A garda she's off with took a shine to him Halloween, right donnybrooks out Malahide way. Her fella had every young one here to Dundalk.

Ordered dreaded pub sandwich, covered with Colman's yellow mustard.

Forever cavorting, a hussy. If she was a married woman there'd be none of that palaver, put his boot down. Sounds like she's from Texas, too brazen for this country air. Garda will have her under control read the riots act.

Midst of musings I left, heading for the jacks and slunk out had my fill of Bettystown mama with ears still ringing. They'd caught my drift. Meandering in street lights could see leaves falling in chilly evening air, not only thing falling on that autumn evening wherever she was. Still hungry picked up curry from Deep Singhs on high street, tried to be strong but that task in vain, my choice in cold fridge blue or black. Inhaled several Black Tower and some fags with Punjabi mash. Shoved leafy plant in empty bottles other plants upended on carpet, one shoved in her supermarket cake. Plantslaughter, her pride and joy under mortal attack. Later that night anxiety with butterflies hearing key working in the lock, Noreen returned. Me trying to portray unconcerned but maybe over did being detached. *Don't reveal too much, skin cover meat.*

Said nowt about dead flowers, with coat on ran upstairs, on the ascent as ever tripped on sword man's step. Lot can be relayed from scent of irritated woman when she's sweat from a man.

"In absentia chopped clamamentia." I shouted. "Did he use handcuffs my Miguelini? Cops supposed to protect not be stealing."

Knowing her history, sodden brain blurted. Confused lacking control, only way to fight a woman is with your hat, pusillanimity grab it and run.

"I'm tired," heard from top balustrade. "Don't transfer demon troubles to me, get help with your extreme behaviours."

Plants beyond protection her plan to go root in other soil. Cherrywood cheval hall mirror gave glimpse of weasel veins set to pop on my beetroot face. Bedroom door slammed.

Alone again up double helix
spiral staircase to widow's watch,
out on a charpoy study ocean life
and my own existence naturally.
Glass bottom served as monocule

for sky that night, Moore in heavens.

With scallywags aftershave on my nose hair *et tu brut* downed Blue Nun, langered till cups runneth over, empty flagon an ashtray. Stared through mists at life galloping past, sang dirges to ghost of Eria on Ireland's eye. That night my bellowing bounced off the ocean, no craic coming my way. Rumpled my hat at the isle, hollered fist in air singing over air waves, isle looked back in black.

"Noro, so made right bags of things never compos mentis. Glasnost, solidarity, perestroika fucking Gdansk, here's to tomorrows we will melt mellow in Cologne."

Drinking deep measures singing 'Córas Iompair Éireann', glimpsed tips of aurora borealis from the north, sure I make mistakes now only gasping for areolas. Sure Janie's Mac aren't we all cousins with freaking monkeys? Can't be rice expert and mushroom expert, 'no longer young enough to know everything.' Shivered me timbers, making sense out of nonsense, signed cheque for five Gs. Stuck a note on marmalade.

Peace in our time babe keep your fork more pie's coming.
Promise to buy apartment for when I'm annoying.
Sorry I drunk foreigner's wine please don't go astray
(Noreen tear down that wall, paper the cracks)

Before daylight stairs tripped three sheets to the wind, as I drifted off realized no sounds of woman's sleep, no warm bum or cold shoulder only freezing sheets with empty feelings. On her down filled pillow a note filled me in, only floored I was.

'In the spare you're scaring me'

Tiptoed landing left note on the door, could hear whispering maybe even prayers.

'In despair you're scaring me.'

Cars passing fell asleep with noise of pounded battered salted rocks, into deep reverie lived in wadi hole untarnished by life's humdrum. Perhaps creaking floor boards indicated something was afoot.

Eleven that morning in the kitchen read the note added to mine, on the bitter marmalade.

'Away to Lourdes weekend with Mairead, Mother's ailing wants holy water.'

Pilgrimage doing what Irish do, her half full cold coffee I finished, sweetened by honeycomb, cheque she read lay on the table. Away over in Lourdes Irish girls recite rosaries unless langered in wine bars popping sommeliers corks. Not a baby washed but gone her way she was. Lay upon her pillow, needed Noreen pull my pint one more time, sweet nectar turned sour.

'Och! I'll roar and I'll groan,
my sweet Molly Malone,
til I'm bone of your bone
and asleep in your bed.'

Spent weekend reading them Agatha Christies to distract mind's eye those emotional times. Nothing on damn TV still got the picture. Wanted to tell her some gadgets in me head needs adjusting not sure which or how, never got a manual. Those evenings Bruce hob nobbing Dublin taverns back carousing with mates. Saturday night phone rang, heartless sister Beth calling from banks of Avoca river.

"Oh it's you," she says. Flea infested vagrant, dog's body dragged in by a cat. Her sister's low expectations.

"She's away in Lourdes, Mairead and that."

Slurped and sucked miwadi vodka ice.

"Oh yeah Lourdes. Okay I remember. Sure."

Twigged dastardly plot, rats working set of mischief's. *Sure nowt, small hay stack easy find needle.* Unwitting whistle blower puffing louder than pied piper, turned by her sister near rivers that babble on.

Noreen that deceiver, people telling porkers poorly practiced in deceptions, she a piker with the master.

"Testimonium Perhibere Veritati' ye bear witness to truth." Informed Beth.

Flung wireless phone at fireplace bricks, harke hear buoys ding-dong bells on rough waves. Agatha 'twas constable that done it, lad from Dalkey harbour repeat offender. Chill wind rattled windows on bleak and lonely cliff, fickle winds of change had changed. Turncoat O'Boyle woman poncy shyster, three card trickster, carny gamer, ponzy operator, shroud of medieval Turin-uncovered. Wood fire set for long hard night, drank into oblivion. Miss Beth knew zip about Noreen's quest for well water, sure divil lady was in Lourdes that scheming trip was true. Essence of her game woman with treachery, as female chimps abandon weak losers only mate with strong. Under nervous duress opened bottle of Alba faithful malt from isle of Skye therapy reserved for maladies.

'King o' drinks, as Scots conceive it', but no not I. I fear it.

Kept working to reveal Bruce treacherous web. Half way through turfy barley case closed, 18th call to cheap hotels in Hautes-Pyrénées revealed Monsieur et Madame Walsh bienvenue guest at 'Le Carpentras Inn'.

"Fair cop guvnor,"Wicklow girl must concur.

Not brave to request to be put through, didn't need to hear hot sweaty wicky girl answering 'coiti interuptii' Sunday morning. Never rosary repeating in Lourdes, fooling no one Bruce and ill-gotten maid communion between sweaty sheets and not pews, bread and wine from service aux chambres. Finished off bottle of booze except angel's steal, slept until early afternoon. Noreen froze remains of lasagna from month previous, devoured luke warm with Brennans white pan.

'Don't waste, each rice grain cost poor farmer drop of sweat'. My mammy's wisdom.

During that evening consumed 20 mgs of valium, couple bottles of blue. Calm and thoughtful, judgment error in game of bogeys. Late Sunday night called la French hotel.

"Woo, woo, Birdie Walsh," says to African on the desk at Lourdes hotel.

"Les pilgrams sleeping, call sur la matin."

Clerk reluctant to put me through, convinced him there was a crisis.

"Alleluia, allez begorrah! There's been miracles sick mother dancing fandangos playing on spoons. Dangling hooleys in glens, uillean pipes and banging bodran, porter flowing free. Cul de sac do I need to call les gendarme relate good tidings? Listen Mandela it's emergencies go ring them silver bells. Sil vous plate and saucer."

Not having yobo from Congo interfero this import momento, I'd stuff on me cranium.

"Monsieur, Irish Madame returned with tres handsome mari dévoué."

"Merci, Nigerian."

Talking damn liberties only mulligans with life of divots.

"Noreeno?"

Wake up Resurrection church, ready to hitch wagon ball and chain. Speak to ruby rose, my scarlet Ibis.

"Yes."

"'tis me, baby."

"Oh, okay."

"bb baby, baile ata cliat calling on big bay baby."

"Brian what do you want?"

Wrestling match with the female get to a point.

"Will you marry me?" Slurred and sang to her, swing for fences no spinning wheels.

'Daisy, daisy, give me your answer do.'

Not complicated, pinch fatted calf from over hills for grand feasts. Full roasts heady fruity wines, gaels be blowing full sail, and *'kiss me hardy'*.

"It's him, leave a few minutes," heard her say, door closing heard the grunt.

"Why are you calling?"

"Your fella Mandela said youse were still up, 'member we met at motel desk, Noro?"

Solo shot woo her back, sub rosa.

"Want to marry you, have papers written a contract. Lawyer in the village says it will be sworn and stuff. It's definitely legal."

"Are you drinking?"

"Elephants from Fossetts in Galway, wooden barrel Niagara champagne. No escapes now." I says laughing, what with pipe of Afghani ganja, drugged, confused with she angry and shocked. Never easily amused female, when mask is off none are. Obviously except Lucy and delightful Maureen Potter.

"Brian it's late."

"You're three hours ahead, time flies like an arrow, fruit flies like banana. Did I get me lotto numbers? Are we rich with black diamonds?"

"Brian you're drunk, I'l be back mid-morning to settle things. Best we can."

"Do it in Howth, Glen da Lough or Grand isle, travel to Toyota have special sushi."

"Have to go," all she said.

"Sure have a go, I'm a man from Stoneybatter." Clicked off, swing and miss for sure.

Dawn's early light woke sitting at the desk, French telephone numbers on note pad recalled some stupidness. Naked woman staring from porn site, went to bed obsessed over another. Late breakfast of coffee toast and regret that Monday morning, did she get to Grotto or stay holed up with concubine? Watching from bedroom window as she paid the taxi, one legged prick from Dundalk curious as to why she'd not called me to haul arse. Right brazen puss, 'belong to no one attitude' over pouty face. Turned on the radio eating bottom of bag cornflakes she liked, one day I'll invent a cereal crusher, that's golden. She hesitated in hall went upstairs. No acknowledgement, neither did I greet her, freed of any man thinking she was his. No check in, only silent treatment sorry room not yet cleansed, I'll get Molly's do laundry. Cried on your pillow, no charge. How long is your stay? Family style shepherd's pie for dinner on big plates.

'Twas curtains for me wide gulf lay between us, this lady from the delta.

Miss Malone alone, left with brown reddish hair returned with fake blond on that body, return 'good time' now blocked by Garda Shiochana. Left house by back door out of sight agitated up the creek, reclined in heather for few smokes and fruit juice. How to protect these women from cunning divil smart Irish fellas? Ancestors long with their wits about them, hid them in those tall boys that round tower in Glen Da Lough. Feeling crushed a condemned lad, Mohangi, our last condemned reprieved in '66, ordered by all Four Courts. Expected no such big wig mercy from ginger locks, threw up breakfast and tea leaves on heather. No need of RTE fishing forecasts, stormy weather clouds had gathered with intentions. She was in the living room oiling leaves both sides, saying goodbye decapitated plants withered on vines. Proud of her adventures turning over new leaf.

"Beautiful out there."

"I wet the tea leaves."

Universal greeting noticed rosary beads on the table, strained tea I knew my fortune. I was in hot water.

"I got that for your mother get them blessed at the Resurrection."

"She'll like that. Thanks." God bless, I'd make peace with McCracken.

Put with dozen hanging in Ma's bedroom blessed by bishops attack heaven by all sides their diligent promise. Withdrawn no anecdotes of frenchy fashionable women compared to umpa lumpa boats parading Irish streets. From slim hippie to hippo as time surely passes.

Ferrice Pickens consigned to dumpster, bereft me joining him amid potato peels. When courting mi esposa, she'd asked to marry being stupid was my problem. That day sparse lunch of tuna sandwich, tomato soup and dreary silence. Our cup of parting soup. She let in cuckoo boy went to work. Off to nest in finer twig and saliva, difficult part over, moving on. Seeing her high tail messed my transit like Jupiter with tiny moon, she carried all the gravity.

Helen of Sparta followed Paris to Troy. Husband Tyndareus sailed in pursuit, slew Paris on greasy street returned victorious. Should have fought Bruce on slick Wicklow roads, fighting Garda would get me in trouble with courts, she'd canceled my authorities.

Pitiful man neglected recluse chancy looking roaming the hill
pig on his own as ever, picayune monkey peeling his own banana
with me hobo bindle and cup unkempt hedge lonely wild grass
garbage piles disturbing villagers, stress and strain come what may
procrastination curse of my life, lazier than Angwantibos slow Loris.

The Irish man sober or soused an ugly creature, in truth worst of all men a garbage-can man. In shark feeding frenzies for a bird demonstrate no concern for a brother. Irish men have no notion of solidarity no mercy offered. A nation divided between gobshites and flim-flam artists. No united men in green, we're un-united, dis-united, mis-united never man-united. Bunch of louts and bollix garrulous grifters, suspicious chisellers, pettifoggers. Blaggura ceart, waggle spewers. Always gombeen men, trickster, bousy, gurrier, quisling, scoundrels, knackers, slouchers, eejits and dogers, traitors and turncoats, maggots, sly chancers and spoofers, hagglers and trader raiders. Country of swaggering bogtrotters born from likes of spalpeens tattie hookers and langered god fearing and twisted misshapen drunks. A land more angry culture not agriculture. No Magna Carta just maggot classes. Oh, go where you are wanted, for you are not wanted here.

'Only thing straight in the county village was the steeple.'
'An Irishman on the spit can always get another Irishman to turn him.'
Never went same direction all the time, bunch of talking horses,
agree on nothing, country forever governed like herding cats.
Countess Markievicz's advised the Irish wench
"Dress suitably in short skirts and sitting boots,
leave your jewels and gold wands in the bank,
and buy a revolver." Words for any age.

CHAPTER 10

Later that night expected her to come indoors resume our simple life. In stupor staring at TV crooking the elbow Kent ale, tasty hops and gold foam. Dear Jackeen call from Wicklow, inevitable but drag on my soul. Throw me a bone tell me all lies. Bruce is impotent went to pray don't worry, Lourdes forgiven without miracles. Put me in a whirl, roll around carpet and drink Chablis. Won't complain, batter or blatter bad things, taciturn but no tantrums. Share worldly goods, what you say? I've stocks in a startup, worth bags. Can be less a nutter than before. Easy for me! All yours take over be Queen Noreen. Four poster, own room, by appointment only, schedule on the door. To comalot. Boss over all you can sea, horizon be dammed. Bus load of Wicklow folks dancing, they'll come to romp. Open doors make jamboree galores. Accordions and big thirsty drummers with mustache parading. Whiskey by barrel, drums of porter. Show them you a big shot. With your Ma so proud. Build gazebo by the dock, have a yacht and sail, swim with dolphin pods. Travel and frolic at ukulele concerts in Hanalei.

"bb it's me, sorry did I wake you?"

Can't just disappear and fade away, sure without you? You're all I got.

She hoped to leave message given the hour. Bye, bye, don't prey on me, don't call maybe I'll pray for you someday.

"No, couldn't sleep worried as ever."

Damn Mr Bell, disturbing peace.

"I'm okay, I've moved to a house near Roundwood."

Damn this world and all who sail in her.

"Roundwood?"

Hardy brass spittoon required in my company, shenanigans unbeknownst. Sometimes when shepherd cries 'wolf-wolf' something is barking 'woof-woof'.

"Closer to my mother better job. Manager of a Carvery in Bray!"

"Wow so much happening, many changes?"

Still a bitch, now living in Wicklow.

"Had we discussed any of this? Kumbaya?"

"Lynchys, one of those old places for the Aunt outing of a Sunday."

How will I manage I've my round wood?

"bb sorry, I needed time to consider after things happened."

Get over yourself, fly by night fling with a nun should count between naught and zero, I'm no two timing Papa, but by Windy hill expect vindictive. Only Kipling had them properly nailed.

'the woman that God gave him,
every fibre of her frame
proves her launched for one sole issue
armed and engined for the same
and to serve that single issue
lest the generations fail
the female of the species
must be deadlier than the male.'

Lot of learin there within, for every male of that species. "Noreen when are you coming back?"

Always the tinker woman, went to bull pen tad early. Like a frog lilly pad leaping.

"Brian you have responsibilities with your new son. We're never married obviously don't only need me."

With two water bucket for three, everyone thirsty.

"I had me extenuating circumstances. Unfortunately."

"Something was extenuating."

Okay had anticipations, no sammy good shoes.

"Other lads saw me in the rescue Father McCracken has evidence, I'm hero out here. Priest will get it sorted."

Sky watchers spied and caught lonesome man in frickin solitudes, searching for comforts.

"It's all big mess."

Lay not up treasures in heart where mott can so easily thieve and break.

"Exactly, monkey loose in a corn field, crazier than a dog in hubcap factory." So she claimed, herself being familiar with those locations.

Another Wicklow broad with moxies casting stones, not my first ride in uppity Garden of Ireland county. Miss Goody two shoes never put foot wrong, with vanilla jocks, hot mulatos and every other yokes? Now getting rocks off by horn of mount Tonelagee, them two langered high on Kippure scrub land. With losing shoes on Burnside, her gra for boys and he more testosteroned than Jamaican sprinters. Right shower that pair, now she burns my butt.

"Not marrying her, don't know her."

"Amsterdam and old Dublin flames I'm sure. Please don't come to Wicklow."

"Noreen you're dumping me because of the cop be honest."

Flabby hide not compared, six-pack cooling in fridge.

"Half pint Astair and Ginger two of youse."

"What in Sam Hill are you ballin about?"

Dial tone down the blower, being oafish never best with dodgy female. Noreen knew I was no playboy on Dublin streets. Departed ale for harder stuff, damn fool, that night rightly jarred called work number in Bray.

'The Cavery,' answering machine, no time for questions.

"Gringo sinoretta so que papsa?
Yo this for Pickens, Suzann
my beauty from Belize comin
kaiso, kaiso, bum bum.
Creole bambinos to fill house,
all jumpin up Carnival time."

Woke pale head ailing, empty state. Hair of the dog required for spinning mind. Her friend Mairead called sometime after one pm, met in dingy coffee shop in Rathmines near red stone library, where once loved dear Enid Blyton. Sisterhood dispatched, consigliere relating world gone pear-shaped. Rollicking coming as flogging her piñata, but heavy male sac delivered plenty attitude. In naff place shared plonk and tasty crust apple pie, cox pippen no golden delicious.

"You said the F-word seven times, now that's not fair."

Boil duck meat soft, mouth still hard.

Sure took my shine away, silence not a good answer.

"She'd called me her liberator, middle name is Daniel."

"You could get her fired sure she only started."

Count blessings, be
grateful for bananas.
Lucky like monkey,
a wonderful life.

"Mairead sure I miss her what can I do forget about her? Give me that break, middle of night. Noreen got the hump sure no biggie, honky dory not never Andrea Doria. We've special relationship she needed to go for the while."

Blew a loon tremolo hoot, all at Mairead's worries.

"Our relationship fiord deep. I love her."

Stay stoic pay bills, be responsible. Doing what's required. Anyway it's nuthin till she calls it. Really calls it.

Don't get ahead of the game.

Don't wash dish while eating,

or make bed when people sleep.

Don't bother work hard people,

or question Olympic when running.

"Remember we've bonds of Shannon waters from the canals, and wandering Viking blood."

Stem winder, man of baloney, a four flusher.

"She's mad with you, Winston the cavery owner listened to the message."

Wow, well now Katie bar the door.

"Floods in New Orleans writhing snakes in streets, Mississippi waters with all kinds of varmints up with overflow from manholes, rode on my shoulders in that thunder storm. So scared to get bit by cottonmouth, bit folks get very aggressive. I'm Howth head man with first class ticket, up high she ate fois gras. Kissed away tears thousand times, all her stuff at my house."

As photons divided, travel separately never untangled that's basic.

"With she in house on Howth head carpets wall to wall worth a ton. Not serious problem temporary, wait and see. We're great mates, take care it will get sorted."

In that greasy spoon Mairead figured I was waffling, as goldfish blow bubbles, ain't tripping on that. On I went with determined good news. *None so blind as the man that will not see.*

"Bray for iodine baths and sea air walks, agreed makes enough common sense. Mother with rheumatism maladies and lumbago, gout got her big toe. Damnable damp air by meetings of the waters."

Even St Patrick let out blue streak stubbing toes on Croagh Patrick's rocks, trying to knock sense out of stubborn pagan Irish.

"Living in dump on Decatur down on her uppers over an art gallery, still with splinters in my arse from those floors, nobody rushing to help sure nobody could. Her life a mess, writing was on the wall don't paper over cracks. New Orleans right tip outside the Quarter and scary dangereux let me tell ye. Abandoned old bats drinking daiquiris midday to midnight, arse pinched to get a tip. Don't go wail on me, don't never stray north of Satchmo, up there is no wonderful world."

I'd see her in Dublin she'd come back, we had rows but we'd overcome. Row, row, row, get ship to shore.

"You've to get on without her she surely told me. Tidy suitcase now, tell him it's over finito."

Such expected windbaggery from Noreen.

'Had me only half skinned with those wicked winds in that lonely place, how could I drive that hill on icy roads, I've not got a jeep? Brian was all inside himself, it's that lonely. Perfect with he and the cloistered nun. In those winds sure I'd be blew in the face.'

Noreen locuta est, causa finita est -- 'Noreen has spoken, case closed'.

Okay, so those were winds crafted by God. Glorious sea breezes.

Like O'Boyle was cow in market shed. Find doppelganger, few quid, spit and handshake carry off green eyed Miss. Plonk Italian no surprise, never buy except out on the boot.

"Friday night in Avoca all there, girls from school, Carol Tetley and she with four kids. 'He's getting the free fuck', Tetley says as you and Nor were not engaged. Noreen was upset here it's more different." Mairead looked embarrassed with life's engagements, as designed by our creator.

No free ride in life for Tetley's old lad just heap of mouths to feed, sucking up Cow and Gate by cart load. How much Tetley charging bareback coitus aficionado? Mucho, mucho. All she could get.

"Ireland's stone age they'd never understand, Noreen and Carol always at 6's and 7's. She damn well married Ferrice at nineteen." Young lass knew numbers by the score.

Mario send fragola grappa shoe polish to Irelanda
fill big potato beer bellies, make love to beetroot women.
Irish women have hard on for Italian fellas
med dwellers honey running in their veins.
Not a fada shared since we departed Olduvai Gorge
we went left for bogs right side they got the Med.
By george different as Caliban and Cleopatra we were.
Chips with me spaghetti bolanaise, grazie senor.

"They're living in Avoca, house down by the river."

Her watershed, now me mentals getting battered, getting swept out like sagebrush.

"Brian I'm sorry at least youse were not together long. You've women all over no more room, now running with a Holland nun."

My monkey business now all got up in Wicklow's business. Go climb on frigging barren hills, youse be exhausted then mind yer business.

"Mairead with uisce baite things got carried away, not only man with that carry on, I'll take care of things get sorted no worries, I've seen it all before and more. Much worse."

Ball o'malt pillar of the nation
builds our rotten characters.
No wits about had my mickie pulled
feckless lad, blue with cold
trickery unexpected blew icicle wad.
Messed my ying yang fang shui
with Mi Wicklow Esposa, still

suffering and mourning that loss.

"She'd be home in Wicklow for the weekend and with you the house would be a mess."

China after Japan soldier departed. Plonk emptied indicated another, Med fellows regard us as wart on arse of Europe, carbuncle of their continent, volgarita chip butties and farting. Incontinent to national aclaim. Romans did sod all but drive us mad with Karloff images of hell, as to believe our creator runs merciless penitentiaries. Sounds non-credere, for heaven's sake is God American? Land of free, and locked up, forgiving my arse.

"She's forever working, you'd promised to do some book? Bruce always excited about his job with chasing robbers. Catching them hither and yon, tracking across hills not as the crow flies. You photographing seagulls she'd complain you'd never do a hands turn nor quit skylarkin." *Now only eating crow.*

Noreen complained I was 'watermelon man', no arms no legs. If not for my draw we'd not have two cents. On her budget we'd rent a caravan on the burren.

Always doing something useless,
feed cake after Christmas dinner
warn starving Africa of cholesterol,
make monkey grow more hair.
Take off pants to fart.
How keep sun, not have dark?
Tell hungry make stomach full
swallow wind on the hill.
Do I need tell egg make chicken?
I have to do everything?

"Mairead I paid bills she paid for nowt, woman would take farthings from grandmother's eyes. Okay, once she bought Atacama cactus, right prick."Yippee!

'never knew a sweetheart spend her money on a chap.'
Minger would break penny in two, iron chicken never lose feather,
jump fence to save hinge, give poor last week food.
She'd sell me wild rabbit if stood still to catch,
she don't like parting with her brass.

Sonesta biddies learned her old wives tricks, acquire their mulla, vitamin M. Marrying 'potentials' focused on earning, chosen men sucked dry squeeze man's money. Made sure her tank was full, paid grease monkey. My hot skinflint watching my shekels. Fair dues we'd symbiotica not parasitica.

"Brian you'd be out flying kites."

Flew chapi-chapi from dollar store in Niagara grand sea breezes abroad on the head, catch four winds, tricky up draughts navigate wafting in sea gusts.

"Doing her U.S. tax."

This citizen still owed Uncle Sam many Benny Franklins, not want her sent to suffer America's bleak hillbilly justice, in today's grotesque 'lock 'em city' Amerikius.

'Essential American soul is hard, isolate, stoic and a killer. It has never yet melted.'

"She likes he has friends, but it's all non-stop?"

Copper hardly had two pfennigs and she with overdrafts.

"A wedding in Donabet she hated, hundreds knew no one. Bruce got drunk spitting peanuts, imagine the likes that man would go to opening of envelopes! Sorry to say she made a mistake, away fourteen year for heaven's sake. Nobody knows real Noreen, a whole side I know nothing even Ferrice and James. Ferrice was devastated sent so many letters she'd never reply, the way she treats men is dreadful fierce hard." Mairead says. "I've witnessed that same with county lads, before she went away."

Sister Pickens knew to mess a fellow.

"Tell Noreen I'll no be pinning, nor jumping over cliffs. Noro ain't all that, big bore in bed with no great shakes." Even with those hips.

'He that speaks ill of the mare wants to buy her'.

For short leg fox high grapes forever 'too sour'.

Not scare tiger have three mouth,

scare partner have two heart.

"All right Brian enough of that."

Well knew who got kicked off that mound, forever switcheroo madam.

"Show up rabbiting about house in Howth, lonely guy then takes me for loser. Flew home on my dime, first opportunity dumps me."

"My lord Brian sheer nonsense! You need to accept responsibilities for what happened."

"When he dumps her tell her don't come crawling up Howth hill. I'm not waiting and wailing, sure not broken hearted. I'll not be needing Christiaan Barnard with pumping contraptions."

We wandered out of dire café having a smoke, other fish in the sea maybe not dogfish.

"She still wants to be friends."

"Shopping clogs for plod, coffee at Bewleys, spit and black polish. Going insane and she wants friends?"

Woman only a friend,

so all just for show?

-drinking near beer

-fishing catch and release

-Pogues and no Shane

-life in Ontario

-driving hillman imp.

Decaf, my arse.

Shoot me now, go on,

no pint to continue.

Already did hard time

with catholic girls.

Oh one sweet caroline.

"Brian she wants Mr. Piggy."

She'd talk to wire tail buttoned-eyed pig, those bed room stuffed animals gave me hebby gebbies. Drop kick over the ocean belly flop in air, more fun times for pinnipeds with porky.

"If she's back Mr. Piggy will be safe."

Elsewise grill his bacon ass.

"She's that afraid you'll throw him out over the cliff face."

Tight in burlap sack tossed in barnyard with hungry pit bulls, I'd be chortling as drunken Kookaburra. Enough, Mairead's strong bones getting on my wick, yapping wind blow my ear. Departed with sisterly hug, wandered canal banks to Portobello bridge. Quite the punchy solid mary hick, right tall totem stand tall in storms. Mountainy woman hard tits to feed army bad form to cop a feel, had battle with the widths. By canal bridge dropped into the Barge, paid for pint with spanking crisp fiver. Needed Alamo quiet as Davy Crockett before Mexican contemplation.

Can stones be diamond? Study why monkeys not human, how cobra survive it's venom? How all world beavers make same dams.

But no chance brawny culchie took one gawk at me green unit, brand new mint.

"Go take your self off, did ya make it yourself like?" Felt full whiskered snarl, knew what he had for lunch. Yesterday.

He sequestered me pint, forged bill tossed back no high stool for me, kept on my toes. Change from naf café buying romany plonk, counterfeit what a pisser. Headed for door, turned knob right as he flew off the handle, legged it fast over lock gate. Bang on perceptive Toronto fellow barging a shambolic island, never meant for me. Loss of face with surly kind, right hump sat out by Harrington street canal banks, leave this celtic viper nest far gone away in exile. Off to Maui licking beads sweet and sour from honeyed Orient, eat moon cake Chinese new year, have her dumpling all year long. Celtic broads do weary souls of Dublin man, pursuing wear down hob nail boot clicking cobble stones. National Geographic had Atlantic island horses run wild, try to ride and they buck. Wild creatures not broken, gaelic women as broncos, decent fellas tossed discarded in the sod.

Better look beyond for love in Tijuana bordellos,
San Francisco gay street clicking females from Kalahari
unrequited subway riders with questions in brown eyes.

Red haired babe stole my heart, her trophy room bagged from cruel safari times. Great white Noreen many lads caught in her web, only prawns in that game. Poems she wanted not poets, matador not bull, needed a ring not bull ring. All I said was 'complicated', she wanted simple man but no more not me. Noreen finest girl to come from Wicklow only wish she stayed put, now found my butt lost in Coventry.

"You caused so much trouble." Says Wicklow princess.

Get off your high horse Tonto, she without original sin only Irish citizen no need for baptism. Don't start war and complain train's late, sorry no Kellerbiers with Gerry's zero beer sales to Blighty in 1942. *Apart from Gerry freak out forties life in Europe warm and pleasant.*

Discarded I was, as used picnic plates on Seapoint strand.

With begging Noreen agreed to meet in pub beside O'Connell bridge on Burgh Quay, mighty building crafted from stone and iron, interior sixties bar cubicles shinny plastic and neon.

Float our Kish lighthouse,
grand head on tin stout briquettes craft from turf,
finally find balls to dispense condoms like gum,
let people come without fear, as normal primates.
Liberty hall my hairy arse blot on our landscape

Strumpet city built best by Victorians.

All gilette best clobber, I wore dark blue sweater she'd bought from Dunne's stores. In jeans she arrived at 8 pm so radiant, no legs in red dress now only for show as ears of deaf man, face as German Hilda entranced by Wagner. Sat in a corner from the bar, I sees culchie pubman pour my pint from slops, annoying fly buzzing. Wager weeks wages tight Wexford man figured me a loser. Not wearing me short pants, but okay with Noreen as boss.

' you a woman came
to soothe a time torn man
even though it be
you love me not.'

"Wicklow hills are best, it's years since I could wear these jeans."

Acting all brand new with her slim self. Who was she kidding with G and T, she full pint woman not Delgany brasser. That evening I cried tears, half filled pot makes most noise, cry baby get milk to drink. Wanted cop out, didn't understand why she flew the coop, me vocals all engulfed, entangled. People stared, Jesus Murphy Dublin man crying over losing a bird. Shame the county saints in heaven preserve us, hardly knew the wee lass. Ah now stop grieving and wailing get yer slops down ye, dry yer eyes Johnny. She sat tissues to spare, her cop doesn't bawl he's real man. Wanted to tell her we'd honeymoon in Pacific islands of Bora-Bora, emerald seas and drink cocktails.

"Bula, Bula!" Laugh with Tiki barman under tropical nights.

"Once you eat cascadoo love woman more," he'd declare.

Breakfast surrounded by cockatoos, bikini birds, drink mauby from boiled bark, roll in waves. But Noreen paid no attention to travel brochures only glanced at her Bullova. No Bora-Bora, Tora-Bora nor mud hut in Kampala desperate to take a hike. Crunching Tayto crisps for carbs, taking it all with grain of salt.

"I'd move to Wicklow, Arklow or Rathlow, any damn low you never gave me that chance." *Only offering poor man talk.*

"You said how annoying Wicklow was, like thick planks."

"Uisce baite bullshit pub fellows, Avoca better than Howth I agree. You know my grandfather is buried away at Glen da Lough."

'There is not in the wide world a valley so sweet
as that vale in whose bosom the bright waters meet.
Sweet vale of Avoca!
Where storms we feel in this cold world cease,
our hearts like thy waters be mingled in peace.'

"Brian you'd stay home, I'd be down there lonesome."

Alone my arse, manky drunk loosy goosey with wanky boyos.

"Your mother's house busy and youse yaking all afternoon, needed contemplations in my own place to hide away."

Cat at mouse meeting, my passion occupied with her by myself.

"See 'hide away'," she pointed sarcastically.

"I'm not broadcaster person if living there things would be different. You prefer quiet, now all 'Mac' Boyle he doesn't want real Noreen. You're a loner, this guy will drive you nuts good luck not being yourself."

Replied nowt, nuff said showed some job adverts, salaries underlined.

"Interviews lined up, right up my alley if I get Shell/BP position I'll relocate to Dubai tax-free. That's a possibility with great swimming, gorgeous sandy islands. I'd be investing." So imagined. *Only advertise speech.*

Only busy supping gin, as exotic spices cautiously sup, sup, supping. Never focused on bogus plan, likely hoped I'd move to Inisfree shelter with honey bees, stung by them wasps again, all slurp with no honey.

"bb I can't accept any proposal." Cocksure she was.

"It's not love I've been there, Bruce chases women."

"Brian which man of you does not chase women? It's all you fellas want to do, talk about pots and black kettles." *Kill chicken don't need cow knife.*

Men's brains only work part time with that Achilles heel forever dangling.

"Don't be so sure, depending on a man more fickle than you."

"Everyone wants to be his friend, you're completely that opposite."

"I met this girl in Canada, black hair, lips with brooding dark eyes. Third date wanted to marry her, month later changed my number. It happens you and I beyond that." Short shallow fingers, broody's appendages bothered me no end.

Noreen sat emotionless, sister Stasi mowing brother at the wall. Not even that personal, only taking care of business.

"You're thinking of marrying a fellow you just met."

"Bruce is transferring to Wicklow." Root canal talk. *Too late! Wood already become boat!* Trounced to stop whining, wheezing.

We had farewell on O'Connell street bridge, many questions unanswered. My dismal dismissal deemed final. Two monkeys hanging in jungle, didn't mean nothing special.

"You have me in tears, Brian sure you'll always be that special."

Kissed teary cheek as school friend and disappeared in the crowd, kept me fork but no puddin comin.

'Some do the deed with many tears,
and some without a sigh
some do it with a bitter look,
some with a flattering word,
the coward does it with a kiss.'

Likely Bruce shiocaning having rough laugh with prima nocta, I'd nowt just pocket of wet tissues and cat cry mouse die tears on my jumper, I'd not take it off for that week. From viaduct threw pack of Carroll fags in liffey, water under bridge, left for rock on H train.

'What makes you sure, have you learned nowt?' Wanted to ask.

All men created equal bad, heaven's sake why make a change? Better she keep weather eye, no Deus Ex Machina to my rescue. Sometimes put wood on ball but no fairways to pursue happiness with this female. Singing carols, as marched the hill, pee in hedge. Against that westerly I'd a fork pissed on my khakis, ding a ling, ding a ding a ling. I'd no chance, only she changing mid stream.

'You've heard of Julius Ceasar
and the great Napoleon too,
and how the Cork militia
beat Turks at Waterloo.'

That night staring at bricks and mortar, outside blasted by prevailing elements. Noreen with her cop beyond the bay, difficult for man to contemplate his woman making love to another, primordial territory dark place to be.

'And when you gaze long into an abyss,
the abyss also gazes into you.'
Wiggling like trout on the line,
unkissed, twisting in the wind.
tensious times for timid mind.

So I had issues, sat on floor of living room, village church chimed every hour. My father's brass ship clock ticked loud only winding me up. Needed those moments cease and desist. That clock I'd no longer wind *'what care I how time advances?'*

Dad promised me summer gig on mail boat
some other ass hole wore the sailor hat.
Feck you wanker, hoped you and your Pa drowned,
so wanted to take cattle to slaughter.
Over the rough waves to Birkenhead.

Watching a photo on stony Greystones beach where they would come Sundays after mass. Her Dad died there of hemorrhage one bright Sunday morning, she'd made sandwiches for lunch. We'd walk Greystone rocks, cuppa from cracked china at caf cuis farraige.

'bb so crazy, he went long ago. Here I feel at peace elsewhere I miss him. When I lost my way he was not there.' She once told me.

"I love you for telling me," I told her.

On the beach she walked away surrounded by waves, white caps welcomed for her. I had sat on stones, pounding waves making rock music from *'wind that breathes upon the sea'*. Her moody blue black dogs would descend, maybe she felt tide turning, our relationship mired in doldrums. Who knows what Irish stew of emotions stirred within her melancholy soul? Freaking Celts handful of mournfulness with ceaseless crazy searching, forever moving why we ended edged perched on side of an old world, even moon man Armstrong descended from Fermanagh cattle rustlers. In China they say freedom is not what it's cracked up to be, only wanted to be little pants man. On sand she wandered bare feet in surf alone by sea-breakers and rain sprays, as waves tumbled in tides and wind. Distant and remote didn't need me, watching her walk head down, disturbing when she wanted to be alone. Maybe I was inadequate not strong enough to put my arm around, never returned to that beach. Fell asleep surrounded by detritus of nights drunkenness, days later she asked if she could come to move her stuff.

"Please, bb. Could I do that?"

This was not life I wanted back on Eireann's rock, fated to be guan fu pathetic man with no woman. Stuck there in amber destined to be long time alone. Sure it was no life at all.

'When I was one-and-twenty
I heard a wise man say
'Give crowns and pounds and guineas

but not your heart away,
give pearls away and rubies
but keep your fancy free.'
But I was one-and-twenty
no use to talk to me.'

Boo hoo, so bad things happen in life, and then there's fleas.

CHAPTER 11

Dismounted number 8 bus outside Whisper O'Neil's professional building on Blackrock high street, graceful building gone only old street façade to hide renovated shell. Quite an affront for town folk, those developers fooling no one. Still retained yellowed sepia memory of that better place. Now full of steely medical labs, opticians, dentists and one office for 'E. O'Rahilly Psychologist'. With her I'd booked an hour, try to sort out those unbalanced yokes in me head, seeing as I was not coping well on me freaking tod being ill equipped for such likes. I'd found her location in yellow page search. Me and her with previous, journey back to source of my wanderings. Given state of fraught cluttered mental faculties chatting with one old friend would help although paid by the hour. Whatever paid many a broad by half hour multiple satisfactions mostly time to spare and no complaints. Elevator grounded for being out of order, not fixed, no good omen. Set me off with anxieties. Stricken panic attack as grunts back from Nam. Hoodie up, withdrawing on the stairs. Outside raining down, rat atat tat.

Abort, abort, abort, abort.
I'd hit trip wires there
telegraphing on nerves.

Don't resurrect that
consigned to oblivions.
After struggles almost
closed doors on them.
Hanging on street lamp.
Get out, get out.
Why are you here?
Face selfie smacked
you stupid coward.
Felt valium spurs
pulling me through.
Then carried on,
as needs must.
Go on! Regardless.

Calmly hoodless anxious in small waiting room listening to Scott Joplins 'Pine apple rag' on radio, at the counter young one by computer reading 'White Cargo'. Wishing I'd me ear plugs then sees dark haired beauty emerging from an office.

"Brian! Oh my god, well look at you!"

Smokey hazel eyed O'Rahilly, she who relieved me of virginity in her parents' house on Bushy Terrace in Rathgar many moons before. Slim pretty woman now 'thirty nine', last time I set eyes she was twenty-one years. Back then rough diamond a generous girl, before dear Evelyn girls bodies remained unexplored territory, nothing presumed. Otherwise existed, occupied in Mother Theresa barren territories. *Irish girls behaved like saints, Irish men wanted girls that's ain't.*

"Evey wonderful to see you," muttered, while intently studied by paperback reader.

Had a hug, musky perfume on my white linen shirt looking sharp casual Italian garb.

"I'm finishing with divorcing couple fighting over a tiny rabbit, had to saw down the middle bone. Everyone departed unhappy but mutually satisfied, blunted my last blade. Made a mess, hope you've no pets!"

Only you babe in those once upon a time Rathgar days, we'd make out in leafy lanes behind Georgian red bricks. Never realize I'd be haunted by her and drag my heels through life ghosting through it's shadows. *To the Delorean! If only.*

"Splitting hares as ever! Sure no worries, hares breed like rabbits."

Got a laugh from paperback.

"I've been looking forward, you and me will have grand old memory lanes." She said with a smile did me nerves world of goodness.

First cut deepest, forever grieving my dark soul
left to beavers and black mailing French
never thanks giving, north passage muskeg and meti,
Anishinabeg 'First Nations', anusic sculptures,
mukluks and Queen Victoria's treaties.
Haida nation, Micmacs, Plains of Abraham,
Potawatomi, piggin buckets and j'm souviens.
Cod fish and caribou, Iroquois birch bark
with babiche and bunkies bunch of coggers further down east.
Somehow in that soup stew a country got cobbled.
Nation my arse, with their four freezin winds,
jackass Canadians dopey hard on for foreigner's Queen,
'alarm' that queenie their highest crime.
Boo!

Finally together again, facing upright in satin covered Laz-e-boy. Both armed with pen on fools cap paper, feeling lost for words.

"My old soul mate, you've a grand tan," she says and poured us a cuppa. "So surprised you came back after so long!"

"Doing fishing off rock pier in Sandycove, salmon bass and flat fish had them fillet fried." Feeling relaxed, recent short back and sides.

'Her soul-mate' once whispered in my ear in rented caravan during rainstorm in soggy Wexford. Then plain man running in fields of Ireland *'when boyhood's fire was in my blood'*. Met her on a Monday night dance in Courtown's Oasis ballroom, Butch Moore and Capitol Showband playing. Sitting all mini-skirted and long hair, legs tanned and shining. Best nature designed, no mirage and life never got no better after.

"Just as well I don't have a couch with you and I," she laughed.

Practiced ice breaker expected, pay homage to our past. Damn fool psychologist with no couch. Ready to pounce! *Hunter and fisherman all stored in my quiver.*

"I've read your wonderful book, all my friends have. All your shenanigans, didn't surprise me one bit. So much our story, you were nasty with crazy things you said!"

Good enough to wipe cat's bum, avoided misery lit with celts stuck wallowing. *Wind of wallows blows forever on our land.*

"Folks don't pay for nice. Have habit telling people what they don't want to hear."

Accent ascended on prosperity scale, keep fruit in dining room bowl she would. Maybe something about Dublin women, first sounds heard in this life. Married well that I knew.

"My daughter Stella and her friends think I'm that cool now." Evelyn laughed. "The MILF at school."

Named after the local cinema, where once we'd watched Elvis gyrating. Good lessons.

"Times of my life babe had to publish in England, Dublin only waiting for Zurich's Joyce to show with his sequel. Don't go sue me!"

"Brian sweetheart I was delighted a fella wrote about me. Hilarious, shagging like rabbits in that VW van."

"Still with writing so struggling unhappy love all that. As ever!

Inspired by broken hearts, last chance honkey tonk saloon." Babbling I was.

Longside Pope, JFK and Book of Kells calendar you need this book.

"Full of unwritten words as always," she says.

My words needing to organize in their special ways.

"Here's the thing wanted something real from paper and pen, somethings down in words searching roots. I'd a set of me grandfather's notes, but only accounts and bits of newspapers. Sure that got me thinking, caught the internal fire. Scorching. At least have the persistence."

Memories survive, else going down,
knew time to escape, or forever be gone!
Dusted or buried, same difference,
when both are grounded.
Full fathom five comin my way.
Down days my history, Irish stuff,
those words not lost. Yet.
Know once I passed this way.

Back then in Courtown asked her to dance, during a slow set pushed her bare thigh between my legs. When music stopped she stayed, we shared a TK mineral and bag of Tayto crisps, tasted salt from crisps on her tongue when we kissed. Next night on the beach we lay on sand, finished flagon of cider. Full of fermented apple juice hearing wild waves crashing, beach dancing with transistor's rhythm and blues, busy with drawing 'love you' in those sands. After she wanted a lot more but condoms never available in Courtown those days. Mad with me but Belfast 100 miles away, had just covered cost of cider. Nothing worse than not having Trojans when cocked and loaded. Like a stallion. Uncomfortable withdrawing, entitled she was. She'd no rhythms available.

Condoms once illegal in Ireland haughty Arch Bishop and De

Valera blocked to deliver, president no dog in that race, his auld one 100 years old. French letters, Durex, Rubbers, Johnnies, overcoats, goalies, Jimmies, all verboten by Romans, did not cotton to likes of sausage shaped balloons when used in vile fornications. Burn in oily lubrications you will according to them pontificating, that was where they had a problem with me. Life too short for such nonsense that class of thinking not worth the candle, fellas vacated in droves needed somewheres else. Randy boys off on mail boats to toil other shores in Atlantics gulf stream and beyond. Tired of being tossers.

So why would they be illegal?
'Ex cathedra' proclamations,
because Casti Cunnubi, guilt of grave sin.
Daft as daft can be mad as a hatter,
our fun loving place, no fireworks or condoms.
Tommy guns and dynamite big bangs aye okay.
Don't spill seed on barren ground
say in latin, say in Aramaic
daft and wrong, in English our national disgrace
grave sin my arse.
Murder is grave sin and stealing
not much else. Dominus Hiberniae.

"We had our fun times walking boreens and beach bonfires," says she.

In that long ago Wexford summer until Daddy took her back to Rathgar in red Opel station wagon. We must have made love more than hundred times, once I got rubber supply from old lady traders down Dublin's Moore street. From her yellow wooden barrow hidden under bananas, green cucumber, thickest carrots, and spuds in burlap sacks. Delicious ground provision items legal in free state, when stewed. *'Today's carrot greatly enlarged less woody.'* Biddies rule purchase tubers with rubbers. Ma's kitchen over loaded with root vegetables in brown bags.

"Eyesight improved, seeing things never saw before." That partial to carrots, tells me Ma.

Me brother's not year older without Casti sarcastic
I'd not be fogging spoons on this planet.
Romans did that for me, mucho gracias mes hombre
living better than hitting trobbing latex.
No holes, barred.
Got to breath air.
Got to breed heirs.
Such matters for me.

"Sure I heard you were back in town, you've been hiding away some neck of the woods? Howth head?"

"On me tod presently not easy with contacting people. Wondering why I was back really. Across in the aunt's place, she's gone these few years. Needed to come, chat get my confusions out in air so I could self think … meself. All my nonsense carry ons."

"Brian to be honest with our histories we should have a rehash, I've even questions for you. Clear the air on memory lane, then set up for some professional work. You could help me." She laughed.

"Bit lonely, that's okay." I says.

"Brian in Canada did you have lots of friends? Maybe not. You're a wandering soul. Independent fellas like you do your own thing, pollinating ideas like honey bee, never get fenced in. Now it's a little shaky as you have the recent divorce, not easy predicaments and you back here."

Traveling lads difficult species to nail down, moving foot gets something even just thorns. Do not venture abroad in search of monsters within to destroy. *New world, same as the old world.*

"Mind you this world needs your types, to take a risk see what's going on, you've been a master of curiosity, I remember you describing strange quarks. Give things a chance and you'll be on your emotional feet. You've been through upheaval, your center of gravity groaning."

Noticed black stocking and firm thighs invoked instincts of men, getting hadrons with such charms. She'd be shocked to realize what got stored in Kodachrome memories, our relationship unfinished as Sagrada Família and starting Finnegans wake.

"I still have your letters, ten of them when I was at Gaelteach in Donegal for a week. Fear on phoist groaning under the weight of your devotion, all your lovely poetry. Under my thumb then my dear, we were mad altogether."

Needling me with those times. Kissing her my euphoria, addiction shot of heroin. Then cold turkey down my years.

"Evey nothing's away, my regret is being gone so long. Wish I'd firm grasp of being Irish, love of the land and my place in it. That's what brought me home finally."

'I have none other home than this, nor any life at all.'

"Brian you're so wrong you hated Ireland then. You wanted to get out go American, you forget complaining about phony baloney middle class Ireland. Stifling competition with severe exams and hoity doity stuff. Believe me it was not for you, living some Donna Reed dream world. Only you booed farmers marching in Dublin. Only you!"

Well healed tax free spongers cattle ranchers in land of struggles. In Ireland only one way to see things, 'array whist boy, that's how 'tis now'.

"I've searched psychology text books, you are not in any, I cannot put a label on you. You do the things that you do." Everyone out of step except my Seannie.

I did want to be Jeff Stone, Donna's son. There you go.

She really let me have it, in truth there was loads annoyed me. Many of these souls gone now to wonderland so RIP, Dev, John Charles McQuaid, Michael O'Heir, Paddy Crosbie, Father Michael Cleary, Charles Haughey, all fathers of daughters, RTE, Gymkhanas and horse trainers, every man jack in Foxrock, every Jesuit school, every one of their pupils, every country politician, every night club operator in Leeson street, that Bishop of Galway, Ian Paisley and Ulster (driven mad by circumstance within their control), all rip off artists (in a land of so many), every b and b landlady. Brendan Behan and legions more. Mostly hoped there was world removed from suffocation starch of middle class Dublin, adult Irish men and obsequious obsession with religion. Radicalized by Vatican's hell bent notions to lodge and flourish vacant minds. I'd still visions of pew rows with nodding merikats. Even me Dad, gone many year full of Vatican, won't pick on him risk clip on ear from the bruver.

Church, one book for learning,
Catholics new chapters only, and
watch Ten Commandment film.
Meanwhile, Hodges Figgis
stacks with books
new school every year
writ by human.

"Back then with girls afraid you'd not collect nuts to get through winter, too casual with serious notions. You took longer grow into yourself."

'Dimes and dollars, empty pocket worst of crimes.'

Growing pains in my thirties, lazy nuts, skinny fellow with that head of popped corn. Middle class Dublin girls convent sheep desperate to marry solicitors and accountants or settle for uppity civil servant or supermarket whiz kid. Ireland's women gave no breaks, judged to have no potential only wooly headed. Those 'tricoteuses' sent me on my way, with cut of their tongue.

'Take yourself away, impregnate foreign pagans have heathen kids,' Mother Erin's girls declared. 'Nothing for you heres about.'

If always lose why join competition? I fled.

"You had that anti-Irish rebel thing, now all gaelic and misty Misey Eire Galway Bay. You've to be away ages to feel that way."

On a roll with personal a tale, all was needed to watch sun go down in Aran sweater, pipe and crooning with Bing Crosby's tribly hat.

"It's in your letters rejecting here, you didn't have to leave. You wanted to disappear in crowds of London, have a flat in Notting hill. You ran away from being middle class in this town, maybe you were so right. A conservative place full of snobs really, tedious keeping up. Sure we are dreadful like that and no mistake. Yes Brian, it's easier to waltz back when those tough battles are over."

Dublin bay vagina of Ireland, rejected cum of the country dispersed on ferries off to England and worse places. Fellows departing on crowded ships at midnight not chosen to swell bellies of Erin's belles. New York Harbour has Lady Liberty as welcome sight for orphans, we erected two piers of Dun Laoghaire harbour as our 'Fuck off' sign. Nobody cared about poor departed, never a plaque placed to welcome home Irish souls.

Begone! Dispatched!
Still plenty of dead wood
keeping male boat busy.
More acres for stalwarts
keep homefires burning.

Get that midnight ferry from Dun Lar, depart away to foreign parts. Slan leat but return for gatherings. *Bring us a few bob.* At first I felt that on the midnight ferry we were as innocents in Pinocchio, not fully aware of our predicament. Scattered as chicken eats cracked corn. But pints of stout aplenty provided on the ship of destiny as we departed Erin's isle. To ease our troubled minds, forget we had lost our loves to better men. Lost lovers to stay behind with these fellows, on our blessed island while we headed towards pagans away. For them they would have Irish children with Irish culture. Our children would not be from Eireann, would never care a jot about that place. Our relationship with these kids could not be the same or as close. TV aboard ship was loud and clear with The Late, Late Show, but as our brains grew fuzzy with porter so too TV signal dimmed and disappeared, the umbilical cord shorn with our green island home. For ever after we would visit the place, sightseeing tourists in the land of our birth. Our home always come from away.

"Christy Ring, GAA played hurley with flat caps. PJ, Peadar and Seanie, alien them old days."

Once upon a time we lived divided in 'Evening all' BBC world that TV signal reached only east coast. Somehow Morecambe and Wise and Benny Hill travelled down Rathgar coaxial cables, freed from Sinn Feiners by Brits, that signal made me. Out in west Munster and Connaught stuck in darker ages, from bits I've observed maybe still are.

BBC made us smarter, alls I'm saying.

"You refused to go to Bunratty castle even one weekend together, I had the dress for dinner and gala. You'd not rent the suit. Only New Jersey and San Francisco, never this old place. I was upset that summer you went to New Jersey, I supposed you'd not be back."

Crazy to leave her alone all that 'hot' Irish summer. Swimming with her lads.

"Needed money that skint."

My New Jersey Wildwood summer surveying American football jocks, bulbous wart planted on arse of male species. Testosterone laden balloons, hazing muscular blimps, semi-literate yahoos, bucket heads, beer swilling yobos, reeking of middling wealth and privilege, anti-intellectual morons, big tempers with steroids. But however mis-shapen they were perfect, I wanted to be a jock. Apartment on the boardwalk, mattress and hash pipes, Boones farm ripple wine and sock hops. Girls come and go all season, condoms used by baker's dozen. Brown skin, white bums beneath blue jeans a fair thicket to ride. Lucky frat-boy oafs with life of Riley, to them I was jock strap. If only my parents had sense to get rich and live in America, send me to the gym, desperately wanted to be all American boy. To mate universal lure entwined by sun blessed babes east coast broads nailed beneath pines under the boardwalk amid dropped cream cones. But those frat boys carried their boners stressed side by side with lottery cards for foreign wars. They'd play life by draft numbers, dangling glands might never fat a loving lamb. We micks only had Irish sweep-stakes and Rockall. We had it much better, then.

On Wildwood boardwalk met a fellow shot in the mouth in Mekong

shattered tooth and gum never cut his grin for hazel eye'd, hard to kiss a girl.

A dark haired in Zaberers diner she'd heard her johnnie boy over there

traumatized, gone native would not come home from Thailand.

Damn Stars and Stripes never bomb those Asian babes again.

Victoria, leg tanned Italian job from Ocean city wanted me to go Florida. Shaved those thighs on the picnic table every day with shaving foam, should have followed her down. Great rides in Orlando, work in a supermarket and had her kids. Midnight swims, cheap Thunderbird wine and five o'clock stubble not too shabby days end, sure did love that Jersey girl.

"I never shared a need to leave from friends and family, I didn't have that courage. You had prospects here, but you'd a wandering spirit. You forget my dear."

Evelyn was right, I'd downright complain all the time.

"If only I had gotten you pregnant we'd not have split."

'Do not abstain from sowing for fear of pigeons.'

"Then you'd never had overseas adventures. Anyway I would never have married you, we were too young. I used to think you were so immature, maybe we were all desperate to be adults, Brian sure none of us knew anything."

Eccentric, core never located, still don't know where it might be. Yeah, you married Chris a year later, third year at college. Evelyn left me and course of life changed. She'd figured I was a loser, even I'd me doubts. But in those intervening decades I wandered tasted fruits of the world.

"Evelyn it's great to talk with you."

Strange but time passed seemed not consequential, bothered with her saying she'd never have married me. Chris from Galway city with blackest hair as if born in Pisa. Always irritating how Irish women had leanings for dark eyed Mediterranean's, tilting at drop of eyelid with Majorca gypsy selling oranges under street canopy. For Dublin girls the world too full of ordinary fellows. Brown hair, grey eyed and bog standard skinny fellows with no smiling grill from Rathmines easily turfed aside. Telephone numbers acquired from Dublin disco girls rarely worked a damn, only costing me tanners, plus punts for pints of courage.

'Sorry is no Mildred here.' Ad nausem Mabel, Agnes, Maud, Philomena, Wendy...

She'd complained I'd no friends only yobos I'd meet in pubs. Hey babe, it's Ireland not some oily desert with pachyderms with hookah shisha smoking. Whereas new man had social scenes by her imagining, my pub acquaintance before he robbed Evelyn. Don't complain I've no friends then steal away my one friend. Your new soul mate once my sole mate. My love affair with Evelyn ended suddenly, later she went and married her Christopher. Endlessly seeing them all over town didn't help, I'd headed over horizons to discover new worlds. All Christopher's are not inspired to sail the ocean blue. Seek my fortune toiling on foreigners soil, that's how God's plan unfolded. She twirled a wedding ring on her finger.

"Sorry to hear about Chris." Bumbled as a galoot.

She shrugged not a subject wanted, heard her husband had been killed in car crash five years previous in Sligo, died and left her alone in prime of life, heart of gold broken. Chris an architect they'd lived for years on Whitethorn Terrace in Glenageary. The man violated a code of men, in my world a bigger bollix never put his arm through a coat. Back then knew I was in trouble when Chris boy sketched Evelyn one Saturday night in Keogh's pub. Evelyn sitting beside me on that time worn brown leather couch. Everyone respected we were an item doing a serious line, officially my bird. Seriously goin constant, taken me chances, deliver as Victorian mail man four times a day.

In the sketch Chris created she wasn't smiling, smart arse called it 'Mona O'Rahilly'. Proud of her rascal's sketch and showed everyone, should have ripped up the sketch and thrown it in his face. Sometime fellow has to fight I pusseyed out, let the bastard take her. In the end rootless, never ruthless enough. 'Evelyn is my girl, go get your own bird. Get that picture?' That I never said. Wind up merchant found doom in Sligo under Benbulben, he who laughs last cruelly thinking with a full set of nashers. *Give me time machine one time, journey make it right again.*

Should have taken Chris out of Keoghs, beat crap out of him on South Ann Street maybe avoided his rotten faith in Sligo. Few days later she told me Christopher wanted her to sit for an oil painting project for Architect school, smiling when she told me. Just school thing 'not naked or anything', shouldn't worry. Butt naked with paint boy was few weeks later, I'd hooked them up as Mr. Lisdoonvarna.

Thrilled being portrayed, hanging with me paid off. Framed my ferry boat ticket stub to Liverpool for a wedding gift.

Hasta la Vista, Sayonara,
Au revoir, Slainte to you all.
I've passport pages to fill.
See if I care, onward
Machu Pichu, Tierra del fuego.
Ontario, Ontario, Ontario.
Yikes!

"I put my poor daughter in Ring boarding school and went off. She has gaelic better than Peig from the islands, went away to South Africa for a year needed to get far away. Wonderful Capetown, living with a fellow played cricket. LBW, long blond waves, forever leg before another wicket for God's sake!"

Banyana knocking bails off some bokette.

"Afrikaners with outside women couldn't get used to. Dublin women with that carry ons, you must be fecking mad. After a big row I came back, at least we can control Irish fellows easier."

Maybe we lads knew cheating was wicked, not cricket.

"They all do it." She waved in a dismissal way.

Stumped by fast Boer, on his sticky wicket.

"Gorgeous blue eyes." She'd forgot nothing then left only with the ashes.

Intimate nostalgia as we hugged goodbye, agreed to keep in touch, book the sessions felt I would not. She'd mentioned dating a lawyer, glad she would not be lonely. Had nod for paperback reader. Not the wisest of men but obvious life is hodgepodge of old quackery organized as dingo's breakfast. On journey back to Howth could smell her body on my shirt, all for nothing my life set adrift. Evelyn and I would have been better left alone making babies, walks among Dublin and Wicklow mountains. Instead drunken nights in Camden town, nights listening to snow ploughs on streets of new world. Raising children in northern American town with no shared culture. When torn from your roots you lose more than you gain. We were in love back then, handsome dark eyed Galway Chris interfered, took away my life with her and lost his life. Chemistry we shared was still there. Of course it was.

'For of all words of tongue or pen, saddest are: It might have been!'
After all our poem is 'never finished, only abandoned',
Invested emotions in Grecian Urn relationship,
long ago so full with weeds.

As I boarded number 8 back to the city, easy to say I was up Kobayashi maru without a paddle.

Miles in Atlantic forever stable island with filly bolted.
Gaels change fair days and foul calm and stormy
in our roughian nation, no predicting temperament of man or woman.
On Dingle's peninsula trees bent molded from surroundings
as parasitic worm. Warm high Arctic Eskimos,
giraffes munching high leaves, obese in all you eat delis,
smart fox's outwitting gentry in Shires, better know what's coming.
Stunted until I went away, never man I could have been.

CHAPTER 12

Month after Noreen's exit obeyed 'sede vacante' request, not to put foot wrong I legged it, departed my abode so she'd collect her stuff. With grievous allegements I'd stuffed Aniky Panky up the pole so off with lad in waiting. Not being stubborn agreed, better leave than witness witless dismantling of life we once had. From a distance watched as Walsh's paddy wagon arrived with two of them in tow. *Damnable second mouse always gets the cheese.* Barbarians at my gate. Horrified as citizen of Clonmel gazing at moleface Cromwell on the horizon. With keys to my kingdom, steppin feet stormed through my door.

'Poorest man may in his cottage bid defiance to forces of the Crown.
It may be frail, roof may shake, wind may blow through it
storms may enter, rain may enter,
but the King of England cannot enter,
his forces dare not cross threshold of ruined tenement."

Bruce square jaw blond hair with big head, what matters to me why she'd ever bothered with my plain poke. Face ugly, only money can repair … for a while. Now vanquished dispatched to sitting in a field wrong side of the fence, scarecrow forever chasing birds away. Listening to Peggy Lee, 'Where or when' on head phones.

'In one word deal with what God gives us, youse grow up very natural

personality appearance,' Mama would say to her plain young ones. 'When youse get old and grey less to lose.'

With the hump ran off with shirt on her back, wishing to remove millstone me from her life. Clothes and shoes from bedroom dumped in the spare piles lay on the floor. Wanted to put a lump of cheese inside give country mice their field day, demurred given fear of rodents having run of my abode. Being considerate resisted temptations to throw stuff outside Simon community gate for rugid vicinity rag-abones. Bathroom bottles swept into bags with stuffed bears, shamed that I cut stitching in jeans so when she bent butt would rip, not a moment bone idle in doings. Rescued only a sweater worn day she arrived, now kept stuffed under my solitary pillow. Should have ripped down and burned misshapen dream catcher from bedroom ceiling dispensing nightmares, those willow Ojibwe stick macinations turned feral, should have twigged lowdown shenanighans earlier. Nightmare persisted in day dreams. One midnight fury beat hard on calypso music with metal hammer, steel pan Tamboo Bamboo pannists whacking oil drums, mashed kaiso disks to smithereens. *Get your crap out of my crib. Canboulay, canboulay, canboulay, canboulay!*

She wrote, confirming I deserved comeuppance, did best I could only follow in that wake.

"I know what you did, I was hiking above on the top of Beig beag. Walking up and bending on steep parts when my jeans ripped. They were brand new. I had no way of covering my ass, I was not even wearing underwear. I had to wait and go to the back of the line. Alright, fair enough Brian, I know what you did and that's childish. I had six long miles to hike with my arse hanging out. Your trick worked real good, I had to put grass and leaves to hide my protruding butt. Why did you do that? You think this is funny, but women see this different. In the company of men it was excruciatingly embarrassing. Father B was there and he probably was wondering why grass was coming from my arse. A woman's bum is her private territory, Buster. You should not

have done this wicked deed. You said the quality of a people is the respect they have for women. Are you proud of yourself, you should be ashamed. Yes!"

Che bono, felt shame but lectured by her an idle waste.

Hypocrite piffle, although she had points.
Many at fault with that hustle,
preacher caught bare arsed in house of rising sun.
Dublin finance minister himself avoiding taxes,
god-fearing Southern gentry baptizing slaves
harping to save they own rotten souls.
Rock stars preaching, blasting paupers
save world your damn self, excess dumbos.
God gave you more, so we got less.

Stomping tom-cat with his trollop, each other to celebrate only left me celibating. Strong arm of law Bruce by her shoulder leaned close telling her to be brave, he'd have me beholden to Laws of vagabond men. Probably had handcuffs, truncheon stored in pants for causing mad trouble. How dare she bring him to my castle, didn't need marauder Walsh in my space close by my hearth, fellow who bought my abject state. Full well knew she was in a relationship, seduced then stole her heart when I was struggling faced with innunendo's bare facts. He'd interfered like bowsie throwing sugar in petrol tank, gummed works done in by Irish man as ever, never pondered vileness of his thievery. All plans laid waste by Bruce, that truculent sneer entered my life with no mercy, stands to reason in time me and her could have resolved our problems. Ragamuffin, a riff-raff man, raggle-taggle rascal creepy cop wandering around the house with my barmaid met in alcohol haze on shifting sands of Louisian. Woman with no bed rock grew accustomed to forever changes from those delta landscapes, damn I'd tried to build future with a broad travelling through swamp of varmints, now smitten lady, gaga like teenager departed our rabbit tail relationship. Feeling dejected I walked over the hill, mournful sad sack solitary man, and wandered rocky paths into Doldrum bay, *'down to sunless sea, sitting by desolate streams'*, reclined there on Buck's point. Only skimming ocean stones, don't need them back. 'Bo ho,' scream bounced over seas to skye, disturbed old folk out walking on the head, glad to resist temptations to erect 'Go back to N.O. Noreen' banner in hallway, feared agitated Bruce with waving his baton would wreck the gaff. Already disgraced myself leaving telephone messages, for her and colleagues at beef Carvery.

'All I ever got from you was scabies, and stabbed in the back.'

Unfair as we had been itchy after b and b weekend in Clare. Visiting my brother in Tarbert she refused to stay one night in Limerick stabbing capital fair dues, carvery worker sensitive to knives. Sure there are good b and b's, never tarred them with same munster brush.

Not left cash with Garda robber about the house. Restless traffic cop out stealing broads always on the hustle, women free or encumbered either way figured rights his way. I'd batten down my hatches. Porno mag stash in press with bolts. Full well needed to count aunt's pewter spoons. It was I who discovered my free bird waif by gulf lowlands, flew back home on my crust directed by her voodoo lady. He a pirate with precious booty, plundered my Louisiana purchase. When Noreen departed from over there no one left bereft, Ferrice did not wish me harm knew he screwed up, she gave everything he couldn't complain or begrudge. Now Walsh would see mocking signs of man existing on his tod, tins of soup, John West fish, fruit cocktail, stewed tomatoes and mousetraps. As an Irish man Murphys tinned potatoes I was ashamed, all testimony to wanton descent. In this land with people I hardly knew, pondered as waves rang rough on dock by Doldrum bay. Missing her pale body crying pails of tears lying in rocks beyond the pale.

Yo ho ho,

'I'll eat when I'm hungry

and drink when I'm dry
if moonshine don't kill me
I'll live till I die.'

Noreen would notice solitary feather pillow, bed never made in yellow walled bedroom where oft admired cut of her jib. Place stank of man-only habitation without polished monastery smell with house keeper gone AWOL. Unplugged ancient gas fridge making shuddering rackets, beer I drank warm. Calm nights with full tide running, chilled chardonnay in ocean breakers. Unwashed clothes littered laundry floor no flowering plants only dusty space, no woman man forever pathetic wretch. Unloved weeds filled garden, nettles shaking nasty leaves only longer by day, braver taking their chances to act out with maggots. One fine day I would come rout them with full strength paraquat for their roots. Sting me if you can. Small ball hiding, resting from mutts. Sure dear old Ron had only kicked the bucket and bought the farm.

Once voluptous prime, branches decorated by green leafs
now soft raked in pile, windfall pears tasted like turpentine.
Saw down eyesore with big axe, only wish I would.
Being single never tasted good neither, pair bond busted.

Half read Dublin books littered space amid smell of stale tobacco and sweaty socks. Low spirits forever thirsty in salty breezes, cleared bundles of bottles lying discarded in living room, hid in garden shed's cooper barrels. Cellar anchored house against wild gaels, but no fine wine was stored away, any longer. Understood despaired citizens downing vodka in Stalingrad to get through gray Soviet times, dispaired as I was from me absent gaelic mott. Hands plunged in pockets wandered off to the village, spa lady Maria Apelin gave blowhards her run of mill workmanlike tugalog hand job, well knew Noreen departed. Ran an eyebrow-haircut place, jack handed lady mastered many trades, appreciated warmed hands under the tap, freezing on plastic massage couch. Listening to band from Tagalog country singing Abba, recalled breasted Hawaiian porno shot a load into experienced hand. Gave tip of the hat for that. Told her music 'turned me on', after calmed for a while.

Made whistle sound, rub blue dub dub
forever panting breathing passion.
'Fuckin manilas,' or words to those effects
Dear Yemanja, mother of living things
knew of solitary ways, take care of me.
Mucho misery spreading about, as
orphan bending bar elbow Father's Day,
teary eyed slobbering downing slops.

When I showed twice every week, sharp clicking finger snap on plastic card knew she'd found sucker to fill till. Fair play, an ill wind that blows, but good for her. Being stressed from pressures of wild gaels. S*nappings head her style.* Only considered going to those islands pick beautiful maiden pay peso pittance bring her to potato country. Walked Howth Hill surrounded by growling black dogs, down much endured emotional rabbit hole. Back at sequestered spot observed they were leaving many suitcase and portmanteau loaded, she had accumulated stuff. With not a bother or backward glance headed to glens, my queen stuck in his honey hive. They'd made a pot of tea with fig rolls, on kitchen table lazy-susan she stuck a note.

'Thanks bb, Noreen.'

Sure thing Mac Boyle messing with my life then haul off with first troll takes a fancy, honey sour as lemons. Left Claddagh ring friendship gone but diamonds not abandoned those stones forever hers, woman iron chicken as ever. Loud as hogs stuck in sand they want jewels not pig stuck in a poke. Could smell after-shave sure he'd reek above with gales on MacGillycuddys, ensuite he took a leak on the seat. Victor gets to soil with bone dry soap, avoided using that room. Needed mollies to scrub. And scrub.

"Saints Paddy ye left snakes abroad on land, do you nay understand we've still got them pagans scurrying in our mists? Like rats. If only Vikings cleared Ireland's O'Boyles and carried them off to Icelands," Hollered for no one, slammed that bathroom door.

Welch lad Patrick, 'twas said,
shamrock or leek either way
he lived among the weeds.
'Where'er they pass, as softly green
a triple grass, chosen leaf
of Bard and Chief,
old Erin's native Shamrock!'

Haida patchwork quilt odor of sweaty bodies familiar coitus perspiration, never kept that truncheon in his pants. Pavlov dog behaviours again exhibiting her fair jig, on reflection mirror shocked by events, scared to look in trash. Left a letter mailed to the house addressed to me, flowery stationary used by women, why Noreen had opened it. Evelyn wrote 'congrats on the book' and looked forward to meeting, maybe Evelyn courting a solicitor only a brief affair.

"Ballcocks," I seethed.
Another bogus charge,
batteries in the sixties,
internet Nigerians,
a light brigade,
Faulkner's infernal internments,
nibble and dimed by banks
in those cockamamie times.

'Honesty' Noreen wanted, apparently I was never wise to deliver, nor she. Bits and bobs of dishonest I'd own, not deny. That letter threw in trash. Drank beers of some consolation.

You say raccoon, I say badger, brothers from different mother.

"Okay, beigh la eile eg on phaorach," being not bananas or nuts.

Whatever salami-tsunami, after blasted by foul chicanery in bitter and cantankerous mood, journeyed out and stopped off at Sabatucci's Continental joint in Clontarf, pretentious snotty place. Despite eatery being half empty dispatched to chilly foyer wooden bench, left fuming. Mark of no respect never surprise with these Mediterraneans, then God shaped Italy to give us all an arse kick. What keeps these med fellows in Ireland away from the boot, living with hounds of uncouth roughians? Know nothing of Sarsfield or Daniel O'Connell, never be more Irish than Irish themselves or befall that pernickedy fate. They'd lucked out no better looking species on the planet, legacy of roman slave trade, bastards harvesting creamy crop of young ones. For centuries. Teams of women manacled marched on latin roads. Mille viae ducunt per saecula Romam (thousand roads lead forever to Rome). Tinned our herd now they must mock us. From Scandinavian, Roman and Brits it's a wonder we have culture, only by grace of celtic gods and potcheen. Now budget airlines, Adriatic cavern cavorting on hen parties.

"Buongiorno, ciao bella," impeccable taste young waiter Alberto beckoned to women entering, such abbraccio. Regarded me as an inferior beast.

Caliban kept in dark shadows,
no shinny hair nor marble teeth.
Adorned with chopped pants from Bray,
down at heal plastic shoes
unmatched nylon socks
no dandy with this world
only known for beanos.

Finally escorted to tiny round table perched near bunch of loud mouths, piss artist Geordies to put label on them. Blow hard half caste rapper 'becoming a power house in music industry', says a mother smug with good fortune, only one would be paying both man and minister.

"No senior," says I, dignified hibernian attitude.

Instead strutted and sat myself down at prominent window table, grand view of bay, appropriations for my likes 'emeritus Professor' from Dominion of Canada. Advising myself don't pit wits with shinny fellow, go to chipper or feed fish in Dublin bay. Unwanted sea changes and me in my prime.

"Table is reserved," yer valentine says, ignored his request.

I decides, not them cooks. Placed my order off the menu, as customary wants. I'm paying, they have a kitchen. Problemo? Don't think so. Do it!

"Few boiled spuds, broccoli, what's yer dressings with grilled plaice?"

"Wrong place, my friend." Handsome smart aleck. As ever.

"Do youse have raspberry vinaigrette?"

My arse on the line, time to head off for few shashlik kebabs.

"Half of Barolo, bruschetta. Per favore amigo." I soldiered on for no reason, a pain in their ass. "Do use wash vegetables, and change yer oil? Regular." Rubbing salt in his gears.

Alberto the spoiler disappeared, surprising apericena starter arrived delivered by waitress member of the clan. Lorenesque with those eye brows, my glancing gawk. Beauty empowered to knock eyeballs from any man's sockets, now worried over my uncouth dressing. Never noticed me a smigen and me that concerned.

Ciao bella chiceta,
let's be in Tuscany
a brass bed, for us
grapes, virgin olives
and melons.
I've meat balls,

spaghetti entwined.

Mustache if you prefer

my sweet muchacha.

In due time the son reappeared with salt and pepper papa, no surprise.

"I'm Mr Rudolph," Papa tells me. Pops with snaps and crackles.

And if you ever saw him you would say he glowers.

Summoned from Bocce or high stakes briscola card games, reckoned from demeanor.

"Mahalo," I says, lashings respecto. "Buenos Aires senor."

Sizing me, shaking in my worn sweat shop suede's. For no good reason shook my sweaty palms, wiped his hands on a napkin. No barbican block another gurrier come invaded his territory, as Barbari, Visigoths, Hannibal's elephants, all manner of Vandals. None worth steam off his piss.

"So what's the problem?"

Oozing disdain clicked fingers fast as Chubby Checker at Apollo.

"No problem now amigo." I says.

Our interaction unfriendly match, no Maguire and Patterson. Chewed bruschetta, appreciated cut of his Savile Row Bespoke.

"You come my restaurant dressed not respectful. No jacket, no tie."

Darn judged by cover, entitled on his manor, wooly jersey sleeves with patches.

"So 'scuse me been with cutting turf all this fine day, macushla." Mick toiling bog fields with sweaty brow, "Real Irish fella with rights of turbery from Bord na Mona. Who's your tailor? I get me garb in Bray emporium, second hand returns. Bargain galore!"

Wine gone to me head, many folks last words.

"My Alberto shows you nice table. My friend you are alone if you have friends a sometime you sit at this table."

Don't hold breath on that old lad else you'll be needing acqua lung. Rudolph takes half eaten grub rest stuck in my craw, reunited plate back on small table.

"In my house there are rules and procedures."

Loud mouths enjoying mortifications rapper boy making notes, all knew one skinny boy doomed to fail. Calm down old dude tempest in espresso cup, let me savor Med cuisine with dreams of eyebrows on your one.

"You've been drinking, you'll not have no more service."

Does he know it's Dublin city? Getting turfed no desserts?

There's fish shop down the road, fried chips at O'Rourkes." Sneered sincerely. "Enjoy our hospitality, enjoy bruschetta. No charge and must leave. Pronto. I buy and sell people like you. Everyday."

No need to settle on that slate. Well that set me off, enough with this Papa, like drunken moron rose and challenged this falutin fellow. Very nerve of him, I was Howthhead man, landed gentry of substance and property. Lord of my manner, I'm saying. Noreen look now at my dreck world.

"Pur pa voir, across in Tuscany once." I started. "Why don't you choke on sun ripened tomatoes from sewage farms in Florida. Spaghetti or pasta who gives a crap, triangular meat balls tastes all the same. Yellow shit that's not potato or rice in dumb squiggly shapes, stick cheap meat and call it rialto, covered in tomato sauce all taste the same. I prefer salty chips, pig with brown hair for that's what I am a proper mental Irish man."

Lost my friggin mind snapping at powerful papa, heading for mountain ditch, ended tossed on feather bed bones snapped like winter twig. Years to come found pickled in bog waters plastic watch ticking, preserved with me brogues set under glass as 'punctual bog man'. Grabbed by Alberto, Rudolph and deputies loud mouth as frog-marched threw in the street. Alberto flung wine dregs.

"World's worst food, hardly pay washers," I shouted from the street. "Eat a spud why don't ya? I'll be stopping by pub for bottle of sack. Bunch of wallies."

Kept me fork as souvenir. Not too shabby. 'Time to say goodbye' followed me up road, on air from Sabatucci's. Wandered the road thinking Irish men despise med dwelers while our woman drool. Problem for the island. Celtic women should realize never in history of time has the boot man loved Irish woman or boiled cabbages so sorry for them desires. In times of high pomp never came to wild bogs of Hibernia. Scared of dreary inclements, for sure our traitorous broads would have kissed their butts.

"Kryshtanovskaya, eigenlob stinkt." I cursed, and felt good on that way.

Maybe rapper boy would create a hit from brouhahas, beats for some. Snagged my chipper batter and vinegar pickle, Howth an ominous hulk on dark horizon, searching for lights of my house. *Lights stared back as wolf eyes on the head.*

Battered by rain checked in b and b in Sutton. Obsessed that black night thinking of her black stockings lily-white skin, took to yellow valium and welcome blackout shut eye.

What about when Jimmy died, her young boy entombed there with grandparents in Grand Isle? Of course never raised those times, with she in fetal position in motel room, four days grief unable to move. Fed her tea and oranges both laden with vodka and cried with her. Darkest times you said I gave you hope, but we were never family easy to discard, substituted by cop pulling his foamy pint. Nothing sealed and delivered to her in a church, Catholic Irish women needed and I'd not delivered unrealistic vows. Noreen I brought you back here to weirdy Eiry isle so you could pick up some cop in a bar? Once she replied.

'Not like you think, he's away lots, different parts of the country.

Need time alone to contemplate my life, I told him. If anything I'll be right back in Lousiana. Seriously!' *Hey babe 'don't pee on my leg and tell me it's raining.'*

Only gaslighting about who was lying in her bed, didn't bother to argue lying inanities. On each morning checked for replies, mostly nothing. Never sure if one sentence doodles helped as she'd mention him. Devastated to hear they'd been roaming in Rimini and Venice on road to Rome.

"Noreen, nothing profound!" I screamed after her words written.

Beside an azure sea
hotel with whitewashed walls
blue window frames.
Sunburned English with accents
Nivea cream over ruddy faces
drone about being abroad.

She'd be topless on the beach, light breeze ripple through brown but reddish hair. Full of anticipation sipping complimentary wine, he a bull with sights of her. Lightly redo green eyes and apply glossy lipstick. Making love after lunch of fish and succulent tomatoes. *Fair dues cabilero, that haunted I was.*

A real man would drive to Wicklow march into her Avoca house. Challenge scoundrel for making off with my woman, berate the cad for callous behaviour stealing like common thievery. Take her home to Howth, inform there was nobody else, leave her to dwell in my house. Go to bedroom put on my old cream Italian suit travel to her mother, relate I intended to marry her daughter. Return and ask Noreen to finish what we started, but weak weasel, didn't do what should have tried.

Bruce with history of 'Jack the Lad', told his friends this was different, seduced by green-eyed beauty. Now in love for the first time in his life.

A Wicklow Girl

Her beam once burned for me
brighter than Mc Arthur's lights
then by silence she sent real signals.

CHAPTER 13

Christmas morning that long year, not well stocked having can of odd tuna, be troubled to cater for unexpected visitors. Even this can labeled 'not for human consumption' better served for pussy cats. Last egg give to visitor, my style. Always relied on what birds eat. Two of my children in Toronto had awkward phone calls with wayward father, consumed several cans of stout early morning to get festive spirit. What we learned Howth was wet and that day cold in Ontario,'quelle surprise with that'. On their long school road trips to New York and beyond, I would sit home waiting arrivals. A ping of the phone. Like Nasa and signals from other worlds. Stranger listening shocked to realize I raised them through Toronto teenage years and not TV weatherman. Things to say, words stuck like dumplings in teapot.

Iceberg city, barely balanced skates
Nathan Philips square rink
noggin wack on hard ice
windchill in train station
white knuckle highway
black ice snow drifts
giant tractor trailers, salters and plows.

Ice fishers stranded floes in Lake Simcoe.
A place where hell has frozen
over every blasted winter, ski it
hills petrification by Horseshoe valley.
Wandering over frozen lakes in
Algonquin blinded by whiteness
no glimpse of a green grass,
all that never cut any ice with me.

Told them I was spending Nollaig with their grandmother, 'God bless' as we tried to be cheery, relief when final 'Merry Christmas' ended their seasonal agony. *Rock the world babies, I only wanted for them.* Relationships with kids like the old Bush TV, always on the fritz hoping it lasts forever. Lying on a couch after breakfast fry up, lots of marg in fried spuds, hoping me ticker keeps ticking, carelessly out of beer staring darkly at clock passing. Glowing turf in front living room, stoked that fire threw on more fuel. They'd be with their mother's family in Etobicoke none upset I'd not be there, already had enough of times when this father would sit withdrawn longing to be away. If Christmas be barometer of families emotional health, we'd problems not solved by wild Atlantic oceans *'ceaseless turmoil seething'*. Things misunderstood in childhood comes crystal clear as adults, *'six feet snow pile not by one day make.'*

'Sure they won't need to dig deep to bury this father.'

Later went to hole in the wall, armed with rubber banded wad of cash took care of nieces and nephews at the mothers, where always had place at the table. Ate mince meat pies and trifle, broke turkey wishbone with roast potato marrowfat peas and sang along with Pogues.

"Youse will have to keep the singing down, your one is on at 2 pm." Mam repeated every childhood year.

Mother and aunts watched the queen, 'get a load of the glasses'. Sister lit whiskey soaked plum pudding, consumed with fresh whipped cream. As considerable quantities of drink were taken stayed over at my mother's Christmas night. Crashed in old single bed, woke at dawn only to contemplate reduced affairs, absent broad controls all them dreams, bedroom mirror knew me well, liked me less with years passing. As I exited Stephen's day washed rasher sandwich down with strong tea, loved sliced pan turnover bread with melted butter and juicy bacon. Lyons tea better as mother brewed, she busy doing the Irish Times crossword puzzle as ever.

"Off to Wicklow?" She asked as I ran through the door.

Wear shoes and go. None of your business old lady, garryowen or Hail Mary pass, bailing or double down. No potted plant, whither stick or twist?

"There's no t in China, there's wan in Taiwan." All I tells her, alls I knew.

Whatever bird I'm shagging for me to know, in life entitled to fill me boots.

Oh happy days of life, never less than a dollar,
or slept on park bench or sold shoe laces
never in soup bread line with tin cup and plate
what more to ask for from Lord and creator?
Times only borrowed, but gave me everything.

So family missed that Wicklow bitch, fair enough.

"To whom should my trouble show
burdened sick and faint
whither should I go,
and pour out my complaint?"

Wanted to hang around Howth house, what consumed me was waiting for Wicklow to call, every whisper of Christmas cheer. Pointy heads trying to figure dark energy need to chat with me in time of muck and nettles. Merry Christmas my arse.

"bb I want to come back,"

imagined that daft sky in the pie.

Rice cake draw on paper look delicious.

Invite gobs of people, celebrations comin.

Knockdown dining room door make big table.

In my mind's eye peace restored returned to Xanadu, no cross words. Our pack drill winter walks arm in arm, woolen sweater furry hat, mittens on string, thick socks in farmer boots. Sardine sandwiches, flask of sweet tea in back pack. Hiking places forever sorry I never saw, Sorrel Hill, Luggala, Turlough Hill and Deputy's pass, vale of Clara and Derrybawn mountains of Glen da lough. Sally's gap (oh never mind), Devil's glen would be first, back pocket steel rum naggin an old time taste.

"Open your legs, pick up the pace." Her style up on mountains.

Wind blown leaves follow on as we jump stiles. Mid those deep places find her secrets have her in rocky spaces.

"Open your legs, pick up the pace." My style on mound ofVenus.

Overnight cosy inns, mashed spuds grilled lamb chops, tinned peas and sup grand pints. Fluffy pillow in bedrooms, deep feather mattress, listen to 'Arrival of Queen of Sheba' behave like wild rabbits on hills, lie exhausted and sleep as coats of paint. But nowt happened, remained tosser in fools bed, still with stones in them hiking shoes and peppers in my pants.

'With such a wistful eye

upon that little tent of blue

which prisoners call the sky

and at every drifting cloud that went

with sails of silver by.'

In plastic bag carried a phone in shower never got one tingaling, sat about and pondered futility. Calm like surface duck paddling maelstroms, ansy as cat scratch screen door. '*10 pounds emotion in 5 pound bag.'* Thinking faster than bells blazing Córas Iompair Éireann fire truck, needed a qwerty slow my ass down. Considered drive by Mama's Avoca patch, dash through Roundwood in search of green Civics. Not be a pylon on Picken's Charge. In the end sat in that bar in Bray where occasionally she'd sup brews. Gathered 'neath the head as Neapolitans under mount Vesuvius, far into Wicklow as I'd dare. Through that tent door shoved my camel nose. Grand old Dublin buttressed by ancient granite, where jackeens butt heads with culchies, where reinforced concrete bump mountains. Wicklow grand neighbour but beware for their women have rocks for hearts, only pump pebbles of indifference. Tribes in their stone age. Being lunchtime 'grilled sandwich' got delivered, wood bowl effort unrelated to generous American hero. Stephen's day feeling pervaded anxiety decreased, no one working except blue job trojans kept things moving. Being of a mind called Derek in Avoca.

"Jeez boy can a swim duck? I'd murder a few pints, sure great to hear from you despite circumstances that's in it. Busy putting messages away in the press, shoveling down the dinner be right over." He says.

So what if I'd stank of want '*I'm drinking ale today.*' Culchie boy keep off hard stuff, avoid 'Jude the Obscure' discussions muse on return of native. Grazing on east coast girls sounding like Noreen, smelling of baby wool cavorting with lads, cure for all what devils ails ye. Christmas sweaters, being in love, glow on plump cheeks swollen and proud with gift for boyfriend opened beneath lamb's wool. Wicklow perfected art of creating these creatures. Childhood spent in valleys of garden of Ireland envy of world. None were thinking about me.

Sound heard first lights of firmament?
Adam's wail ribs intacto.
'Nice paradise but what's me balls for?

Something good, right?
I'm feeling it, bring it on.
'Ok, she's nice, no navel.'
(Maybe Eve was Swiss)
Still floated his boat,
as we are here.

Skinny bobble head girl chin pointed giving her man bedroom eyes, more emotion than Shakespeare. White bright teeth, nervous not to yap a lot. Girls breath wild air and breed for Eireann, Irish men without one of those babes wandering nomads with terrible desert thirsts. Life soviet coal mine without them, *so be it*. In my time those Wicklow birds always somewhere better to be. *'My boy friend's a drummer in the band, otherwise we could shag like carpets'*. As with other wildebeasts sudden migrations required.

Recognized Noreen's niece, Niamh sitting at bar suckling vodka soda, one of those broads so tight they'd not make two pennies rattle, red hair, orange sweater and green eyes. Farmer boyfriend kissed way long, hand placed high on her thigh. No settled face still room to grow, but no dime's difference between two O'Boyles. Stop, pause, so okay go ahead, enjoy it ploughboy soon you'll be old fart beaten down raising young ones. Measured by weight of crust hustled from forty acres. Take care peep of dawn milking 'twill be you and them, never enough scratch for appetites. No randy hand up skirt when she's mammying and that never stops. Pray in days hence there might come a neglected milk maid, pretty Tess to help molest hard aged wood. Busy musing when Derek showed through the door.

"Hidey?" He says with manly shake, culchie lurch in his gait.

"A man of easy leisure, taking the walks secret to success they say."

"Arra then I've a few old farm dogs should be running the world."

Animals tedious with blank stares.
Gibber, whoop, bark and screech.

Can not one of youse talk? Feck sake.

Hey monkeys we've been to moon,

take a gander. Time to move a notch up.

"At least we can drown lost love sorrows, that's worth the drinking," ordered the pints. "I'm only taken cold showers."

Snaggle tooth grin, shook his head and smiled.

"No no, she came back man, she came back."

Laugh tears in his eyes, like he won sweepstakes after gorta mor times.

"Yeah things changed Brian."

Whales search mates across oceans but three legged horse don't stray far.

"Hey congrats man, like any man need how's your father to keep young."

"Cop a load of them street scrubbers in Bray? Look like centurions."

"It's okay I still existing, Canada doc told me one can of beer a day, so fine stay with pints of porter."

Resented his enthusiasm, feeling chill of alone, now he's back in the saddle. Damn nowt in my chilli bowl, needed bird of my feather.

When hungry don't watch people eat meat,

when people poor don't show how you fat,

when fall in well don't throw rocks at me.

No food to eat, don't offer luxury coffee beans.

Derek was quiet didn't dare disturb man gummin for his pint, with savvy decency not to enquire why I was hanging out deep miles from home. He knew I'd to be close breath county air. Pints arrived and we drank deeply.

"Advantage of life on hills, sun always over yardarm. Porter good or bad for memories or good for bad memories can't remember which."

"Sure I'll give it one more lash, know well what you're dealing with," restored man says.

"So what happened?"

"One day she tells me hire van and piano movers, don't dilly dally just like that. I didn't question only danced the wild jig, all the better since. Try to do right after trying everything else, high on the hog begob. My daughter learned to play a load of new songs, 'Tears in Heaven' mad talents for Rose of Tralee."

Niamh sashayed by, smiled sweetly with her farmer, plough boy watched how I lusted at his O'Boyle woman, knew she was my type.

'Made real bags of it, pig's arse,' said only with his sneer. 'Right haymes of it.'

My arse hurting with life's speed bumps.

"Finally she copped on with undertaker, forty never been married. Busy poaching other fellow's birds." Wiley operator.

"Happy new year Derek and Brian. Hi Brian, missed you!" Niamh waved and blew her kiss.

Mesmerizing, nectar from gods that scent of a woman. Farmer boy would make sure Wicklow breasts had Bord bainne for grand babies, taste her Wicklow gold and think about that on his tongue as he milked cows in the barn each morning. Prized wife content in farmer's bed with red haired babies, only farmer man knew to tame O'Boyle wildness. Niamh moved with legs through crowded pub, farmer furoughed ways through unwashed sea.

"Fair dues them Roundwood broads," I said.

Bothered by Niamh's curves and how she moved, bothered by loathsome lonesome tumble weed feelings with tail between my legs. *No bread, want to eat biscuit?*

"She's got all of that like her Aunt."

"Say nutin, and saw wood as they say." He says.

Know what you get in to, with one of them. Take boys to good men.

Niamh never wandered to Louisiana places, only walk down Glen da lough's church aisle on her tarot cards, put on blinkers keep sequestered from human rat race. Sometimes they make mistakes to live in reptile infested Louisiana amid gators and rough wild elements.

"How do they keep making them in Wicklow?" I queried.

"We've that demon Viking blood flowing, drown ugly ones in lakes or shove 'em off mountains. Then steal their gold."

Kidding that Derek boyo, maybe undertaker should not go a hiking in lonely hills with slippery slopes.

"Them fellas always screws up, rutting chimps."

"Never interrupt enemy when screwing up." I tells him.

"They all come back man, soon as the other fellow messes around they know we're waiting. In tatters, wanted her back whatever, other fellows won't be like that." Derek off on his favourite rant.

'Some blessed hope, whereof he knew and I was unaware.'

"Not convinced." I says. "Every good time in life involved a woman."

We sat staring at the pints, needed a hush. Inclinations for silver clouds.

By outer Mongolia once Mr. Si possessed horse of beauty. One day horse bolts. Man despondent. Week later horse returned accompanied by herd of animals. Happy Mr. Si.

"After she left I was that scared needed viagara to have a pee." He says.

"I've laid more chicks than the hen house." Says I not crowing, only for the laugh. "Ah sure ye need emotionals. Can't seem to get tired of her."

Asail on our rocky island in wild ocean, gael male set to deal with wildest women. Went to jacks for slash, hoping women likes of Niamh would spell waterloos for Walsh lad.

"They call him the operator. All pell mell, phone in each pocket. On his turn for the drink, gets his urgent calls. Heads for the door. Even ex-quare wan he'd still see, they'd go to the pictures. I saw two of them down in Gorey having tea and marietta biscuits. What carry on is that?"

Mixing stealing with removing, some pots have lots of lids. Let him now hang on his petard and dangle from church cupola. Derek with family connections beyond in Cymru, another Welch fellow in my life. I too was equipped with Viking's horn.

"A brother named Pious, same off in the Thailands doing their prostitutes."

Busy with bodies their stock in trade, business and pleasure.

"Sooner or later undertaker will come again."

"Brian I've heard them all, I'm only wedged in that edgeways. Sure she's wearing me Y fronts, let these fine days pass on by. Have everybody settle down with these circumstances, without her I'd be having beer for breakfast."

Nothing like porter to wile away lonely hours, I'd come to appreciate it's goodness. Rueful Derek knew his place in his world dictated by women, now playing wack a mole with local men.

"What are we Brian us fellows? Once I was stringing along a whole bunch. Right now I make porridge, drop of Lyles golden syrup, drop the kids then off to the job."

"Us boyos are zoo tiger, not jungle tiger."

Screwed, as DIY furniture. Rather be tiger tail, than chicken head.

Derek wiped his cheek, Irish men crying for their coileens. No wonder the place is a sweet green boggy mess. Yet there was life in the man I'd not seen before on sponge island.

"I got the tourism job on the council in Arklow that helped no doubt. With the arse gone from the economy here abouts."

Don't matter what manner of cat chases mouse. Catch mouse is good cat.

"I know Jenny that swims there, take care of the pool."

"Asked my sister to tell her I'd the job with a pension. Hey man best what I can do. If it was nine days in a week, I'd be working them nine days. When they put their arms around you and say they're sorry and they love you. Feeling alive man, these days."

Wandered in the yard for smoke, watched cars go south to Glen Da Lough. Us old lags released dumped outside gates, never wanted such freedom, they had us as nature designed all gummin for the broad. Like heroin, like her on my own.

"Have you seen them at all?"

"Christmas at the mothers. My missus said Noreen looked stressed, can't relax a friggin minute. Trying too hard, uncomfortable to be with fidgety with talking. Never a quiet word spoken, talks over everyone. Yapping with drink repeats things even yer man looks annoyed. When youse were together we had them great Avoca nights, old Danny boy sure that was the great night!"

"Yeah, I can't sing a note, flat as a pancake."

'Teach pig to sing, wastes time and annoys the pig.' "All's the better, they're not around, parents place in Dalkey I hear tell. O'Boyle women fickle creatures what we've to put up with."

Noreen with other pipe dreams, that hat I now have to wear. Imagining Noro and Walsh wandering in that village over looking the island, wondering if I'd be happy citizen if row boat busted a leak as they headed on over. *Aye, aye sure an 'an eye for an eye leaves world blind'.*

"They make little phone calls does Noreen never do that?"

"Yeah so maybe, get lots of junk mail." That girl did fool me good.

"She's making sure in case he strays in her heart she knows he's not fly paper type. This undertaker fella calls now she won't talk to him, before very bee's knees."

He was thoughtful again with the drink. For us all life load of old bollix and way too short.

"You know I've never left the country, up to Dublin still the big trip to be honest like. Never did the week in Benidorm and Lanzarote. I know there would not be many places like home, never had that want to roam like ye fellas. Tell me this 'n tell me no more Brian a fellow like yourself was I right or not?" Country mouse scare city life.

Why bother travel, when home has it so?

My lord even butterfly make wave.

After swim in ocean cannot wash feet in small river.

'All in gutter but some of us looking at the stars.'

Partridge in bamboo forest never know season.

"With Dublin and Wicklow you'd be hard put to find better. No better city than Dublin, now many Dubliners I can take or leave. I've flown over bible thumper square states, only see line of fences. You know there's no swimming in the Pacific with that cold."

"Begob that's the thing now, I heard you were away in Japan, Van Diemens land and them places. Listen now I'd that feeling Cill Mhantáin to give it respect had the whole thing. You think now I was right? Sure that's grand your saying didn't miss much?"

"Never cared about Cuba or those North Korea." Preference of Irishmen have balls swing free. Ding dong bell.

"Well I mostly copied Lennon and he married Japanese. Actually Chinese from Chengdu, best I could do. Sure every village has Chinatown. Japanese rare species abroad, tend to stay put."

"Sure is there any difference?"

Ladies divided by sea of Japan.

"Not that I could see, anyways. Aberdeen to Cork, same difference. Either way you'd hardly go wrong."

Saki, saki, saki, saki.

Need hips like Elvis

dealing with them babes.

Shake, shake, shake.

Meantime Greenwich not my sole compass on this life voyage. Remembering mongolian spots on arses of Asian babes, that stringbean from Chengdu in school they told her be proud of her yellow face. Derek missed lots door to door. That meager fare on ferry from Dún Laoghaire opened the world, pity the lad with only National Geographic for exotic women. Tanned girls never faded come December, screw Copernicus. Studied Asian ladies as jockey on Curragh plains knows footsteps of thoroughbred. World of difference beneath my finger tips, take that gallop early morning, under sheets with 'In Steppes of Central Asia' playing a long time.

"I'll tell you one thing for nothing always put extra in her account no question asked, sure that's their romance. Mostly didn't have the price of a pint, borrowed from my brother. Solid on that." County man insisted, understood them single days he was hard up. Noreen once claimed with dollars I was squirrelling nuts.

"Ah sure once sold my Bob Marley tickets on Kilburn high road, instead with cash went to Camden dances, met my future wife." Left with eternal voices of one love.

Finished a session with happy lad Derek, two of us couple of old soaks made decent dent in barkeep's keg, only a drop in the bucket. Busman's holiday slept over in Victorian b and b by Bray head. Next day stopped off at the bank set up monthly transfer for Noreen. That wedge fit all as pants at Clerys, them days I'd still afford the pint, but still hard up.

On death bed old chinese lady lived as vegetarian,
her daughter in law fed her boiled eggs,
'the taste is so wonderful, now everyday I will eat eggs.'
That night she passed away.

I'd let Noreen slide through my hands, and that's how we left it. I straggled back home to the Northside.

Back on the rock early morning checking Geographic Khajuraho pics chanced skinny arm with winterwood, tossed one off. Noticed snap to the air, tough with them knuckle hard balls and strikeout days.

Checking works in fine fettle.

Chug, chug, chug, chug.

Turn over engine cylinder

hand cranked machine shaft.

Needed chick-handle me motor.

Midday neighbor Robert appeared at the door with invite to his place New Years Eve, grizzly old schooled neatly bearded fellow married few times. Ex-military served blue helmets in Belgian Congo, Jadotville Jack fought Bantu Baluba with Bren guns, out gunned infantry radioed HQ for whiskey! Six month dark jungle POW, malaria then shot in the back poison dart by Luweyeye river as he tried to turn and skedaddle. Rescued by French missionaries armed only with gospel truth broken Swahili and Gauloises. Enough said, had brave army silver medals minted from alluvial river deposits rescued on Slieve-an-ore in Clare. A beer in kitchen, depressed as his dog 'the second Charles' died previous week grieving with his loss '*so little cause for carolings'* them seasonal days.

"Chas was only ten, run over down the road," he tells me.

Should keepa dog, sure only busy with mostly barking myself. Sad pair that day, felt for the man but cold porridge comfort those dog days of winter.

'... a man of constant sorrow

I've seen trouble all my day.

Wandered to his place that New Years Eve, house in disrepair party happening in enclosed gazebo, red hot pot stove, view of heather and drizzling rain. Over half hour previous polished bottle of cheap porto bubbly endeavoring melancholy not trump holiday cheer, enjoyed being out in conversation with folks get attentions distracted. Team of guests gathered, my 'intersection people' shared only tip of hat on walks, pally with none. Perfect guy, Olympic hat guy, Tilley hat lady, arm swinging all weather guy, fast walker fat couple trailing various long haired mongrel mutts. Few front porch Joe and Jane heard on the hill checking azalea blossoms. 'Saw up metal guy', suspect he had a foundry in back yard, wanted to wack him on the skull with hefty tire iron. 'Rejected friend' popped up from back steps, 'Welcome to neighbourhood visit'. Worked on Kish lighthouse, sold raw chickens from rusted VW van, only one head light. Started parking poultry van outside the domicile, pissed me off no end, put note on his windscreen. *Hey spot, blocking Kish bright light.*

"Your aunt never had a problem," he replied on drive by. Vacated gravel spot forever smelled of wet feathers, sturdy new padlock for back gate. Got my poultry from Greek deli with trimmings, no inard gizzard or beaked head.

At party gathering determined not be boring turnip nor carry on about Ontario's stumped trees in swampy lakes and glacier scraped barren landscapes. Under imperial orders loggers and skidders long ago scarpered with good wood. Gentry lords built shire mansions, laid scullery maids on hard wood courtesy of Alqonquin forests. Residents of that province once confined to Speakeasies, blind pigs with bootlegging, Ontario now proud to boast bars with three beer bottle limits. No where for thirsty Dublin man, being that displaced. Someday lord of my manor with hard red wood, rows of pretty maids from Thailands. Turn up and turn over.

'Hell or Connaught' Cromwell put upon gaels,
each surpass north of armpit Ontario.
Once their land of temperance
'lips that touch liquor shall not touch ours'.
Mosquitos, every pesky flier in pure air Canada
buzzing deer flies, sphagnum mosses.

Dear lord wriggling water snakes
snapper turtles, massasauga rattlers.
Canyon cold as Valles Marineris,
no cold beer on brief summer beach, $$$$ fines.
Comfortless barren mill dewed taverns
stubby beer served by the neck.
Are we imbibing like street ruffians?
Barkeep! Fill that glass with golden amber,
have it shine most shiny bright.

Evening wore on only Daniela, Robert's main squeeze, tolerated my guff. Daniela, vet in Rush, forever trying to unload some 'rescue' mutt. Spend days flinging twigs. Not I. Fancied her no end, coveting a neighbours wife. Put sins on the slate, so pay later.

"England is Antarctic, Ireland once part of Africa has excessive copper, need to wash this toxin away. Scientists tells us soil makes people different."

Conversation veering from bedraggled cannines, desperate to wedge in 'glacial isostatic adjustment rebound'.

"Okay Mr. Pointy head," she says, exasperated Daniela put finger on my moving lips. I'd even bore small dog with coloured ball.

Spanish, low forties, black boots, stiletto heels. Slim ass thanks to no kids. Tall willowy, pounding running machines, power walks hot and bothered, rolled with bells on, deep dark set eyes. Spent time styling short black hair, rings on fingers and painted toes, keeping it together. Never had chick like her, lot to play with in her prime never glanced at thin specimen likes of me. Bone to pick with recording my bare arse on heather cavorting with lowland lady, entitled lonely man, keep home fires burning.

'Two macao bonobos.' Professional scatology opinion, she told McCracken. Caused lot of grief, I said nowt about spying glass. I'd pick battles, or forever I'd hold my piece. *'Never mistake malice for stupidity.'*

"Bobby has no lead in his pencil," pushed me in corner near doormat.

"I've warm extremities," alls I could muster talking weird with village Porto.

Watched Robert smoking his pipe, kitty korner discussing Andy Warhol with French polisher, had his framing shop in Sutton.

"Can't get it up only drives me bananas, I get all that edgy."

Made L shape with her finger, angle of his dangle.

"Bendy, bendy." She'd nothing to grip gripes.

Dear oh dear floppy pot Bobby boy. No potter wheel, don't take pottery job.

"Erectile dysfunction, E.D, smoking blocks veins, rarely use fags." I tells her.

"I know Mr. Ed, he tried fucking Viagra. Gallons," what she said, what I heard.

Of course, of course, patience low now dealing with village's idiot. I'd not fail a dope test.

"Yarchagumba from Nepal, seal penis from Dildo island (does exists), cow testicle, fertility chair from Lubumbashi, Brazilian wandering spider venom. Shanghai doctor stuck needles in his balls, holes all over the scrotum to make 'iron tiger'. Honestly six thousand years not even paper mache kittens." Desperate laugh in air of pot stove and fags.

Down tools, poor man jacked, janked, swindled, jangled and shaghai'd, succumbed to lot he had. The hard life. Nothing worse with broads complaining you're not on the game, and nothing available at hardware store. Understood Old Chinese geysers motivations with boosting equipment. Once took Havana's 1950 Yank Tank cab Chevrolet Bel-Air to Ambos Mundos Hotel, hemming and hawing that way. What's a few rhinio horns? Plenty more.

Facing Florence David so exposed

why that small size for big boy?
Can't we touch feel it's width
and girth, only babes do wonder?
Flaccid thru' centuries uncircumsized
relaxed contrapposto,
never member so gazed upon
more than Hefner or Genghis Khan
sexiest man hewn of rock with bone.
What's his pleasure long silky hair?
Men know shrinkage when too
much gets chipped that way.
Too busy hammering and removal,
artist masterpiece got cocked up.
Michaelanglo why humiliate him so?
(with no skin off his catholic nose)

"In Rio boiled soup from frog skin worked then balls got huge." Daniela went on. "So all for vain again."

Her quest, blessings and curses in bada bing bada boom of life.

"He won't drink that no more, waddled like ducks for a week."

Quack quack,
baculum needed for Bobby boy
ninety niner, flake in cream cone,
Mr. Softie, old man strikeout.
Bobby boy drink the damn toad,
keep her from wandering with tossers.
That's a good lad.

"On his birthday I paid a Polish lady in Hamburg, after half hour she returned my cash, it was his pole. I never had a problem with men. Before."

Good woman had tried hewers of wood.

"Just a few kopeks."

Licked her lips.

"My rocket hasn't cleared tower many's a fine day."

"You go to the spa in the village with my friend Maria," she says.

"Lower back pain, deep oil massage from Taipei or Bangkok. Uses her elbow works wonders clears head unblocks my chi."

Next might try needles for carpral tunnel.

"Maria and me like to share bottle of wine after second we don't have secrets. You're horny one begging for happy endings."

Astonished spilling beans by long tongued women. My reputation flapping on clothes line. Objected to being bandied about. *Just one touch, just one touch. Again.*

I was bachelor boy.

"Do you want hand job or good fuck grey eyed handsome man?" Brazenly what she asked. "My life high and dry, bang me with cock," pleaded in her whispers.

Bird in bush worth two with hand known by everyman.

"My bird has flown," all I says. Not only my pupils expanding.

"Sometimes sights on the heather makes me miss bulls on streets of Bilbao."

She'd observed utter shambolics on goldenrod heather giving bonker business to Aniky, advertising wares left on that park. Uncomfortable brief activities, as Venera on Venus.

"Get what's on tin babe," says thin man.

Heard rumours of her and 'frame shop boy', maybe not hung well enough. Whatever, I'd be third man. Noreen had duets with zitar player in the Arms.

"She who asks is fool for five minutes, she who does not becomes fool forever," says philosopher Daniela.

Wanting to be good neighbour ride pole position on this latino, bounce that fine ass.

"Me and Noreen were planning a Wicklow hill walk, why she did no one knows."

Now Noreen high tailed up down stony trails with master plod.

"Noreen's a dumb waiter."

"I know that gobshite she's with, we did it on a Dollymount sand dune. Really I could spit, he'll cheat every live long day."

Playboy of his eastern world, more stray pussy than RSPCA. Catching volleyed sandy balls, entitled she was.

"I'm not proud of that, not what I'm looking for."

"Damn."You too.

There is a pub nearby Bull island, more birds than seagulls on the strand. Salty beach times where seamen roll, sun down to sun up.

"Miss Impetuous, married young now out playing, if a woman feels you love her she never forgets, she'll be back realize mistakes."

Daniela older broad vision, likely from sandy bum good times and life's errors.

"I'd love to kiss you," I said.

Needling a hardy woman, heavy bedraggled conkers had me in a rush.

"Not tonight darling, sleep only with my husband. A Catholic girl I've to meet my maker."

Tipsy broad leaned on rocking hips, creating mayhems. Toe her line, finger those assets, *go configure a 'beast with two backs'.*

"Canadians like donut early mornings."

"Maple honey nibble and dip."

"Wednesday he'll be in town, Fernando no more spa so I ride rocket."

"I shoot massager," assured her.

She'd sways about her, me and Moet poppin that morning.

"Bobby will be furious if he sees me smoking."

Another drag to relish sandy fling memories, glanced at husband pipe in hand. What would he think and her on my pipe getting nuts roasted, come Wednesday?

"I'm not unfaithful with spiritual commitment's but it's physical world."

Rubbed that rack against me, and me crunching Jalapeno crisps feeling heat. Desperate for trickles from ripe mango. Feeling as toucan's beak.

"I'm out on a limb to ask," says she.

Weaving leaving gave scouts salute.

"Job for Bob, be prepared." No DIY, I'd all I could handle.

Wednesday morning, heating jacked, granola plain yogurt with honey and fried johnnycake. Pink stripped boxers nuts dangling free, unicorn rhino horny, balls not drooping that New year's. To tip the balance, mad Viagra imbibed, wings for briefless meetings. No boneless wonder.

Thinking 'bout that dream girl
from Bangalore selling tickets,
Tiki bar on coast of Malabar.
We rode seas under Arabia sun
on deck of the Sally Anne
stem to stern that catamaran,
joined hulls below deck bang galore.
Stole my private parts but
muggins happy that trip.
[Sights of girl from Malabar]

Daniela arrived T shirt cut off blue jeans tricked out rigged for fiesta corrida de toros.

"Coffee," she says mug in hand, painted toes in sandals.

"Instant?" I'd queried.

"Don't be silly we've all the morning."

Need to be undressing old shawlies survive that long.

"I've nuts grinding, percolating."

Venetian blind living room rattling drafts from bay's breeze, poured herself Glenvidic dram from shelf. Stretched on the couch, caffeine hooch flowing in veins, 'Summer wind' on down low. 'Real' tattoo'd inner thigh of fine barca legs, anticipations something coming, Me and her do mango dance, our grand slams.

"In Bilbao neighbours borrow sugar, in confession my priest will only hear cream sugar. Robert has time share in Bridgetown, we're heading next week."

Her fella okay with sharing, from a bag she took out swimsuits.

"Tell me which is best."

Disappeared up stairs, reappeared as curvy girl with mature woman confidence.

"Come now gentleman, I'm never Noreen or any of your young ones, be so kind."

Ripe fruit vary in size and color, plethora on my mind. Serious intent to hoist my pecker flying full staff wafted in sea breeze. Feeling she could she pull it off.

"Looking good babe."

Living dog better than dead lion, don't give pearls when rich only rice when poor. Batting order Bobby pitched with foul balls, needed a closer. Wasn't stealing emotions nor violated codes of men.

"Champagne before you get wicked," she whispered.

Propelled Moet cork sabered by poker bayonet, filled glass in hand, toasted bubbly grape. Carpet grope pulled my elastic boxers, knocked my socks off.

"Birthday suits," all I told her.

Propelled in action hardballs showboating. Moved as bacon on spit, somehow she was naked. Took a mug in hand then bull by the horn. Dog with a bone, only fit to be be tied.

"Relax a while, don't go all bonobo." Bing bang boom she'd not wanted.

"Won't jump the gun."

Long time in desert arrived at oasis, two rounds with Enya a goal. Brighton rocking.

Almighty repertoire begin
ready to fly on that handle
blunderbuss and squeeze.
Willie stay perched up awhile,
lady in mind sanctum breach
no hockum no rope nor cellotape.

Bobby cuckolded under gaze of blue footed booby. Guttersnipes we were on that day. When deed was done Robert's life relived of stress. On sofa sharing a fag saw mouse disappear under fridge. Grand-Father clock innards moved twelve chimes.

"Brian you can't forget Wicklow?"

Scar not gone forget pain?
Ride donkey after horse.
Hunt meat, discover tofu.
Lose watermelon pick sesame seed.

Our rendezvous could never replace.

"You help."

Wondering if somewhere Noreen was reciting Angelus, hoped she was. Ginger hair pale skin green eyes, missed her more than ever. Once I'd her right of way then took her hike.

'Bell ringer haul on the rope,
smite the metal,
make huge long sound.'

Later dozy and drained, contemplating mango chutney, and strange words of Galen, '*Every animal sad after coitus except human female and rooster.*'

'I'm pressing on the upward way,
new heights I'm gaining every day,
still praying as I'm onward bound,
Lord, plant my feet on higher ground.'

Viagara a world wonder, Niagara prettiest waterfall I ever did see. As they go.

That's how we rolled in them days.

CHAPTER 14

Hollow echo from brass door knocker, austere imposing red brick on Clontarf road that cloister full of nuns. Great fan of those Angels of Mercy, yellow starred graduate from Muckross kindergarten.

"Sister Aniky," I told grey hair house keeper, attired in trim speckled pinnie as befits that post.

"Bernie," she says, likely Waterford.

"They call me Mr. Boldwood." I gives a raffish wink, messing with the woman, all my braggadocio a real spoofer.

"Oh aye we know that, she's *expecting* ….. "

Caught her drifts, older ram stiffer horn, think Tramore's ancient metal man. Rolled in long halls pimp swagger as if fitted out with balls too big for britches. Bernie kept her distance, knowing fullsome nature of dreadful exploits but beneath machismo bravado I'd fear in my bone. Ushered into wood paneled library study, surrounded by polished drift wood sculptures pulled from bay. Musky books smell of incunables recounting worthy lives of saints, and Pope John XXIII: '*men come to ruin in three ways, women, gambling, and farming.*' I'd vowed forever to stay clear of hoes. Given long half hour contemplating errors of my days, sowing my oats, now encircled by pious. Those nuns acting the maggots.

'Stiffest tree most easily cracked.'
Blotted me copy book, beiseiged I was
flee house head for airports,
out with snow shoes till kid's grown.
Bone up Farley Mowat,
Iniqautuit teepee with first nation metis.
Howlin wolves, on snow blue highway.
Whack noodling seals burn sweet grass
whittle on them Haida totem poles.
Drive huskies over frozen tundra, fear polar bears
ptarmigam for supper, scratch schrimshaw bone.
Work black jack table, easily less taxing life.

Plan B have the kid adopted by Nigerians, grow strong and run with those girls of colour. Fat lady appeared in doorway ushered by grey locks and sentinel heads, eyes popping due concerns. Gadzooks it's her, large as lard 'fatter than tick on coon dog's butt' as Noreen would relate, now reassembled as seal from Arctic lands. Dressed in civvies, doubled in size as steamed bun, damn frikandel and waffles. Giving Aniky the business caused this grief, hot barley toddies did me in. Shocking behaviour, appendage too long in socket, never heard 'hurry up'. Not bluffing, she was in the family way. She had 'creation in her keeping' an end in sight.

"I'd to leave Bruges with my bulge, my few things packed. It's a boy, Mark. Due in three weeks, what do you think?"

Testicles ascended from whence they'd emerged, best they feck out of sight.

I began to weep and cry.
Showed her my willie
hit third rail blew a fuse.
Oh she perished in rough waves,
egg cracked, mashed scrambled

against sea-torn weedy rocks.

Maybe preferred that omlette.

"The boy should be an Irish like his father."

Way off mark stay in Schiopal with moeder, not me on burren rock with lambs. We drove away in silence.

'Oh sick I am to see you, will you never let me be?

You may be good for something but you are not good for me.'

'Treat her as a b and b guest,' departed aunt voice from mystics clear as bells from bouys. 'Child birth been done before, hospitals know what to do. You'll not need boiling water or bust up sheets in master bedroom. Fry bacon, tinned stew boil a few spuds. Methylated spirits and needles, doctor's bag and syringe not required. Don't seal the deal I'd not want you hen pecked. Do what the world does in family crisis get a Filipino lady.' Still her boy in this life.

Decent nuns sent a Young one everyday on the bus to help, novice in gray garb starched white hat. Hailed from Magherafelt tells me, basket case them times suffering in my cups. On my instructions Young one kept tantalus topped, days and nights, searching dutch courage with being discombobulated. In stupor fully detached shuffled to attend luncheon with Aniky then retired to study. Taken to the sup with brandy, spirits lower by the day. Dine alone with plate of fried rice. Reading 'To kill a mocking bird', Young one kind soul love for all.

Aniky register with Jesuits move to Blackrock,

dreaded semi detached, ducks on a wall

culture shock snobby yobby Dublin.

Mother of god, pram pushing and pulling

up-down hills to sea.

Where certain nothing to see.

Cannot go that road where every wrinkled biddie think she's Queen's mother and two up two down's their palace. My brain chucking mud pies at notions of bairn raising, interacting with Dublin people. Oh my lord horror of birthday parties with wee johnnies and maggies, neither was I Walt Disney nor Solomon. Parents sending kids to Tuscany at eight years, get Seannie Mac leg up brass ring. Never matters a damn kid got schizophrenia, heard voices in five languages now wears tin hat with hollow ring. Staying put.

One evening in living room we sat on rattan amid dull terra cotta décor to face facts.

"What should we do?"

Bruges planted bruise on my existence because of malarkies. No prick teaser, well knew havoc loads coming. As if I'd control, hanging machinery churning serious ounces of testosterone, got nobbled bollixed. Should have zipped blue jeans, stitched pecker in Hazmat suit. No longer transferring genes, embargoed for mixing or mingling. By dawns early light innocent in my own bed became unguarded by belly of whiskey, bare-assed recovering from heroic briny's trauma. She'd stooped over to conquer, right there under cover spied rocket red glare and trust herself upon, predictably causing bursting in air. Their cunning arsenal had me overwhelmed, our creator's design. Impeccable, for my vantage.

"Hard to get employment as nun and mother in the twenty six." Wth skills monastic, bare realities stated.

Lighting candles 4 am lauds, matins later
dispensing alms fruitcakes and raisin bread
honey bee keeper, book binding,
weaving, pamphlet printer candle stick making.
Worship night and day every nook and cranny,
pray for Africa missions our eternal basket case,
Heaven's gate, Bill Gates mercies needed.

"Maybe adoption ....?" I queried, after broadside swipe.

"Of course not brainy. What do you intend to do?"

Emphatic nun, no surprise no wonder. Damn if she still had a sexy side.

"I've kids away in Canada, wasn't planning on no more."

"You did this, now you have to. I've no place to go, only destitute alone with carrying your son."

Ten grand minutes in crime, life to be penalty,
sentence too harsh for conker misdeed,
like stealing Trevelyan's bread,
Texas jail for smoking hashish.

"Tough call for me, never had real relationship just few days. Barely."

"Our marriage arranged by fate of traveling, I'm ready with my heart."

Caught in headlock soldier on times pass, events never engraved on walls of history, started with bang ended whimpering. Brain wanting to grunt hoot clap hands, drum sticks on hollow trees. Don't sweat stuff today, tomorrow likely worse.

Early morning no white smoke, noise that fierce, Florence use steel clampers and take Heaven's help. She'd been violent labouring all night at Rotunda by banks of canal. Pushin like hooker, get ball popping from mighty scrum amid blood and gore. Good on them ladies, fierce strong beasts women, God handed men an easier ride, with them bringing angels and devils into this world. *None of us arrived easy by rocket.*

I'd only experienced birth canal's purge passage in transit arriving on the planet, declined earnest invitations from midwife nightingale to join delivery room activities. To stand around as a mook feeling guilty with mayhem created violating nun in distress with carnal demands whilst in me cups? I'd dozed off on vinyl couch in hospital waiting room, late night drivel on the box. Telebroads giving a come on, away ye witches. Don't always do what it says on the tube. Dreaming, surrounded by distressed and judged by oriental nurses.

'Only my mid-wife' I appealed, 'no ironing or BJ's. What's a summer day without swallows?' I do ask myself questions even when drowsy an aroused.

'We're pregnant', well my arse
men out source that skilled job
our notre dames give life,
harbour two beating hearts.
That separate men from girls
our sac race can't compete.
When can I pick it up?
Whose a goo goo boy?

Snuck off to have fry up at Big Charlie's all day breakfast in Parnell square, blustery day on the street, cupped hand with match lit a Carroll. Surrounded by Dublin's workers bellies fattening on victuals before days grafting. Lingering ear wigging, watching our show unfold. Grand fried potato, egg yolk a bit of sausage and black pudding, Kerrygold, Johnson Mooney and O'Brien turnover for mop up. Cup of Lyons tea with hot scone from an old molly, hair tucked up in a bun. Scrawny lorry driver cap in back pocket, fag behind ear nibbling at his bacon. Dodgy unshaven fellow doing security work off in Croke Park drinking coffee from steel cup, each gulp followed by facial contortion as chewing wad of potato. Apprentice plumber boys checking Moen faucets, fresh faced students stubble and hangover rolling joints for later. Saw and heard solitary man eating bag of large carrots, wore red jeans. Grifters from Abbey moving scenery, needed to get a grip myself. Bicycle helmet fellow, bustling lycra leotards faced to disturb everyone. Heard he was a solicitor, watching shape of his articles beneath briefs figured he was jewish. Sweet Fanny Adams here come the judge, turn speedo bulge from respectable folk, partaking early mornings victuals.

"All girl's want a brother." Pretty Carol-Jane saying to mates.

Eats like a pig, hogs TV with sports,
takes more space everything bigger.
You're 'the sister', inferior species
never bothers to talk.
That's okay he is a brother
having one makes girls different
no fairy tales coming they've realized.

"I've to get off the island with talking distractions, ruination in Dublin with likes of Beckett."

Pontifications from goateed Charles Dickens the younger. Like beatnik emerging from beat dive on Harcourt street in fifties, Phil Ochs for the week bring bongos and rizza. Roll your own. Can you cats dig it, dig the changes? Hippies are soon arriving. Spied molly hair in soda bread with jam. Nightingale called to say bun was out, mother and child bonding, Marky sucking grand tits having whale of a time.

"Dad needs to be there too." Mister fish out of water loafing though life now with an extra child o'mine.

Right pickle, itchy underarms stinking palms, brain set sweating turmoil. Despite and in spite that order desperate need to partake of ointment, deal with predicaments. I'd a pint off in Windjammer an early opening watering hole. Shift workers having tipples before home to ride sleepy mott or shifty fathers greeting new born bairn, never cold sheets of a morning for shift man. With the pint I'd contemplations.

I've bourne witness to rare events
unexpected beer back of the fridge
particularly wise Dublin man,
smile from a radiant blond,
girl's wallet out on dinner date,
chinese man with a fork,

Japan girls drinking pints of plain.

My favourite far and wide.

Me old mate in Toronto thinking I'd be struggling for company. Ha! Drip in his eyes never do a tap, now Micky Fawcett making babies. Marched back to Rotunda, face me consequences like manjack, picked up few roses from auld one with barrow full.

"Boy or a child?" she asks, nowt to relate to those old time blarney blather.

From nursery window beautiful being got born, women do all that creating from spec of nowt. God knows how. While hardy men shoot their breeze. Look on with awe and be quesy.

"A son," ginger nurse from Cork says.

Mama dada, ga-ga, da-da, ba-ba, itsy itsy spider, patty-cake.

Marking red ink files Florence and Cork gathered to watch contortions with viewing of the lad, my radar twirling like egg beater. Caught clutchie sneer all a twitter beneath their surgical mask.

"Looks like you, congratulations!" Florence says. "Absolute spit."

Taking the piss loud as carnival barker. No wonder coppers have trouble with eye witless.

"Image of his grandfather from Barcelona." Sharing mirths and myths with nursing jokesters. I'd wear my mask panglossian with wink and nod.

Two things struck in nursery, heavy stomach burp from fry up and no court of jesters could fix my pus on such handsome wee lad. No need to bother Watson and Crick, manual construction instructions not determined from on lump micks in my ancestry. To state bleeding obvious kid had flat nose, no celtic cyarno. My honker designed to warm Atlantic air embellished further by life full of fibs.

We here are winners

infirm, down trodden vanquished and spoofers

in race for life.

Put together miracles by Mama
to hold our own and have another.
Bears serious ponders.

"Me old lad Geppetto was Galway with Spanish in the family. He'd clean up at bull fights."

Sure play along, take a toot on their tune. Knew I was set up, slim nose held high not out of joint. Whatever imaginings of ladies with the lamp, landed on side of angels. Maybe with time chimps could type Newton's *Principia* but no seed of mine would create that young one, echo click bats knew better. End of days 'twould be Father Salvador midnight with Woodwords gripe water for colicky brown eyed baby, rocking in the chair. Spoon for you, two for me. One 'butter side up lad', shine on. No 'Charlottes web' readings for shortie. Escaped wall duck semi, still time to get ducks in a row. Ole, ole.

More of what Chengdu man unbuckled,
chicks and hard liquor
between sheets of satin red and gold.
Wind chimes and her charms,
what else does man want?
Supreme power not worth candles.

No surprise, pair of copulating yokels hardly knew what they were up to with willy, hobbled by principles of casti canubi: go forth with 'joys' of raising kinder. He cocked up deserved gold medal, I a participant so give me a fucking ribbon let me go on home. Mea culpa appendage intrusions, we both had fun with fair maiden, no celtic blood in those wee veins he'd qualify for Malta red shirt or Walloon, boy was a mutt. Got bag of malteziers in corner shop, chocolate balls not melt in cool hands, I escaped scot free as Windsors at Balmoral. On that hospital ward happy second fiddle, as Aldrin, Gore, Scott, Franklin and Stu Pitt. Aniky turned blind eye, feigned oblivious.

"It's jaundice, they'll have him under lamps a few days. You'll see."

Haywire panic in eyes, mighty powerful lamp if kid grows me schnozz. Well no lassie no, will ye go lassie go, Señorita I'm no Agatha or Sherlock or Joe Friday but 'tis Malta man. Shout over mountains, Noreen a woman I cheated with had another man's baby, 'twas mugs game. No nappies flapping round my Head. Man of the cloth got collared, Salvador man of the match could have no gripes with them sour grapes. Back on the rock sent baby mug shot off to his order in Rio, gave man heads up. That day his son got born on sweet emerald isle, one bonny Irish lad. Although many a scoundrel hid in South America barrios never doubting clergyman would come espresso to Dublin city. Make Aniky an honest woman and not be left with her disgrace. Heavy b and b tarrifs would serve to dispatch her, obviously family deductions deemed not appropriate. Them's the rule.

On yer bike laddie take over reins,
to victor go spoils nappies to wash.
Congrats you won the swim meet,
head start my handycap you got mugged.
Mind you Clerys don't take no jungle beads,
sell sweet banana, baby needs sugar daddy.
Car seat, walker, you'll need notary wad.

Short order took Aniky and offspring to b and b, only wishing do right thing, spared no efforts. Acquired Victorian wicker basket from Quirkes antiques in village, still fair nick, hundred seanie and Jeany macs counted sheep in comfort. Soiled, solid car seat crafted by East Germans from Vincent de Paul. *Think only other people benefit, that's high class.*

As good citizen week later stood with 'Salvador' sign by Airport Gate. Surrounded by wheeling suitcase commotions lad and lassie returning, mammy hugs galore. Disheveled sangria dossers cavorting back from bonga-bonga parties in Canaries grasping plastic bags of Bacardi, Campari and Marlboro. Sloppy kissing sandy bum molls glittering shinny grills, high jink latin ways acquired, still flowing as dead cat bounce.

Party over youse are back where pint needs down payment for grim dispenser. There'll be no good time carry on in this pub. Begob, I'll be having the guards if ye persist. Orthodontist Eireann 'Mucho gratis' for white beams in red lips. Beautiful work, babes hot like Tenerife lava. Perfecto. Had my sap flowing. Where were yees years ago? Not down young street on my watch.

Right out of the gate no mistaking jungle meerkat trapped in head lights.

"Un momentito señor." I says.

Tall lanky drink of water not filled out, bumpkin arrived in big city. No suitcase, armed only with Neil Armstrong's backpack, dressed with roman collar no need to tax a razor. Younger than Aniky, spitting image of his new born.

"I'm him, how is she?" Her odd bed fellow.

Breath disturbed air, no smile no gas, no airport pint for pious man. Strong armed into landing at Collinstown. But felt sorry for the young lad, we're all God's blessed children. One glance mise filed 'inconsequential' confronting irritation, know nothing rumpled gombeen. Tourette's tic forever about to sneeze. His roaming jig was up, mine dangling free.

"Mother and son are fine. How's Dad doing?"

He had gotten screwed.

Turkish cig airport bench hands shaking nails dirty
rain forest grime, as bringing gurriers to this city.
He did the crime whatever mano to womano,
I'd not rub his nose in it, needed to pin down.
to nitty gritty consequence.

"When I got your message I was up river Awá-Guajá in Maranhao. My life's work, important you see?

Get a wee grip Charlie, checking canaries in coalmines life's work?

Digging coal at the coal face was the work, lad was a nipper. Bearly knew yer furry polar mammals from pandas.

"I must continue evangelical works for Amazon tribes, you do understand that? Please you understand they're endangered."

What's their contributions? Mumbo language? Pounding guave, spitting fruit juice, with mushrooms for Shamans. Big dollar tourists partaking these potent brews.

'*Me brain got scrambled could see 3 D colour, trees talking mumbo.*'

Brown tits for nature mags, not to be misunderestimated.

We need hyper drives to get to Mars, do youse jungles know any magics? Zoomer, zoom.

"Let me speak frankly man to man." Bright eyes pleading.

Admired priestly noble dedications, desperate to get back on plane, be with doomed pagans fighting vandal loggers. With his form, jonesing for birds of paradise, bedding Awá-Guajá brown skins on green leaves beneath canopy with gayly coloured skylarking parrots gawking over carry ons. No skin off my nose where he got up to, I had my own road of tumbledown rocks.

"If you've passion you must have her, I'll not stand in the way. Can we not agree? I understand you do not work."

Don't clock in, no contribtions, no dole, but still get good Friday, anxiety Sunday evening feelings.

"I'm married already Father. Separated only."

To confuse threw that bluff, collared he'd understand. Passing granny dropped her luggage made tall man more giggy.

"I eat a lot of fruit." Effort to segue, while I'm thinking.

"Aniky says she has feelings for you, I'm not interested in having ordinary life with woman and children. I am Father Victor Cheman Maria Salvador with a vocation. Senor can't you continue with her? Only once I was, Aniky says abundant times with you. I don't have that time, don't have mere animal feelings like you. She a woman of desires, I'm out in the forest no one will do my works tasks. Take her, can't you do this? Why not do this? She's young, you are older. A good deal, lucky for you I think?"

Fresh fish flapping bladdering widget, wasting time water off ducks back logic, hardscrabble beyond here, bored with life's silly games. We both were in the honey pot, for me bun was rising, not interested in life with yer bird. Distressful raising new ones. Raised enough shorties. Only once? My arse. What they all say. Like eating single tayto, never been tried or done successful by any man nor beast.

Whether pints
wet dreaming
Niagara strippers
balls for mongrel mutts
or shampoo
we all repeat,
thank God we
confess in a box
light penny candle
repent our sin
keep with truckin.
Father I'm bad
some more again.
Back baby brand new!

"You've handsome wee son across on the hill waiting to see his Dad. Let's go."

Got the man to the car like dragging tot to kindergarten. On back seat only a wee glance at coast road, some stagnant back water compared to his grand river. Armstrong's back pack lay flat in the trunk, no tranquility where he landed only more boulders to navigate and celts to contend.

"Have you been to Ireland before?"

Negative finger wave, yapping dog to him. Eyes closed in his nightmare only damage his pecker had wrought. No man of world despite Amazon travails.

"Your son is a beautiful baby."

Jarring words conveyed to his shell like, explain life of facts not shaman's magic. Buddy pull up yer boot straps, rift between us wider than Amazon delta. Move on I've quare one to hustle back, you and your moll and human that sprung from join of loins need to skeedadle, sayonaras. B and b fully reserved by me, I've to get mollies clean every spec, not hair from her head must remain new baby smell to vanish. Hasta la vista talcum powder, nappies vamoose. Then repeat. Salvador concentrate this is no tribe down a trib on big river. Deal with it damn you.

Prove up my boy roll up sleeves
hunker down macarena at Maracanã
whatever works, yelps do not help.
In the byre patch bier rabbit stuck,
I'll help youse on the way adios forget tariffs
you are chosen one go forth multiply,
my seed hit only on barren ground.

Drove through Sutton's Burger joint, no baby on board.

"What ye fancy?" Gurrier on the speaker.

"Three hamburgers and bucket of chicken with chips and dressings, large orange juices." I says to the machine. "Give us few ketchups."

Collared man had big hands, ear phones like stethoscope, choral hymns playing. Maybe for dealing with pigeon english fellows.

"Mother will be hungry."

Despite ennui detachments I'd glimpsed charismatic passions, took him by Church of the Resurrection. Have his talk with the boss get sorted, light a few roman candles. No words uttered only an appreciated nod, foreign coins in box like a shawlie. Crossed himself meticulous, signing in, deal with hic-cup in his life. Later outside on bench with leather pouch, inside floated gummy fluid potion. He swallowed a wad like spoon of honey, offered nowt.

"Light and dark separate," he says.

As well poured stout.

"Vibrates the soul, get above."

Like a grand stout.

"Give us a chew."

"Not for you. You need shaman guidance, Ayahiasca bark for divinations shows right roads."

Fun for rain forest boys over there they'd lot going on, feet off the ground in vines of high canopy, apart but part of it all. Sure Yaweh watches them too, entwined we all are.

That evening after hamburger and bucket two of them yapping in the kitchen, Young one from convent bottle feeding baby. Victor putting decent dent in wine supplies, avoided Blue Nun only reds for him. Fair play Malta man taking break from bacurai fruit beer fermenting in Amazon waters. Resorted to French brandy for anxieties biting my ass. In his cups painted spots on his face like Awa, figured Aniky would control that, knock spots and socks off him in the sack. Get his mojo working, regular.

"We have good news Aniky and baby will join me in the rain forest."

Smart lad, take her far from Bruges street vendors dispensing bruxelles waffles wrapped in newspaper. For a long fellow he was big man, iron back bone required in jungles.

"Our grand adventure." She was not waffling.

Made sense out beyond Vatican harsh rulings, far from approving their activities. Dear Aniky avoid rain forest capuchin monkey hunt, curare woonari blow dart might have her rotund ass as target, succumb to double blow excommunicated and exterminated. Victor had wine and bread and stone cold from tap, wee young lad yelled with shock chill on noggin but saved and absolved from original sin. That's a good deal, best there ever was. Forked over for one way to Brasilia, bade them fond fare well. Of course slipped hefty bill fold and Noreen's Lourdes rosary beads for baby, after all I was designated 'God father'.

Also fear of God's wrath messing with front line workers. Intruded as lout escaped as limber lad, that month craven gave McCracken extra to atone with debts to pay. I'd not abscond church obligations, made efforts wished only to strengthen weak timbers. Later I'd fit of bawling loud as chuffed tufted titmouse, never heard from her again. Aniky remains in my mind desolate as that currach strayed off course alone in deep Irish sea. Go wander under the canopy, she has Lord and savior in her blessed heart she'd survive fine. Why not? I'd no doubt she would be a mother, superior.

CHAPTER 15

Seated at Grafton street's end savored brief periods from our pale sun, well solar power my arse. Busy Dublin sky reflecting pace from shadow to sunshine, *Dublin weather change like child's face,* moment to moment. Surrounded by beauties walking their beats, Dublin women knee high strapped boots as if marching on GPO demanding free stamps, for wayward males. Tall Chinese with short tartan skirt, adorned with nails painted black white legs in furry boots. Whitey with swinging pendulum pony tail, *swish, swish,* sucking bubble tea. Just for show as QE2 pint of porter with his nibs. With x-ray specs I'd see that ass, pale as fish belly Madame Curie where are ye?

"We don't come ready made we're created by life together. No freak, lonely fellow, give me a break from empty Ontario."

Gaggle of Cantonese with two friends doing their oriental walk, born ashore Long river, baby eyes filled by Himalaya streams. Hoped they appreciated my stare and good celtic nature, suspect I scared them like Japan soldier at Nanking.

Dublin street tiger rose hair tied by rubber band
pig-tail squirrel bobbing. Arm in arm synchronicity
tippy tappy Strumpet city joined by ear bud music
make up Buddha eyes lips with no quarrels

such dancing bundles of joy. For each an all.

Honorable Minister open borders let foreign girls pass, replenish our famine weakened nation. Stuck in mud of paddywackery, benefit their history 6000 years of passion skilled Emperor breeding skills.

"Babes don't never go home."

Hurricanes rejuvenate

bayous clear out.

Dead wood forest

chopsticks, every twig

California fires burn.

Long river girls

ourland green shoots.

Fill our land with mandarin ladies from spicy Sichuan, red hair green eyes, Mongolian spots on every arse. Our symbiotic destiny.

"Come one come all, I've great hedge. See from space."

Later waited alongside Quay riverside Dalkey bus stop in case Noreen heading to Walsh's, a waste but needed the chance, carried with gravitas and little content plastic briefcase. Her Saturday shopping, later he'd bring the motor from Wicklow. Up that night debating this barking idea even with light of day seemed worthy, tumble weed clutching at straw strands. If a frog needed no push to jump.

Caught in switches of picayune, drinking mavrodaphne with Beethoven, dreaming of Venus of Willendorf.

Liffey swans below mate for life, no flights of fancy 'free will' for them birds, our motts should study them creatures. Made few cheese sambos for nourishments nowt one crust to Liffer birds. Then she appeared all got out with brown suede skirt and diamond ear rings wearing deep red lipstick, shaking Louisiana redneck for Euro-erin chic. Nice bit of skirt, still rusty Pickens to me.

"Did I miss one?" she asks old dear in the queue.

High steppin Grafton street shopping bags, Ireland good for return of this native. She rested by river wall, I wanted closer to the bling.

"This man waiting longer than me," old biddy big mouth says.

Welcome as cold rice told by her stare. Silk pillow lined with golden thread, filled with cold, cold water.

"Yes, but not too late." I tells her, giggy with nerves.

Wondering why I was there, folks not on same road even half sentence too long. Despite old biddy yap I persisted meeting by water coincidence, swanning around, sauntering by sweating in plastic brogues. Not stalking my prey.

"Ahead of schedule on my way to the train, lollygagging." Pointed to Loopline railway bridge across the river. "Working back in the grind, carrot and stick cross to bear on my back."

African bling home on that ear lobe, better than buried fathoms under grinding Africa grime. Paused to breath Liffey air let my heart rhythm get steady as she goes, bitch smelt like a woman. Need tread gingerly.

"You're wearing diamonds."

From my sweat and blood, one stone shy of a load.

Pulverised carbon lumps symbolize love?
Too eternal for many pressured souls
bewildered in fraught relationships.
Only those stones to stay rock hard,
where all else fails and goes to dust.
So sad.

"Make me feel luxurious even though I'm forever poor." With hands over her ears.

'Why does it matter about ear-rings, does he want them back?'

"What are you working on?" But she hardly cared.

You Noreen, life without you sucks.

'I git up long before the sun

I grab my dinner pail and run
I have to hump myself and scoot
and git there 'fore the whistle toot.
My boss he smokes his fine cigars
and rides in automobile cars.
He gits a dinner nice and sweet
while I can't git enough to eat.'

"JFK thing, talking to people I've heard intriguing stories. You'd laugh! Ones that looked after him, partaking details. How he liked his tea did he leave tip for the maid. Shower or bath, pinch any bums. What did he leave behind? Before they all die off. What did he do at night after brandy with Dev? His favourite drink was frozen daiquiris never once served in that ancient Áras, still a hot topic."

Blind yank Eamon and ancient moll Sinead no jet setters in them bygone days.

"Getting brief notes he wrote, all minutiae lots of support from old Dubliners. Poster for three quid might use for a cover, need to go to a pub by the Park. Enthusiastic! That's my 'Tis."

But had done nothing on 'Tis'nt, lacking motivations preoccupied by green eyes. Being so besotted. Windex bottles would fail to have me see clearly, those times. Blind as chimney sweep in Chile coal mine.

"Collecting conversations, have to piece it all together."

"bb that's great, glad you're busy hope you've a big seller." She looked panicky.

'*I don't care nothing about Kennedy why is he bothering me?*'

Wanting to yank a chain, make me disappear down river.

"Expect lots of rejections, sure that makes it better in the end. Polished up. I'll go back out to New Orleans see old Felix before he croaks. We spoke over the phone he has lots of bits and bobs. Next week."

Black security agent with JFK in Ireland, running Asia where lovely Suzann plied her trade.

"Let's have a coffee, have sambo rolls." How I travelled. Desperado.

Sat in a caf on Quays, she wiped plastic table with tissues. Grasping, gasping for precious moments. Rejected my baloney and cheese roll, peeled an orange split in two, handed me pulp and pits. *Always smaller half from her. Seven apples she'd take four.*

"Brian I should really repay for the plane ticket, money is terrible compared to French quarter. You have to know that."

"Forget it, I had points." Once top tier Air Canada high roller.

"What's with Irish leave a few coins? Bunch of misers never a paper note, I'd everything in dear ole Louisiana. We need to have a golden coffin? A poor woman needs to squeeze money till the eagle grins."

Broke, but still the copper lass.
No one has everything in this life
Venus de Milo beauty with no arms,
no fingers to feel strength in her man.

As she checked her phone I threw a hefty wad of folding money in fancy bag, coin from realm of her old dope. Hoped Bruce not comfortable flat cap earner. Money uncomfortable dwelling in poor pockets. Low wage could put payed to them, pay check to pay check, honest working stiffs, one jobbing peeler and her. She'd appreciate my sharing swag.

Woman prefer inside Mercedes cry, not on bicycle sit happy,
money abhors poor people, as mother nature with vacuums.

She'd rightly trouser that stash without a bother. Like guinea or bakers dozen and long tall sally, always looking for sumeth extra. Even when smidgens on offer.

"bb you look tired, losing weight."

Not a pick on me sister, women in droves departed with pound of flesh. Only left my boney ass, more boney.

"You were skinny already, maybe need more sun." Bonny lass figured.

Maybe move to Africa, join Bedouin's caravan in Sahara. Don't have your ass to burn arse off cajun roast, that dinner stole from my table. Fast food menu now garnished by sauce of hunger.

"Is it the hard work looking after your new baby? How's that going? Daniela told me you'd all moved in together? I saw the birth announcement born by grand canal. Congratulations a boy! You must be so happy such exciting times at your age."

Blather mouth neighbour that Daniela cooking with gas, had her own agendas. Busy lady. *Stupid people think they are maximum smart, maybe she was only with saying I'm the fool.*

"I'm on me tod, all done with long times. She messed things, that crazy Aniky gone off to Malta never my child. Father big shot in Valletta well set up. Ten year a nun never was anything. Mark away, father with son misunderstanding confusions nothing much between us."

"You messed things yourself, finally really got found out. Talk about putting socks on an octopus."

"Look I rescued her from drowning. I had me badges and certs from Tara street baths. Without me she was a goner."

Repeating like Blackpool ferris wheels, circa late July.

"Don't have head nor tail for whiskies, to warm up. You know how long that was there, fierce over potent with long years aging, chilled to bone. Only for special occasions. After I went to bed freezing, obviously nothing happened. She with her vows I should have been warned." Warmed by naked lady, trouble coming.

"Two days after your big rescue youse were lying in the heather, spic and spam," she chuckled where nothing was amusing.

Foxy heads nutin but spiteful cats, woman's smile no truth, in false red lips.

"Daniela watching with binoculars.You'd not keep your hands off your dutch one, on the heather arse naked waving your thing around that peninsula."

Seeds splatter as shower elephant, spilling seeds as blind pigeons.

"Never wanted such hard liquors in my beer. I'm that devastated. Hardly touched a drop since."

Porter was my only man. In trust. Don't bark at me.

"Mr. Jack in box with people out and about, complicated life across there in Howth. I also heard you were drunk in a diner on South Ann street with some other woman. Three bottles of wine with pair of you, I know Lilly the waitress I was there for lunch last Thursday. Evelyn she said a widow woman, some of you fellas never grow up."

We'd bawled tears over tiramisu.

"I don't know what you are up to at all, you need to calm down with that mad behaviours. All on rotation with me bottom of your line up, I'm not batty."

Move garbage under carpet, then have no garbage. Only room for more garbage.

Dublin gossipy wee village, not one of us can shut it for a minute. Like Miss Noreen was ever St. Bridgid and she never was, as if I was wandering streets with wrecking balls. So I'd bumped into an old girl friend, my active shrink. Damn gift of gabs and all who sail on this island. Ear growing blisters with such rough speech.

"A right Benny Hill," on she went, "zebra never changes spots, a hard dog to keep on the porch. Better suck it up buttercup."

Falsus in uno, falsus in omnibus 'false in one, false in everything.' What she was saying.

Wow, not living in a cage, free man baby out exploring me options as needs be. Never claimed to be Cisterian monk, neither had women chasing me.

"All Chinese whispers, Aniky and baby long gone, got mollies clean up and clear out. That woman on South Anne street was an old friend with grown daughter. I was seeing her for me lonely mental issues, she's a psychiatrist. Her husband died but she has a boyfriend, he's a lawyer. Two big shots. A professional meeting, chance to offer sincere condolences, I once knew the husband Chris. Just intersection people I don't have nobody, on me lonesomes. Only having a doze in the church box, can't see clearly with liquors, with yellow valium for me mentals. You well know that."

Gabbing ninety to the dozen, windbag let loose from pillar to post, case of projectile vocals. She'd seen me negotiating 'huge assed beers' on Bourbon street, hope it gave some immunities.

"Howth was so windy," heard that Noreen whine.

On RTE forecasts Noreen O'Boyle hears winters fierce out on the heather but never been for those climes. This fair weather friend suggested I go to Florida. *Better skin cold not heart grow cold.*

"Orlando with fish restaurants might be good rather than isolated with no friends. Nearer Toronto for your family, after all you're mobile," she offered. "I'm worried, I do think about you." *Chicken die fox cry, real piece of work. Progressing.*

Be gone so I'd not wait hours for naf coffee and cake, park my arse on a condo balcony in Florida. Once she ran from southern places now Noreen walk again with me in Dixieland with dolphins and corn-syruped dessert. Split this hovel, ocean pad in Coral springs, Cubana siesta, cool guayabera for swanky steak houses. Elegance, wine from Aconcagua chilly in crystal. Surf and turf, not briquettes from this sodden island. Lift our spirits ride down turquoise Keys, escape Quays and muddy liffey. Rust or tan? Breakfast of mushroom omelette, fresh coffee in Miami beach family style. Brand new silver Cabriolet *or* Buick, what's your pleasure? A wee rumbustious doggie named 'pup', shopping at Piggly Wiggly. Do Disney and be together forever and ever. Her message diffident, silent eyes told me things were different, *'things which I have seen I now can see no more'*, now a toad she'd not kiss again.

No chanca señor, move along
no need to visit Disney
for fantasy worlds.
Tell him intimate things not you,
call for no reason.
Sees me naked in the morning
when I brush my hair,
mate with my pretty body
like you used to,
when he sucks my nipple
I love him, not you.
Sayonara my fly boy.

She drank coffee, slice of tipsy cake with her satisfied mind. Maybe and finally on some lonesome lash I'd drum up some shawlie in Spiddal, Gortnamuck or Inismacsaint. Live in thatch down a boreen, staring out hump of three Aran islands, Inismor, Inismaan and Inisheer. Drink boggy yellow well waters and flagons of Blumers cider, sit quiet smoking a fag while she'd kneel with rosaries. Collect warm bainnes from farmer Costello and days fish catch, read postcards from young ones off in Toronto. Wonder in those days where it all went wrong and not shinny anymore.

"Me feng shui that screwy since you left. Just big mess."

"You'll end up always on your own. Secretly I think Daniela has a thing for you."

Deflecting attentions, eagle doesn't catch flies now reckoned I cut Daniela mustard. With double decker Dalkey bus heading gathered her kit and headed out. Determinedly I got on and sat together on top at front like a kid. Favourite place to ride.

"What about the train?"

"Bus needs me, I'm our pilot." Keen as mustard. "Ding, ding."

Along we sped past Sandymount to Blackrock and beyond. Past Booterstown where often take sea baths in shallow waters, as a lad put pennies on Bray rail track flattened to get tuppence, dig for lug worms on Sandymount beach for fishing off the pier. Pointed to mound of Howth across the bay.

"Noreen nothing happened why did you leave? I explained things, broken hearted without you."

Woman washed her hands of me, she still with the hump. *I'm good person. Annoying is no sin.*

"Everyday and night without you."

Gave wee dram from my flask to relax one uptight broad.

"Just for the nerves."

Put her head on my shoulder, given her patina cried croc tears. Silent until Bullock castle gates above the harbour.

"Sweetheart I've to go."

Once foreign soil soul mates, now junked soiled mate. Dog was barking but her caravan moved on. Downstairs saw her on pavement as bus turned a corner. Stop later got off, see what she was up to. Wandered through Dalkey streets in twilight, noisy seagulls from the harbour. Walsh family house on Martins Road in that village, passing Pav Borrzer chipper got myself portion of fish and chips. Hot Med babe golden olive skin, sure papa has firm grip, daughter with blond hair job, no messing with Dalkey lads, drawbridge up at night. Italian and Irish together like oil and vinegar, no paddy's malarkey with her. *Catenaccio!* He'd be sending her to Roma, some lucky lad with Tuscany café. Evenings in Pisa piazza, operas for supper, singing Nessun Dorma in shower with jarring Dublin accent. Leaning on strong shoulders, sturdy hips for bambinos.

"Large," I'd informed her.

Took fanta from cooler for vitamin C, spawn of Azurri despise us for our crass diet but they are purveyors of les chips magnifico. Like opium Brits in China, Southern farmers hustling Alabama 'baccy, surly teetotalers owning pubs. Mild evening in developing darkness street lights switched on, as glimmer men passed on by, invisible through gloam of evening *'clouds that gather round the setting sun'.*

Sat out on end of harbour wall unwrapped battered fish, ate thinking with smell of chips of that spring evening this was greatest grub. Devoured half and covered the rest with ketchup, threw crumbs to perishing gulls. While sucking the mineral imagining her twin C cups, finished off with few fags. Wanted to tell fake blondy loved her big chips but fizzy juice gave me no spirit, tin flask on drip dry. Remembered me and my brother fishing for plaice with rag worm bait, got from shop on Abbey street, now buy fish in tins or Italian chippers. Down harbour steps washed hands in weedy sea water wandered back past tidy terraced homes. Ghosting through shadows, there's weirdo on their streets, call out Dad's army, Free Clothes Association (FCA, our home guard). Easy to get into Walsh's back garden, climbed stone wall in laneway. Pitch dark in leafy branches of pear tree, foolhardy didn't care wits with me motivations, *die pig never scare hot water.* Bunch of kids kicking football further up narrow garden, adults by open veranda enjoying evening, Noreen ensconced with golden haired Walshes arrayed in a bunch.

'I wandered lonely as a cloud
When all at once I saw a crowd,
A host of golden daffodils.'

Skunk at their garden party, got impression three sisters married well, 'Foxrock' accents annoying for faux Canadian ears. Kids interrupting, young mothers in their prime with patience unknown to my parents or myself. Noreen clueless how to communicate with those stoic harridans, she an exotic beast, knew her past divorced from a gambler. All mad with Bruce for invading their comfort, none wanted to hear shenanigans at carnivals and carnies. Nor to ever know she slept with chauffeur of mulatto lover in one room sheebeen back of Gentleman's Jazz club drunk with tequila and lonely birthday pearls. Their's world of draining costs of catholic schools, keeping up with high stepping yobos, run of mill lads and laddettes pushing paper charging bucket loads by quarter hour. Mother's so proud, kids with scholarships. Sweating exam results for Blackrock run by high class Jesuits. Give us the child and we'll guarantee poxy narcissist, pirouetting fuddle duddle behind the Queen. Keep us on their right paths, helps too if your Daddy's rich and powerful gentleman of substance and property.

Barbecue king Bruce yammering pars, eagles birdies with merry mates, flipping chicken, flapping beef slapping sauces. Tools of the trade, brushes, lackeys and German's lager. Wiggle worms in Dalkey not found only in the seas. Could see Noreen twiddling ice in wine none of her kids playing, knew secrets and scars of her heart hearing fog horns across an ocean. Eyes too dark to see back with oil tankers and hearing James call out to Captains on Mississippi barges. Returned home folk leave much away but never escape old pains, sometimes better to lighten the load discard that suitcase of knickknack amulet baggage, bric a brac serves to trigger old wounds. Finally Noreen enough Mammy chatters took herself over to Bruce, captured attentions of pasty faced husbands. Tools for her charms gaspin they were with tales of beads collected on Frenchmen street. Desperate to see grand tits, sure I was no different, suck like grapes not grab like Tokyo salary men. Damn missed sucking those red nipples.

"Perfect!" Bruce laughed. Ha, ha. Ha, my feather in this fellow's cap.

Bruce's father, school teacher hitting glass with spoon, milquetoast from my angle.

"Today Margaret and I are proud parents. Finally my son has found his true love wandering days over, a new leaf he'll be turning."

Distaffs cheered, I cowered behind green leaves.

"This lovely woman Noreen has come back from dreadful Mississippi places and I welcome her into our family."

He gave Noreen a hug.

"If I was a younger man I'd marry her meself!"

Felt like tossing rotten pear at his bald head.

"Noreen is a Wicklow girl, ah sure that's were they make prettiest girls. Please now raise your glass for Bruce and his lovely fiancée Noreen."

Clinged and clanged big stupid pear shaped glasses.

"Bullcocks," I heard myself.

Stuck like scrap yard dog, report do nothing no flipping yelp from me. Took my leave slunk down the lane as sly raccoon.

'Fancy' Noreen got on my goat, my troubles lie in deep roots not fluttering leaves.

Long way back around the Bay, stopped off in Keoghs for few pints. From phone box on Stephen's green called Evelyn, man's voice answered. I headed home. On that night train saw couples, young ones out on life's adventure. Gorgeous babe with young fellow, he looked besotted. Best days of his life. Lose her and you'll be likes of me, for she was too good and knew well her rights under Magna's old Charter. Give her love with hope in his heart. Poor sod, maybe win a lottery his only chance or else walk in many days alone. Set her up on Vico road God's right away for Jesuit boys, holidays in Grand Turks. Maybe overlook ordinary mug with she distracted by vista of the bay. Remember Aristotle married Jackie, Rainier and Grace, Sophia and Carlo, Marilyn with Joe and Arthur. All blessed happy lads. My pursuits of happiness seemed long ways off but I'd bottles in the fridge. Another day had been only on errands for a fool, punished for one error of judgment made with lowland lady. Never asked to live this life, lost soul to end of my days. That morning I curled on the sofa, pulled blinds on back porch no interest in belle vista or Wicklow hills beyond. Like a hit-and-run drunk found sober in jail cell morning after, hoped telephone would ring and warden send me home.

Hoping as planting feather grow chicken,
grow golden wheat out on the muskeg.
Just kidding Noreen loves you.
You big lug, go on. Get out of here,
no more mourning on that morning.
Go make love to her!

In heel of that evening needed drugs to dim memories, longing for lost love and felt my dormant staff losing patience with lack of business.

'Oh what can ail thee, knight-at-arms,
alone and palely loitering?
So haggard and woe-begone
the sedge has withered from the lake,
and no birds sing'

CHAPTER 16

Winter days spent living on beans with buttered bread and strong tea for breakfast. Silent abode where nobody tinkled piano keys, enveloped in beany bag, meat ball in blankets to protect from drafty chills. Watching football games, re-running Sideways and Love Story activities that rendered pallor of Nosferatu, 'On Golden pond' reserved for searing Ontario lakeside memories. Pre-war toaster gave up it's fiery ghost, resorted to three bar electric fire in living room to brown a few buns. Added papryka to Johnny West for dinner or barbecued tasty German sausage with YR sauce, partial to Birds Eye fish fingers given our sea air. *What's the point in eating corn seems so indestructible?* Walked those rooms wrapped in blanket cowl as a monk, melancholy haunted me like lonely aunt before. Played Thelonious '*Blue monk*' softly in background, needle crackle confirmed this as her favourite. Lying in bed dead of night, winds through drafty walls then I'd hear Roses of Picardy picked on the ivories. Aunt near and dear, for her I left Emu port on the side board. Valued final postcard to Toronto, her eyesight failing.

'Man without a goat, ship with no rudder.'

At Easter time overnight I'd run Mise Eire on TV, she'd never tire that vision. Kept the place a fridge, not to heat the house with only mise and aunt from mystics 'when she yearns deep in labouring night'. Showered with stone cold pumped from belly depths of the hill, cascading icy chills served due warning volcano remained dormant. With scruffy facial stubble celebrated my birthday in shepherd's pie family style by Clontarf. Pie had mince and peas with light crusty pastry covered the spuds. Previous times Noreen would do hash pie, stuffed tomatoes with corned beef, there's no home cooked in a tin needed to kick that can.

"Wake the feck up." I'd hollered across the bay having birthday beer for breakfast, as clouds darkened a sluggish rising sun.

Checked if Noreen might send a note, didn't bother with such likes. That day little by slowly trying to be upbeat, given myself féidir linn 'yes I can' pep talk determined to shed blues, embrace brand new days. Mentally shagged but needed to behave moving and shaking, not be confiding Irish men didn't do such likes. On those streets no sympathy given for Dublin man with woman troubles. Unseemly to scorn schizophrenics but mental disorder induced by flown bird nowt worth uilleann pipe symphonies. Already with enough struggles for citizen, like share of decent crust few spuds with bit of fish, where next pint was coming from.

That day after my birthday I'd sat my arse while bicycle postie dropped a card from a dentist, showed some pearly smiles. My mother mailed a cardigan and book on Irish fathers which I never read. No longer interested in that dire subject, sorry ramblings from sons of Eireann and drunken fathers. Done with roles never suited and according to my kids not good at, always remembered them on birthdays and ex which cut back Dublin carry ons.

Money go everywhere disappear like steam, generous spread as pepper on steak dinner. Even if yer Ma and me took youse all about the world now no one extremely happy.

Occasionally ventured for fags and booze, for victuals tins of dace with black beans keep me living vital and keep pecker up, nutella with dates ain't so bad. Tried to tidy garden, from cold spells fountain burst dragged it where van men in a lorry carried it away. A yard tree lay straddled over the path, perished from gales and age, wasn't that bothered was heading that way meself.

Now a week after such events passed by bumped into Tom Kelly on Grafton street.

"Jasus sure you've been a rare old fart comin round about these parts."

Staring like he saw a ghost, scared bejasus out of him.

"Donkey's years." I agreed.

"Brian sure cead mile failte. So conas ta tu a cara? Howya?"

As we shook hands he gave a hug, unusual on land with shamrocks.

"You're skin and bones, a Biafra man."

Like he was weighing scales owed a few coins.

"Looks like you lost a shilling and found a tanner. A bit off colour."

Always that look about me now with holes ventilating in me pockets.

"Naw is mise go mait man, okay just bleedin cold. Foot loose and fancy free!"

Out with light corduroy jacket and freezing a bit with chill wind coming up from the street. Outside Bewleys café savouring aroma of toasted beans took a drag on a smoke hoped I wouldn't fall apart, having difficulty finishing a sentence with nervous tremors. Determined to brook no hints about harsh demons, I'd not expected to be meeting up with curious folk.

"I'm looking after meself," significant problem all by itself. "Farting thru silk."

I'd come to be withdrawn hikikomori man, them times I'd not get dog bark at me, hand shaking as I lit another smoke with kill of the fag. That late morning I'd been heading to C.I.E rail station hoping for a 'mystery train'. Although afraid those trips would deposit me in Wicklow 'Garden of Ireland', only fit to sit in the station wait for return, should better boarded express plane visit orientals by red lit Soho town. Tommy looked uneasy witnessing disintegration of a soul given the state of me. Cursing I'd taken no valium, always needs to wear spurs in case I meets a horse. I was a strange article in his realm, he almost bailed a prospect to be avoided finally got going on the babble.

"Me dermatologist, a female, said to keep my drawers on, what if I had a wart on my arse? I'm a bit stressed, do they's ever play John of Gods on RTE?"

Chirpin brain helter then skelter. 'Why don't cat fish have kittens?' was coming next.

"Bloody teller at bank asking me about weather and weekends. Man trying to focus on me finances, few bare bob what's left after the ex."

"Our quare wans keep us skint right enough." He says.

Tom, dodgy old acquaintance from college, beer gut and bald no Silken Thomas. Unvarnished son of the soil as if raised entirely by wolves, same even in younger man's clothes. Wore shoes too big stuffed with newspaper, better value he'd lay claim. Foreman in Balbriggen's plastics factory since he dropped out of school. Even to him with elastic waisted pants I was a mess, chronic 'go by wall fellow'. Always with tendencies now blooming, dark shadow traipsing down black roads.

"I've a throat on me, gummin for the pint." I managed. "Good day for high stool."

Get gargle in me stressed brain, pair of quare hawks to shoot the breeze.

"In floods and drink now your talking. Sure very man indeed a grand gargle, drop of the crater."

We headed to Keoghs, in truth if we met any ladies I was beneath sartorial grand, rode hard hung up limp wet category. Bag of bones unshaven phaorach appearance unkempt, Johnny Forty coats brother avoided bright mirrors. Needed a haircut with confidence low.

"Sure fellas that head off to Americas never do come back to live. Back to haunt us all here's abouts!"

"Yeah sure I was brewed and stewed in Ireland. Them bridges in Ontario and me with vertigos, then with those ill considered beers. Kids were alright and wife gone off."

"Ah indeed."

"Right enough never expected to be fetched up back here."

As he understood twenty years of goings on and wives going off, like she was left in sun and rain too long. As if I traded for '57 chevy which I never, like I changed tyre and still with the flat. But the man experienced many wretched Ontario 'lager'.

"We're all Liffey fellas days end, born bred and buttered. Thought me hard yards were over, now days they're putting less wine in the bottles. It's one thing after another." I says.

'She got the Merc and you got an ass to ride?' Noreen once declared. 'Better deal for me!' I'd declared.

I'd never driven no Merc through Queens highways of Ontario. Maybe Noreen had points although with the garda she'd not be gallivanting Saint Moritz boulevards. *Princess body with domestic life.* Unless bent copper with hollow spaces for swag her fine arse would polish no bar stools in Bregaglia trattoria. Remembered Tom lived in Ashford a town near Avoca out on Wexford road. During our conversation I lied and said I was heading to Marsh's library near St. Patrick's Cathedral.

"Research for a book."

Unspecified but imparting raw gravitas for special business, no doubt he understood I was thick as mince exhibiting too big for me britches. Tom didn't comment nor pegged me proceeding opposite to that Cathedral, nor query for what research a gurrier would be requiring that exalted library. Cultured fellow he was to understand. Viewing the Caravaggio on Leeson street was worthy plan B, enough to know I was baggy in the arse. He had the air I supposed knew my problems, loss of face down dumps with the birds.

"Two plain my good man," Tom indicated to bar fellow.

Negotiating pints in Toronto with Canada man.

'What piss do you have on tap?'

Deep ponder, more complicated than pursuing a condo.

'Is it local? Is it fruity? Could I get a taste.'

Jeez in ages, be a man, pint of plain, be done.

Craft beers universally are crap. That's a law.

We sat on barren oaken stools familiar with my arse. *Lucky no dress code, that bar not set high.*

"G' day," fellow countered. Genuine GAFA escapee (Great Aussie Fuck All) as they say. Down under matched my very mood.

"How's Frank Ifield? Still yodeling?" I enquired.

GAFA'd not remembered that star man.

Porter's wait

are you dry?

PAPOTM

are you dry?

PAPOTM

are you dry?

PAPOTM

are you dry?

Go on you bugger.

Put A Pint On The Mat.

Jeez in ages.

While waiting those on pints Tom volunteered he married the

'quare wan', plain broad he met at college. Mousy with greasy brown hair, features not in natural location far apart eyes studied like goldfish but liked to knit. Called me a 'fecking loser' when I passed a joint at a student party in Northside bed-sit near Dalymount. Couldn't argue that point of view the woman was not stupid mainly ignorant of the future, no seed knows what happens when grows tall. My wealth then consisted of two Bachelors pork and beans cans. Pauper man, but world in a playpen was waiting.

Don't scare mountain high
or know to climb mountain.
Only does brain have road
to travel and sense to arrive?
Successful.

Dated her best friend she with big tits, bubble bum and unbeatable sweaters never partake one without the udder. All full of potentials, unraveled as I had my odyssey loafing thru' the colonies, 'the eye altering, alters all', while they stayed behind in our dirty old town. Most follow water to low land, not climb heights, knew I'd be someones gopher if stayed put, my life catch airplane, bicycle to SUV. Footloose, not march in time. Admired he was married down all the years, old country Tom probably still loved her. Quare wan said I was puny and weak with weird accent, all before I left for the Dominion. I did a bunk, sure what did Ireland ever do for me?

"Paddy Esperanto," that smart arse called me.

She'd insisted in pointing out to all and sundry I'd an unsightly wart on back of my hand. Stumped I was still have burly scars, no wonder I wondered who I was those early days what's me attributes and talents. Trying to figure out which beetle I was, brachinus georgio crepitans turns out, great bores of the genus.

`Oh, at home had I but stayed
'prenticed to my father's trade.

Had I stuck to plane and adze,

I had not been lost, my lads.'

"A dry shite," what I heard she said.

'Twas scary what she now looked like, cruel but in her twenties hit the wall, early closing for quare wan never a hit on prime time.

'Nay, she must be old.

She cannot choose but be old.

Certain she's old.'

Well fortified over pints *'as a means to let my mind conceive visions that the unaltered sober brain has no access to'* peacefully listened. My contact with human face so long only on flat screen. Didn't ask much not interested in making plastics but happy to bullshit, in foam of second pint connected dots making Southern cross. Mentally meandering obsessed with image of Chinese girl's legs down steps on Howth double-decker, pale thighs in furry boots. Men's minds only work part time, yer eunuch man has free will rest of us get screwed. Eunuch should be doing Einstein work, enough with the choral singing in the cathederal.

'How are ye me old China', should have rendered.

'let's boogaloo Tokyo

eat fragrant guavas

by land of the Malay.'

Drink aussie Shiraz

a wine that travels

down gullet opposite

make her dizzy 'twould.

Worn out lace shoes

but with beds to rent

go from a Jackeen

to prince of her heart.

I hears Tom all blasé telling he attended wedding of Noreen and Bruce at Meeting of Waters near Avoca.

"They're married?"

"Sure the missus was at that nun school in Waterford, like yer old flame old 'lumini they are."

Well pickle me head proper, busted and bashed me mentals. Violated shafted with a shiv as gipped by grafter at flea markets. Ton of lead bricks landed on me sac, my life's journey a quagmire, only now with circling the drain, dizzying.

"Brutal day was had for it, lashing down whole friggin time. Deadly never let up for a sec, drummin on lead roof of that old church such a bloomin noise. That racket right as yer one was singing her 'Power of love' solo and two young ones fiddling on violins. Put a proper blight on festivities, grand marquee up and all. Real pantomime felt sorry for the lass."

"Good luck Noreen and him," I said with long draft.

Shocks to me system stomach objecting. Fellow was a stool pigeon dropping such news.

"Yer one was upset, no chance to get pictures down by the river. Him in the tux cleaned up nice."

Rabble meeting by waters babble on and on see if I'd even care or give a damn. Sunahara to all them Wicklow activities.

"Paid through the nose for camera fellow. '*God's work*', he was claiming, soused in the bar seeing as we'd met foul elements. Still have to cough up the few bob alright like. Sure it's gas a decent crust you can get from taking the snaps, they did the business with the bar I'll say that. Scuddin down it was in stair-rods, splashed out you could say."

Then sure Tommy heard about my troubles probably her bestie Mairead, likely in bar parlour after gordian knotting. Mairead delighted telling Tom how I once cried in the pub getting a heave ho from my Noreen.

'I think Brian might drown his self in sea waves. With the rocks and rough tide below.' Mairead likely told the fellow.

Tom would pin me pathetic, tragic morose, broken-hearted left with nothing at all. Still intact wits my loop-hole, there'd be no dangling from ropes in my life.

"Jasus me old son you've bad dose with women," Tom said regarding me pallid pallor.

Never believed I'd be instantly ashen faced, shade of pale in bar mirror betrayed me. Fisher woman from Guangdong province with firm fist grasp once told me I'd hairy chimp arms and pallor of fish belly.

'Sex with you', was said,
'like England take over this world.
Only two minutes, then India still India.
No difference and no jewel.'

England's empire did sink one afternoon in the sun. Still shinny.

"Need a smoke desperate." Old cara's doing my head in.

Out on South Ann street sucked a fag to butt ash get heart beats ticking normal, looked like he was holding back more scraps.

"Go on say it, can't get no worse, lost the bitch in anyway. She pushed me right in stinging nettles." I told him. *But human being improve ask monkey for help?*

"Hard place right enough. Do yez want to hear any argie bargie? Are ye up for it at all? Maybe I should shag off and shut me fecking gob."

Dublin wee village not one of us can shut it up.

"Go on already, I've hide of albino rhino." Tell me crapola. Why doncha?

Tom told me other stuff, rewarded for supplying his pints, decided he was creepy fellow, breed commonly found on the island.

"Her sister Beth said you were a weird recluse, should have stayed freezing away in that Canada. Honestly a right pistol, too hard for the woman."

Face of a right clenched fist.

"She was putting you down desperate, funny how you love one fight the other. Noreen with the looks alright, a bit of fancy stuff on the day. The mother saying Noreen made the big mistake marrying that Bruce fella. Mind you jarred she was with uische baite, nattering craic with old talk."

Good for the mother, grand black pudding and fried tomatoes in my few Wicklow days.

"O'Boyles have not taken easy to Bruce, a big loud mouth, I'd say Noreen is sinn féin with that one. She said Noreen needed a mature fellow, you fit that bill, savior of her family. The mother had a grand time in your garden last summer, bottles of wine from Canada galore. They're all a bit mouthy."

Gave the fellow fist pump on the revealations. Must think I'm a tourist on the planet.

'Dreadful wild streak all ended bad in America. Life of O'Reilly over there in Howth. Brian treated her like a princess, running up and down to the village half dozen times. Welsh rarebit was grand, Tom what is she looking for? I'm sad at my daughter's wedding! She must have hurt Brian, I feel sad for the lad never understand what happened betwixt two of them. My daughter is the divil truth be sold. Since the day she turned sixteen, it was putting her away with nuns that I believe. Misshapen with unnatural experiences. Her father's wishes no less. For me I'd have her in the national college up the road, always with gra for the boys. A wandering mind.'

"She says if ye see Brian about town tell him I'm fierce sorry for his troubles."

"Tom thanks good to know."

Entitled Noreen was, I waved dismissively as if disinterested in doings of Bruce and Noreen.

"O'Boyles are in the past," I insisted. "Always liked the mother a good old soul."

Unfortunately with no influence over wayward daughter. Seemed Noreen kept my baby troubles under wraps, appreciated her discretion.

"Trying to decipher women is like decoding Voynich's manuscript, Yonaguni monuments and Baigong pipes."

"Me very words, there's a pair of us in it." He agreed as any man should.

"That's my life back motoring on black top, doing a ton with the T bird."

"Mairead said you were having hard times since over in Howth?"

"Naw doing okay man, tough for a while now water off duck's back. I'd a thing with Dutch chick, another one in Bettystown although bit loud. These days computers are full of ones wanting it. Fish in barrels."

When selling three legged trotter

set up in middle of market.

Home run hitter have high strikeouts.

Wink and nod to convey I'd be getting it good. Better than most for sure.

"Oh aye, Beth said you got a Netherlands one up the pole."

Sly bastard caught me off guard. Throwing tommyhawks, caught me in goolies. *Bury the lead, my bruver.*

"Is he going for a rugby team?' she was saying. 'Tossing his caber, waving it about all over the city. Debasing me sister, needs to put his rain coat on."

Flooding basement compartments I was. Like to air it out, doncha know.

"While Noreen was still coming back and you on a tare through the city. Mairead showing us all on the phone, you got caught on video out there in Howth on the heather. Some auld one was walking her dog she said some one should put the garden hose on pair of youse. Her round arse bobbing in long heather."

"Well flamin nora," I says.

Trying to please a young one when blind drunk, appendage caught in the dyke. Peeping neighbours made me look a damn fool, Tom took me to the brink, prickly that weedy heather was. But okay, right enough.

"Rare bit of gas alright, fancied that bit of stuff meself." He says.

Butter face woman with grand ass truth be known. Back in pub he was checking Weckler-Schkeel clock, finished the drink for emotional sustenance. Likely his missus Tom's one and only, neither about to be wandering with gallivanting.

"Noreen wanted us to get hitched sure once hobbled out of that jail, God gives us forks heading every which way. I'll be taking care of business there'll be la eile," I says, "other days galore."

Wasn't bothered chasing after me fling, serious man with other priorities. Shook and parted ways with my casual demeanor in tow.

"Always is a cara, slainte for now."

He knew I'd screwed the pooch on that scene, meandered through Stephen's Green digesting news of Noreen's wedding.

Crunching twigs stomped chopped sticks,
threw up pints of stout behind locked toilets, by railings.
Damn you Dublin not a single public bucket for citizens,
another needy fellow was watering, ranting and railing.
Some scoundrel closed the WCs,
'Victorians provided facilities, our lot filled with cement.'
Wondered if mystery trains went to Knock,
I'd visit Mother Mary for troubled mind.

Computer café on Tara street saw wedding pictures, only needed to torture myself.

"What about me Noreen?" Queried loud, alone with Pakistani owner.

Later picked up off license beer and smokes, booked into Drakes hotel off Harcourt street. In my room cried buckets, lost as burst ball in high weeds. That morning finished off the booze, retreated to my hilltop redoubt surrounded by water. Withdrew like turtle inside my Masada fort with ceilings of hefty wooden beams. Annoying high pitched gulls, given half a chance I'd blow their tiny brains with laser guided pellet gun. Screw waves on a turbulent sea, screw wind and hill heather willows, gloom descended shivered with me timbers. Lifer returned to his cell denied parole all hopes evaporated, Noreen and husband ensconced in valleys near deep waters mixing.

Read about Chinese man with ball of gold, everyday for 40 years he'd hold it then hide for the night, one day ball was stolen and distraught the man was. A wiserman instructed him to cover a stone with golden paper keep on living. But this wise yarn did not help one bit. Mama would ask about Noreen, upset no longer saw her dear friend, I'd drink pints start a querulous tone. Remind her of injustice things not done in my childhood, as if raised in Aberfan valley and rarely saw sun down the mines being so underground. No laughs or whale of a time for her with Noreen in Murphy's pub of a Sunday only mournful son with much on his small mind. She'd be off to Wicklow if I told her, her disappointment compounded my failure. Tom said they'd a lovely house, hoped it would be a hovel, fireplace you could sit either side and watch turf burn both side. They'd sit together most of their times, *tibi focvs splendet 'for them hearth-fire glows'*.

"Rain forest plants maybe from Loosy Anna, Connemara marbles must own the bloody quarry off in Spiddal." Tom said having a laugh.

She ordered him to remove his shoes, he'd holes in his socks mixed with fermenting moldy disintegrating Irish Times.

"Socks smelled something rotten, she busy spraying air freshener. Sure it's Japan and them places where you'd be doing that. Rural Ireland, what's she ever playing at? With farmer's wellies and big yob old trout creatures like me? Like it's Buckingham palace and it's far cry from that. Spent an hour hovering she did."

Come from away folk always with their queer notions, needed to shut that voice. They should teach kids about love warn how to handle it and absence when it's over done and gone. I'd fanned on the puck now pylon duster ridin' pines, end of day sat with tray of ice and white wine in my garden of remembrance. Twirling ice kitted in green orange T shirt exhausted by emotions. Across foggy waters imagined hearing stout fellows in Rhondda Valleys with hymns of praise.

'Shine through gloom
point me to the skies.
Heaven's morning breaks
and earth's vain shadows flee.
in life, in death,
O Lord, abide with me.'

Woke in a chill drained the glass corked the bottle wandered to bed, wind picking up listening to Enya, house braced with rattles. Recognized one peg's taxi with labored gear changes passing a dark road, ferrying sloshed goosled, jaded and jowled. Maybe I reached an emotional nadir resolved to consider options, where pressure makes diamonds. No longer bide my time for now never she would bide with me. Never wait for sky to drop cake on my head, *'Don't expect owt for nowt.'* Drop rice on road, maybe birds follow you home.

No more blubbering I'd go dancing on that wild side. Had anxieties nervousness being national trait, as an Irish face. Bunch of friendly lout, love 'em all. Let be-medaled Generals fight last wars my privates were moving on. Like ice cream van need sunny day.

CHAPTER 17

Driving Clontarf road windows open enjoying mid-day breeze from across Dollymount strand. Distant Dublin city pelted with rain, soon streets were slick as tyres glided over their surface. Had rendezvous at Gleeson's Bar on cobbled Fitzgerald street, squeezed between Phoenix park and river Liffey. Days previous spied a bronze skinned girl in blue jeans opening wooden shutters on the old pub, wistfully remembering cheeks of her fine ass. Meticulati of the male in pursuit, focused as lions on Serengeti springboks. Carrying out my plan, crafted to escape turmoil of life gone wrong. Nervous but determined, passenger side littered with empty packets of cigarettes. Business to carry out, to maneuver is to live was that days mantra. Following up what New Orleans spa owner Felix Walcott described. Jack Kennedy had been on this street during his stay in the Park with President De Valera, summer of '63. Walcott related that Jack blew off old Dev that late evening, a tale told often among citizens of the city. Jack with stomach of boiled spuds and little whiskey.

Early afternoon pub was near empty, sat at river view table, photo of the American president hung on the wall. Down through Louisiana that old blue Mississippi river would shine like a mirror, our river Liffey was backside of tinker's fiddle. Feeling positive with my 'Jack

Kennedy in Ireland' manuscript, 'African' quarry busy behind the bar bored with herself, in her sweet time she carried indifference to my table, thirty, breasts and wild tussled hair like popped corn, filled water tumbler on pink plastic tabletop. I wanted to rock her world, she communicated by moving that body, not a girl of mixed emotions.

I'm best goddamn lay in this city
old white guy you ain't got any chance,
don't knock on the glass
don't park your arse.

Maybe potboy girl all shop window and no stock room, but better young mouse than old lion, even Crested Argus come from small nest. Not doubting sooner or later she with some cop or fireman would have great nights in semi-detached out Lucan way. Detected hesitancy and dubious confidence, knew she was broke there was no ring. Million dollar body wrapped in rags, broken tooth on top row tried to hide by keeping lips at awkward angle, needed a manicure. But no chance encounter more encounter by a chancer, Walcott revealed he had a daughter, born from one nighter in Dublin park. This beautiful creature was Walcott's granddaughter found by the park, some seeds land where rooted.

"Are you the writer?" she asked looking at my papers.

London accent also tincture of raggedy poor Dublin.

"Sure I know 26 letters and ampersand," an acting jackass, "verily I say unto you dot over i is called a tittle."

On a bar-stool taking a butchers, familiar stare from women how amoebas feel exposed beneath a lens. Wore my Italian away strip fitted nice, looked half decent for that change. *Rabbits don't only eat grass close to home.*

"Are you takin the piss like?" She queried, with likes of me saying *tittle* to her face.

Threadbare thong strap appearing over jeans slung low on those hips. Hook and reel her in, how we take care of things in Howth when fishing on Liffey banks, likely breasty already had belly full of me. When lacking peacock's plumage with superior broads guile is your only man, honesty or deceit too obvious and lame.

'Sometimes I'm up, and sometimes down,
if I get there before you do,
I'll cut a hole and pull you through.
Swing low, sweet chariot.'

I'd got drunk with Syd Martin her tattooed ex-boy friend in a bar on Kilburn High road a lad on life's low road. She was born in Dublin grew up on Abbey road went to school in West Hampstead.

"You're from England?"

"Nil aon tinteann mar da tintean fein," says she with a gaelic laugh.

Not surly one I anticipated, lots of down easy folksy Felix influence on display.

"On bfuil any ocras ort?" She smiled some more.

Interesting hearing gaelic from black bird. Bord Failte should fix tooth and nail post her all about. Tiny kilt with green panties. While she was a nipper at six years her poor mother fell overboard Dover to Calais ferry, high jinks with intoxications newspapers reported. She'd spliced the mail brace cavorting with two gills tot and more. Trinidad puncheon rum cruel mistress crossing high seas, that Atlantic sailors knew, feared and suffered more than most.

"Oh aye my bean an ti agus ta terrible tart orm."

Not to miss a beat ordered grilled tomato sandwich with the stout, noticed gold fainne ring on fly of her jeans, pin badge displayed by fluent gaelic speakers.

"Just cupla focal?" she asked.

"On third date darling if lucky," what I was angling for.

She looked at me giggling, hand on my shoulder.

"Love a fellow that makes me laugh. Bualadh bos."

Standing close as damn to curse I pushed eraser end of my pencil through the fainne. She flounced around examining this gold ring protrudance.

"If I get pregnant baby would be a writer."

"Used a rubber," I says, she laughed again.

Making moves, my route out of chaos. We had that chemistry.

"Gillian."

Handed her an envelope, coming down to the wire be long neck horse. Her look queried how on earth I knew her name. Syd in London had written, awaiting sentencing on burglary charges asked me to give it to her. Back at the bar she paid no heed concentrating with reading. Humming away, pencil in mouth and back to me, that denim arse wriggling.

"Old bill won't let me go to Eiry. Never been, knows I'm not stopping over. I love her man but with getting nicked and likely sent down she pissed off. Back to Dublin the paddy bitch."

Smart gaelic coilean but losing her should be enough punishment for decent tea leaf.

"Looking at a stretch so she went off. We wus getting hitched an all that."

When finished reading she carefully folded pages of the letter.

"Gives a right old bollicking she was the missus, I think she's gone looking for some Mick. I drove her from here to Glasgow with that Irish dancing, 'cause of her, I'd do anything for her. When she won those contests I was Alf Ramsey proud, that was her thing. Listen mate she takes me to the dancing shops, we look at shoes hard and soft. I'm a f'ing expert on gaelic dancing. She'll do hornpipe hard jig and treble reel." Laughed at himself. *"She does gaelic fusion with flamenco, castanets and all. Me mates take the piss, but they know."*

Nodded simpatico for the man.

"Never expected nutin like that, Gilly got me sorted. The stuff I got done for all before her she wouldn't stand for that. I'd turn around, they'd be going

down Millwall or Hackney marshes when I'd be at a Céilí dance in Liverpool or Nottingham. Gilly Dillon in all her gear banging, flinging it out on stage. Smiling, them judges gave top marks for personality. Pairs and singles. I've all them dancing trophies at me Mam's house till she comes back. Me and her in Irish clubs on stage with solo them places go nuts. Fiddler and accordion boran, Phil the fluters ball. Magic. They love her, like I say she always got a big smile and legs going crazy. All over up there biggest attraction."

Men get emotional over lost broad, more than gizzard prospectors losing nuggets.

"Went with her to Holyhead then off on that ferry, stayed in Liverpool for a few days. Lost really, I didn't want to be back in the Kilburn kip. Give over, brutal man, desolate don't mind saying so. Fetch the pints in good lad, got melancholies remembering."

Gillian glanced in my direction, she went to serve some customers, knew Syd told her who I was. A man lonely in his soul as any I've ever seen, pinning this gaelic coileen his black bird flew away home. Week after our last encounter he'd been confined to Belmarsh prison in Woolwich. Citizens of Camden town, Kilburn and West Hampstead could sleep undisturbed in their king sized for ten years. Beak that sent him down lived in John's Wood, too close for comfort, tough break for tea leaf. Back she came all serious.

"So Brian I've a bone to pick with you."

Then planted beer and sandwich with herself smack down at my table, Roses from Picardy I was humming. Despite callaloo blood woman got wacked by shillelagh, she'd not needed shamrocks on her ass. As green a leaf as Bray goes through a stick of rock.

"Failte romat," she says and threw letter on the table. "Did you never have your heart broken?" she demanded.

"Yes, Miss Gillian."

She gazed tears falling down her cheeks, ink smudged on the envelope.

"You've something to tell me? All the blamass? Fuck all of you too," scared a few rubber necking fellows at the bar.

"Why are you messing? What's on your game?"

Brown eyes a blaze.

"I live on Howth head."

"So what?" she said. "Why are you spying? Your big wellies all got up in all my business. Go on."

Getting a rollicking, prepare web think like spider. Syd told me you were wounded and single seeing as he got sent down. Arms folded covering her chest, knew well she was not just for show. Candy beneath cotton, unbutton two by two.

"Gillian, I'm nervous fellow with beautiful women."

One false move I'd be Mallory sliding down Everest.

"I've important stuff." I says.

Only wanted a peak, tongue in cheek.

"What?"

"So listen."

Picked out strategic pages from my JFK manuscript:

"A night in summer of 1963 pub was closing, staff cleaning up and in walked President of the United States. Handsome with that full head of hair, tanned sat by the bar threw Boston Red Soxs cap on the counter. Matthew Gleeson not turning from washing glasses explained closing time.

"Feck off now, you shouldn't be on the premises sure the guards will be by. They'll be out what with your man up there in the Park, full of jitters. Have you no home to go to?"

Jack Kennedy didn't budge, from leather pouch took Cuban stogie.

"Home for the week," Jack said with Boston toothy smile, not a man from Castleross.

Smelling cigar smoke and that accent Matthew turned and looked at who was in front of his face. Handsome man, confident yank smelled of better place. Different from usual no hope Jackeen creatures frequenting pubs those grim black and white times, ha'penny dropped.

"Holy sufferin Mary."

Matthew sturred and slurred as Jesus himself sitting his arse at the bar, Jack stroked the stogie.

"So 'tis yourself," Matthew managed, gave Kennedy slap on the shoulder and firm handshake. "Sure it's wonderful thing to meet you Mr. Kennedy. We thought you'd be locked above with Dev and his old one."

Jack pushed over the cigars.

"Take a Cuban."

"That's very grand, I'll take one for the missus as well if you don't mind now."

"Salinger got me a stash before I signed that embargo. I'm good for the next two years!"

Matthew put the cigars in his shirt pocket, precious San Cristóbal de La Habana stogies, family heirloom never to be smoked.

"More power to ye now."

Matthew called up the stairs for his wife Mary, that fine looking woman.

"Mr. President sure you are so very welcome. We all love you in Dublin city and sure I have the niece over there in Massachusetts." Mary says.

"Eamon and Sinead were going on about his prison escape with a soap key, so I made my escape! Needed a night down in the town." Jack puffed on. "Slid past the garda."

"What can we get for you now, make you welcome?"

"Mary let me have double shot of that Bushmills scotch on the rocks."

Amid tables Matthew shepherding young bar maids, Brenda

and Maureen. Before Mary could lock the pub door a large black man entered.

"Jack ! Jack be nimble, Jack be quick, Jack jumped over Garda, know you well. Garda and embassy going crazy. It's mayhems above."

"Walcott enter the parlor sure we're Irish here on this tonight, I'm sure Dev will give us all the pardon," said Jack.

"Where's me porter?" Walcott said putting on a brogue.

Handsome man, special presidential security agent Felix Walcott occupied studying Maureen and Brenda.

Gillian appeared transfixed with my spiel, I paused.

"You know my gran is Maureen."

"Look," I said, "that's most all I know."

Matthew Gleeson was gone and Mary with dementias, only knew what Wallcott revealed, getting to interesting parts.

"Need a smoke," I told her.

She took care of me pint.

"Smoke, nobody cares get on with it."

Researching JFK's visit had my travel back to New Orleans, Walcott told me Maureen was dark haired beauty.

"Those Irish girls a lot of fun, first sight I fell in love with Maureen sweetest thing I've ever seen."

Continued with my reading, why not with audience of one? All I wanted.

JFK and Felix had a good old time drinking and singing up with two young Dublin girls, great craic all on the house. Pioneer teetotlar Matthew and his reluctant Mary disappeared up stairs. Felix remembered one of the old ballads as he sang out on his porch in Baton Rouge.

'Fare thee well old Erin dear
to part me heart does ache well
from Carrickfergus to Cape Clear.

I'll never see your equal
although to foreign parts we're bound
where cannibals may eat us,
we'll ne'er forget the Holy Ground
of poteen and potatoes. "

Felix laughed as he remembered that old time, with the girls they got rightly jarred.

"Those days Jack wanted to be in Ireland," Walcott said. "Khrushchev banging that shoe gave him a headache, Cuba nearly blew it all up. Then Jack got done, killed by a dumb coward commie redneck. LBJ was never no JFK." *Say it ain't so my brother, even then we got no RFK neither.*

Eventually they'd stumbled from the pub and walked through Phoenix park back to Deerfield the U.S. ambassador residence. Somewhere near the Monument Walcott said he was delayed with Maureen, spent time in soft green grass.

"A taste of old sod." He'd said with a gleam in his eye, that gleam lasted long time.

I sat back nothing much changed in years gone by same bar stools as with Jack Kennedy and her grandfather. Pregnant Maureen sent to her sister in London, baby girl was born. Of course Maureen had written to Felix telling him he was a father and of that there was no possible doubt.

"Maureen in Louisiana Jim Crow times would have been crazy. I still ain't over that Dallas, 100 years and I still ain't done. That Oswald did a lot of damage, messed up lot of folk."

Never had no lunch counter
segregation movement,
never had no Jim Crow
only abroad we had 'no Irish'.
Then we had more class

first, second and third.
Who needs segregations
when you got class?

Felix lost himself in whiskey bars and prison bars of Louisiana. As I finished reading a distillery transport river barge let out loud blast.

"Mam never said much, only Grandad was from America people did not talk."

"I've video with your grandfather, he had a band."

Perversely gathered my things although still fishing with shark on the line.

"Well I wanted to meet, promised Felix and Syd. If you've memories that could help let me know, I'll put it in my special notes."

Handed business card prepared for the occasion.

"Yeah, you know so give me a call, always appreciate helping hand."

She became all flustered, waving those hands.

"Brian I never see people likes of you. You just can't leave I need to talk."

Only with the porter I was calm, she grabbed my arm examined dial of my 'Taiwan Roolex'.

"I'm out of here in an hour can't you wait? I live in Chapelizod we can have dinner, I'll get Chinese at Yim Cha Hap. Do wait, they've great Dim sum by a Sunday."

"Always good for spicy Chinese."

Long legs in furry boots, with dark eyes, my go to Japanese porno.

"Go raibh mile math agat."

"Hey failte romhat no problem. I'll get the champoo."

Maybe wounded ones easier sat back in the car happy as Larry, earned my corn. She could be taken by dawn, early or late. Noreen vacated from thoughts. Wanted to say run from Dublin open grocery shop in Tobago. Sweltering West Indies, wee cottage overlooking Scotland Bay, watch Scarlet Ibis of an evening. Swallow me bunch of beers in hot sun, sell Carib to tourists and nights with salty waves in Gulf of Paria, 'when evening's fan of sea winds rustle'. Why struggle in Dublin city, when I got the readies. I would write and each night take to bed this nubian beauty. Sweating in tropical heat I'd not be thirsty, towards midnights I'd take her again. So done with red headed birds.

'Skip across the ocean
Dere is a brown girl in the ring
Shi luk lakka sugar and a plum
Plum plum.
Show mi yu motion
Tra la la la la'

CHAPTER 18

Light from silvery moon shone through basement window of the flat. Room mate Shirley gone, city gallivanting as birds have mind on fine evenings. We sat in kitchen shared heat from two bar electric fire, Gillian wearing white cotton skirt changed from industrial tough linen, now with mahogany legs to cheeks of her bum. Curious sight, nubile pendulous beauty and skinny beast. Strange kettle of fishes in Chapelizod. *Old white pork and young dark chicken.* From whose hammer and furnace was ebony woman cobbled? Where that anvil had created quadroon girl 'and shaped my burning deed and thought'.

"I don't know who you are but you made my day." Gillian told me.

Put her through turbulent time, she opened wee metal box with her stash lit a joint, moved my chair closer making scraping noise on lino floor. Outside street heavy lorries changing gears on the hill on the way south.

"You know I'm turned on." I told her.

Can you knit wooly jumper?
Can you mow a green hill?
Can you feed my soul?
Can I feel mahogany, love?
Felt sure I would.

Entertaining her gentleman caller grand style, drank chilled champagne, take away roasted pork, chicken with fried rice steamed broccoli, esteemed veggie by my book. Watching her chopstick machinations, reminded of three legged mutt taking a stroll. I pitched with heaped fork, famished from days anxieties. Best learn to eat rice one spoon at a time.

"Brian you need a few squares, men by their own selves are that hopeless, I'll cook real Sichuan hot spicy chicken. Way before troubles with Syd I apprenticed with Dad at five star in Chelsea, Korean banchans my expertise."

Busy, with developing munchies.

"Nowadays eat like a dog from cans even with spuds."

"I'll do stir fry with anise, peppercorn and dozen fresh herbs."

Irish men rarely concerned with grub's geography, she wanted to cook spicy on the wok. Hic-cups with hot spice but home cooked and she *wanted to see me*.

"I'd love it."

I'd not want anything chili in my bowl, I'd handle the heat.

"Drinking with Syd, strange you even did that?"

Notorious O'Gradys, paddy watering hole in Kilburn, stayed on liffey waters.

"Everyone in your family in that vaunted pub at some point."

"You tracked them down."

Clues from Felix, spend few quid get pints in they're your friend.

"Syd forever going on about some bird that left."

Detected no revealing response from brown eyes, she knew when to close them.

"I've lived life as a ferry girl, sea between us and England, Baile ata Cliat and London my small world. I don't know Lake district or Connemara only Hampstead heath, Notting Hill and here. I'm Irish but know nothing, I'm never a Sassenach."

"Not just few quid ferry ride, Irish and English are different. You know all that."

"I feel me and mom were betwixt people, never belonging to no where. The black sheep!"

Play her on that game. Confused, mixed up as platypus. Raise stakes see her and more.

In that TV room she lay on the couch, naked legs, shiny polished muscle gladiator rigged for battle. Watching those thighs causing mental confusions in the flat. Lucky dogs men only to pity Castrati and value equipment, mighty loins rarely sleep through the night. She'd get taken, again. Feeling anxiety, not wanting to get off on the wrong foot. Heard deep ship horn blare on that Anna Liffey.

"Queen Aideen is buried out there in Howth's Cromlach, I've been, do you know? One summer day learned it by heart from a Cork boy on Hampstead heath. Listen." She closed her eyes and off she went.

"Leave her among her fields of fern
a spot to sepulcher a Queen.
The music that alive she loved
shall cheer her in the tomb.
Humming of noontide bees
lark's loud carol all day long
and borne on evening's salted breeze
clanking sea bird's song."

Took my turn to finish, all I'd remembered of legendary Aideen's cracking poem from school. A blessing in the skies

"A clear pure air pervades the scene among the sparkling brine!"

Gillian's smiling high five telling me together we had more chemistry than found on Marilyn's mole. On account of drink recklessly I made a promise.

"I'll take you down to Wicklow, garden of Ireland I know mountain trails and secret places. We'd have a gas time of it." Altogether.

"Climbing hills I'd love that," she said. "I've seen lots in the films, 'Waking Ned Devine' was so beautiful, I need to see more. I'll do a picnic, I love the exploring."

Confused by Isle of man like many whales dashing channels betwixt main lands. An island for no man, no pussy tails surely no place for me.

"Mostly dated Irish guys in London those moody introverts, I'm spiritual to feel their souls with me they'd know what love is."

She with copy of Bedells gaelic bible on the shelf and bio of Sacagawea.

"Off the boat meet up with you, rub of green for them lads." Shot in dark bush, into the pink.

"Damaged goods cry babies trying to figure why they were dumped by some colleen, run to get away ferries." Hiking down losers lane, relating my life's experience, as ferry fodder.

Once desperate to spend life with some plain culchie girl, freckle face beetroot arms down old rutted boreen. With lofty ambitions to be shop girl in Dublin, find fella with a Leaving cert. Get uniforms job, stand grounded before you start in this life. Smitten fellows never witnessed thousands of tanny leggy babes on Wildwood boardwalk of July evening. Greater than caribou herd, locusts swarming, penguins marching. Migration of Philadelphia birds down Atlantic's shore, wonder of world visions for minds of men.

'Cape Cod girls ain't got no frills, they tie their hair with codfish gills.'

"Briefly I dated an English fellow from Welwyn Garden city, used one tea bag for two cups. Hours smoking his pipe, displayed an enormous stamp collection in his garden shed. So proud of his match boxes and those dinky toys organized on shelves." Gilly says.

Welwyn man sports coat leather patches, knew that mainland species, Sundays an anorak watching trains. Drove Morris minor convertible, 'collectors item end of day'. She slammed an open hand on the table, din lit up that room.

"More interested in penny blacks, I need their bags full!"

Baa baa black sheep, Yes sir yes sir, bags full for this dame who lives down the lane. I'd give many a fair penny for black babe them days.

"Only strong Darjeeling for me, no bainne." Drunk darkly she'd tigum.

'I've all those ancient Ireland Cú Chulainn fantasies from night classes in Kilburn. I met a Galway fellow, gorgeous white teeth played GAA all religious. Kissing those stormy boys, scent of a fellow early morning breathing salty spray from Atlantic air."

Licked her lips, she'd suck gaelic roots from lucky boy's to get what she needed.

"With a firm bum."

"Never saw the likes of you, I need to brush up those gaelic sagas."

Running hills to village for smokes, I'd buns of steel.

"One Roundstone lad of a Sunday took me to mass, met at that Saturday's Camden dances. A fisherman, during communion with rafters organ playing 'Fields of Athenry' he asked me to marry. I told him he was crazy, later in the papers there he was leaving for California with a supermodel. I let him get away, do you think I'm that strange fish?"

With me wriggling caught on that hook.

"No Irish fellow wants to stay across in London, Swiss Cottage bedsits not a cottage and no friggin snowy hills. No Piccadilly circus clowns or acrobat, only dealing with daft land ladies fussing with hot water rules, endless coins for the meter." I says.

Britannia always with rules, truth be told many Irish man's wallet stuffed with UK notes. Lucky we got painted pink those times. From what I have seen of the world.

As Ireland pickled spuds, Brits picked the world.

Waspy Brits made life betterplace for me,

wherever I wandered shared commonwealth.

Brits were worst just better than anything else.

Cheers ! For old English.

"That's Syds mom with hair curlers, does bangers and mash for renters."

"Your Syd's not gaelic?"

"My exception now my mistake."

We sat to watch video of Walcott her grandfather, meanwhile Suzann's arse bent and touched her toes on the TV, focused on a mongolian spot. Hit fast forward.

"Belize bird," I told Gillian, "excuse shoddy editing."

"Flat like a boy," she noticed, no dark continent influences.

"There's your man," I says. "Gilly Dillon this is your life."

Old Walcott sitting on his porch wearing his Dad's sharecropper hat.

"My grand father?"

Walcott in Louisiana, drinking Carib brew watching oil tankers on the river, sweet magnolia in air that July, sweating swampy land between New Orleans and Baton Rouge. House on stilts elevated over briny bog land, heat splitting stones air blast from oven roasting turkey. Iron mouth buzzing aedes aegypti mosquitos feeling breeze from gulf, eating worn porch screens. Felix Walcott never returned to Ireland since that JFK summer. With me he recalled a night in 'Fenix' park and being with Gillian's grandmother in Brighton years ago. He stared at my camera and spoke to his grand daughter.

"As a baby you gave me a kiss all those years ago on the pier in Brighton. That was all the time we had, Gilly enjoy your life. I spent too much time wasting, too much time off the main line, now living many regrets. This man here with the camera a real scallywag, be careful now. I will get to Ireland again and see you someday over there. We will take a walk up in that fine park, I do often think about you and your mother."

She took my hand, excited tears were falling.

"I see my personality, I'll have to go see him."

Maybe we try to borrow too much from that which has past, *let it go my brother, let it go my sister.*

"He made a few records, have LPs at home. Grand voice backed with calypso band from Port of Spain. Great stuff."

"Lord I am all shook up, Mr Brian this girl is shooken all up."

On the couch her eyes closed, hands and lips trembled.

"Brian you must half fancy me with all your work?"

In the village I've a butcher, baker and farmer's market, locks on my doors open from inside.

"Mile failte always gra in my croi for mna! I've a nest over looking the bay, come that way and rest. Castle brand pots and pans even a gas oven."

"I'll do shopping for veggies."

"Maria, my spa lady makes pyellea and bread, if she has a mind she whips up a mean and spicy chimichanga." Kneads the dough, with those bare hands.

My strategy to leave in full rapping flow, hit the road. She'd come to my place that week.

All I had empty house with feather bed. This game worth the candle, all I really wanted was shirt off her back. Should have cashed post office bonds for bouncy castle.

Ireland, sometimes direland.
'She's not a dull or cold land
No! she's a warm and bold land
Oh! she's a true and old land
this native land of mine.'

One Saturday after we'd been seeing each other few grand months went for drive deep in Wicklow county, desperate to see country this lassie was.

Smooth landing on that bod?
A stretch even for Armstrong.
Lots of folks would never believe
had the stones for hill and valley.

Picked her up at Chapelizod she'd packed picnic lunch, uisce baite my contribution all I was good for. People would be surprised we spent time together, didn't burden her with questions. Seeing me no lateral arabesque, maybe now searching different boreens. Stay with plain Howth man, less competition. Not incarcerated, my bonus. Clothes appeared in bedroom closets, empty drawers got re-stocked. Ceilidh dancing gear and piles of patent leather shoes, long plaid argyle socks, dresses and Spanish accouterments, castanets. Strange foods, spice bottles arrived in the kitchen. Fridge stacked with artichokes, sprouts and other vegetables never plucked from muck in an Irish farmer's field. Whether choosing mates or tubers the woman not stuck in a rut, cast a net far and wide. No stuffed toys in her bedroom sturdy virile boys much preferred, with exceptions. My roads scholar traced her finger on our teddy bear 32 county map.

"What's best way to Wicklow?"

Like many a lass she'd no find her arse with an atlas.

"Travel ye down south." I says, "motor down the old bog road."

Signoretta not so easy for mise, previous dalliance to deal with, nerves raw yet with that blister. We wandered along Dublin and Wicklow hills late on that spring sharp chill on the air. Past rocky Scalp and Sallygap over Feather bed, that scalp forever serves due warning to beware how you go.

Passing kids havin wooden toboggan sleigh ride
an odd patch of Wicklow hill snow left to play.

With Noreen I'd driven those roads,
now getting rides in bluebottle's squad car,
slaying her copper with hot rocky times
bully for her getting charge from a peeler.

Gillian stared out at the landscape and river in valley floor, dreaded to see likes of them.

"Canada is so big if you get on a plane in St. John's Newfoundland, takes shorter time to get to Vancouver with earth rotating."

"Not as crows flies, food for thinking,"

Curvy better than flat.

"On those Grand banks sailors once reported cod 'so thick by the shore that hardly have been able to row a boat through them', you know St. John's is nearer Galway."

"Where are you taking me, Mise Eire?"

"Mysterious Glen da lough, my lady."

"What's special?" she wondered.

That Glen tugging my compass as ever. Your man E=Times square claimed objects curve space and affect reality, that Württemberg brainiac stumbled on something spooky, as we mortals barely imagine. God gave Einstein kick in the arse, shoved his nose in barrels of weird. Saw the light, but even Albert remained confused. *Too much info! Not enough info!*

"Tower erect beside sultry lake. Get there get sorted, feed your confused Celtic soul."

Oz Abos have Corroboree
Markawasi in Peru,
Acropolis Greeks and London marbles
Blacks Senegambia gates,
Islam make Hag to Mecca,
America's claret fields of Gettysburg.
Ontarians sacred hockey rink

now supermarket, no surprise!
Damn Burgermeisters in big O.

Accelerating down county roads in top gear with my woman, over no man's land into enemy territory, beyond long shadow cast from Sugar loaf. Seeing 'O'Boyle' on many village shop front as we joined mountain roads other side of Bray, thinking of secret places Noreen promised, all those mighty what should have beens.

Yeah, yeah, yeah, yeah,
many days offered not lived,
summers laid wasted and past
seasons gone, futures withered on vines.
Never ice cool shandies nor
warm showers in green marble.
Sunday afternoon under wraps
sleeps with sheets of black linen.
Nor picnics filled to brim, prim
glasses perched by mountain rocks,
wicker-baskets soda and griddle bread
potato salads with beetroot
scallions and cheese from Cork.
Hope you had times of your life.
Noro, stark butt naked for that peeler.
So maybe I've me doubts. Face it.

"What will I feel?"

"Tough question babe, soul of beholder. Japanese and German tourists traipse through seeing ancient stones, nowt more for them to know."

Them with raft of monuments to conceal, although Erin stone Victorias long banished to dusky barns. Those statues had limitations monarchs once beloved on Dublin streets as Pathe news record, now we destroy our history like Taliban. Subjects my arse, no divine rights to rule o'er us. Take hike off old Dunleary pier back to blighty.

"Portal to our celtic world, without Glen Da Lough we'd have hole in our souls. Places where boundary between living and spirits is porous." I tells her.

"My lord Brian it's Tír na nÓg?"

Trapped in that timeless valley
our spiritual place in this universe.
Something that vibrates also
in Glastonbury, Lindisfarne.
Late late show in Gaybo's day
Ireland souls gathered round
Sinn fein from Montrose Donnybrook
wherein beats a country heart.
When I was only sixteen.

"So what about your Scottish?"

"None of Dad's lot have been to Ireland you know they've got issues."

'Come up above the crags and we'll dance the highland reel'.

Insular tribe those Scots never 1916, no Pearse, Clarke, Connolly and them god fearing rebel boys to give the final lash. We'd made the escape and captured bogs, never seen Eire without itch of divided Ulster.

"They so resent Ireland only Celtic nation dumped the crown, mad jealous of Free state. Can't be living in Aberdeen and have kids named Tam and Murdoch, I'd be lost in highlands with Craggie and Kyles. You can't waltz in on them they only look to Westminister. Gra geal mo croi."

"Helps us being an island."

Scot hard-on for England barely hid by furry sporran, their lairds fenced off highlands now wooly sheep welcome for roaming. Towering country only for show.

'English steel we could disdain,
secure in valour's station
but English gold has been our bane
such a parcel of rogues in a nation.'
'Please sir we want more porridge.'

"Their thick brogue and wee phrases sure it's only bearla."

Let her vent, their high hills were not my hills or valleys. Dispatch our stone Queens on the mail boat, maybe some Scots to appreciate them.

"They have their red haired feared warrior Calgacus, Scotish soldier Andy Stewart on London Paladium and Cináed mac Ailpín. I like Scots but don't have brotherly feelings, they never encouraged." I says.

Passed my mind, never cared much. Caledonia high lands, Hibernia on steroids.

"Donald Where's Your Troosers?" Her favourite. "Dad bleeds tartan blood, more Scottish than Robbie Burns drinking Campbell soup."

Past weekend we'd been to London to visit Aberdeen Keith, Gillian's dad. Jeans and T shirt, long streak fellow with curly hippy hair rolled his smokes, highland stock. Gillian could do better said with withering gaze.

"My family were travelers." He'd announced.

Lived in Twickenham detached house near the stadium, not pleased with me sporting hochmagandy with his daughter. More favoured fellow with double glaze caravan, tinkering, knackering and trickery pilfering trades in his pocket. Passion for cars including Jaguar parked in the drive, had broken side window and smashed bonnet. Liken for bevy sitting in his living room drinking Newkie Brown, explained he lost his temper with Indian girl friend and belted her with his fist, broke her front tooth. She refused to come out of bedroom that day. Through the door she said her glamour was destroyed, we could only see photos of her now extinct smile. She slammed his motor with his Ailsa Craig curling stone. Jag deprived of glitz and glammer, stone never lost a chip smooth as ice. Despondent bad lad busy judging me. *We can't chose our parents, that design mores the pity. I was only thinking.*

"So we've tempers." Keith told me with a laugh. "That's the culture I have, through thick an thin."

Figured I weaned on hind tit, felt silence would be wisest choice feared Glasgow kiss on me front choppers. Nevertheless fellow genius in the kitchen, grand feast on his table.

"Like white fellas in Nashville I'll try influences, food is jazz put Coltraine in the kitchen that's me fella. Golden age of grub with those avocado and mango, plantain and kiwi on High street for any of your neds living as hobo kings."

Being raised by liffey muddy waters never much valued jazz, appreciated his philosophy obsessions.

"Our Gilly has a palate, I gave her that. Gilly watch out a pie eater this one." Aberdeen reckoned. "Gilly does it all fusion today's word, Ethiopian ingera."

'Where's your fucking rice,' my Ethiopian cuisine.

"Always fancy a stir fry. Utopia." I replied to confuse.

Hoping I was dropped like chopped bacon on hot wok, no potential with micks like me.

"Stir fry ups me arse, where's muck there's brass. You've no taste, stir fry stews! Last night's veggies left over, rice from customers plates, pig food mixed like scraps. Do youse not know? Oh my fecking sides."

Gilly's old lad had a fart fit laughing, served as his jester absorbing jibes.

Emperors eat many dish, peasants hog around one big bowl, pig monkey style.

"Youse Irish no nothings. Paddy in Chinese restaurants waving chopsticks like shinty sticks. Swapped daggers for forks, now eating fan with kuaizi. Bunch of tripe eaters."

Coming from haggis eater. Fella felt exhausting.

"1983." I says with a final handshake. Try bonding for Gilly.

"Good lad," says he. "12-22, I was there myself."

North of Hadrians wall, what they all say. Last Calcutta victory for Scots at the stadium, likely never see another one. Anytime soon.

Newspaper 'Docs baffled'.

Lovely couple off by Clew bay,
young one hanker for stir fry,
then settled with the bun.
Oh Lordy,
wee bairn spots on the arse,
docs don't know what to say.
Parish priest pulpit declared,
'Sun screen and the chipper,'
or there'd be a hell fryer.
All knew she got 'take away'.

Finally parked by that two lake Glen, wandered over stone bridge quiet place would shut her up about Caledonia, land foreign in Hibernia, took gravel path around lower lake and sat looking back at St Kevin's church and round tower. Horses grazing, sun bright as clouds slipped away for that while. Felt goose bumps on her thigh from valley air as she handed me a joint, she examined the wooden door above on the tower.

"Village girls protected in the tower with monks for many days." She read from tourist's guide book. "Men dispatched by sword or battle axe."

Take that pick on stairway to Valhalla gates, six of one half dozen of t'other, to be fair.

"Eventually they'd have to come out, frog marched into the lake, I'd have jumped to get away from fat old monks, heat me with mead and god help them Iceland boys," she laughed, "fellows passion and rowing muscles. Get a good Viking!"

Lusty woman appetite for worldly pleasures, fat balls on those Nordics invade waterways, march down our boreens. Hibernis hiberniores not our ways for Vikings, only delivered many annus horribilis for peace loving. Armed with hardest steel forged with dead bones from comrades, gave them the edge. Broad sword proved mightier than quill, whatever claims of bard Will. *Their blade strongest steel. To chop us down.*

Fertile valley nourished by blood of many Irish men, doubtless my existence set in stone from impact of these attacking Neanderthals.

Mari usque ad mare, our nation conquered, sea to sea. A pedibus usque ad capu, posteriori, head to tail.

High minded Gaels every monastery with scribers copying Greeks, hunting words in texts to save souls from darkened worlds, 'we pray dear god inspire us as we inscribe on papyrus'.

Old empire collapsed, Ireland saved Christian worlds.
I've my doubts never a Thomas Edison among us
what we did was copy. Copy our game, Etc, etc, etc.
Publicans, solicitors, money grubbers,
accountants by abundance 'developers' a plenty.
Excess saints dispatched to Iona isles beyond.
Inscribing on vellum ecclesiastical fonts
ink soot dried dregs of wine gum and eggs,
peaceful monasteries medieval xerox machine.
Latin Greek, Virgil, land of nonescience
no Silicon valley only culchie's bogs.
Chips are from the fish and chipper.
Steam train travel puff to puff in Erin.

Only O'Boyle to now rule, gas altogether.

We don't do Einstein job.

Viking boys had it handy departed with treasures, precious women, sheep and nuggets of Mayo gold. Brave monks sequestered glorious books in bogs of Kells and Durrow. Sea faring pirate invaders not read a focal skilled only with slaughtering and stealing, head home navigating on wet sail, roasted lamb feasts, women conquered moreover on beds of polar furs. Empty their sacs spawn rotten blond hair sons to plague us, return to defeat us with kin, from our own blood, from our blood loss. Eire's many points of entry promiscuous old whore, marauders cursed the nation, no wonder Dev wanting dear Eire left alone mired in deep Atlantic. Every rock of ours has seen destruction.

"Some women did get back according to sagas," says she.

Home sick, sea sick, morning sick, women piloting rowing long boats across Baltic sea, broad sails and red hair catching winds, wise tacking in northern seas. Heading for a Rathlin island connect.

'Bitter is the wind tonight
it tosses the ocean's white hair.
Tonight I fear not the fierce
warriors of Norway
coursing on the Irish Sea.'

Those Danes cut the nose of those unwilling to pay their danegeld tax. Off with our armada Clíona, Meabh and Mucha settle ancient sores. Smack snot nose kroner Norwegians, give us oil barrels alls we have is sodden turf. Reparation for stolen women folk mea culpas give us back our golden ore.

"We never pay any-one Dane-geld
no matter how trifling the cost;
for the end of that game is oppression and shame,
and the nation that plays it is lost!"

Later beneath the tower we sat at a picnic table.

"Brian let's eat, I was up since wee early hours."

Laid out plastic tablecloth and plates on lopsided wonky gouged beat-up picnic table, presented her exotic feast with lashings of strange. Menu set with bowls of Korea bachans and dim sum.

"Bibimbop, gimbop, dooboo kimichi, yang jangpi and dakdoujiib. Takoyaki."

A taste of everything. Like a man in deep throes with a woman.

"Love that MMMbop!" Sings I obviously.

Had hoped for chili con carne carrots a few Tayto crisps. Woman packed full container, bird nest soup, enoki mushrooms and others size of plates, dark buckwheat noodles, green onions and soya sauce, grilled sea trout with pickled vegetables, eggplant stuffed with spiced pork, stir fried vegetables and roast duck, sticky rice and buttered broccoli. Beef marinated. Full passion from blood line on display. Dang proud she was and her skills.

"Fermented Schichaun beans to complement sourness of eggplant you'll notice la difference. Kitchen spices from your Loser-ana friend with mumbo jumbo. Peppered with a spiced vingerette my Dad makes for me to steal, made from Lough Lomond waters. What do you think?"

"Five star, baby."

Salt the Irish spice raised in nation of fish and chipper vans, spuds with melted butter to fill empty stomach. Our tribe of folks down the years rightly terrified not to have food on the table for young ones, culture framed of empty spoons. Not long ago.

"I climbed tree branch's in the Park for mushrooms," as she showed her tongue. "I'll do an Asian haggis for Robbie Burns day, my Dad says it's the best."

Desert rice wine in decorated Chinese bowl finished our feastings, home runs galore in these woods, woman covered all base instincts.

Our nubian Princess gifted to Erin, her path forged from when JFK once graced Ireland's shores.

Ready to pitch tent but buckets of rain started, heavens lashing with ear pounding, tour buses in torrents tore back down the trail, curious eyes abandoned pouring over our precious stuff. *Sayanora, auf wiedersehen peace in time, my brothers.*

That valley soon needing Noah with his boat to rescue daft pair of us, rising wind sang with gurgles rivuleting thru' drains. *'Make thee an ark of gopher wood.'* instead for rain coat cut three holes in fertilizer bag retrieved from mulberry bush, only with dashing I was. Distressed Gilly wrapped in tablecloth, paper plate hat secured atop unruly mane with bit of twine.

"Scooshing down tent would get flooded, I know where they hide tower key better shelter in that pillar than get drowned. What?"

Noreen promised to take me up the tower but decided not be trapped with pillock, prospects better with plods on level paddocks.

"Get it."

Wild tinker's gleam in brown eyes, potent fearless mix of gypsi traveler and African voodoos. There beneath graveyard slab wooden box inside iron key, heavy as mallet once carted by St. Kevin himself.

'Tower haunted from mayhem times, Ye be so warned.'

Ignored lid warning, deviants words carved from devils anvil, enough fears with physical elements pounding. Erin's isle astride fickle oceans nothing predictable all things fluctuate. Land of thousand weathers, no weatherman can predict. *Sure they only have a go, even with fish forecasts. Confusing us all.*

"My dream come through, get me up there. Bring your whiskey share spirits with souls departed. We'll be dried have a hooting hoollie be never afraid." *'some cursèd thing unknown must surely lurk within.'*

Abroad on land where every pile of rocks pops with fairies, pookas, leprechauns, banshee, changelings with more bally bogs to shake a shillelagh. More of them critters abroad on dark wet pastures than regular folk.

'Up the airy mountain
down the rushy glen
we daren't go a hunting
for fear of little men
wee folk, good folk
trooping altogether.'

Armed with sleeping bag and knapsack, climbed steep steps to tower door hefting stout lumber branch to gain lever, twist that hefty key. Timber door yielded atmosphere fermenting through thousand years buzzed by agitated bats and spider crazy webs. Table cloth discarded plate topped Gilly tore on hauling ass up sturdy ladder, followed cut of that fair jib, briste togail for spirited man. *Dream on, dream on hard boy, so aligned only impeded upward progress.*

"You stay down!" My plea in vain, "only need dry shelters just one night, don't need intruding on them elevations. Feck it."

Lacking caillou inspired bravado better show no fears. Natural scardy cat coward personality I'd fear of dark high places, nervous poltroon with such activities. *On river new water push old water.*

"Twitchy webs with spiders." I says. "Meow Master Pangur ban?" Ancient scribers cat, girl jeered knew her level best.

"Spiders and heights give me feckin willies." Rightly they should.

Only solution, swallowed healthy slug of hootch, headed up conkers tight fisted, as once grasped by that hefty dame from Guandong province. Never same since, got nervous.

"Water for tea will boil cold." Knew she needed her Darjeeling hot.

'A man does what he must
in spite of personal consequences,

in spite of obstacles and dangers and pressures.'

Confident I'd have King's shilling fought Turks at Gallipoli, if alive them times, if clobbered dragooned as common fodder. More likely hide down boreens in the hen house, with other turkeys eating eggs. Hiked past three pine floors arched windows exposed to elements, ears poppin breath short downpour echoed through granite cylinder. On top tatty red carpet, bare essential Van Gogh table straw chair, outside church slate roof, flat yards of dandelioned acres. Gales play that clarinet tower, strange tune by reedy lake shores, sounds once heard by St. Kevin himself. Above crude bell suspended from rafter beam, hammered pummeled crafted from bilked fir bolig iron bucket by oaken shillelagh team, rough hewn bent and tarnished. Enveloping chill huddled in sleeping bag, calor gas mantle with sparse yellow light. Crunched cheese and onion supped uisce baite, dropped angel's dram through trap door. Short orders oft neglected Nancy whisky invited back with Bells on, two of us hamper jarred giddy-giggy with only maggots tomfoolery. Laid back astro-beings heading other worldly hollering like piggies. Wiles and motions on pines her nibs had me pinned grinding sturdy pins, defiling druggies rocking rolling coming in that wee spot. Two lagered blaguards playing hell fires riotous rackets, gunga din ruckus. Nothing righteous roared between pair of us in that empty clearing between rows of trees covering hills, perturbed beasts mooing in moon lights.

High on thin air and ganja two daft birds in belfry
banging pot with spoon making right old tennis racket
mad like Pussy riots in church. Huzzar, Huzzar!
Shouting more ole, ole, ole than boyos in Jack's barmy army.
Worse than Tasmanian devils got loose in top paddock.
Gilly's stoned gaelic dirge gizmo with celli's tunes
danced her moving legs tip tap tapping skull jiggery.

Under study PTO tattooed on her ass, hammered as Noah's plank did what I was told, fllled in blank what best I could. That whole shebang I'm saying, I remember spinning tails, loved her round towers. Post coitito shouted till hoarse scarifying ponies being drenched in fields.

"Feckin bulls and heifers jumping, moving yer very arse. Norse men coming down from Dyfflin go hide yer women."

Commands rained down, evening's darkening flashing warning bells before closing time, *get yourself in order.* More booze on tap. Finish up!

"Brian, we'd better halt dumbassery mad gallivantings. God knows what we're stirring up with. What possessed us at all? We'll burn in their hell."

Gas mantle revealed walls covered with Cil Maintaen wishes, thousands listed in neat rows. Scribed by duitiful female student hands.

"Your old flame, see." Eagle-eyed Gillian.

County girls in those learning days before they determined to harness useful lives for boys or create emotional hazards for useless pilocks, or discard good ones.

"When I grow up I wants a pink pussy cat, gold fish and make men cry. Boo hoo," mocked dear Gillian.

Overload of junk ganja flowing through those veins, read dear young Noreen's dreams inscribed on ancient walls hopes to be fulfilled.

'I will world travel search for a man like my Dad, Sergeant Frank O'Boyle. We will have a family and live forever in Avoca. I will miss him terribly when he is away, never want to be without him. Mam and Dad are apart now but I wish they would love again.'

Marry her cop live in old Avoca, wished we'd not intersected in those travels, I'd never be her garda-angel.

"Let me try see if we can be welcomed in this old place, I've cantations." Gillian whispered, "make our amens proper, keep me with the angels."

Sat on blanket tits swaying nipples erect with cold air, orange ribbon gathered unruly hair. Almighty lightening storms armed from all directions. Focused as demented mechanical Turk shifting motion wild fists flying. Jerking, swaying like Jolly Jack Tar at penny arcades, this islands dark Rosaleen twisting twigs.

"Wicklow's figured out this immortal portal betwixt and between kept for them damn selves," she says.

Damn tight lipped bastards with our secrets. Pale ditch man stay in your place.

"Check point culchie no jackeen required."

Lady knew the jig, her voice rough amplified echoed rock walls.

"I saw lofty raven,
we breath here this night
sister and brother
guardin of stone of time.
We know each other,
come forth from dark domain,
make a bridge across
tonight, with two of us."

Noreen's sean-nós dirge followed ways of rapid ranted rosaries rhythmic burren shawlies, Tibetan beaders mantra in sync.

"A bhui le Ri na bhfeart go bhfeiceam
Muna mbeam beo 'na dhiaidh ach seachtain
Grainne Mhaol agus mile gaiscioch
Ag fogairt fain ar Ghallaibh."

Beyond my focals to comprehend know enough to shut me gob, mother Eireann would approve this soulful creature occupying our mystical space.

"Come forth!" she demanded. "Keep the light shinning they're rushing in use energies to manifest and reveal. I'm pushed back and elbow, waves like storms from a strong sun by cuis farraige wave after wave."

After caterwauling she fell back, floored with wanton carry ons flaked out under sleeping bags, warm as turf fire knowing mad energies doing locating, hugging against her like wall paper, having dreams of wet spaces.

'light thickens, and the crow
makes wing to th' rooky wood.
Good things of day begin to droop and drowse
whiles night's black agents to their preys do rouse.
So, prithee, go with me.'

It was tapping that woke me, persistent like flapping in a wayward breeze unnatural rhythm then impatient ringed finger on rare wood. Shuffling feet as if odd creature stirring from darker side. Right as I gives Gilly elbow nudge bleeding rafters bell starts shaking, clanging slamming on tinkers bucket with iron hammer, deafening to folks in tower cone. Each strike banging my skull vibrating jelly cranium innards, intense thousand old hen solid penny coins clattering high mass in Procatherdral with Keith Moon winding pile drivers in metal band.Very air vibrating in pale light intent on bemaunching molars.

"Gilly wind's up right doing me frickin head in. I'll stop the damn thing, else we'll get tinnitus."

She held me back, keen African eyes cutting through shaky gloom of cluttering moon beam.

"Hold your horses, Brian we've a visitor."

Demented furry varmint squirrels through an open tower? My head cowering under cover nothing to offer but rabid fear itself.

"What ye saying? I've no glasses on."

Squinting in darkness something moved by the table, too blind to focus foggy gossamers in the midst.

"Specky four eyes no time for tomfooleries, time of times has come measure up! Take up your head sure we've roused Quasimodo."

I sees shadow arm moving the bell rope.

"Hoodie fella," she whispered.

"Oh jeez 'tis monk Malachy with warning the village."

Cowl head shadowed hermit fella in tall house, tale once told by Noreen, them days figured she was only winding me up.

"Killed in 709 by norse sliotar thru' window, many Viking slaughtering in this space."

Through the monk with me thick specs saw granite bricked wall, such vision not expected with robust parish monastic. No trick of light, no propane intoxications. No dodging that spirit.

"What does he want?"

"Worries with enemies from North ways, fir an cloicteach keeper of the inn bangs a fecking bell or borhan, warns villagers of any invader yokes. Searching for bad reputes. Thinks you're Barbary river pirate and me from fjords."

Ice and fire baby, rock Kasbah and Reykjavik.

"Tasked to warn living souls, Paul Rivere of them days."

"We've to account for sins, belligerent coming here with all your nonsense." she says.

She the one busy interfering rousing from mystics, never was I comfortable with those spooky activities. Although found comfort with Aunt Tassy in Howth house.

'Man should not know of God's private affairs.'

"Cloicteach maybe wants tariffs for our lodgings."

Villagers would understand monk blowing ghostly gaskets, strangers out habitating where they'd no damn business. Like weekend yokes wandering on Howth head.

Clanging on each toll,

get out, get out, get out.

Clang-clang, icy foreigners.
clang-clang, Africa woman
barbary barbary bang bang.

Cometh that hour and one brave lass blanket wrapped walked steps to cowl man. Deal with our whole shebanging.

"Tell Malachy stop clanging, no knives needing sharpening." Says I in bearla.

"I've maybe to save our very souls. See what he needs."

Enveloped by dark figure, strong brave face close to hoodie fella. Gilly rapping gaelic as sagart mutters latin, Malachy by female company agitated, strident bell tempo signaled distress, effin and blinding in my head, incessant punk rhythm all abandoned. That monk never seen the likes, his day broads were snow whites, likely never had his way with one by any hue, not on his balliwick. Malachy's arm pistoning harder, blaring bell noise thru'out breath of that sunken valleyed land. Saw her as Eve leading only to temptation on pitted rotted road to hell. Powers she held o'er me never worked on old Malachy, never taken in by tricks of her trade, them wicked palavers keeps me beholden. With me bags full.

"Malachy no bell, peace with icelands many's the year." I heard in the bearla.

Rightly saintly monks don't cotton much with buxom birds sailing with marauding pirates. Cowled figure swung back an arm and she goes aflying, flippin heck noggin over heels and lands sprawled in barebones chair. By same miracles she and chair do flipping summersault with she sprawled on that bubble bum. Floored like punch drunk gurrier KO'd at north side bar fight. Babbling though flummoxed gibbled gob gaelic still flowing, flashing stars she was seeing through those flicking moon beams. Not counted out but no más stay in your corner woman, enough for me. Heart thumping arse naked knob nobbing steered clear of old bell ringer, picked her nibs off ragged tacked carpet.

Donnybrooks lakeside fair old tumble rumble,
once St Kevin himself shoved quare one in nettles
arse over backwards as writ in our annals.

Covered her head and tail with burka blanket, abundant provoking assets with breasts barely out of sight. Hell's clapper bell quiet, silence reigned ringing only in my ears. Then I hears cars, pubs emptied farmers dispatched bad seeds about wide boys charlied up, fir boligs abroad on land of saints and scholars. Malacky's job done for valley of villages, hob nailed soles, drunken army afoot protect old turf. Feared empty bed boyos, dander's and cock up, man with no lady always wanton dangers. Head bangers, wild oafs sowing mischief's couraged with belly full of beers, constant heart hammering goings on, clanging commotions echoed as they'd gathered below. Ladder shaking heavy man's boots pounding like dragoons coming. Cultchie radar boyos on red alert for Dyflinn jacko's smacking a jackeen would be right craic. Where scribes copied on vellum Greek works my hide would be taught a lesson. No place worse than tower for hiding, trapped we'd get turfed out. Culchie has it for jackeens forever be it so.

Indicated a silent zip it to shocked Gilly, her focals already proved foolhardy with lumps and bruises, fine exotic lass on board these lads need not know. One fellow pushing trap door, hard task seeing I was lying with my arse, yammering I'd violated their space. Through crack in the plank spied contorted face of Cathal Sweeney, once tried to pinch my bird now out hunting on a lark. Big mouth with crocodile smile.

"Take a hike farmer or boiling oil on your head," I warned Cattle. "Away to bed tosser nothing to see."

Continued pushing mutters and cursing, aimed high beam flash light in fellow's eyes.

"Listen lads I'm garda Big Jim Larkin from Dublin castle, few of us partaking sheltering from inclements. We were above on Devil's glen surveillance pursuant for drug gang doing shenanigans. Take off now be aways home, I'll have youse done for salts and batter. With infrareds we have youse car number plates, all be arraigned in Mountjoy by morning if yeas persisting. We're active following enquiries, don't be interfering right now bunch of rubbernecker rednecks violating laws."

Heard gibberish louts hollering from windows to fellas below, grumpy lads dangling wrong ends of the mental bell curve.

"It's fecking Dublin coppers, take off home." No craic here.

"Only mighty fierce burst of winds bell got loose rattling now dismantled. We'll be gone first lights, better away off home bang the missus. If you block us I'll see you'll be done for garda kidnapping. Strung up on College green, we're loaded try your luck boys. Be hero."

Bald head backed down my crack prevailed. Fair dues.

"You'd need to be keeping your gobs well shut we're sleuthing out. Cracking down on tomfoolery."

Drink wearing off legs tired, they'd not be hanging around. Skeptical maybe, leave it to beaver. With them driving away I shouted.

"Youse stickybeaks could not hit cow's arse with long necked banjo."

That night still shaking wrapped around Gillian, protection from bitter wind. Stalwart Gilly insisted we stay put what with copious drink and drugs partaken, being done in by spirits. After caterwauling now silent like two buck eejits dark shadows gone, drifted into wary sleep. That morning down on tower's second floor, Y fronts discarded having desperate morning pee, styrofoam cups filled to brim. Gilian kicked me off the floor above to take care of obligations. Ancient monks never built a can, they'd not discovered Tommy Crapper's ballcock. So early no living soul save steeds of field, ears picking up stomp and whinny, nostrils flare manes shaken like teenage girls, later human beasts will ride them. With aid of early morning hard on considered jet flow arching through stone opening but figured disrespectful in celestial space, checked if way was clear to throw warm styro contents on bushes below. No wretched Vikings gathered to be trench coat drenched. Following that emergency a morning fag, gazing at hazy drizzles faint promise of sunshine. Optimistically wondering if I'd juice for another round with Gillian, double shifting lazy sac, *from soft clay she could make pots.* Images of brown nipples dancing in my head, Ys straining to a T also desires for county inn fry up with black and white pudding. Bedeviled by breasts and breakfast an ass between bails of straw drooling and jonesing on those fronts. Lo and behold spied coming through the hay field one and only Mrs Noreen, she with her high stern gob. Knew immediately it was her when my heart skipped too many beats without the paddles. *Sashiburi (long time no see)* muttered my very words. Bold Noreen carrying roses, red cape covering head, pushed the gate to enter graveyard. Come in I didn't lock no gates for you '*gin a body meet a body comin thro' the glen.*' On she went strolling paths between stones, close by she walks legs so smooth to touch.

"Sometimes a woman comes across the grass,
bare-footed, with pit-patterings scarcely heard,
sometimes the grazing cattle slowly pass,
or on my turf sings loud some mating bird.
Oh, plotting brain and restless heart of mine.
What strange fate brought you to so strange a
shrine?"

How Noreen could steal from lads their very souls, envy all not tormented by thoughts of her.

Her soul in her eyes, heart on her sleeve,
more precious to Wicklow than blubber in Samoa,

nonsense in Inuktitut, girl's bare bums in Ipanema,
Polish blonds by red lit Hamburg. Required.

"Brian burn a spiff," Gillian called as I climbed the ladder back, from beneath covers a crocked arm raised. "I'm that disjointed, light me with fire. Jah?"

"Okay I & I rastafari."

Shared that toke and from an opening watched married lady heap roses on a Dad's resting place.

"Come lay down otherwise away with Morpheus in dreams with lads from long boats." Mellow Gillian warned. "I've learned how they folks came from Africa on planks of hard wood, I've bruises to show."

Malachy and mise with rough housing shared that blame. Restless, surrounded by pine, still needed see wood. That is my girl.

"Having juice hang on, hold your horses I'm your cocksman."

Stoned, sat with cheese crackers and mi wadi, feeling need for Daniella and those Brazilian Rio frog potions. Just gimmie, gimmie, gimmie. Only on my last legs with her.

"You're worst lover I need you again," heard muffled giggling. "Later we've to go to a hotel fry up breakfast a real bed, leave these friars to their worlds."

"It's quiet no one around." Lied as Gillian lay waiting wood in bush. "Only pine cones falling on needles."

Shivering Noreen sat on a wooden bench short hair tied with a red band, sunlight that morning was cold. Sometimes early worm watches the bird, felt like a CCTV camera following her from on high. Guilty low life acting the maggot, *'watcher of visitor not listener from tower window sill'.*

Nearby nags not spooked expecting ginger to pony up treats, she fed carrots from brown bag, white tailed rabbit waited his turn. Curses for them horses in fluffy's mind, they'd scoff the lot. Amid brief periods of early sun, tower shadows reached across. Noreen wrapped her coat tight and lay back on the seat seeking warmer rays, close to her Dad sharing precious silence. Finally stirred plucked flower from the bunch and wandered to older parts of tranquil space. Searching she found the grave of J.P. Brennan where she placed a red rose. Noreen heard from me about my romantic grandfather, damn cold Avonmore did him in from fly fishing. *Back then in Ireland everyone had to push cart.*

From my family history
his father a stowaway
from Southampton
had shy disembarked
the Titanic in Cork
twist of faith for me
on that port of call.
Our bodies hold reminders
of those folks never met
we are never all alone.
That our children carry on
for carry on is all we do,
and be Johnny hit the spot.

Sure Joseph approved plaintive waif gifting red rose that morning, had big effect on me crying for roses, tears of nostalgia.

Wandering eye in his prime
in or out that pine box.
Memories of long ago klapper babes
giving good time kiss at the Gaiety.
Collinade girls in Milltown
taking care of business
behind shadows of Glenmalure.
Cha cha cha,
bottle of stout at the Barn

on the hill, off on the motor bike
Sam browne belt for waders
with fly fishing in Carlow.
Baskets of bright tomatoes
spuds from Tipperary blacksmith farm.
Whocheecouhce,
lot of bright sparks resulted from his doing
job well done thanks for memories grandpa
no child left behind.
Yeah, yeah, yeah, yeah,
we took care of things in our time
from Carnaby street beyond Y2K.
Glad I lived miniskirt times,
Mamamia, I said that Mamamia.

Noreen took out her mobile and immediately wondered if by any remote chance that was for me, then with my phone vibbing in my pocket. Noreen that early morning thinking I was across in Howth. Good vibration togaill in the briste as she clicked off and departed through squeaky rusted gate. Noreen moved slowly no spring in her stride, she and Eria suffered from defeat? I'd gained a jaunt in my gait.

'All are keen to know
who'll sleep with bold Noreen
all Noreen herself will own
is that she will not sleep alone.'

Little red riding hood parked on the road and not spied my old tub in field beyond, later I checked her message.

"Brian wanted to say hi see how you were doing, nothing profound you know me. Hope to talk soon."

With dueling bangjoes playing in my head made love to Gillian, still her wildebeest, her hungry gnu.

'Hope to talk.'

For what?
Coffee in Bewleys?
Dire cake on quays?
Be castigated for sins
worse than
teetotaler on Hogmanay.

Had Bruce come cropper on road to Courtown blasted by farmer cuckolded with wifey getting Wicklow gold milked in hay shed? Had my hell angel touched ground by Tír na nÓg? Bruce dating Miss Borrzer boobs nearby Bullock? Feeling annoyed with this Mrs Walsh stop yer messing with me karmas. Never interested in yo-yo'er women, like Studebaker don't know if tis coming or going. Odd ball Noreen kissed all on billard green neither did she play by rules that coileen played with too many red balls, getting snookered. As we departed the tower wandered to grand-pops pay due respects, knelt and said an 'Ave', sure he heard soft tread above. Happy he would be I avoided hoosegow or pan handling, now knew my hands were full. Cleared stone mason carvings, headstone covered by green moss. Picked the rose, pricked by thorn and claret blood spilt, old man checking see if I was related with doggerel haired celts fellas never for sure.

"Passed away long time ago favoured pint by O'Sheas in Clonskea. Green fingers put red rose under his hat took tram from Milltown, platonic affair with woman in civil service on Stephen's Green." I told Gilly.

Buddists tell 49 days death to re-birth.
Same as lent, I'd give up a second life.
One life, holiday in Cuba but I'd no go again.
Stay on Vatican's plan, Heaven's gate or hell,
reincarnation's never for me, Brothers banged on that.

Drove to Avoca checked into b and b Peader Fergusons's bungalow on Dublin road. In the parlour we hit breakfast buffet, crunching buttered turnover toast. Navigated strict paths of white linen sheets cut to save 'deep pile' red carpet, place smelled of fried eggs and Jeyes fluid.

"Exhilarated can't believe what happened. Did you have a son pass over? Brian?"

"Yes."

"I saw him smiling."

"Three years ago. Paulie got sick, we all tried very hard. But it was too late."

Horrific experience go on living. Suffering.

The blight man was born for what I mourn for now waiting, my turn made easier.

"Pretty boy handsome dark hair."

Pushed on all buttons when confused, got secrets revealed.

When you lose a son
God puts out a different road
a spiritual journey
different than before.

"Mother was Chinese from Guangdong province, fine lady, fine lad."

Infused with great joy for I do believe in angels and lost souls.

"My Canadian son would be here by this desolate place?"

"They're together."

Look after my son old man, I've still some days to pass.

"Children pass before parents create hair pin loop, eventually together. River takes flight to sea of souls. So Paulie is waiting."

That boy Paulie away in mystics always and forever young, on one day I will pass over from this place, and tear this wall between us.

My son passed on
I'm still here sort of.

He knows unknowable
about God before me.
Maybe he whispers things
voice appeared in my head
I know who that is.
There's a place that's not here
that he has made clear.

"You never mentioned anything? You and Noreen both lost kids."

'Thoughts that do often lie too deep for tears.'

"Away in Canada where I left those memories, had to all that's too forever. That's past no longer, my task is done."

Except down all the days to always regret, never allowed to forget. She gifted her vision of smiling boy, something from beyond was near. Felt glory in my peaceful heart, beag la eile over there. I was floored our cosmos cracked, glimpsed forbidden mansions of things not yet to know. Me and Noreen once traveled on that Damascus journey.

"I'm drained," she said so I was.

'*Death must be so beautiful. To lie in the soft brown earth with the grasses waving above one's head and listen to silence. To have no yesterday and no tomorrow. To forget time, to forgive life, to be at peace.'*

None of which I agree, dear Oscar. Due respects.

After breakfast lots of clattering dishes, bed room close to kitchen, heavy delph by dozens getting washed rinsed and stacked. Through ear buds listened to Enya singing 'If I could be where you are' lapsed to almost twenty winks. On feather bed we slept away, lost my fear of dying that tower night, forever believe violins play in heaven that divil plays the fiddle.

'When hearts lie withered
and fond ones are flown,
who would inhabit,
this bleak world alone

soon may I follow'.

Is there God?
Are you with kidding me?
Every life a miracle.
We're from two big bang
bouncy strings, life as fertile egg.
To live, as photon flies
minutes from nuclear monster,
born in peace full-time
bare years from Evil man
for a life given to me
yes caught a bouncing ball.
With dis life. So far.

CHAPTER 19

Later that afternoon refreshed wandered streets antique shops of Avoca, bought hifalutin wooden horse and high tea with buttered scones at Olivia's 'Cat's meow' café with sweet strawberries. Still needed to calm down from our lost souls brouhaha.

"So where does she live then this Noreen?"

"Don't know, somewhere about. Must be." I imagine.

"She never contacts you?"

"Jimmy crack corn and I don't care, she's away married with nice life. Them's folk no longer on my bailiwick." Capiche?

Under the table I put my hand on Gillian's leg, safe in that harbour Dalkey days be damned forever. Me and Ferrice on the 'movin on' train journey through happy valleys, by silver streams and no melancholy airs.

"You still keep her letters."

Yeah, delivered when her male man.

"Locked up."

Meant to secure when gandering gawking Gilly goes plonking poking around.

"Brian you left the key, I like the poetry for her." Laughing, even shed her few tears.

Mott reading craven words for another mott. Mon Dieu, world misshapen without proper order in affairs of men. *Sulcus intermammarius, mons venus, bootees maximus and love letters. Why reveal such private parts?*

"Once she threw glass of rum and coke, lost me computer kits and caboodle."

Land of rising sun babes zapped by sugar cane, now only in dreams.

"So you often came to Wicklow with her?"

"Naw only a few times." Too few times.

"Noreen can leave here no more
feral Rialto youth, panda in Chengdu
Pyongyang Kims. Capiche again?"

"Show me where she lives."

"Nil fios agum babe."

Left the café spoke to red haired young one in Quiky Mart next door. Got choc ice, vanilla ripple wafer with directions, surely she knew me.

"Make a dogleg turn at triangle. Glendown ye'll see their sign with a crocs head. Sure you just missed Noreen out getting messages and fags. Menthols."

Holy smokes, *ciggeregrets.* Noreen?

Little later afraid Gillian would hear heart thumping as we drove past 'Walsh's' sign engraved in wood, topped with gator skull. Pretty bungalow to have and hold long legged barmaid from New Orleans, Brucey rocked her boat moved across the bay took ship to shore. Gave the house a bitter look their den and carry on, Noreen killed the thing we had so losers be weepers.

'Then felt I like some watcher of the skies when a new planet swims into his ken.'

Garden filled with many shade of bush, chilly air red roses blooming. Neighbour's worn grass and swings for kids.

"It's for sale."

Holy moly, Nantucket fucking with sand buckets.

"Coors beers blimey," says I dealing with shagging mentals.

'For Sale' sign in bushy yard yet they'd only arrived in that 'hood, must have gotten bigger piece of Wicklow's pie? Sergeant with arms on the make? Carvery's queen cutting thinner slice?

"Call the agent take a peak," she said, and for what benefits? Pray tell? For me?

Never miss a trick,
cat's curiosity
nose to ferret
hawk eyes.
Sherlock a piker
compared to nosy parker.
Smart X ray eye
see to bone
what's going on.

"Gillian give me a break don't need to see the likes."

Not out of the woods yet. Spare me burdens only wanted to be pegging back to Dublin. A lad with tough beefs, nerves not connected by steely wires. Somewhere temptress Noreen puffing fags.

Chardonay, oh my sweet chardonnay. Go ye down my gullet and make this world feel shinny again. Like always do. Keep picking fat grapes under Cali sun good Mexicana man. Gratias. Do all you can hope you get a decent cut of my ten bucks and don't send you packing. Sometimes take a fill of Niagara tasting. Do prefer wine to roasted caffine. That don't take you no place and no shut eye. What can a pour man do? When cup is empty and bottles are so few?

"Have a nose around see how Wicklow girls live," her daft demand.

Live by rules, sling
smooth leg over

a fortunate fellow.
Lots are doing it
made life interesting
these women seeing how
God designed them,
rare genius with spare rib.

Hand Darwin all creation, platypus ducks, coyotes and polar bears, ostrich feathers, jelly fish and beetles. Okay with aardvark, armadillo and asparagus, even Archaeopteryx as well. But broads assembled by the big man not left to chance, had them on potters wheel for rotations. Nothing random with those shapes, but them creatures shipped with no manual, set in motion for life's commotions. Many delivered short a few screws, same way with book cases. Fair enough, keep fellas busy puzzled for generations. That's what they are for.

You'd say God artiste with sand grains and galaxies.
But hanging balls? Ugly pus? Limp dick? Varicose veins, tortured colons
spaghetti arteries, dementia junctions, bald heads, grey beards and sciatica.
All to plague us higgledy-piggledy with chancy graphic designs? Why?
Oh why? Does it have to be so? So much pain on Sagan's blue planet.

Gillian called the auctioneer.

"Looking for a pied-â-terre."

Proper West Hampstead touch of class.

"Fabulous, that'll be grand Walter," she said.

Pseudo foxrock Dublin, soon she'll do culchie's shuffle.

Suspicious glare sly wink knowing nod,
sparing words costs quids worth.
Never look jackeen in the eye
eternal suspicion of invaders
fair play given their deep valley.

"We can see it, no one's at the house," she told me.

Half hour later geyser arrived huffing puffing in the diesel, rotund gut, ridiculous handlebar moustache with pork pie hat. More chins than China, corduroy jacket smelling of booze and BO, transfixicated with Gillian, Black Magic chocolate with cherries, she would never hold that against him.

"Clutch dodgy on the old auto, I put out the sign this morning youse have first dibs."

"Need to get delux Studebaker cruiser more robust." Says I to blank stares.

Figured I was foreign with weird irritating accent, let Gillian deal with him, Wicklow man familiar with a surly kind.

"My husband's a writer looking for something quiet."

Gave my customery nod, being busy composing.

"I like them horror stories," Walter says panting.

"My husband writes horrible," says comic Gillian, close to the mark.

Got a right laugh from the Wally man.

"Penny dreadfuls," I says, "half priced. Do illustrations, can draw flies."

On the door I sees a sign taped to the paint.

'Remove Boots, Owner.'

Sock it to 'em baby, carpet saved black shoe polish by her red red rose.

"Clean and nifty, woman's touch always key. Does the trick we know that." Fella gave a wink.

Worlds colliding feeling strange entering their retreat, mesmerized seeing wherein my demons gamboled and festered, King fans at Graceland would ken as replica Cavern voyeurs in Scouseland.

Only full of their lives turf blackened fireplace middle of room.
Gaudy Med souvenirs, in skimpy togs. Gordon Bennett !
Photo of our lady in grotto, my grotty lady in Pyrénées
where she had a knees up. With him.

Given checkered past chess board she pilfered, now my stale mate.

Snap of Jimmy with parents on a pirogne in marshes.

Living room wall regaled with framed pics as they arrived horse and carriage to church. Ex-bride of Ferrice Randall Pickens pretty in white, watching dark clouds over head.

"Handsome husband," heard from Gillian as they went to investigate the kitchen. Irritated I sat on black faux leather naugahyde sofa, repelled by scents of Bruce. Gas bill lay on coffee table addressed to Mrs. Walsh, beside a bowl of grapes. Seedless they were.

"Connemara marble tops all brand spanking new," says Walter, grinding peanuts in worn out molars. *Cracks nuts like shower elephant.*

"Needs renovation, I prefer some bright orange mixes. Sure the county is already so with green, can we spray paint or get sandpaper busy?" Gillian jerking bulbous gent having gas time with divilments.

"Anything's possible," ruddy face bewildered by coffee lady. "Many honest crafts man about to assist, ready with days labours."

"Any colour as long as not white."

My two brown cents, after those Canada winters.

"I'm off white these days."

Savouring tower good times. Took slug from shelf Jim Bean, rough waters from Tuckasegee river. Did not approach master bedroom where Bruce lay with my babe.

"So why they selling?"

Brazen nosey not even entitled to rake over them coals.

"Separation, that's the affliction these days." Pistachio gobbler says. "Scourge on county folk, no room for priests with today's orders. Progress, so our betters do tell."

Daniela's older broad wisdom coming to pass. Something crocked the relationship, smart money blaguard shiocana boy the perp.

"Mrs Walsh will be here shortly we'll have the cup of tea. Friendly woman born and county bred, she'll be one to tell youse things here abouts. She left kit-kat." Desperate to get stuck in, then hum from garage door.

"That'll be bean an ti come abaile now."

Panicked I was, freaking nut job, green around the gills.

"Out back Brian, I'll pick you up down the road." Gillian whispered. "Hide in the greenery." *Then how will you see me?*

'Bring us that biscuit luv.' Indicated that delicious crispy wafer.

Scampered past large scattered rocks and stones, love's labour's lost unfinished testimony to rocky times.

Chapeau l'artiste!

Came a cropper with garda

life not cast in iron surprise for her.

Better stayed with my Castle brand

aluminium pots, and polished stove.

Slunk through backfields, conflicted with life's difficulties, waited on my arse behind trees by roadside ditch. Mind's eye seeing black-white, green to brown eye, same rice but different bowl, well they knew about each other. Thirty minutes later Gillian appeared with the car.

"That's ridiculous, off Kilburn high road you'd get a lovely fixer upper semi for half price," she said.

Head for Jubilee line, nail down one bed room over hardware in Westbourne, share loo with artful dodgers.

"Noreen looked sad never wanted to leave. He's gone off, I'd a poke around the bathroom she's on the vallium."

Let her rabbit on, knew more than ever I would have told.

"She's pretty, her eyes. You just want to hug her."

Storm and strife on the ball and she without Jackson Pollock and Brighton rock.

"We'd be great friends, sure I was going to tell I stay across in Howth."

Stared daggers at Gillian, in a pinch she did fill Noreen's drawers, now tight squeezed.

In dis life keep eyebrow and beard separate.

"Walter said the bank owned most of the house, she's moving off to somewheres in Bray."

In a nutshell, feather pillow stained with tears, them were no crocs.

"I hope there she's one happy bunny."

We drove away contemplations beckoned quiet pint for buck eedjit. 'Be happy nursing pints in snug without intrusions'. Woman moved house as rain forest ants move nest, she had expected life of jamboree. Now on her lonesome, financial burden in hedgerows. Read Good book baby learn to forgive decent fellow, proven not guilty only knowing, not begating.

"In the bedroom there's a photo of you with a young kid on the night stand. Fishing by a river."

"Young Jimmy Mississippi."

Didn't wish to know more about that from her.

"She still carries a torch for you."

"To burn my arse."

In rear mirror saw different light reflected from Sugar Loaf, sometimes my guardian angel protects from harm. Noreen alone wasted time with immature oaf, introduced to fertile county seducing farmer's daughters swaggering in sheds on hay bails. Milk, cheese and floral honey in their pastoral Wicklow world. Fresh-faced girls never tarnished by roaming on Bourbon Street with pearl tooth or sunk by Tuckasegee bourbon or entangled with cajun river denizen Ferrice Pickens. She'd took her fox to hen house place full of birds, her cock up got his cock up. *Maybe don't open noodle shop on noodle street.*

"Dumb ass bitch all for nowt." Mumbled deep throat.

She missed me? Maybe she missed me? Doing daisy chains, not dandelions.

Stopped off at Roundwood tavern. Entering the old pub Gillian raised many a 'bed-room' eye from local lads, we sat in a corner near the door. She happy to be out and about in those hills, seeing as her dad a highlander. While gulping shepherd's pie YR sauce and green peas observing as is my want, needed energy restored Gilly being organ grinder, stare at me tits do monkey tricks.

"Spud grandest food in all the world. Mashed fried, baked crisped roasted or boiled. Lashings of butter and sauce, can take a fancy to a stir fry but love my spud."

"Mr. potato paddy all everything mashed in a pie, all you want is your brown sauce. My efforts lost in vain. Me with searching ferreting mushrooms, fermenting yeast and spices. Only me Dad was right, all for yer bangers and mash."

Short order back end of the pub group of bar flies, Bruce Walsh smirking lad barnacle blond on his arm with that reputation. Wherever he ended up in the world armed with his gang of useful idiots to kiss his blarney arse. Noreen was correct penguin and polar bear, that opposites we were. Sergeants carry on his maggot pack was back, hail fellow well met, shinny flower surrounded by green leafs.

"That's Walsh so fill in rest of the tale," I indicated to Gillian.

"In the flesh!" She says.

Tin-horned braggart, never gave tip of the hat, dark shadow for his world. As I ordered beer and 7 Up bar man offered culchie's nod.

"Out again for the day?" He says, starting awkward rap.

"Aye for the drive."

Forked over cash, notes and coins.

"Did youse enjoy your night in the tower?"

Anger all over the fellow, maybe seen me parked motor or had robot camera situated on the pines.

"Rain fierce with the tent," excruciating alls I felt, getting battered.

Busy protecting his turf from divots like me, jackeens sticking snouts where they'd no business. If he got me up that tall pole I'd be debollixed, pair of bruisers pummeled on bony ribs, sucking Cow and Gate sustenance many year. Always with fears of violent boyos in boonies if they'd all piled on. Out top window on the gurney and Gillian wailing by stone wall and me lowered by crane.

'Accident in the tower', explained back pages of Glen Da Lough Press. 'Uisce baite taken, took terrible hard tumble, local lads rescue. Lucky man to be alive. Thanks to the gang Murphy, Kelly, Byrney, Macs and the O's.' Fierce steep on them tower steps. Trespassing disturbing spirits, witchcraft and key theft charges pending. Sergeant Tommy Wafer investigating. Drug dealing suspected, from the butts.'

So wanted to preach to them Roundwood folk.

"Okay up your creepy tower so whats? No Pagoda. I've been up Eiffel and Toronto CN, that thing in Osaka, Cork's four faced liar, WTC in it's hayday pomp and Nelson's pillar. Paid my silver tanner, poor Dublin's not been the same. Made from Wicklow finest granite, should have fixed the stump charged trupence. Bunch of pillock bowsies from the north knocked it down, our very own pillar funded by every upstanding property owner citizen of the city."

Many's a bird met at the pillar
meet there no more.
Sinn féin philistines, need a celtic
Kazimir Malevich paint Black Square
for O'Connell's street, not aspire much.

Downed half lager and pushed car keys to Gillian.

"You're raising chicken farmer's cocks."

"Incoming," Gillian warned, rolled her eyes, giving white 'fish belly' eye.

Blondie walked past on way to spend a penny, buxom lass fertile hips make eggs like chicken. Tall drink of water never sized manicured polished nail in rubber boot nor stepped in cow pats.

"Blinded need shades," Gillian laughed. "I'll bet she tastes all lickedy minty."

Idle miss from das fatherland not trampling hay fields nor cleaning pig sheds, face that could freeze and make sharp edges on icebergs. To sink ships.

"Reminds me of priest at forty foot."

Reeked of expensive hand bag, more silver spoons than located in aunt's dresser. Too cool for cucumber, hard work for defrosting. Frostbite for old zucchini, either with comin or goins. Bruce had to pick on my mott, took advantage of stressed time no idea of mayhems caused. With plank of hefty wood whack him upside that noodle, afraid I'd miss with my sucker shot then battered and arrested. That he stole my babe no judge would care in Hibernia's 'alright jack' culture. Hauled to Mountjoy another slammer lag in Gillian's life.

'Crazy recluse Noreen dumped him, mad bastard.'

"You're thinking about her."

Prison named *mountjoy* to be well feared.

"We came here for chicken pie."

"Are you surprised by the divorce?"

"It's leap year."

Indifferent shrug being so Mr. Smug. Minds eye leaping longer than Bob Beamon, maybe betrayed too much longing, so maybe did she.

Wicklow girl can't deliver no stork her albatross, even field mouse noodle would ken.

Bruce once blinded by green-eyed babe entangled in emotional dementia, fair dues. But Noreen had young Jimmy and that was it. Bruce sees fathers playing with their kin, garsuns running fields catching lizards, honey bees, fish and eels, jumping dams in streams. Bushy trees and flowery plants do not play games or win dancing competitions or make homemade cards at last minutes for Father's day.

Plants don't say 'hi dad' or 'bye dad', and that's what we need. Holy See L'Osservatore Romano would unfetter fecund Bruce make an end Noreen's unfruitful liaison.The man's seeds rightfully yearning to fertilize catholic souls, icy blond eager to make beds for sour krauts. Gilly took us over the mountains as I dreamed, dilemma of photons bouncing off mirrors, no enlightenment for dark windy roads. Gillian dropped off at her flat in Chapelizod, I'd not stay on that night.

"Brian sort yourself out." Fix that doggerel brain.

Tired she was with fresh mountain air, kindhearted woman made a sandwich to take to Howth. Chopped scallions, sweet tomatoes, cauliflower pickles with tasty mustard. Scottish bread cut in two with salty butter, flaky spiced ham and grated cheddar.

"I don't want you in greasy spoon chippers with fishy butties and mushy peas."

What's the matter with that grand feeding buns and fishes?

Monkey meats in Swaziland
reindeer bits in Lapland
squirrel brain in Missouri
dog days in Koreas
there I won't never go.
Only angling for dreams
of burgers at Shoeless Joe.

Desperate to munch batter fodder not weird vegetables, once bitten twice shy. Did question my feelings of proceeding to Howth alone, Noreen still with grip of alligator jaws on my ass, fool to be that fool again. Once bitten twice shy?

"I hate to think of you alone, you'll not starve."

Hugged, kissed and let me away.

"Brian thanks for taking me to Wicklow, you were right about that Glen Da Lough. So spiritual by the tower, I know more who I am. More than evers."

On drive home my Wicklow horse sitting pretty on the passenger seat, realized I was still galloping at the races, unsure of my mind. Noreen took that fork in her road, only ended in cul de sac down on boulder road, exhausting in her quests, two of us in witches brew messing with karma. Bruce has you in Avoca, hammer and tongs to burnt out embers, whole deal with parents, in-laws, new sisters, relationships gone sour. On the beat meets a trollope, now buxom blondy seated in Dalkey harbour. Woman is most dangerous creature in god's creation, not maligned shark nor black mamba, big cat or bears. As long as I decides not to go Africa or jump in monkey house in Dublin zoo likely not be mauled by hairy primates. If desperately need to see elephants, turn on the telly. Women we live with them inside the house, gain access like stealth bomber like Trojan horse, most faithfully sleep on dark nights. Of all living beings they are most likely to do us harm, by leaving they can kill.

Me mate shook my hand, at 17 his mott scarpered
to escape that pains no rocks too hard
poison pills promise only so much.
Stuck his head in an oven and kept it there
that's his motivation, boys in blue took corps away.
Okay I'd bang her in a minute but not top myself
for missing that ride, broads come and go. After all.
Post card comes from Cape Verde, dame wanting to talk
oblivious to his oblivion, she'd cook paella now 'authentic',
[matched now only by 'for heavens sake !']
her new fella now flirting on vacation with Lorena,
she made that rawkus scene by Boa Vista beach.
Called his mom in Letterkenny, could have sent a card,
that week gas bill took a hit an extra fiver.
Drunk his wine from under sink, solo. Hang in boys
or miss good parts of women 18 and out beyond.

"Bruce will you come to Lourdes?"

Started with gleam in her eye call squad car, his heart would wobble, skipping beats.

"What's up babe?"

"I was to go with Mairead but her mother's feeling poorly, sickly."

"What about old guy on the hill?"

"He'll be in the library with books, I've three days, Brucey I need excitement!"

Wished me no ill a punter in her life. Deep Pyrenees valley safe from prying eyes, on Dublin streets stressed. *Leave early spring, why sow winter seeds?*

"Should I fix flights?"

"Book 'em Noro."

Then on the plane to France.

"I had a major fight, he's that unstable."

That cool evening turbulence for my soul. These hot broads make you sweat. Noreen better stay home get library card stamped, try knitting jumpers.

Jackson Pollock, Brighton rock
tools to march in symbiotica
how they know there is a yoni?
Lots of them out there somewhere.
both care for each other.
Us the host need to find so
fix up yer mug and smile
shave, thiner better look fine.
Or waste wither on the vine.
Yes, Bonaboo fuck all the time.
Mindless, not us. Of course.

CHAPTER 20

Driving up Howth head with weather turning bad gazed on a figure, long green raincoat hunched over in wind and rain. Woman struggling on her roads passed on by thinking she looked weary in gloom and drizzle. Maybe not surprised when there was a door knock a little later. Wayward Noreen on porch folding her brolly, a wench for my works. We stared a moment it had been many months, apart from preening with high tower peering, maybe beam of light from her eyes faded. She looked forlorn tired with herself and where she arrived in life, less high minded once big shot molly star of her Milky way. Things happened in beloved county damaged by love, drenched by eternal drizzle. Bonanza day of days never done.

"Will you leave me on this stoop or can I come in from this? Plum tuckered out."

'You who are weary come home.'

Collar up maybe green around the gills. No fata morgana, more Louisian than Avocian, two faced woman like every darned female on the planet. Of course she'd know lots from old talk in village with young ones and hard men. Nothing stands still in this nook and cranny shady lady, if I knew you were coming I'd shake green rushes like

I use to do. She understood my gaze taking nowt for granted on her mission to rescue me from African lady.

Birds return to their nook
fish, eels and caribou do,
not only Wicklow green-eyed girls.
Leather back turtles, Indonesia to Oregon,
Hindu to hippy for them bad boys.
Canadians, monarch butterflies to Mexico
return changed from latin influences,
Montezuma's bugs and airport sombreros.
A mott come back to lamp on Howth head
sans fickle friends, I'd kept that flame.
Only that for two of us.

We did not hug, came close as damn to curse, turned and hung the coat warmth inhaled cherished sommelier complexities, beside aunt's sou'wester and gabardine beneath sturdy upright wellingtons. Shoo in for me.

'I feed horse on other mountain, horse is full, now come back.'

Emotions haywire as hash pipe addict, English man feeling Jules Rimet being so long apart. There was tension odd not to embrace this life of my love, high county wicky girl that laid me low. *Wacked by south paw from Grand isle.* Blind sided surely as Cassius decked old Sonny, no phantom KO.

She sat on sofa near fireplace drying hair, towel from hot press. Having a leer noticed cold plated legs back in business, apart from walking. Toes in Gillian's slippers, nice fit so far from midnight, shoe now on another foot. She sat on the couch and removed stockings, fatted calve revealed, grips on my soul. Still on hook for her.

"Your legs must be cold."

Gawking as ever, appreciated seeing curve of that knee. She with the pair, I was only needing queen for full house.

'.. stand like greyhounds in the slips, straining upon the start. The game's afoot.'

Whatever, waltz back prodigal lady. Woman give me back those bouncing balls.

Dear in head lights transfixed, mesmerized where bare legs went, maple tree sap rising. No smarter than big ole halibut to this broad men 'catch and release', only saps fellas were.

"No taxi down there, I called these few times," said she.

One peg with feet up. No second shoe to drop. Entitled shifting gears. Relaxing.

"I'm only in the door out and about, might have passed you beyond on the hill."

Fiddled with poker threw fuel for red cinders. '*Called so many times'* how many evenings waiting for them ding dongs. She'd put me through that wringer. *Wringer!*

Some might say much ado about nothing.

Ahouy, ahouy not me boyo

I'd given the chance dance their dance,

poke hard me boyo on this my la eile.

"Got the fire going to heat the place."

Always coldest bastion on that rock, now one more to haul wood, get bigger heat.

"Oh it's always comfortable and warm, Wicklow houses are more drafty," she says.

Thinking what Daniela had said 'that bitch will be back' to Howthhead.

Inner thigh birth mark red from the fire.

Dizzy with brobingnagia phantasmagorical

wanting to touch deep like doubting Thomas,

I'd mark down that twain. Pronto.

'C'mere till I tell, many tall tales betwixt those legs.'

"Mostly me and old cypress tree, give hug some evenings."

Keep a tree not bark myself. Hard bark winter tree no substitute for single man, went off to the kitchen aching from her. Feeling skittish.

'under her breast lies a mole
right proud of that most delicate lodging
by my life I kiss'd it
and it gave me present hunger to feed again.'

Beaujolais opened returned ASAP with 'Gillian' sandwich sliced radish and carrot, wine fermented from grapes crushed during our only summer together. Feeling like Millers first night with Marilyn and hat trick Hurst in '66. Noreen smoking flicking ash to embers as her hand shook could feel her sunken spirit or maybe all that jitters was just cold.

"Brian."

Our sandy footsteps brittas waves washed
but emotions engraved as letters stamped in tempered iron.
Hewn like commandments burnt in Sinai mountain rock,
Hawaiian pacific rollers could never yet them erase.

Girl on no fixed allegiance an Alsace-Lorraine women, changed commitments more than Hagia Sophia. On paper a taken woman kidnapped by hawker of Xanadu whispering false promises. Not for a second did I consider Bruce, bung things up he did that golf club manatee. As Normandy onion johnnies returning to land freed by allies, fields roughly ploughed by nasty invaders.

"Brian!"

"Fire needs turf. Right."

Lobbed briquettes cut from county bogland, buzzed not to calm down getting rights of turbary restored, sat on each end of sofa.

"I was worried you'd send me away."

Confused me with you my dear, feeling nobodies would freeze that night.

"What if I wasn't home?" I managed.

"I have my key."

Changing locks not my style, country of half door in land of thousand welcomes. Crazy if I'd stumbled on ginger head back on her pillow.

"I like the shorter style."

"It's easier in the morning," she'd changed her locks. "Bread is wonderful and mustard."

"I found a good deli, " dear Gilly.

"He has a girl friend, Caroline. Are you surprised?"

She looked with those unguarded eyes, took a quaff of wine.

"Yeah, very."

Fickle contender staring in unwanted snaps a one hit wonder, knew her story in my history.

Brucy in real pickle
lady is free to go.
Why doncha beat it?
Slapin tickle turns out.
Wedding palaver
all now quandaries
better end than fighting.
You did that when
Ferrice turned bad.
Hard feelings those he
don't have no more.
So that wheel turns.

Watching mustard drop on her thigh, reached scooped and licked. Gillian's spicy mustard warmed on Noreen's naked thigh. Blimey life is taste of hot women on my thumb.

"Starving didn't dare go to the Arms, anyway their food is truly the pits."

"They've rubbish Filipino pies, better we'd split Denny's steak and kidney with pastry."

Tried to say more but muttered too much, maybe caught the yips. That happens, yeah.

'Woman much missed, how you call to me,
saying that now you are not as you were
when you had changed from the one who was all to me'

Needed tread softly softly not mention the copper, already trashed in bitter twisting winds of her mind. Don't be remote, we both knew control by her hands.

'In peace there's nothing so becomes a man as modest stillness and humility'

"He first left two months ago," she shrugged.

Shook my head and pulled on a fag, hardly prayed now with wishes granted.

"Brian remember lunch at Mulates with club sandwich?"

Who cared about triple sandwiches and zydeco Skillet Lickers playing *It Ain't Gonna Rain No Mo?* in Big Easy town. Tell me about breaking bad with macho man, rogue cop that stole you, no less than container hijacked on Belfast road. Catch more than you could chew, didn't you? Went wrong direction like arm twist in Oz.

Why are you here?
Stick dumpty humpty back?
Ding my feng shui,
mess with me a more?
Our horse done bolted
I'm shagging another
more stable.
Don't double cross
unless saying an angelus
passing a church.
Genuflect.

Aunt Tassy would have judged his sort never suitable, down road from country mile. Better she'd trod cow pucks by Peader Brown's meadow.

"Turkey on rye," she said.

Oh mercy's sake use your loaf.

"Pumpernickel with corned beef or wheat, slice of Swiss with honey mustard side order of fries and onions. Loaded pickles hot peppers and me with hic cups. Bottle of Mateus, listen to Zideco lazy afternoon by big river. Lean back and think about taking a fine lady to my bed in heat of hazy Louisian nights."

Breath darkness down there they says. As long as men have desires for soft breasts of fine women there'll be sinning galore in that city of New Orleans and blow in Katrina be forever damned.Visited that place for carnal knowledge forever student keen on learning and improving. Often times butter face babe and bottle of porto plonk plenty enough for likes of me. Down south in a hurry. In that bang bang six shooter business always over charge, realize you might never come back. Soon enough, after leaving for home.

"Maybe Nawleens ruined us, bad spirits followed me home. Sure Mam never approved much."

Lay blame on an old river, *'he must know sumpin but don't say nothing'*. Remember waters that once nourished and formed you flowed from hills in Wicklow not stagnant Pontchartrain. Remember there's fella running around up there pulling levers directing us all. Also remember me this *'our union must and shall be preserved'* as stamped on Andrew Jackson plinth of statue in French quarter.

She ate every crumb of the 'Gillian', had a chip on her pinkie acrylic nail.

"Ferrice had a son with a twin, I was that happy. A man should have a son."

Showed me a photo, mother and child. Mighty Cajun Mama, Ferrice moved grand style, bulky but that's how they style 'em in delta richness. No silicon valleys with Louisian women in the bayous.

"Well?"

She asked all curious, with Ferris negotiations plan B, don't care if identical, it's extra. Two heads better than one, thinking alike.

"Looks like James," no freckle no spitting image.

She stared into space took deep breath, bolted her gulp of wine.

"God I'm pathetic, bb no deep sleeps."

Lonely broad needing manicure, topped her glass hungry by sea airs, fig rolls on a plate.

"Bruce started not showing up for dinner, sat in oven for hours."

"Cajun style," three legged cat cooking.

She laughed enjoying banter soon as she crossed front step knew I cared fig or two. As high arctic fishers locating open water surrounded by ice, their polynya, we too would find our way. Beaujolis most reliable ice breaker, more happy then relaxed.

"Eat with RTE, nervous not knowing what on earth he was up to. Wondering what the heck was wrong with me."

Maybe you burn birito, always hot to handle.

"She's stylish, she wears hats, went and bought a Murcielago for him."

Emperor daughter have handsome husband.

"That's a duesy, but prefer Countach. More racy for the buck."

I'd not know Lamborghini of any stripe even if walloped in the arse.

"Easy for them to cheat, never know where they are. He'd call say there was an accident Glen of the Downs, 'bunch of Dublin arse holes going to Courtown. Pissed drunk.' Then be late and sleep on the couch. Smell of a woman and never accident reports in the paper. Come on I'm not that stupid." *'A woman wailing for her demon-lover.'*

Then Bruce told her about the blond, by then he seemed to not even care or give a damn.

"I was with Mam and Patty having dinner, Redmonds in Greystones. My birthday without him."

She stopped to gather thoughts, recount difficult times.

"My worst day, they dragged me otherwise toasted cheese sandwich and late movie. Mother and aunt on my birthday!"

Thirty three years baby.

"Mam wouldn't stop how she never wanted interfering, then Brian this and Brian that. Life with my Brian was perfect according to her. You must be paying her!"

What was wrong with hill top Utopia? Those polyanna times, exasperated with this broad all because Aniky got preggers. Not with my ball and wick another man carries that ball and chain. Mucho gracias Malta hombre, not all down to me. I came late to that game.

"Bruce came over cool as mint julep and introduced her, they'd been to a film. Not a bother on him, she stood there like a Princess Grace with her arm around him.

'It was a great flick made in Ennisskerry on the streets, gas seeing those places. They needed a garda.'

That is what it came down to, bit part in her life as an extra, *relationship brief as dragon fly dip tail in calm water.* Noreen stretched out on the couch, set back on her heels, felt her warm legs to reassure, listen to yer Mammy. Cad Brucey away laying hands on cold Fräulein, so Noreen barked up wrong tree as squirrel chasing a dog. Remembered to click the blanket, warmed half mattress enough for that night.

"All I knows her father owns golf courses," deep pockets with holes.

Her finger moved slowly up and down contours of Polish glass. Penny had dropped about the copper.

"Never said a word about my birthday, Patty said the girl looked just like a ghost, so pale."

Be advised how you go limits to your snare, sisters come take it all away. Some things in life common sense prevails, *'mother wit'* as Orleans folk have it.

Don't visit Arabias any time
if you must don't stick neck out,
there are no good bootlegs,
never build church with pointed arch
don't steal cold man's snow shovel
don't honk at bikers
don't ring bells round old boxers
don't build furniture with rotten wood
don't name pig you plan to eat
don't learn to salute or square bash.
Don't drink West Virginian hollers moonshine,
only child is slow eater.
Don't dig for water by outhouse
yield to man in the white van.
Lose weight? Don't bake cake.

Remember also no human ever regretted drinking less night before.

When you lie with woman don't lie to that woman, by the way don't never fall in love with gigilo.

Quiet listening to clock chimes, solid hands on that big clock, in time she would feel that.

"Turn bells off nights with windows open bells confuse fishermen give fish time for escape, sometime leave them for company if up and about."

Stayed mum about seeing young blondy in Roundwood pub.

"Sure I was mortified, just hadn't said that much to me Mam."

She looked little girl confused, strategy commonly employed with big girls.

"I mean I lost a second husband, this does not happen to us Wicklow women," she paused. "I would think I was a good person but realize that's not true entirely, I've hurt folk."

She sat fig nibbling looking through French doors across dark sea, feeling loss like sister Eria. Consoling broads could feel sorrow with loss of men, maybe we're more than hairy chimps.

"She never liked Bruce, I was red with embarrassments wanted to scream and run. We're still paying for the wedding, I'd sell the very ring worth a few brass nickels."

Don't want monkey? Don't go in monkey forest.

I wanted to tell her how much I underestimated feelings, outside waves crashing, her fortune lady said rough followed by smooth.

"Anyways that's all for him now off with his bunny boiler."

What would tea lady do? Have a cupa Pukka pie calm down, try swap shirts with her.

"bb I love this place, I agree with Mam I've made too many huge mistakes. But so did you, you must admit that very fact! Rewind your memory on that."

She ran fingers through her short hair, despite turbulent times Noreen changed and stayed the same as albino polar bear.

"She's fed up only doggin on me."Tears rolled on freckled cheeks. "Truly need to catch myself on, things only gone cattywampus with my life."

Distracted thinking of meandering walks on bright evenings with Gillian in Phoenix park, we'd lie in grass by the monument looking back at the city, her family tradition. She'd relate dreams of a restaurant with her Dad, there I'd peal spuds and bone up on Robbie Burns.

'And I will luve thee still, my dear, till a' the seas gang dry.'

On mantelpiece Gilly left the metal box, from hot poker lit a joint once licked and rolled on ebony's thigh.

"Brian don't get sleepy." Noreen never interested in any old dope.

High as a kite sailing over sea wanted to take her in shallows off Ireland's eye, bone up and board her in surf, Mother Eireann would tigum.

"A few times I came to walk the head and sit by the church, I'd hoped to see you out and about."

Likely out on the piss
barely head above carapet
head pounding them diems
tatani style wall to wall
left sunken Titanic style
in for copper in for pounding.
Happy to wake in a bedroom
and not a jail cell, my success.
So measured.

"To top it all Bruce made a pass at Beth at the wedding, drunk but she managed to tell half the county. Bruce is leaving Garda." Tragedy unfolding for farmer's daughters.

In quiet of the living room implication hanging, bb can we start on over? Well knew to screw with emotions Noreen was searching, I represented worst of men to sleep with wife of another man. Coveting, stealing and adultery I wanted her that night, whatsoever Moses commands. Rooster go crow all night. Never considered code of men violations seeing Bruce was a rat. Don't steal money from banks and complain banks have no cash. Don't steal fellow's bird and wave adultery flags, married in ratrimony did not count on my beat. Mea culpa.

"I'm tipsy," she whispered. *At least that bottle never stopped working.*

We didn't speak profoundly reached and put my arm around her relieved of tension she reacted and hugged. There's limits to understanding, tomorrow's problems would wait. 'I'm in a relationship with Gillian' what I should have conveyed on the portal sent her off back into inclements and slept alone. Only if I lived on planet Bizarro circled by two moons bizarrets. Now wanted to lose my shirt. That night she felt warm and familiar legs stronger thanks to mountains, bog of Allen babes have flabby caboose. Well jeepers bardarbunga this sorceress conjured new tricks from somewhere going everywhichways, that chick could Katmandu. Climb in them Himalayas take peak at Chomolungma, in that cold bedroom tossed her my heater. Hardened stick, drip technique easel with brush, not easy, but that's the man I am. Had bendy Brighton rock that night, barely wits intacto. Afters with 'Danny Boy' playing Noreen singing, remembered driving in snowy Toronto, years of being away.

'come you back when summers in the meadow,
or when the valleys hushed and white with snow,
I'll be there in sunshine or in shadow.'

Accompanied by banging of rickedy plumbing, in truth pipes were calling.

"Oh Brian I often think we're strangers in this land, Tom Kelly said you've so many girl friends."

Right squealer Kelly should have mouth washed with carbolics, give it to yer quare one stop gossiping like battle ax. Feel widths of quality plastic for peat bags fat boy thick head, busy sticking his oar in everywhichways.

"Only Gillian."

"Where is she tonight?"

"Across in the city."

Gilly and two bar electric fire by her chimney in that town of chimneys.

"I don't know if you will come to Wicklow I know you've things to think about."

While thinking of dreaming, fell asleep listening to 'Amarantine'.

Day break happening one more time on Howth head, early morning feeling anxiety, confusing life rushing back.

On cliff edge wrapped in blanket, coffee with honey. Once read sperm helps broads sleep soundly, she'd be out cold. Stared at silhouette of Bray head determined to push out independently like Gibraltar. Forever more Bray kids with tight fathers will sail paddle boats, and carnies on the make, candy floss, sea weed, skipping stones and yellow beach trains. Thoughts of Grand Isle and small breasts on dark skinned Indo girl from Belize and spells she cast in my perfect world wanted to give her sandy bum in Dollymount. Brown eyes said money not her object. My patchwork life tested many waters, a soul of good fortune. Where river suddenly have bridge, someone forever hitching my horses. *Sunny boy, a sonniger junge, one Johnny on the spot.* Beanie bag with blanket on my back trying to cope, nights thinking about them in hard county beyond. Noreen's surly sayonara in morning mist, blue jeans on, off to the cop. Likely now sent by her mother to rescue her life. Would I put gas in car I already wrecked?

'Brian could buy the mortgage keep the house, there is a man still loves you. Away over there with you now.'

I could be in Aughrim, Carnew, Kilpedder or Tinahely, any Wicklow town, with family buried all about.

"Everyone would be happy if you come there." Noreen had said.

Except every county manjack but she'd control them boyos, Bruce off without bother easily as wiping cow pat from polished shoe. Noreen not treasuring photos of forgot husband, bolt from the blue, fast rubber from that soul mate. Marriage banns so fast wedding snaps got blurred, made Casanova look like a piker, speedy Gonzales gone before coming, made Henry VIII like virgin king. If a ship he'd be Titanic never finished his maiden's voyage, if a place on Repulse bay in Nunavut. But fair dues out smarted O'Boyle broad enjoyed her charms and walked away, kudos to him cock of that walk, no laments. *Next!*

By hook or by crook you can steal man's soul, perhaps like Gaul divided in parts, go through life missing what you stole. Part you never returned, part woman never knew she had, that price of love baby. Was I providing haven from a storm, love till she can find someone better, only shelter for battered wet traveller? Maybe there'd be roads not taken with Gillian, we had no commitment now me cheating with fellow's wife. Listening to 'Miss you nights,' emotional song written by Dave Townsend while his bird was away. Watched the Ferry return from England with worn souls, stressed with returning and facing gatherings and judgments. Small islands run busy ferries with worn tread marks on those oceans.

'Oh, that's an Irish voice I hear,
and that's an Irish face,
and these will come when dawn is near
to the belovèd place.
And these will see when day is grey
and lightest winds are still
the long coast-line by Dublin Bay
with exquisite hill on hill.'

Noreen happy once to see me depart our granite land to live in Orlando, sit alone in hurricane alley trailer listening to storms batter mobile home. On trails where tumble weeds meet dead ends, all options terminate in deep Atlantic.

"I heard waves and music, the song you love so well." Noreen sat with her coffee. Gathering her dressing gown nibbled croissant with marmalade, woman had tolerance from lame tossers like me. No sperm whale, my journey man tack and caboodle.

"I know I'm worse bitch altogether."

"Ah there's pair of us in it."

Held her hand and sat watching rough waves, I'd not know if that would be our farewell times.

"Let's have breakfast," I told her.

Cobbled together eggs rashers sausages white and black pudding, toasted brown bread with chunky Gilly marmalade and strong tea, presented on willow pattern. Not feeling blue.

"My favourite b and b, sure why not when it's free." she says.

No tariffs for kitty, but naught was free.
Busy washing sheets and pillow cases
rod on my back, massa day done gone.
Hombres. I won't do windows,
only apple pies, easier job.
There were costs slamming my emotions.

On the coffee table she picked the framed photo of Gillian, I'd not bothered to conceal.

"Everyone saw you with her, Walter told me you ran out of the house like it was crawling with termites!"

"Okay I was intruding didn't feel like seeing you there, Gilly saw the sale sign. She is the nosey parker."

"She knew I was sad we had a nice cuppa, after she left I heard she was with you. Do you love her?"

"Too early to tell." Parroting Deng Xiaoping on merits of French revolution.

As I ate soda bread my mind was hearing dance steps on wooden floors, seeing Gillian in kilt with gold fainne. Maybe unlike prarie voles we can have enough love for two of them creatures, that was how I felt. My head might explode in that process. When they would always get too hot to handle.

"Some Scottish guess she's a mutt, gave me a book of porno in gaelic. Imagine craiceann a bhualadh means collision of skin." I laughed, Gilly liked rough with tumble.

En garde trust and parry
touché, touché mucho.
Glide to hilt raddoppio
longsword lunge rapier

right of way. Seconde !

Noreen had to depart for Bray, with working later. At the door we hugged, felt a togail, maybe dead cat bounce given nights steamy activities, old combatants fully armed, unlike Venus De Milo. Drove Noreen to the station nothing resolved, perhaps she felt her magic worked, back on track. She left by train but still in my train of thoughts, felt like flower on silk that moment wanted her cobble stones be bars of gold.

Does nested sparrow owe oak tree rent? For the bough. I'd say yes. But what?

CHAPTER 21

Later that morning after Noreen's departure found myself back on Camden Street outside Lange's Jewelry shop, mind wandering in beadledoms. Hour later again shook Joe's firm hand a deal struck, lighter in pocket sporting springs in steps, peaceful state of mind. Not to screw up dropped ten Gs keep brown sugar sweet, keeping broads happy always worth value, life strategy of forever paying women to keep my peace proving ruinous. At this rate should now have owned chunks of African Veldt, patch of Table mountain over looking busy colours of Capetown. Zipped along streets past lady feeding two swans in Stephen's Green and students loitering park benches, listened to 'Here comes the sun again'. Passed shady trees in that park where Noreen and I spent too few warm afternoons, felt no angst was home free.

As violet Elvis on velvet everything perfect, two birds dance card. Hog heavens!

Brisked stuffy Suffolk Street crossed Halfpenny bridge, threw twenty note to traveling lady sitting on tartan blanket.

"Wish me luck." Old bean of roads for I'm time traveling, all of us on solitary journey.

"Gur a mile amait agat sir. God bless you, oh god bless you," turbulence heard in my wake.

"Get your wee bairns Cow and Gate." Commanded like amadhan ceart knowing for certain she was going no wheres.

Sitting on a bridge begging for mercies, give don't judge with your farthings pittance that spirit needs no commands. Woman clearly needs fair heat of a naggin, not exposed to nagging ways. You're no holy Moses not even bright spark, got better deal buying karma. Run on quick count your blessing. *'As soon as coin in coffer rings, my soul from purgatory into heaven springs.'*

Lucky part of my brain took over harness, inner angels voice provided clarity. '*Do on to others' I'll not be telling them words again, dimwit.* Whatever perceived circumstances I was not to be leaving Gillian, didn't have cojones to make that switch up. Strode alongs Liffey's bridge glanced at Clerys clock face, on up quay wall to Phoenix Park swung around Monument down grassy knoll, past school bookstore onto Fitzgerald Street. Gleeson pub was open, Gillian not due till later so said related bar maid Ruby, pale skin version of Gilly. Not my cup of tea, gave salute of affection to JFK over quick pint. Sat on top double decker to Chapelizod, youse need ticket to ride, full penny ha'penny. Ran down six steps of basement flat an eager beaver, before I rang bell of that green door weather-beaten postie appeared handed me letters. All happy with sunny elements and current blessing in skies. Great job in outdoors, then again old phoisty and coal man gets the sack everyday.

"Grand day now," surely he would ken vagaries of fickle climates.

There with utility bills was brown envelope from old Belmarsh jail.

'Miss Gillian Dillon' it did read.

Serendipity my being there realized the problem, wish I was your lazy bugger not crafty badger, nor gobshite with energies for mischief. Better of an evening be gummin me choppers on kippers watching Coronation street. *By flipping 'eck!* Understandably panicked dropped bills in letter box and lickedy split with 'Belmarsh'. Away in my chambers nervously contemplated Lange's 4-carat diamond ring and words from prisoner BM-9749, aka Syd Martin. Felon asked free Gillian to be his lawful wife, long and short of it. Gillian who earned meager workman's wage had dispatched 500 quid to Syd's prison account. Me throwing money at her and she busy exporting to incarcerated, mise keeping Syd's larder stocked Golden Virginia, red leb, Sun for page 3, Mars bars, Fairy soap and Mc Vittes jaffa cakes. Things changed and hoped to be out on appeal, keep lad in longer it's banana skins out here. Syd's lock up set my soul free, dreamed he'd get stabbed by lag in bandana while showering with sharp stiletto crafted from toilet rolls. Syd promised to do social work prevent kids from thieving, going straight and didn't want getting robbed by bandits. He'd leave big smoke for Liverpool grow veggies on square allotment with tidy shed. Syd would have windmill with vanes rotating in winds, listen to country ballads, take the kid fruit of her loins to the Kop. Rent a caravan near Douglas on Isle of Man for two weeks, romance weekends in Blackpool with illuminations. She'd leave for new perch in liver bird city?

'the sun is on the harbour love
I wish I could remain
I know it will be a long time
till I see you again.'

Syd would hammer engagement ring using gold teeth from incinerated old lags and cubic zirconium smuggled in relatives arse-hole. Send crafted ring inserted in barnbrack from Belmarsh kitchens, conjugals not permitted, but for a ton a screw arranged medical bed to get bun in oven. Gillian with stank of prison on a cot, through slot in door screw would admire her moving arse. No chard, no candles, no satin sheets and no Dublin bay view from sun-filled bedroom. No

Enya or negrinho chocolate from Brazil or Vacqueyras wine for dark lady, just determined felon that loved her uncomplicated. Meantime live with his mother on Wilberforce by Finsbury park she would, with legend reggae street beats from windows in summer. Syd messed up but now figured things out, he was London streets ahead all things considered. Maybe she forgave him, after all never had benefits of Christian brother's education. Never had ears boxed for divilments or six of the best whether or not deserved. Never had spirits broken by cassocked rottweiler's on Rome's sole business of terrification, herding souls of sheep. Many days of fears in my youth but never wasted day incarcerated. Good on the brothers, under their strict tutelage my spirit kept free.

Made right fist of schooling
tempered by Brothers
toe party line gombeen.
My head in way of culchie mit
neurons scrambled, brain battered.
Can do Virgil and Pythagarous
Sarsfield beat Normans at Waterloo
Carrantuohill high all the time
Macgillycuddy reeks with diet of worms.
Math easy as gooseberry pie,
good for soaking spilled beer.

Syd's tintean a real tintean, tigum ceart, felt she'd give Syd the focal and he with no word of gaelic. Needed wisdom from wise soul's departed acquired on auntie's deep cushioned settle, item salvaged from Dublin mountains, Hell Fire club she'd claim. Not to forget Noreen called florist to send red roses to Carvery.

"Sign 'em Danny boy to sweet Noreen O'Boyle." Keep that pot boiling.

Considered telling behind bars Syd, 'Gillian got killed on way to work lorry heading south. Died instantly, suffered no pain sure we're pained with loss'. Never did, instead anon sent the man a decent tenner to cover few milky bars. Honesty to be best policy, reassembled the letter as departed from H.M. Belmarsh now with extra glue. Returned to the flat, slunk down steps discreetly delivered female's mail. Lurking with intent no one to know devious shenanigans, no harm no foul postie doing overtime. In battle with broads need strategies, to out fox an old dog needs new tricks. Sometime later Gillian called said she'd journey to Howth that very evening.

"Meet at the station, 6.30 don't be late we've things to talk about." Thusly was informed.

What was afoot? Always wanting she'd bring white stockings in those Irish coffee legs, old dogs see best black and white. Laboured to cover signs of Noreen's visit, even after one night dames make changes. Had all necessary tools windex brushes and bleach. Wicklow left her pink razor in the shower and that pale chick's as smooth as baby's bottom. Preparing to tackle anything as catchers mitt in batting cage, spiced by my varieties of life.

'Gilly it's mine a very fine Gilette blade easy on complexion. Keeps me skin like babies bottom! Noreen has a key, now I'll be changing them old locks. First thing."

Hide garbage under sofa. Surveyed scrubbed house confident Gilly would have no reason to cop shenanigans. Picked up quiet Gillian wearing black and white striped dress, stretched to cover hefernesque curves. Unruly hair wrapped with a scarf, like Pukao moai head piece from Easter island. *Afrorodisiac!* In the house barefoot on sheep skin, pampered and plied her full of grape for distractions.

"Varietal recommended by Frederick at Donabate wine store ...."

"Shut your cake hole," says she, not tap dancing around. "You took my letter."

Came fierce torrent as New York summer's hydrant, heavy brass from sugar babe. Doing it like rabbits might not be on the table. Now engaged with her Kabuki dance.

"Begob," says I, only ready not able.

Needed slug of puncheon sugar cane desperate, dealing with *woman of plus air persona.* There was me Connemara farmer in thunder storm, narra hedgerow to hide, *'land too poor for snakes to live upon'.* Right hairy nosed wombat all got up in her business. Re-opened 'Belmarsh' shoved in my face, could smell fresh glue.

"Are you Gillian Dillon?" she asks.

In her blowing steam tirade throwing jagged rocks I'd not get words in sideways. Verbal's felt like head butt, male sac tightened in a crunch, them two yokes butting like steel marbles.

"Shirley saw you." *'t'was him not old postie with delivery.'*

Why read the letter, man missing his broad, ramblings of damaged soul, no idea why women gave damn about me. Didn't dare venture to ask why Syd was writing as she paraded all toil and trouble. Designed from slave captured in Sierra Leone, Walcott's sluggish ancestors transported to whipping posts in Dixie. Cotton pickin lives toiling, entangled with each other as determined by their Masters. Gran Maureen emerged from dog haired rabble of Erin, celtic high stepping mongrels from Lucan. Motley crew mixed with down trodden high-land Scots, little chefs with mental tempers. She walked tall, hybrid vigor of callaloo woman, coloured not pale below Brazil.

"I don't spy never open your mail," she claimed.

Except old girl friend letters locked in a safe, parchments you studied as rabbinicals poring thru' Dead Sea scrolls, I should have inscribed in Ogham script. Likely had that text covered in Kilburn night classes.

"Your mother never told you how to behave? Brian you seriously need to catch yourself on. I ask you."

With me bent as old copper from rail tracks. Honesty had let me down. Again.

"A real long hand man, forever interfere other people business."

Wrong to eavesdrop words for serious mott
bare souls to broad when needs must
fellow deemed pathetic when men read
they'll know you've lost both marbles.
Kings, beggars, emperors, salarymen
in throes of battle with the bird,
kiss the arse of main mott.
In time, needs, will, must.
Zap it, all the damn days.

"You need to know I get marriage proposals walking sights of Grafton street."

Common as muck gurriers whirling whistles at her ass. Then fascinated as she sniffed like thirsty komodo dragon, monitor with no good intentions. Searching she was in anyway I screwed up. When she shuts up I will give her the ring, but plan went awry, then being askewed fell off rails.

"Is mise African sensitive on Serengeti, see one leaf know season. Elephant, gazelle, wildebeest we each know how wind blows."

Tapped her skull as if Queen Nefertiti her very self.

"Hunter ancestors gave me that, we've brain like atomic radar." She says.

Skewered and impaled, too much yabber jabber from this black bird, wiles of woman having right giraffe.

'Hhayi asibesabi siyabafuna (bring it on),' mulling only my middling Swahilli. 'Niyabasaba na (be not afraid)', described my demeanor.

Flipped barbeque one meat slipped on deck, my mistake. Well done with splinters, beef rare for her, croatia gnocchi and porky pies from village deli.

"Only giraffe you've ever seen was above in zoological gardens not those wild plains of Africas."

Me Dad used to bring us watching animals thru' zoo fence. Oh so hard happy and life was back then! From his pocket rarely cough up gate toils. Familiar with giraffes, never once a zoo hippo. Salvaged admissions for ball o'malt and pint in docks pub, club orange and Tayto for us. Me mother never came, too scared of python house. Only affluent childers watched monkey eat apple, and *Impalas?*

One day, if aliens come,
by then us half robot,
zoological all emptied
only pythons and rats.
Nowt from hedge rows
only photos to remain,
giraffes, rhinos, camels?
With the trunk?
All due respects, natures folly
should have been more handy.
Rejected by fire brigade
did youse not realize that
China loves ivorie keys.
Tinkle, tinkle.

"Brian you had someone. You changed sheets, couch cushion smelt like Wicklow house. She was here."

Juiced for her war path with regal bearing of Kori bustard. Should have opened ajax bottles. *Cat away, mouse think they are owner, if no energy don't touch tiger.* She downed glass of chard. My goose sizzled, angry raptobird in my abode talons of an eagle. Minefield no tranquility, she grabbed a cushion and flung it.

"Basket with towels, shower with red hair. Fox having a bath? Gewürztraminer in rubbish, perfume office phone."

"You say James Dean I say Jim Bean."

Wave off such whole palaver, rhubarb time in that ball park. Cornered heading back to barren hills of old tosser town and endless troubled nights of draining wet dreams. When complexity confronted preferred strategy do nothing, still hoping to bamboozle survive nefarious escapades.

Houdini where art thou? He'd always keep escape key in orifice.

"As soon as I saw 'For Sale' sign I knew what you would want, then I could see intensity in her."

Big tears falling, loved she cared a whit. Surprised she cared that one whit.

"That Sunday Noreen told me she had an old boy friend in Howth."

'I'm going there now to see him.'

Well Mary and her carpenter, stitched-up, she'd been tipped off. Set up by mother of my peril. Worlds colliding full of hard knocks, life entered asteroid belt mashed in blender sucked through straw. *Not ex, but 'old' she said.*

"I knew she'd show up and you off by yourself that night. I cut the sandwich in two, hope she enjoyed. Two of youse, round her you're all little pants," she mocked.

Broads make it difficult for man to maneuver, unity in their battle. Bollix a common foe something that stirs the pot.

"Coming here I could feel her arse warmed the car seat. We had our time Brian that is all the time there will be, it's not me you're looking for." Blowing her stack.

Warm arse beats wandering lonesome abode in thick blankets. Alone.

"Go on back, go on back."

Fishing twine entangled best cut that line, loud as hog stuck in quick sand. She took my New Orleans crying mask down from the wall.

"I need to vent anger that I need to do."

She flung it splintered and shattered, nose lay on floor sniffing Wicklow in that baloney air. From the couch threw my only fast ball.

"No idea she'd come here I was that gob smacked."

Late in the evening, I'd no warning
showed on the stoop inclements rolling in.
Distracted by storms had me befuddled,
bone drenched with no trains home
access for her of course had to let her in.
There's no excuse, one decko at bare legs
'Once more unto the breach, once more'.

Noreen drunk the wine, wild bacchus, cupid and our previous led us away into temptations, she had it coming, me lacking powers of St Kevin. More jumping with leaping than Knieval in Grand Canyon's.

"Wicklow wants you back, I can't replace, no woman on God's earth can do that. Not even Eria her very self."

Brass yellow wallop from this black bird.

"You came by my flat with good intentions even after night with her. The letter unhinged you, what I would do if Syd was back in the picture."

'.. a tide in the affairs of men
taken at the flood,
on such a full sea we were afloat.'
Come hell or high water
till cockney tout do us part.

"She's beautiful I can see what the fuss is in your head and elsewhere."

I took her emptied wine glass and put in a glittering dazzling ring. If that bird comes mocking *'Daddy's gonna buy you a diamond ring'*.

"That's for you my angel, you rescued me from my nightmare."

Syd in a cell and I an emotional jail, painful places. When pressured give diamonds, she looked at the ring engraved *Gillian.*

"You're offering the wrong person, file the name give fainne oir to Wicklow."

Stakes forever high for me, no mistake.

"Listen Brian go to her, Syd may be a crook but honest with me."

I'd fears of jailbird Syd hearing what I'd been up to. His twist and twirl Jill and her Jack, didn't fancy getting crown broken falling down Howth hill. Me getting laid an he being tucked up. Silence welcomed as we ate the steaks.

"Will you tell Syd about me?" Better she with gold fish memory.

"Not a focal to pass my lips."

Gobble, gobble.

"Thanks."

Of that I hae me douts.

"Gillian it's odd each of us going to where we started."

To where we belong.

"Brian you'll live and die in Glen da lough agus bás in Éirinn, I've my own fears going back to England me and Syd so poor in Birkenhead. I'll help him get going with landscaping, it rains all the time there must be business galore."

Sticky fingers to green thumb, aiding and abetting rhododendrons when droopy.

"I'll try to keep this ring and not go pawning for weed wackers!"

At that time of night tucked up Syd would be shooting his wad to Miss White's perky tits from page three red tops.

"I better make most of tonight, always feel so cosy here. You're not putting me in the spare a girl gets scared. Put up with me one more night and your patchwork activites, run my bath and bring some bubbly."

She looked again at golden band, played Chieftains cellis and danced bare feet on wood floor. We did our ruckus business one last time, twisting and turning doing loop de loop like Coney island rocket roller coaster. On our last legs. Africa's that hot, blimey I'd rare old time in south Africa. *Honeydew and cantaloupe. Man go.*

Again early dawn had hot cross buns and later breakfast. Gillian released me and I love her for that.

End of days only game in town
they know that for sure,
not gold or fame, damn they
have us joined by short and curlies
like Velcro.

CHAPTER 22

By time I got to Avoca it was eleven that morning called Walter the agent to put an offer on the Walsh house, after selling Howth I'd be bank notes ahead. Hoity-toity Howth scored higher, folk high on the hog always looking down on unvarnished rabble. Feeling well pleased.

"I'll contact both although Mrs. Walsh she's boss." Wally man insisted. "If she decides you'd be on the pig's back. Grand cosy house, lovely spot with your lovely wife. Youse will be welcome in the village, quiet for a spot of your writing. Keeping busy."

Dubious glance getting spotty scribbling credentials judged, he'd not be borrowing me ramblings from village library van. Damn searching knowledge highways no place to hide, if in time a Shakespeare monkey can scribe folios surely I can do sumeth?

Either way bang it out
papyrus with hieroglyphs,
paper and quill in lime light,
Bic and carbon copy days.
Remington selectric golf balls,
mighty exclusive Wang
'Dear miss typing pool

is the reply letter ready yet?'
Then me Mac did the work,
forever more jobs never finished.
Life is either short or too long.

After signing papers in the office on Pearse street drove on to Bray, jewel in crowded crown of Wicklow. Sat on concrete seat by that Victorian Esplanade built by steam punk mighty machines, those boys once held dark world by scruf of the neck. Built fortunes by letting off steam, celebrated ice in uisce baite, splashed and splattered cash. Their brass era bestowed froth from Empire prosperities, grandiose Dublin city with grand share of looted spoils, jingle jangle in citizen pockets, more power for them. Steam barons in hot water, shocked by power coming from Shannon river dam, harnessing and shifting damn electrons. *What?* Never could see them type of yokes comin down the wires.

From pink globed empire to turf fires,
sinn fein for what? Pourqui, ce fa? Eh?
Decades lorded by Roman heel of fine leather,
bullied by pompous compulsory gaeltoire, nil fhios agam
belittled, shunned on UTV by belicoise Stormount.
Worn down freestate citizens, me ma and pa
sustaining bairns on praties, turnover bread with jam
gooseberry, rhubard and home made marmalade,
raising run of the mill mail boat ferry fodder.
Train Heuston to Euston, 'so farewell my son'.
'Don't drop any H's' over there.
Dublin bay and coastal hills, see you some fine day.
Poor land left to fairys and worn out shawls down boreens.
Raw culchie Pucheen more power to yee, thank goodness.
That's the way it was, culture pounding me everyday.
I'm connected to all that, set me up nice. Reconciled.

End of the day.

Should have gathered every twig and stick, stayed with coal from Ballingarry, leave Arabs on camels. Not be gouging us to poor house, only copperless.

'Please Mr Saud we need more, cheaper'
our harness treadmill, punts for Lamborghini.
Do youse take aunts old farthings and florins?
All we need is spuds and fishes.
Conquered, we're accustomed what with
Albion and Rome and Euro.

On account of blinding sunshine and cloudless sky that rare day Irish sea was cyan as if green land leaking, cuis farraige. Treated myself to roast beef in Lacys grand hotel off Esplanade. Mash loaded with milk and butter, chopped onions, parsley, beetroot, side order of green peas and carrots. Dash of gravy on beef lean done to my liking, ancient aunt would well voice approval. Dining room wall papered with photos of Bray 100 years past, grand hatted ladies getting the air, well to do posh Dublin folks busy developing precious memories of Bray, days of their lives. Couples processing sea-side promenading, brollies, bowlers, jitneys, hansome cabs and hackney carriage lined in waiting. Poor auld ones would make do with tuppence day out at Sandymount Waxies' Dargle. For afters looking above at the head scoffed '99', needed peaceful, no need for tranqs. Wishing they'd the chair-lift to Eagle's nest when my mobile sang, soul reeling from events.

"Hi it's me," Noreen said, paradise bird.

"Having ice cream in Bray." Soft pale, taste divine.

Broad's voice created euphoria, held phone so she'd hear waves crash on shore.

Bray carnival slot machines
always our holiday gamble
take jackeens for a ride and

dance, waves, wafers and chippers
early training days for wild wood.

"Where are you?" I asked.

"At work, it's quiet. Come on over?"

Spotted red dress in that Carvery sat out on patio, early summer wind came and ruffled, collections of folks with beetroot complexions, weathers that grand. She in black stockings knew what suited, smile like tooth brush advertise. Nearby two kid family kept her on edge, changed seats 'sun was in her eyes'. In deep blue air.

"I was thinking I'd never see you again."

Did not approve Gucci shades, she'd borrowed his.

"Maybe future is what it used to be."

"You really wanna buy my house and furniture?"

'Whitener come to cleanse the nook.' Have mollys clean that nest with ketchup, works with skunks.

"They full know I'm a jilted woman."

Ruthless staff wagering on gaffer's shaky happiness pendulum.

"What do you want?" She asked, searching menu.

Let me take you some hot afternoon by old shebeen, rain belting on hot tin roof.

"Sweet red would be nice."

Her sadness had not disappated, she pointed to something French for gambling waiter.

"I had lunch."

Not a time to mince words, dikey dicey times. I've come to take your future.

"Brown soda bread with argan oil," she told attentive young fellow.

"Yes, Mrs. Walsh."

Love name changes these Irish girls, will she be back to O'Boyle? Passport with more changes than dyslexic's spelling bee.

"From Morocco." Sunny hollier with gone one.

As much as tattoo on her ass Bruce left his mark, run life's gauntlet get influenced even Aniky departed with her Mark. I'm not bothered that's what happens, watch what hefty blacksmiths do when impress shaping wrought iron, I'd come to realise there was only one of this beast in God's mansions. Hair crossed her brow Wicklow freckles make her look like a kid, how different they are as needs they must be. What is it about grains of sand that makes babes whip out boobs expose bum cheeks and lie about as sea lions? It's what broads do to feed on man's hunger. She put on her shades emerald eyes dark behind, cheater I canna see your soul. These shades could not hide how moody she was, yes I was still being inspected. Whenever she fell on butt end of life each morning got her ass back to take another shot. Chatoyancy, I was missing, even when she don't say nuttin, I knows what she says.

I'm the prize, show me your cards Dublin gurrier. Don't dare feel sorry, I'm a hot babe. What are ye packin skinny white potato boy from Rathmines, it ain't so posh. You ain't no mulatto nor creole, don't smile with pearly white teeth no cajun cool style. But you're all I got, so I'll settle for likes of you what I ended with. I'll have regret, memories and dream time. No more time for handsome men, I've been to med lagoons, pan handle and down all the islands, take it easy. Generous Brian will do, we talk he cried and wrote poems. We're Irish maybe understand each other, I will love him. Again and again at least I'll try for a long time. Until I'm old when it don't really matter no more. We are both going to hell. When that bell tolls.

Learned my lessons enough, outside cat inside tiger. Added hair tint, exercising, wearing sweater, pants and Italian shoes Gillian bought, with 'designer' shades. Done with smokes, never going to look better. Felt balls hanging loose relaxed swinging by summer wind, prolonged active life, later gamboiling. They'd have work cut out for them.

"Eating well at Gillian's deli I must say."

Beats mongrel from tins, airport scanners screaming thin man passing. Waiter came fine fellow filled glasses, Viognier grape, added water splash make time longer, and clocks run slow.

'I sat me with my true love
my sad heart strove to choose between
the old love and the new love
while soft the wind blew down the glade
and shook the golden barley.'

Dipped bread in olive oil, there was no toast.

"You'd think beyond in Cork they'd grow grand grapes?" I queried. "Insane Kinsale plonk, Blarney's Beaujolais, they've full grown palm trees in Kenmare. My good man this wine has corked. Yes, well 'tis from Cork. I'm returning this because the cork has corked in wine from Cork. Are ye takin the piss? Cork wine is awful and glasses so small. Yes, another high fill my good fellow. Would ye crank the frickin elbow."

"Did you have to consider lots of things?" She wondered.

Shove a cork white boy, concentrate terrafirma don't act lad insane, no sour grapes. Not amused Noreen, female with no time for trivialata generated by male cortex, they're more focused than hawks, can he feather a decent nest? Glad when shades were again shoved back, seen enough she had, like many Da Vinci portrait felt we were left unfinished. Get discipline be her disciple.

"Yeah, well lots."

'Her hair was a waving bronze and her eyes deep wells that might cover a brooding soul'.

Looked directly into endlessly revealing eyes. Same colour as sea waves beyond as if I'd see through, being naïve in the breeze.

"You know we mostly accepted the offer although a little low, for vale of Avoca!"

"With old green kitchen and one shower?"

Rub in tub, tight-squeeze with green eyed lady. She with half a smile.

"Bruce in hurry to get rid of me and mortgage, mostly me. Learning to sell golf stuff to Hamburgers."

'Jasus now hit the fricking ball far as you can now. A good swipe.'

"More better he concentrate on handicaps."

Rootless weed blight in decent woman's garden.

"I'm selling Howth, windy old place, now someone else can sit there after me."

Shrugged like it meant nothing, abacus in my brain knew our score. To Spanish lady, Daniela offered a good price for 'mine field'. Memories of wall to wall carpets keeping her bare arse warm. Haunted with mystics, bricks and mortifications, kicks with mournful times.

"Too fierce them January winters." I says, with me from Ontario.

No female Chinooks had me balls blue with inclements, one night on that hill deep in the settle heard aunt cry in my head.

'Whoosh, go try
go on be happy,
I lived lonely times
did not want that for you.
Be big man in high county.
Belt out all the days,
we never get enough.
Make waves now.

Only bloody Wicklow could deal with restless longings of moody bitch Noreen. Old Mother Eireann ruthless manipulator gotten grasp on the broad's ass, two stormy bitches left in my life.

"You never brought Bruce up the tower?"

"Brian that means nothing to him."

Load of old bollicks for him, castrati grazing tits in harem.

"Never read a book since back at school, for him poetry is Jack and Jill. Y'all are that different," eclectic lady with her men.

Y'all, wants me to recall happy times with Jimmy south in Yatland, wandering bayous in Terreboone parish chased by speedy gators. Flying on airboats with swamp folk, pilot high on sazerac hootch in land of scary monstrous snakes and angle toothy criters. Scared to death by nature's gross swamp insanities festering moreever in Everglades.

"Added my name near yours and Mairead." When addled and elevated.

One of her special places in valley of ancient scholars.

"Lord above I should never told you about county secrets never realized you'd live up there. Next thing a satellite dish with laundry flapping in the breeze, I mean really!"

She with phony killjoy exasperation. Could well have been turfed from top instead got Glen da lucky two short times.

"Jackeens not to scribble drabble on those stones, bad to be wandering there with spirits good and bad. Upset the local boys, heard youse left a fertilizer bag full of empties and marijuana butts. I've got to clean up. Brian do you hate me?"

"I love you."

Far down that rabbit hole, bikini girl.

"Do I have to move from the house?"

"You can stay."

Don't go astray. In the night lay down on that county bed, under cover keep home fires burning, give up the fags.

"Is she coming with you?"

"Lowland or Africa?"

Feckless me treating her as fool, as ever.

"Brian I know Felix and family. I lived in New Orleans for nigh on 12 years, lest you forget? Gillian's grandfather a big tipper, liked to pinch my ass. Had a thing for Irish women, loved to hear my accent,

J.D. splash of water on the rocks in crystal glass. I've heard lots about you and Gillian. She was gorgeous, I was impressed when she came by the house although you've boyish charm."

She meant I was old as Habakkuk but pulled a bird like Gillian, not only with my mug. *End of day, only evening vegetable left in market.*

"She'd charm dew off the honey suckle."

"She's not around, departed for foreign parts."

Syd's parts, jittery emotions with Gillian gone. From my brief case handed her the real estate contract no time for caution give mademoiselle drawers a twist. Hoped I had this planned to a Tee, patch with super glue let it be so. Needed to tip-toe through a mine field.

"I love you Noreen since Picken's motel." Kracatoa times.

Head down Cill Mhantáin boreens to conquer valleyed woman, took re-jigged barge to Wicklow shores,

"It's your house," I told her. "You gave me second chance."

Messed up, now do right by this Mama.

"You're giving it back! To me?"

"Fully paid and your Mam should move in."

Put that mill stone around her neck, load down with kitchen delph. House my Venus fly trap alls I had end of days, none other may invade that valued threshold.

Feather nest with baubles and diamonds.
Clip this bitch's wings
learn from bower birds on Tasman islands.
When vagabond hard-chaw
Irish men sniff her wild scent
make plotting plans as they surely will
I've poor man's castle for protection.
Get me best moat maker in Ireland
salt water with man eating snakes,
and gators. St Patrick is long gone.

"Will you come to Avoca tonight?" Her ridiculous question.

Kissed her cheek tasted bayou tear drops, crocs maybe but making no allegations.

"Sweetheart sorry I was that terrible to you." She says.

Hard like granite under foot women of Cill Mhantáin.

"bb, I will build back our love if you let me."

Task done took that long draft, no pearly gates but closer to God's heaven.

"You've bricks baby."

All I could muster, true to form had me emotion flusters, tears flowed like Powerscourt's waterfall, as ever. Maybe gaffer done a freaking Lacrima di Morro d'Alba wine switch. Should have requested dry white. Emotions hobbled by foreign vino, as ever.

"You've been through Pickens, O'Boyle and him. I'm mad as a hatter, why you'd still want me I'd not know?"

Only want one happysac life.

"I've suspicions you'll never be reformed."

Practiced me Prussian virtues. 'Mehr sein als scheinen, be more than you seem to be.'

"Remember that was me living on my tod waiting for you to arrive."

Wretch forever on prowl, misshapen as Caliban. No more catering for knocks of strange travellers. Whatever affiliations. Perhaps exception if Victor sent me one of those trophy brown skin amazons. To learn them the shambolic ways of an Irish man.

"Drink that night of the fancy dress and dressing me like that? In future I'll be staying home those Halloween nights."

Her tricks and treats only for mischievous me, looking for divilments. Relaxed and looked across our bay, her mobile rang.

"He hasn't killed me yet, he'll have to be stripped and searched for his weapon", she said to the phone, "Well know where to look."

Styled fringe brushed aside with manicured fingers, heard laughing.

"Mairead, I'm busy, I have my life to mend and Brian's heart."

Hit nail on the head, '*time to repair roof is when sun is shining*'. All my world Jim Dandy, but don't wag tail, don't be happy early. Empty vessels loom largest, striding at corner of my eye spied Bruce uninvited wanker, uneasy the clown to wear his crown. Intimidated to spoil ambiance, she firmly held my hand.

"So buy my house, take my wife. Busy fellow."

Balls on the bustard, must have drunk Amazon's soup. No Brucey no Mac their contract ended. Well water separate from stream water, their pillow wind done. Get your rocks off with middling birdies cratered in sandy dunes, I've bucking bitch back. A many feather peacock, lose one? No value for him.

"How's golf?" Being my lummock self, enquired behind shades.

He gave a quizzical look, wondering if a weasel would cadjowl wits with likes of him. *Knock on rock won't scare tiger.* Learn to stay in lane buddy boy, let him depart to das fatherland he's above your station. Fine line piss him off with slagging he'd march back haunting every month of year. *When dog bite, you want to bite dog?*

"Prof take a hike, I need to talk with my wife." Grumpy git. *Wood pecker with hard mouth.*

"Right I'll head off on down the town," says I to table with one flat track bully.

Once bright shinny copper, now tarnished no rub of green for them. Contemplated sending scoop of vanilla ice cream topped with raspberry for desert, my complements. Went off laughing, he-he haw-haw. Lordy, oh lordy. *May this muggins last beer be half full.* He freed her positive karma releasing caged life, fang-sheng for him. Walked rocky cliff paths to Greystones, county with nooks and crannies. Lost on slots in arcades watching carnies. Spent coin for gypsy fortune teller lady, mechanical hand moved across the board and dropped a card.

A Wicklow Girl

'Sit by river long enough bodies of enemies float past.'

Being anxious downed few pints in pub garden on Bray road. Sun coming and going, warm with betwixt and between.

"It's me," heard her on the blower.

Minutes later she picked me up.

"How's Danny boy?"

"Pints in sunshine and shadow."

Our mega embrace what no man could undo I'm saying. Milky way and Andromeda colliding becoming, Milkdromeda. Put my hand on black stocking, she with seatbelt off.

"Sweetheart keep those very wicked thoughts."

Words spoken by Wicklow girl as we headed into hills under weak yellow sun.

"Mam put a beef pie in the oven, kept a fire going, didn't want you coming in a cold house. Your one's taking him to Hamburg then Naples."

Auf Wiedersehen. Her ma had cranked the heat, so once again I'd no get chili.

"Pastry pie, bon appétit and grand fire, this is the life."

'I'm a goin to stay
where you sleep all day
where they hung the turk
that invented work
in the big rock candy mountains'

Harsh winds on hard land, those combatants shaped each other many year. Elements working so we'd keep county girls warm, turf fires could only expect so much. Kitchen table set with solid crockery, pastry delicious extra gravy knowing she was browned off with her louse. Cinamon apple pie with fresh cream for desserts. Their monogramed silverware B-N, B or not to be, her man must fit that bill. Iron chicken take back old crock to keep her crockery veritas. Lucky for me.

"Often wondered what you were doing over here." I says.

"Mostly crying, I'd wonder about you?"

But those days had prized calliloo assets to gaze upon. Keep blood flowing like Niagara, over the falls.

"What men do cry in dark shadow, remember you gave me chicken soup when I had flu. A lot to miss. Afterwards trying to get laid, pestering Chinese girl in a kilt on Grafton street. Listening to Abba, looking for Tom Waits song."

Gleam of 'long river' in mind's eye, gave me a togail, up Erin go brea.

"Wanting you back."

"I'll have Mam put rice in the stew."

"Keep spuds, happy with praties."

"Lion doesn't change spots."

Irish man days end, pushed plate away. Later with street lamp's orange glow reclined opposite ends of couch, enjoying red Bulls blood from Hungary.

"Blanket is turned on."

Finagled inside old leaba, up beyond the pale. As hockey player Wayne Gretzey with the puck, I cared where woman is going to be not where ever she's been. Felt her calf under dressing gown counted toes, now to be forever under her thumb.

"When we walk Greystones beach I'll give you solitary time, but want your Dad to know. Don't hide me!"

"We'll stroll that surf, I talk to him there Dad knows. I never forgot when you cried in the pub."

"Too much onion in those Taytos." Don't flatter yourself. "You know I cry at 'Love story', I've seen that 100 times!"

Jenny Cavalleri, every time.

"These days I can't watch the news no more neither."

"Brian once I did ask you to marry and you said nothing, I didn't want to be a mistress forever you have to agree, it's important when a woman asks. You rejected me remember I'm a convent girl, it was always on my mind."

"Yeah, I often told myself."

Of course I cried no you in the morning
cold sheets on her side, no you getting ready for work.
Slept with your T shirt for weeks, sick on my own them days
no soothing chicken noodle and you to gaze upon.

"Noreen do you still love him?"

"No Father B is definitely getting it annulled."

Yo, give broad a break eat a muffin, no need to be gumshoe dick or Perry Mason. Or try to hit nail on head, have a bruised thumb now and then.

"Noreen will then you marry me?"

"Yes dear."

"We can go Tobago this Christmas, there's a tiny church Minister Bernard has grand voice. He'll raise bamboo rafters with hyming, paper confettis." No rice.

"I'm not dreaming of white weddings! My old dress is darned and wine stained!" She laughed.

Dress like Trini girls, boozy calypso nights wear wee green kilt. Do hoochie coochie like you know, I'll be goochie man. Shaken all about.

"By the way Walsh's neighbour in Dalkey spied you in that pear tree."

"What did they say?"

Some strange fruit no doubt.

"Ordinary bloke, thin with owl glasses. Walked the lane kicking a coke can, didn't look like a burglar, lonely looking fellow!"

Out of my tree that night, standing alone. Chestnut hard conkers preference, wood qualify. With me wicked melancholies.

"I'd fish and chips sitting by harbour wall."

Low tide seeing you kiss Bruce at toasting, musta busted few springs in Dalkey's bed on that night. Didn't you. 'Fiancée'.

"Tell me more about Gillian."

Dumb struck reluctant to relate such tales with her.

"Oh go on, I'm so curious, amazed what you get up to."

"We've had great times, an Irish girl." *Many flicker in my mind as will o' wisp pixy lights.*

Syd will go from Belmarsh grub to emperor's table. Together some hotel in Liverpool tonight, likely the Cambrian. *Dublin dalliance complete. No malice.* Some days by the park, wear shades to watch cousin Ruby in Liffey side pub.

"Things changed when you appeared that rainy night. She knew I changed sheets put them in the machine, later she found wet towels in laundry basket."

Should better separated whites from coloured.

"Syd her old boy friend in London released on appeal."

Beak that sent Syd down had leg over a juror, caught flagrante delicto hole in wall at Old Bailey. Absolute pants for him, let his hair down with wig on, a public mischief.

"No more porridge."

Wads of syrup coming for brown sugar.

"Old emotions came back she had to decide, empty Gewürztraminer tipped our balance."

"I caused confusions."

Worse than Michael Fagan by palace four poster,
odd ball Paisley lambasting popery in St Peter's square.
Hollering as Allen Ginsberg Pentagon levitating.
Pentangle stayed put, got shook up 9/11.

"Away on Liverpool ferry this night. Syd to leave big smoke and mates, settle in Birkenhead, has sister there runs sweet shop. He'll have his allotment for veggies."

Heavy price to pay, but beats morning slopping out H.M. lockup.

"When you finish garden rockery I'll sit summer days, drink beer watch lads hurling. Have a fountain and grow the spuds."

"Heaven's above sure Mom will have bushels, she grows gorgeous orchids from granite pebbles."

Put her arm around me snuggled closer. House braced with aches and creaks.

"Rough housing out on that sea tonight." I said.

Wind whistling through the tower, those souls beyond harm. No Vikings sailing astride the waves. Coming to get us.

"Maintain our union," I whispered.

That night. She could handle the knob and gypsy rolls, no need for sassy loaders. Felt her pear shapes. Sugarloaf tough climb all manner slips and bumps sweet on top. I'd surrendered again.

Next afternoon from hill nearby watched Bruce and mates loading stuff in a van, lot of gym equipment. 'For Sale' sign uprooted threw in the ditch, by the door Noreen motionless. As he waved and drove away, my phone rang.

"bb, come quickly."

Door off latch calypso in living room, she ran from the kitchen.

"I've made a cuppa, so glad you're here."

Sat in bright kitchen, tea and fig rolls. She'd kept delph and nawgahide and dented king sized, varnished furniture.

"Brian, what disasters we create on ourselves."

Ebb and flow ways of women in old Wicklow, bay of fundy times. She being the willing host.

"We lost a lot of happy time."

No longer girl from yesterday, had tomorrows back. Balancing wine glasses on rocks and sleeps in eiderdown.

"Amuit fein spear."

Squandered birds lose their way
penguin's tack ends baked on Cook's isle.
Police target practice terminated Bonnie,
Charlie's women caught helter skelter,
Nancy's vicious stabbing by pistol Syd.
Winnies primetime lonely in townships,
Marie Louise's emperor in Longwood.
Ditzy Diana never to be queen
fortune no better than poor Wallis.
In the end no fundy times. For them souls.

CHAPTER 23

Woke that morning stout front door receiving stick beating, wild fellow up about disturbing slumbered naked village folk. Making dents in oak salvaged by ironmonger in Carlow.

Dear lord let citizens lie in their pile at peace
wanting no rude dawn awakenings from visitors,
when man kips with woman likely up to no good.

Oblivious to noisy clattering, Noreen a broad that valued sleeps, under strict instructions 'not to bother her' before 7 O'Clock. Hard to leave warm bed and body early, hopping down hallway pulling my pyjamas. Day's young sun streaming thru' lead stained glass half blocked by hatted stout feller silhouette. On door-step her uncle Gerard, battered jeep out by the road, old lad himself retreated to rest on the garden seat by our chestnut tree. Face battered by elements and time, creased more by lonely times, a mug left intersecting visitor folk with contemplations. Likely not spied morning wood, hardly concealed by cotton pj's. His flumoxed doggie expected pat and treat from kind hearted female, instead spied doggerel gruffian. Got mutt stare eye, shoulders then ears drooped, tall tail half-masted. Doggie instinct, I was leader of no pack.

"Beautiful day we're with having." I offered, best Wicklow. "Seems anyway."

Rightly aware of randomly waving my hands to distract center point attentions.

"Fast asleep above in the bed." I informed him.

Gives me understanding wink, shakes the blackthorn door rapper.

"Right enough, keep 'em tired out good man yourself."

Dog shuffled off, disappointed to hear the boss had greeting time for dreg likes of me, something some mangy cat dragged in. No accounting for gaffer taste shocked head to tail, loss of furry face for mutts.

Gerard, short legs dangling on garden wall busy filling pipe with wad of Players navy cut, happy to be in that garden that morning, enjoyed pipe aroma evidence of honest hard toil from bachelor content with life allotted. Knew pack drill retreated to supply glass of warm porter, returned wearing my gabardine. Himself never bothered with such carnal activities we all relish, such gusto. Man made decent pile renting barns to Dublin hashish gurriers, under-table siring of Shorthorn bulls from Newtownmountkennedy. By now my own horn shorter, size more convenient for yapping with a batchelor of any age.

"Ah, sure that's grand now." Quaffed long draft. "She's had hard knocks in a youngster life 'tis glad I am to see yourself back. Didn't take much to your teddy boy Tommy Steele, flash Freddy fella. Better off to see back of him now if honest truths be stated and pervailed. Without fear nor favours let's hope she's learnt from them hard lessons, t'will be for betters and time passing. You'd never be sure with them article, sure never got much involved with one meself."

Never have yearnings for likes of a woman? Get hardened conkers workin stuck in as nature intended. Aye, mostly demanded.

'Sure never found time what with farming.' What he'd relate eventually.

A life gone by without giving them the business, strange creature by my angle. Maybe his equipment got chopped, many sharp bladed farm implement. Old boy bachelors always have 'sweetheart' from early days, involving separation fiascos, love remain unfulfilled. Only dedicated to laboring in fields, most favoured his own company.

'These days women don't stay back on the farm, they're away up to Dublin. Bright lights and dances easy life now. Cows and crops needs dedication, someone had to take over that like. Sure I'm only glad to do it now. No better life.'

Old baloney hooey, those circumstances I'd blow a busted pressure cooker. Essential to keep living vital, not my nature to be ploughing lonely furrow. Old Gerard leaned his head closer.

"Not from Frank she gets brains her other side few bricks short of a hod, Tipperary if you catch my drift, they let her down."

Wink and nod, indicating perceived hereditary defencies responsibilites of folk in that far off county.

"Arra, different class all together, nothing for poor Noreen there."

"My old fella was Galway."

"Youse are a well suited pair, said same to Sheila. I've something for ye now," he says.

Heard a dog bark out in the jeep.

"You'll know Frank had a scottie, wee Ramsey they had it. Grand little fella. Over on the farm we had a litter, I told Sheila I'd keep one for Princess herself. Come on here now."

From back of jeep he held a wicker basket, tiny pup with big attitude, barking demanding attentions. Tall tail swagging to beat the band, *wagga, wagga.* Reminder to be back in the sack now gone past 7 O'clock. Wagga, wagga.

"From same line as Ramsey, she can take him out on those walks with pair of ye above in the fields. T'will be all the good put a smile back in her."

"We both need that, missed her right enough." Sweetest girl I know.

"Get her up on the mountains tired legs so she won't go gallivanting off up to Dublin."

Stay long ways from that Tipperary.

"Keeps them back down here on the farm, fit and healthy." Gerard gave another wink.

Handed me a furry little bundle, Ramsey the second and bag of kibble.

"Keep on hard tack now with an odd carrot treat. Only if they earns it now."

Wasn't sure if he was talking about me or new Ramsey, I think with all my heart he was talking to me. After all dogs bark and won't never speak, after all I possessed an odd carrot. Gerard telling me to train Noreen, maybe be a bit smarter myself. New Ramsey's ears perked hearing about carrots.

"He's lovely," I petted the pup, fella won litter lottery.

"Grand now, Noreen knows tricks to train 'em well. Be a good lad now in your new home, it's not good if they're too frisky, I'll not be keeping you now."

Then Gerard was gone away down the road. Put basket by the fire, pup looked around with sleepy eyes, seemed approving then off back to his bit of kip.

"You'll fit right in with this house," informed his doggy dream world.

Arrived at right spot, that in common. Hours later Noreen arrived in the kitchen. Little fella jumped from basket and ran across the floor.

"Well who are you?" she says cuddling her wee fella.

"Ramsey the second, Gerard dropped him off."

"Have you come to live in my house?"

Little fella had no confusions knew who was real boss, and his waggely tail. Dogs don't say nothing but bark usually means 'listen stupid'.

"You're too small but sure we'll get you big."

Wagga, wagga feeling, three of us in a hug sun smiling in my heart.

"Sure I've everything now. Brian put on the kettle I'm famished, let's have a grand breakfast. Three of us go roaming over mountain pass."

"I've special places to show both of you. We'll be fit as a fiddle."

'Coming round the mountain, when she comes.'

For now I'd not walk alone. Stuck to Noreen like barnacle, better me than you! Maybe ain't nuthin but that hound dog.

BIBLIOGRAPHY

p. 7. Samuel Coleridge
p. 20. Thomas Hardy
p. 21. Edgar Allen Poe
p. 28. Abraham Lincoln
p. 31. Proverb, maybe Shakespeare
p. 34. Traditional
p. 50. Brewster Martin Higley
p. 55. Henry Longfellow
p. 68. John O'Reilly
p. 73. David Shaw
p. 73. Thomas Gray
p. 79. St. Augustine
p. 83. Banjo Paterson
p. 86. St. Augustine
p. 87. Sam Walter Foss
p. 90. Traditional
p. 92. Thomas Hardy
p. 105. William Shakespeare
p. 114. Traditional
p. 120. Countess Markievicz

p. 122. Rudyard Kipling
p. 129. D.H. Lawrence
p. 133. Thomas Hardy
p. 134. Thomas Moore
p. 135. Oscar Wilde
p. 136. Percy French
p. 137. A. E. Housman
p. 154. John Greenleaf Whittier
p. 155. William Pitt
p. 159. Traditional
p. 161. Thomas Moore
p. 171. Charles Wesley
p. 172. Oscar Wilde
p. 177. Thomas Hardy
p. 182. Traditional
p. 192. Johnson Oatman Jr
p. 195. A. E. Housman
p. 211. Traditional
p. 219. William Wordsworth
p. 222. John Keats
p. 229. A. E. Housman
p. 230. William Shakespeare
p. 237. William Monk
p. 241. Traditional
p. 246. Traditional
p. 249. Traditional
p. 253. Samuel Ferguson
p. 257. Thomas Davis
p. 262. Robbie Burns
p. 266. Kuno Meyer
p. 266. Rudyard Kipling

p. 269. William Allingham
p. 270. President John Kennedy
p. 273. William Shakespeare
p. 278. Emily Lawless
p. 281. Ancient Irish scriber (amended)
p. 284. William Wordsworth
p. 284. Oscar Wilde
p. 284. Thomas Moore
p. 288. John Keats
p. 303. William Shakespeare
p. 304. William Shakespeare
p. 306. Thomas Hardy
p. 313. Traditional
p. 315. Katharine Tynan
p. 321. Traditional
p. 328. William Shakespeare
p. 334. Thomas Hardy
p. 336. Robert Joyce
p. 336. John O'Reilly
p. 342. Traditional
p. 353. Traditional